"YOU SAID ALL I HAD TO DO WAS NAME MY PRICE."

He caught her just above her elbows and stepped forward. His eyes were dark gray and depthless, as turbulent as a summer storm. "Well it's time we settled up, sweetheart, and what I want is you."

Abby's mouth went dry. Her breath came fast, then slow, then fast again. Her heart began to pound so hard she was certain he must surely hear it.

"No!" she cried. "I won't let you do this, Kane. Do you hear? I won't let you!"

"Sweetheart—" that arrogant smile still hadn't left his mouth "—you can't stop me."

His mouth came down, sealing hers like a hot brand. She tried to bring her hands up but it was no use. His lips plundered the softness of hers, raw and hungry and demanding . . .

Praise for Samantha James' MY REBELLIOUS HEART

"Explosive emotions fill every page of this book . . . raw primitive passion and exceptional love . . . not to be missed."
Rendezvous

"Told in the unique style that marks Samantha James, MY REBELLIOUS HEART is a delight . . . rich in emotion and warm in details, it's enchanting."
Affaire de Coeur

"Scrumptuous . . . readers will be entranced . . . Samantha James delivers a fast-paced Medieval that crackles and sizzles with sensuality."
Romantic Times

P9-DXK-620

Other **AVON ROMANCES**

BELOVED PRETENDER *by Joan Van Nuys*
DARK CHAMPION *by Jo Beverley*
FLAME OF FURY *by Sharon Green*
LORD OF THE NIGHT *by Cara Miles*
MASTER OF MY DREAMS *by Danelle Harmon*
PASSIONATE SURRENDER *by Sheryl Sage*
WIND ACROSS TEXAS *by Donna Stephens*

Coming Soon
FOREVER HIS *by Shelly Thacker*
TOUCH ME WITH FIRE *by Nicole Jordan*

And Don't Miss These
ROMANTIC TREASURES
From Avon Books
FASCINATION *by Stella Cameron*
FORTUNE'S FLAME *by Judith E. French*
SHADOW DANCE *by Anne Stuart*

Avon Books are available at special quantity discounts for bulk purchases for sales promotions, premiums, fund raising or educational use. Special books, or book excerpts, can also be created to fit specific needs.

For details write or telephone the office of the Director of Special Markets, Avon Books, Dept. FP, 1350 Avenue of the Americas, New York, New York 10019, 1-800-238-0658.

Outlaw Heart

Samantha James

AVON BOOKS ◆ NEW YORK

If you purchased this book without a cover, you should be aware that this book is stolen property. It was reported as "unsold and destroyed" to the publisher, and neither the author nor the publisher has received any payment for this "stripped book."

OUTLAW HEART is an original publication of Avon Books. This work has never before appeared in book form. This work is a novel. Any similarity to actual persons or events is purely coincidental.

AVON BOOKS
A division of
The Hearst Corporation
1350 Avenue of the Americas
New York, New York 10019

Copyright © 1993 by Sandra Kleinschmit
Inside cover author photograph by Almquist Studios
Published by arrangement with the author
Library of Congress Catalog Card Number: 93-90345
ISBN: 0-380-76936-0

All rights reserved, which includes the right to reproduce this book or portions thereof in any form whatsoever except as provided by the U.S. Copyright Law. For information address Pat Teal Literary Agency, 2036 Vista Del Rosa, Fullerton, California 92631.

First Avon Books Printing: November 1993

AVON TRADEMARK REG. U.S. PAT. OFF. AND IN OTHER COUNTRIES, MARCA REGISTRADA, HECHO EN U.S.A.

Printed in the U.S.A.

RA 10 9 8 7 6 5 4 3 2

Prologue

Wyoming Territory, 1878

Stringer Sam.

There wasn't a man, woman or child west of Deadwood who hadn't heard of him. Some said he was spawn of the devil. Some predicted that— good or bad—he'd end up a legend. But for those unlucky enough to cross his path, Stringer Sam was more like a nightmare come to life . . .

His nickname was apt. Stories about his trademark display of deadliness soon spread from barroom to barroom, from parlor to parlor, from cow town to cow town. Little boys listened in terrified awe as their fathers recounted grisly tales of Stringer Sam's savagery. Women shivered in fear whenever he was mentioned, while little girls hid their faces in their mothers' skirts.

But it wasn't Stringer Sam sitting in the Laramie jail that warm May night. Instead it was Rowdy Roy, reported to be one of Stringer Sam's gang. There were two deputies guarding him, Andy Horner and Nate Gilmore. Andy was a rangy youth of twenty who had decided six months ago to put an end to his cowboy days. To Nate, who was nearly ten years his senior, Andy had a tendency to run off at the mouth. But he could draw and hit a target with a six-shooter faster than a man could spit, and that was why Marshal Dillon MacKenzie had hired him.

"Don't know why the marshal insisted both of us be here tonight," grumbled the younger man. He thumped his boot heels against the wide-planked floor, his lips twisting in a grimace as he glanced at their prisoner.

Nate puffed on his cheroot, then blew a lazy ring of smoke into the air. "The territorial marshal should be here tomorrow night at the latest to take him off our hands," he said with an idle shrug. "Besides, one thing about Dillon. He usually has a good reason for doin' whatever he does."

Like Andy, Nate had drifted into town several years ago—and promptly been accused of cattle rustling. Buck Russell, who owned the Triple R ranch just east of Laramie, had been quick to accuse him. It was Dillon who'd rescued him from a vengeful lynch mob and ferreted out the real rustlers, several of Russell's own men.

Nate had been quick to gather that there was no love lost between Dillon MacKenzie and Buck Russell. He'd later learned that Dillon's daddy owned the Diamondback ranch, which shared its northern boundary with Russell's. On that boundary was a section of rich grassland that Russell coveted for himself, and it had provoked many a harsh word between the two men.

No one was more surprised than Nate himself when Dillon offered him the job of deputy marshal. He had reservations about working for the law after what had happened, but Dillon was willing to give him a fair shake and Nate felt obliged to pay him back. Three years later, he was still here in Laramie, but now he had no thoughts of pulling up stakes and moving on. Dillon had become his friend as well as his boss. Rumor had it that the governor was thinking of appointing Dillon county sheriff, and Nate couldn't have been more pleased.

Andy blew out a gusty sigh and glanced once more at the cell where their lone prisoner sat huddled in a corner of the narrow bunk. Gaunt and thin, with an ugly puckered scar on one cheek, Rowdy Roy Parker stared through the barred window at the inky sky above, as he had throughout the evening. It was odd, Andy thought vaguely. Though he was spike-whiskered and dirty, Rowdy Roy was anything but rowdy, as Andy had expected. Instead the man looked almost . . . fearful.

Roy had been caught yesterday trying to steal a horse from the livery stable. He'd been quickly recognized as one of the men with Sam when they'd pulled off a bank robbery in Rawlins last month. Incredibly, he had most of the bankroll still with him. Unfortunately, Stringer Sam wasn't with him. Sam was a crafty one, all right. Sometimes he worked alone; other times he had as many as five or six accomplices.

Andy inclined his head slightly. "Roy there's as quiet as a stone wall," he mused thoughtfully. "To tell the truth, I expected a little more trouble from one of Sam's boys." His eyes narrowed. "You don't think he sent the marshal on a wild-goose chase, do you?"

Nate hesitated. He didn't want to think so. Damn, but he didn't! Dillon had at first been skeptical of Roy's claim that he was breaking all ties with Sam and his gang. But when Roy blurted out that he knew the location of Sam's hideout, everything had changed. Dillon had grilled him for hours, determined to find out if he was telling the truth.

Apparently Dillon was convinced, for he'd ridden out late this afternoon, intent on capturing Sam once and for all.

Nate scraped back the chair and stood up. He pulled off his hat and dropped it on the desktop, running his fingers through his hair. "I don't think Dillon would have gone after him if he didn't think Roy was telling the truth," he said finally.

For the longest time, neither one said anything. An uneasy, ominous silence descended. It was as if an oppressive black cloud had dropped its smothering folds over the jail.

For the first time, Nate wished fervently that Dillon hadn't gone after Sam. Sam was not a man to be crossed. He was unpredictable. Wily and cagey, as the lawmen scattered across the Territory knew. For Sam, it wasn't enough just to steal and rob; it wasn't enough to cold-bloodedly shoot a man dead between the eyes.

But to think of Sam inevitably brought thoughts of death . . . and dying. Nate was rather grateful when Andy cleared his throat and turned the conversation elsewhere. And so the two men put Stringer Sam out of their minds.

It would prove to be a costly error in judgment . . . a deadly mistake.

Andy's eyes lit up like firecrackers on the Fourth of July. "Say, Nate. You seen that new singer at the Silver Spur? Now there's a lady makes a man hot as a ruttin' elk."

Two fervent gazes looked as one toward the open door and down the street. Most of the town's male population liked nothing more than to bend an elbow at the Silver Spur. A constant hum of raucous talk and laughter reached their ears. Someone pounded out a bouncy, slightly off-key tune on the piano, trilling along with the melody.

A sly grin etched its way along Nate's mouth. "Done more than seen her," he offered casually. "And her name's Tina, kid."

Andy's chair thumped to the rutted wooden floor. He gaped in astonishment. "What! Are you telling me that you . . . that she . . . that you and her . . ."

Nate nodded. His self-satisfied smile spoke for itself.

"Why, she told me she never mixed with the clientele!"

Nate just laughed. "That's 'cause she's looking for a *man*," he drawled. He chuckled when Andy turned red clear to the part in his tousled blond hair.

Andy's jaw clamped shut. He regarded the older man suspiciously. "Oh, yeah? Well, I think you're all gurgle and no guts."

Nate chuckled and arranged his hands over his belt buckle. "Oh, yes," he said. "Tina's a mighty juicy little piece. Fact is, she gave me a ride I won't soon forget."

Andy nudged his chair closer. This time he was all ears. Unable to resist, Nate went on embellishing the tale.

Outside, the ever-present wind had not yet ceased its restless scouring of the plains, though the hour was past midnight. A half-moon spilled translucent fingers of light down upon the earth, where a chestnut stallion broke free from the waist-high feathery grass along the dirt road. In the gloom, his rider appeared dark and featureless; his build was wiry, lean and tough. The man wore a black broad-brimmed hat, dark clothing and boots . . . and no spurs.

The man was alone. He passed two other riders on their way out of town, but spoke to neither. He betrayed no hint of stealth whatsoever as he guided his horse toward the small building squatting near the end of the street. Indeed, his was a bold and daring approach . . .

But that was his way.

When he reached his destination, he slid from his horse. Inside the jail, two male voices joined in laughter.

A shadow spread through the doorway. The man stepped inside.

Nate leaped up in startled surprise, a hand already reaching for his gun.

Andy never made it that far.

There was a deadly staccato of gunfire. Andy's chair tipped backwards. Nate slumped to the floor.

Inside his cell, Rowdy Roy began to pray for the first time in his miserable life.

The man with the gun blew a wisp of smoke from the barrel, then slipped the weapon back into the holster at his hip. An expression of distaste on his face, he stepped around the pool of blood on the floor. With the toe of his boot, he flipped Nate's body onto his back, then bent to unfasten the ring of keys at his waist.

Eyes as black as hell slid toward Roy. An instant later, the door of his cell creaked open.

But Roy made no move toward freedom.

The intruder inclined his head. At last he spoke. "Roy, Roy," he murmured. He shook his head. "Did you really think you could rob me and get away with it?"

Roy fell to his knees. "I was bringing the bankroll back, Sam, I swear. But then my horse went lame and the marshal caught me trying to steal one—"

An odd gleam entered Sam's eyes. "The marshal," he repeated. "Where is he anyway? I have to admit, I was hoping that son of a bitch MacKenzie would be here." His gaze was utterly remorseless as it encompassed the two bodies lying on the floor.

Roy blanched. He could almost feel the tickle of hemp against his neck. "I don't know," he hedged. "Though it seems he might have found out where your hideout is . . . I heard 'em talking, you see . . ."

Sam had gone very still. "Is that where he is? Gone to the hideout?"

Roy swallowed, unable to tear his eyes from the other man's face. "I—I don't know," he whined.

"The hell you don't!" Sam's shout rang from the rafters. "He went after me, didn't he? MacKenzie went to the hideout. And you told him where it was, didn't you, you squirmy little worm?"

Roy's skin was as pasty-looking as flour and water. "I—I had to, I swear. Sam, I had no choice. He—he told me he'd blow my head off if I didn't—"

Sam ground his teeth in order to keep from snatching his gun from his holster and blowing Roy's head off himself. Goddammit, he raged inwardly. Even if he'd wanted to leave the Territory, he couldn't—not yet. He had a fortune cached at the hideout. He couldn't leave without one last trip there . . .

Sam's face was stripped of all expression, but the fires of hell blazed in his eyes. "When did MacKenzie leave?" he demanded.

"I—I don't know for sure. He just found out this afternoon, Sam, I swear." Roy was whining like a puppy dog. "I—I heard one of the deputies say his old man's got a ranch just east of town . . . the Diamondback or something like that . . . Could be he's gone there for the night and intends to head out in the morning . . ."

Sam's mind was racing. Maybe, he decided, Roy had done him a favor after all. It had been an unpleasant surprise to discover that Dillon MacKenzie was still alive, and a lawman yet . . . Why, not six months ago the bastard had killed two members of his gang.

And that same day, MacKenzie had found out for himself why the legendary Stringer Sam had never been caught. No doubt *he* was the one MacKenzie had really been after, but so what? Sam had slipped beneath the long arm of the law too many times to be bothered by the likes of Dillon MacKenzie.

His mind sifted back. MacKenzie hadn't been a lawman two years ago . . . He recalled that long-ago day he'd hauled MacKenzie from his stagecoach, him and his ladybird. Shit, but the man had a mouth! MacKenzie had sworn to see him in his grave . . . A smirk curled Sam's lips. It was with a great deal of pleasure that he'd decided MacKenzie deserved a slow, painful death . . . He'd taken even more pleasure in taking MacKenzie's woman as his own . . .

Cruel lips flattened in a vicious sneer. But the bastard hadn't died, God rot his soul!

This time, Sam vowed coldly, he wouldn't fail.

Roy's eyes darted back and forth between Sam and the door. Could he make it? he wondered frantically. It was worth a try, he decided. But before he could make a move, Sam lifted his head. His smile was purely malicious.

In his hand was a length of rope.

Roy staggered back. "Please, Sam." He was blubbering like a baby. "Please don't kill me. Please . . ."

Down the street, the merry song-and-dance at the Silver Spur continued. A shout of ribald laughter drifted on the air as Rowdy Roy choked his last breath . . .

The townspeople found his body strung up from the gnarled branches of the old cottonwood tree behind the jail the next morning.

Chapter 1

The house was two-story and sprawling, set back among a windbreak of towering cottonwood trees. Beyond the house and cluster of outbuildings, the Laramie Mountains rose in shadowed silhouette against the backdrop of a cloudless sky.

Abigail MacKenzie stood on the porch, her slender figure garbed in faded brown cotton. A gust of wind blew a stray strand of hair across her cheek; she pushed it away and flipped the thick chestnut braid from her shoulder to her back. A faint frown marred the honeyed skin of her forehead as she anxiously scanned the horizon.

Lord, but she regretted her argument with Pa this morning! She had stewed and fretted since he'd left, so much so that Dorothy had finally chased her outside.

Yet it wasn't all her fault! Her life revolved around the Diamondback ranch, and her marital status—or lack of it—had never concerned her. But lately Pa had begun to bring up the subject more and more often. It didn't help that Dillon had begun to chide her about it as well.

"No one could put up with you, little sister," he'd told her just last week. "You're too damned full of starch and sass. And no man likes to be told what to do—especially by a woman."

The usually soft line of Abby's lips tightened. Just thinking of Dillon's lofty tone and mocking grin infuriated her all over again. And now Pa had practically called her an old maid, too!

Her father's approval was the one thing she'd always sought—and most of the time she succeeded in getting it. She could ride and shoot and rope as well as any of the ranch hands, which was why she'd gone after that stray calf yesterday morning.

Sure enough, she'd managed to find him. He'd also managed to get himself cornered by a timber wolf; a skitter of excitement had raced through her. They'd lost a dozen calves and yearlings the last few months. Lucas was convinced a wolf was responsible. Could this be the one? And wouldn't Pa be glad if she nailed this critter straight through the heart?

But the wolf had bolted, and he was a wily one indeed. He'd led her in circles for hours before she finally found his trail again, which was why she hadn't gotten back to the ranch until well after midnight. Pa was pacing a hole through the rug in his study. Lord, but he could boom and bluster! He'd shouted so that Abby was certain she'd heard the windows rattling in their frames.

"God Almighty!" he exploded. "What possessed you to take off like that? Do you know what's been going through my mind? I thought you were lost. Lying hurt somewhere—maybe even dead!" Duncan MacKenzie ran a meaty hand through the thatch of iron-gray hair on his head and glared at his daughter.

Abby dropped her gloves on his desk. "I told

Lucas where I was going," she said coolly. Lucas was her father's foreman. "Besides, it's not the first time I've chased down a stray calf."

"It's the first time you didn't have sense to come back before nightfall!"

He leveled a gaze of fearsome intensity upon her—not that she showed any signs of backing down, or even bending a little. The seconds ticked by while they fought a silent battle of wills. Finally Duncan swore silently. Abby was a strip off his own hide, all right—and so was her brother.

"Isn't it enough that your brother risks his damn fool hide trailing outlaws from here to kingdom come? And all in the name of law and order!" He snorted, and Abby was heartily thankful Dillon wasn't there to hear him. "Now you're chasing halfway across the country after a five-dollar calf!" he finished. "I'm not so greedy that I'll miss that five dollars, missy!"

"But it wasn't just the calf," she proclaimed with a shake of her head. "There was a wolf on his heels when I found him. He ran off when I showed up but I tracked him down." Her eyes gleamed. "I found the wolf's den, Pa—and his mate." She thought of the pelts tied to her saddle and tossed her head triumphantly. "I made sure we won't lose any more calves to those two, Pa."

It was a hollow victory. Pa remained unimpressed, and Abby slipped upstairs to her room, more than a little disappointed.

When she'd come downstairs before sunup this morning, she had decided it might be wise to say no more about the whole episode. They planned to start branding out in the summer pasture today.

Abby had taken it for granted that she would be present as usual.

Pa had curtly refused.

Abby shoved back her plate and regarded him with narrowed eyes. "I haven't missed a branding in years, Pa!"

"Well, you're going to miss this one," he shot back.

Abby glanced at Dorothy, who stood at the stove in the corner sliding flapjacks onto a plate. Dorothy was Lucas's wife; she and Lucas had a small house out behind the barn, and Dorothy did the cooking and cleaning for them as well. Was it her imagination, or were Dorothy's shoulders shaking with laughter?

Her gaze slid back to Pa. "You're still riled up about last night," she muttered.

"Damn right I am. I want you close to home, Abby, do you hear?"

When Abby said nothing, his eyes sought Dorothy's. "Dorothy," he said more quietly, "would you go out and ask someone to saddle up Brandy for me?"

Dorothy flitted from the kitchen, her lips twitching in amusement.

His gaze returned to Abby, who hadn't relieved him of that accusatory stare. Her chin jutted out, a smaller, more delicate version of his. "Why?" she demanded. "Why now?"

"Because I can't trust you further than I can see you, young lady." Duncan's chair scraped against the floor. "Maybe I ought to marry you off to Buck Russell and be done with you!"

Abby gasped. Buck Russell, who owned the

neighboring ranch on their eastern border, had made it known to Pa that he wasn't averse to uniting the two families—and their ranches.

"Pa, I can't believe I heard you right! You don't even like Buck Russell. Besides, we—we're a team, Pa. You always said so and we—we love this place. Why, what would happen to the ranch if I weren't here? Dillon wouldn't be here for you like I am . . . you were right when you said he'd rather be off chasing outlaws than chasing stray calves!"

An odd expression crossed Duncan's features; too late Abby wished she hadn't spoken. While there was a part of him that was proud his son was Laramie's marshal, she alone knew how deeply it pained him that Dillon had never been interested in the ranch. But she didn't dare say so, for that very reason.

Instead, she let an uneasy laugh escape. "Besides," she went on quickly, "you don't like Buck Russell. We both know the only reason he would ever marry me is to get his hands on the Diamondback!"

Duncan let his eyes drift slowly over his daughter, taking in the rich mane of chestnut hair that tumbled down her back. Her shoulders were stiff with pride, the tilt of her chin defiant. Her eyes were snapping, as blue as the summer sky outside. She was a beauty, all right. Oh, not the conventional kind—she wasn't frail and fragile. He thought of how she'd grown up right before his eyes, and somehow he'd never even noticed until lately—or perhaps he hadn't wanted to. But Abby was full of fire and passion, just like her mother—the kind of woman that drove a man to heaven and hell and back again . . . the kind that made each day better than the last.

Duncan plucked his hat from the peg on the wall. He stared at Abby, fingering the wide brim in his hands. "I'm not so sure about that," he said slowly. "I don't think there's a man alive wouldn't give his soul to get his hands on a sweet little thing like you, daughter." He saw her eyes go wide with shock and knew he'd startled her with his bluntness. A grim smile etched his lips. "But Buck Russell knows how to run a ranch, Abby. And at least the Diamondback would be in good hands when I'm gone."

When I'm gone. It was odd, the effect those words had on her. Pa . . . dead. The chill that slipped over her penetrated clear to her bones. She shivered. She didn't like to think of it. Nor could she ever remember him speaking of his own death before.

Now, hours later, that same prickly sense of unease ran up her spine. All at once the wind began to lull. There was a peculiar stillness in the air, as if the entire world held its breath. Even the bluejays ceased their screeching, as if in warning . . .

Abby's hands tightened around the wooden railing of the porch. Something was wrong, she thought vaguely. Her reaction was more instinct than conscious thought.

The sound of drumming hoofbeats reached her ears. It was then that she saw a buckboard rounding the last bend in the road. Hazy clouds of dust spiraled skyward behind it. Hitched to the back was a strawberry roan that looked just like Brandy.

Abby stood as if paralyzed. Some strange force beyond her control held her rooted to the floor of the porch, like an ancient tree. She could only watch with a horrifying sense of inevitability as the buckboard drew nearer to the house.

There was a tall male form stretched out in the back, limp and prone.

Her first thought was that she'd never seen a dead man. Her second was that this was a dream . . . A dream? Dear God, a nightmare . . .

Because the man was her father.

Nor was he dead.

There was a low moan as the buckboard rolled to a halt. It was that sound which finally galvanized her into action. Abby flew down the stairs and climbed into the back of the buckboard. She sank to her knees and cradled her father's head in her lap.

A thin aborted cry tore from her lips. "Pa! Oh, Pa—" A crimson stain darkened the front of his shirt. His skin was as white as snow. Her heart lurched. "Pa, what happened? My God, what happened?"

Lucas hovered across from her, his leathery face lined and anxious. "We got worried when he didn't show at the branding site. Grady and I rode out to see where he was. We found him out near Sparrow Creek. He's been shot, Miss Abby. Grady and I . . . we did our best to stop the bleeding . . . I sent Grady into town after the doc . . ." Lucas swallowed, unable to go on.

At that, Duncan's eyelids fluttered open. Abby stared into blue eyes so like her own. Only Pa's were dull and clouded with pain.

"It's too late," he rasped.

"Don't say that! Don't even think it!" The words were torn from deep inside her—a cry of outrage, a fervent plea.

Duncan's lips twisted, more grimace than smile. "You'll never change, will you, Abby?" His feeble tone tore at her heart. "Always . . . have to have . . . the last . . . word."

Abby began to shake all over. "Pa," she whispered.

His breath seemed to rattle in his chest. "Got to listen, Abby . . . Stringer Sam . . ."

"Stringer Sam! Is that who did this to you? Did he shoot you, Pa?"

His eyes closed once in silent assent. His lips barely moved as he spoke.

"Honey, you got to listen . . . Late last night when you were gone after that calf, Dillon came by . . . Had a prisoner in jail by the name of Rowdy Roy who was hooked up with Stringer Sam's gang . . . Seems Roy knew where Sam's hideout is. Dillon got Roy to tell him, so he rode out late last night to find . . . the hideout. Dillon said he'd catch Stringer Sam . . . if he had to wait forever. This morning Sam rode out here . . . after Dillon . . . I wouldn't tell him where he was . . . only Sam—he laughed and said he already knew . . ."

Abby's head was spinning. "Pa, wait! He knew that Dillon went after him?"

Pa nodded.

She groaned. "How?"

"Sam said Rowdy Roy turned tail on him . . . so he hunted him down . . . He broke into the jail last night and killed Roy and the two deputies . . . But before he did, Roy told Sam he'd already let

Dillon know where his hideout was . ... that Dillon intended to ride out after him today . . ."

Comprehension dawned with a sickening rush. Sam had come here to the ranch to kill Dillon. Instead he'd found Pa.

"Abby, if Dillon manages to find Sam's hideout . . . he doesn't know that Sam's right behind him . . ."

Oh, God, she thought, sickened. Her blood seemed to freeze in her veins.

Her mind traveled fleetingly back, to the time nearly three years ago when Dillon, based at Fort Bridger, had still been scouting for the U.S. Army. Both she and Pa had been surprised—but very pleased—when Dillon wrote to say he was engaged to be married. Rose had been the daughter of a captain stationed there.

The wedding never took place.

With a twist of her heart, Abby recalled how he and Rose had boarded a stagecoach headed for Laramie. Not far from the fort, the coach had been robbed—by none other than Stringer Sam. Beyond that, Abby knew little. Dillon had always been very close-mouthed about the details.

But Rose and the driver had been killed. Stringer Sam had shot Dillon and left him for dead, but Dillon had survived. He'd recovered at Fort Bridger, then spent the next year in search of Stringer Sam, to no avail. Pa had begged him to give up the search and come home. Eventually, Dillon had, only because Pa had asked him to.

But he was a changed man, moody and bitter. Abby recalled how Pa had once confided that he suspected Dillon had taken the post of Laramie marshal in the hopes that it might someday put him on Stringer Sam's trail . . .

Dear God, it had.

Abby shuddered. It was a miracle that Dillon had ever survived; Stringer Sam had left him there to die . . .

Now the outlaw had done the same to Pa. A dizzying fear swept over her. Surely Dillon couldn't be so unlucky a third time . . . But there was a saying—that bad luck came in threes . . .

Pa moaned. "Don't want you to lose Dillon, too. Got to have someone to look after you . . ."

Abby stifled a sob. She could see him straining desperately to breathe, trying vainly to drag air into his lungs, struggling to hold on. He clutched at her fingers.

"Abby," he gasped. His chest was heaving, his breathing a mere trickle. She had to drop her head close to his lips in order to hear. "You have to find him . . . Find Dillon and warn him before Sam kills him, too." His fingers twisted around hers. His expression was tortured and imploring. "Promise me, honey. Promise . . . me."

Tears streamed down her face. "I promise," she choked. "Pa, I promise."

His eyes closed; the grip on her fingers grew slack.

"Pa," she screamed. "*Pa!*"

This time Pa didn't hear.

Abby was only dimly aware of Lucas leading her into the parlor. There she clung to Dorothy.

"Dorothy," she sobbed. "He—he's dead."

Dorothy found it difficult not to break into tears

herself. "I know, child," she whispered. "I know."
At length the older woman eased her down at the
table. She squeezed the girl's shoulder, and went
to fetch a cup of strong hot coffee.

After that first small storm, Abby's tears ceased.
A curious kind of numbness overtook her; she stared
listlessly at her hands, so neatly folded in her lap,
and let her mind wander at will.

She noted distantly how tanned her hands were,
the color a rich dark honey. It had never concerned
her that her skin wasn't milky-white, which was
why she took no precautions to shield herself from
the sun. She wore a cowboy hat when she was
out riding, but the only bonnet she'd ever owned
had been given to her on her twelfth birthday by
a schoolmate, Emily Dawson. It was white and
frilly and decorated with pink satin ribbons. She
remembered how proudly she'd paraded in front
of Pa and Dillon. Pa had tried hard not to laugh
aloud, but Dillon hooted openly. That was the last
time—the only time—Abby had worn a bonnet.

It was Emily's mother who had convinced Pa
that her education was sorely lacking when it came
to ladylike qualities. When she was seventeen, her
father decided maybe Mrs. Dawson was right—
maybe it was time his Abigail learned to be a proper lady. Abby had argued and cried and pleaded,
but he'd packed her off to that fancy girls' school in
Chicago despite her protests. Mrs. Rutherford, the
headmistress, had been shockingly appalled at her
golden skin—and frankly dismayed at her loose-
limbed, leggy stride.

"This—this *creature*," Mrs. Rutherford had sniffed
disdainfully when her father came to collect her a

scant month later, "will never be a lady. She can't sing. She can't dance—but I'm not surprised since she walks like a cow!"

Abby had lost her temper then. "Look who's talking," she retorted. "Did you ever hear yourself laugh, lady? You whinny like a horse who got his behind stuck on a fence post!"

Pa hadn't been pleased that Mrs. Rutherford had dismissed her from the school. It was only later when they were on the train and headed back to Wyoming that he confided he shared her opinion of Mrs. Rutherford—her brain was surely stuffed with chicken scratch.

Abby watched her fingers curl into her palm, so tightly her nails dug into her skin. But the pain was like nothing compared to the ache in her heart. For as long as she could remember, she had relied on Pa. She was seven when her mother died from pneumonia. Dillon had been seventeen, already a man. But Abby was still a child—with a child's tender need for shelter and protection—and Duncan MacKenzie had taken on a role not every man could have accomplished. While Dillon was off scouting for the army, Abby and her father had clung to each other and shared their grief. He had taught her, played with her, and indulged her. Abby had grown up strong and proud, and when she'd needed someone to hold her, her father had always been there. Abby had sometimes teased him that she'd probably never marry.

"I couldn't bear to live anywhere other than the Diamondback," she'd laugh. "Besides, you wouldn't like it if you and Dillon weren't the most important men in my life, would you?"

A wrenching pain ripped through her; it felt like her soul was on fire. Now Pa was gone. *Gone*. And all she had left was Dillon.

Abby couldn't suppress a twinge of bitterness. Dillon was never around when they needed him. Her mind screamed in silent outrage. *Damn you, Dillon! Where are you? Where?* It was just like him— just like a man!—to think he was invincible.

Stringer Sam had already proved that he wasn't.

Yet she didn't wonder why Dillon had gone after Sam. To her knowledge, only once had Dillon ever considered marrying and settling down—but Stringer Sam had shattered his dreams. For Dillon, in this instance, at least, it was less a job than a vendetta . . .

But she had made a promise to Pa that she could never hope to keep. A debilitating sense of helplessness seeped through her. How on earth was she to find Dillon? The only man who knew where Stringer Sam's outlaw hideout was had been killed!

"Dillon," she whispered. "Oh, Dillon, why are you so—so reckless? And why can't you love this land like Pa and me?" A hot ache constricted her throat. She battled the overwhelming need to cry.

Behind her someone gently coughed. Abby jerked around in time to see Lucas step into the parlor.

It was a moment before she was able to speak. "Is Dr. Foley gone?" She'd seen his buggy drive up just after Lucas led her inside.

Lucas pulled off his hat and nodded. "He asked me to pass on his respects, Miss Abby." His voice sounded as rusty as hers.

Abby looked away, unable to bear the anguish

in his eyes. The burning threat of tears made her chest ache.

She raised trembling hands to her face. "Lucas," she said on a half-sob. "Oh, Lucas, what am I going to do? I promised Pa I'd find Dillon and warn him Stringer Sam was after him. But how?" she cried hopelessly. "I don't know where that—that damned outlaw's hideout is! No one does—not now!"

Lucas was at her side in two steps. "Don't take on so, Miss Abby." He patted her shoulder awkwardly. "I know it sounds crazy, but maybe we can find Dillon and warn him after all."

She looked up with a gasp, convinced he was only trying to soothe her and make her feel better. But his grizzled expression was deadly serious.

"What do you mean?" Her breathing grew jerky. "Lucas, tell me!"

He half-turned and beckoned to someone in the hall just outside the door. Abby watched as a sandy-haired young man stepped into the parlor, clutching his hat between both hands. It was Grady, the man Lucas had sent into town after Doc Foley.

He tipped his head toward her. "I'm real sorry about your pa, miss."

She murmured her thanks.

Lucas nodded. "Grady, tell Miss Abby what you told me."

The young man shifted his booted feet. "Well," he began. "The doc wasn't in his office when I got to town. I went over to the Silver Spur to wait 'till the doc got back. It wasn't long before this guy comes down the stairs."

Excitement began to mount in his voice; Abby listened intently.

"Things got real quiet all of a sudden. You can tell just by lookin' that this guy's mean as a rattle-snake. All dressed in black, he was, with a pair of Colts strapped to his legs. And his eyes . . . I swear he's got the strangest eyes a body ever saw—kinda silvery, like a looking glass that'll slice right through a man."

Abby's brows rose slightly. "Who is he, Grady?"

"Seems his name is Kane—that's all he goes by—Kane. Roger Simms was sitting next to me and he told me town gossip has it that Kane rode with Stringer Sam's gang a few years back."

Abby's jaw clamped shut. "If he's an outlaw and everyone knows it, why isn't he in jail?"

Grady exchanged glances with Lucas. It was Lucas who quietly offered, "Abby, a man values his life above all else. I hate to say it, but after what happened to Andy Horner and Nate Gilmore last night, Stringer Sam and every one of his gang could probably walk straight through town and not a single man would raise a hand against him."

" 'Lest he was a fool," Grady chimed in with a faint smile.

It was a smile that was extremely short-lived. One scathing glance from Abby banished the inclination, while inside she seethed. Was this why Stringer Sam had never been caught? Were people so afraid of him that they would turn a blind eye to his treachery rather than see him put behind bars once and for all?

Fear was a powerful weapon indeed. It was an acknowledgment Abby made bitterly.

"Maybe this man Kane was part of it, too—maybe he helped Stringer Sam kill his man Roy and the two deputies." She glanced at the two men for their reaction.

To her surprise, Grady appeared uncomfortable. He shifted his feet, his gaze trained on the rug between his feet. "Begging your pardon, ma'am," he muttered, stumbling slightly. "But it seems a—a lady can vouch for the fact she was with Kane most of the night. And someone told Roger he's looking for work."

Abby's eyes had gone wide. A lady. She was under no illusions as to the type of "lady" he meant. Grady's cheeks were flame-red—and so were hers. She scarcely heard the last of his words.

Instead she considered the information Grady had revealed. As she did, a burgeoning hope began to blossom inside her.

She laid a hand on Lucas's arm. "Lucas," she said slowly, "if this man—Kane—really was part of Stringer Sam's gang, do you think it's possible that *he* would know where the hideout is located?" She held her breath and waited.

"Indeed I do," he said grimly. "That's why I brought Grady in to see you."

"Then there's only one thing left to do." She turned to Grady. "Grady, would you go out to the barn and saddle Sonny for me?"

He jammed his hat on his head. "Sure thing, ma'am."

Her steps purposeful, she strode from the room. She was halfway up the stairs before Lucas's voice halted her.

"Miss Abby, where . . . what do you think you're doing?"

Abby paused, turned and looked down at him.

Another time, another place, and she might have laughed at his gaping astonishment.

She smiled faintly. "I think you know, Lucas."

His face had turned dark as a thundercloud. "Miss Abby, you can't. Why, it's crazy! The man's an outlaw! No doubt he's a killer just like Stringer Sam . . ." He stopped and cursed silently. He'd known Miss Abby too darned long not to recognize the stubborn set of that pretty little chin.

Watching him, seeing the bleakness creep into his lined features, Abby felt her heart rend in two. Pa had been gone . . . what? Only a few hours.

She felt as if a lifetime had passed since then.

And yet there wasn't time to see that Pa had a decent burial—she would have to leave that to Dorothy and Lucas. There wasn't time to mourn him . . . to say a last good-bye.

There wasn't even time to cry.

Lucas continued to stare up at her. "Miss Abby," he said finally, "you don't have to do this. Let me go instead."

A hot ache constricted her throat. Her heart brimmed with misery. "No, Lucas," she said, her voice low and choked. "I need you here at the ranch. Besides, I promised Pa. I made that promise, Lucas, and it's up to me to fulfill it. I know it's risky, but this may be the only way to save Dillon—Kane may be the only man who can save my brother's life." She drew a deep tremulous breath, her eyes full of quiet desperation. "I have to find him, Lucas. I have to find Kane."

Chapter 2

❝**L**et's go upstairs," she whispered.

His lazy slouch against the bar was deceptive. Standing, he was a full six-foot-two inches of lean, spare flesh with the instincts of a predator. His hair was black as a crow's wing, but whether his coloring came from his mama or his papa, he had no idea . . . because he'd never known either one. His mother was a drunk who'd left him on his own when he was just a kid; his father had never stayed around to begin with.

"Kane?" The voice came again, a sultry invitation close to his ear.

Soft feminine arms twined around his waist. Daisy draped herself against his back, thrilling to the intimate press of her stomach against his buttocks. She remembered splaying her hands against him last night, glorying in the way he tensed and flexed with each sinuous motion of his hips.

A smile of remembered satisfaction played over her full, rouged lips. *Such a man*, she recalled. *More man than most*.

Her fingers toyed with the thick dark strands of the hair that grew low on his nape. He hadn't been inclined to talk last night, but that was all right. And for all that those glittering silver eyes

29

gleamed icy and cool, he was a superb lover, not at all selfish like most of her customers. Why, it seemed almost a sin to take his money!

And it wasn't the thought of his money that was making her burn inside again. Her hands fluttered over his chest. She rotated her hips and whispered his name huskily once again, hoping he would take the hint.

Kane released a long, pent-up sigh of frustration. He turned, trying to ease free of her cloying grip. Christ, she had hands like an octopus! When he would have stepped aside, she raised her head and kissed him. Her fingers plunged into his hair, shaping themselves to his scalp. Her lips clung— like a leech, he thought disgustedly. God, and she tasted like sour whiskey.

He finally managed to tear his mouth from hers. He stared at her, his vision blurred. All that registered was brassy red hair and a figure that had started to go to fat. His mind groped fuzzily for a name. Christ, was it him or was he drunker than he thought? Or had there simply been so many women—in so many towns—that they'd all begun to look alike?

Dolly! That was it, her name was Dolly.

"Dolly—" he began.

The furrows on her brow deepened. "Daisy," she corrected with a pout that might have once been pretty. Now it was only pathetic. "Don't you remember, Kane? I'm Daisy."

When he said nothing, only continued to stare at her in a way that totally unnerved her, she eased back from his chest. "Kane?" For the first time a hint of uncertainty underscored his name. "Did I . . . do something wrong?"

Wrong. The word roused a soul-deep bitterness. His jaw clenched so tight he thought it would crack. Here he was, back among humanity, such as it was, and he wasn't sure he belonged—he wasn't sure he was *fit* to belong. So who the hell was he to judge right or wrong?

Daisy started to step back. The movement reminded Kane of her presence. Some of the harshness left his features as his eyes met hers. She looked so anxious, a twinge of remorse cut through him. He had used her, he realized. He had sought forgetfulness in her arms and her body . . .

If only he could find forgiveness as easily.

"You didn't do anything wrong," he said softly. "But you're too much woman for an ornery old cuss like me, Daisy." He pressed a coin into her palm at the same time he pressed a fleeting kiss upon her lips. "Find yourself a better man than me for the evening, sweetheart."

He picked up his glass from the bar, turned and walked to a table in the corner . . . alone.

Hands on her hips, Daisy watched him disappear into the crowd. *Lordy, but he's a strange one.* She shrugged. With a flounce of her skirt, she twirled to the man on her left.

At the table, Kane wondered why the hell he was here. The ladies were getting to him. He was tired of their simpering and giggling. His head ached and the air was thick with smoke and the smell of stale whiskey. No one else seemed to notice. Everyone was rowdy and rambunctious and having a whale of a good time.

Yet the thought of his room upstairs held little appeal. The room was too small, the bed too empty . . . and so was he.

He studied the glass in his hand, aware of a gnawing pain in his gut. The glass was chipped, the contents dark gold and faintly cloudy. With a brooding half-smile, he tipped the glass to his lips and drained it.

When he lowered it, his eyes were watering. For the first time, he understood why this stuff was called rotgut. He'd tasted some strong liquor in his time, but this was powerful enough to burn clear through a man's belly.

Maybe it wasn't the whiskey at all . . . but guilt that forged that searing hole inside him.

But right now Kane didn't care. He didn't give a damn about much of anything these days, and hadn't for a long time. With a flick of his wrist, a tilt of his chin, he raised his glass high and signaled the bartender.

In the back of his mind, he wondered if he'd go to hell for what he had done . . .

Shit. Maybe he was already there.

For the second time that day, Grady crushed his hat in his hands. He wasn't sure about this—he wasn't sure at all.

"Miss Abby," he ventured, "you sure you want to do this?"

"I'll be fine, Grady." She squeezed his arm in silent thanks. "Tell Lucas and Dorothy to take care. I'll be back as soon as I can."

His reluctance obvious, Grady took his leave. Abby watched him round the corner where their horses were tethered. Only when he had urged his mount into a trot did she let out a long pent-up breath, marveling that she'd managed to sound so convincing.

What with the piano, the laughter and the shouting, the noise was enough to make her want to cover her ears and run. She'd managed to conceal it from Grady, but one look through those swinging wooden doors had given her the shock of her life. Of course she'd expected the Silver Spur's patrons would all be men; after all, it was a saloon. What she hadn't expected were those women—and so scantily dressed yet! It had been on the tip of her tongue to blurt out that they'd forgotten half their clothes at home.

Again she cast a furtive peek inside. This time there was a woman seated just inside the door. The reason for the smiling cowboy across from her wasn't lost on Abby. Her dress—what there was of it—was made of scarlet lace and barely covered her knees. The bodice was completely sheer. Why, she couldn't possibly have on a single stitch beneath it! And the way she leaned forward provided the cowboy an unobstructed view of what was clearly a very ample—and unfettered—bosom.

Abby bit back a gasp. Lord Almighty! Now the cowboy was sliding his hand beneath the hem of her skirt!

Abby fled unthinkingly. Once around the corner of the building, she collapsed against the wall with a silent groan of distress. She couldn't go into the Silver Spur after Kane—not dressed the way she was. Why, every eye in the place would be on her!

The shuttered doors swung open. With a swish

of silk and the clatter of heels, someone swirled around the corner.

The girl had clearly just left the Silver Spur. Abby tried to keep from staring, but a nervous giggle bubbled up inside her. Mrs. Rutherford wouldn't have called this girl a lady either. Her red satin dress wasn't as revealing as the one the woman near the door was wearing, but it was still rather daring . . .

That was it! If she was dressed like one of the saloon girls, she wouldn't look out of place. But what if someone recognized her? She squared her shoulders. It was a chance she'd simply have to take.

Her feet moved apace with her mind. She tapped the girl on the shoulder. "Excuse me," she said.

"Yes?" Painted red mouth pursed in annoyance, the girl turned to regard her.

Abby was stunned to see the girl was several years younger than she. She cleared her throat awkwardly. "I know this may sound rather odd—" she began. She leaned forward to whisper in her ear.

When she finished, the girl let out a cackle of laughter. "Honey, that's more than I earn in a week, so say no more. Why, I don't even want the damned thing back!" She linked her arm through Abby's. "Come on, sweetie. My room's right over there."

A scant fifteen minutes later Abby poked her head from a small boardinghouse and hastily glanced outside. The dress—or lack of it—made her cheeks flame with embarrassment. The full skirt dipped only halfway to her ankles; the black silk stockings on her legs made her feel indecent as sin. The bodice was so tight that with every breath she took, she felt as if her breasts were about to spill free. All in all, she felt as bare as a baby's behind.

Thankfully, the streets were deserted. Praying that her luck would hold, she hurriedly stuffed her clothes into her saddlebag and led Sonny into the narrow alley behind the Silver Spur. From there she retraced her steps to the front entrance.

Then a flurry of anxious panic gripped her. Could she go through with this? she wondered frantically. The morals of a lifetime stabbed at her. Pa would have been horrified to see her dressed like a—a soiled dove—and going into a bawdy house yet! And Dillon would have thundered from here to kingdom come if he'd found her here . . . Dillon. Just the thought of the danger her brother faced from Stringer Sam made her cringe in fear.

And she knew she had no choice . . . no choice at all.

Eyes dark and anguished, she stiffened her spine, gave a futile tug at the top of her dress, collected her courage and stepped through the swinging doors.

She was scarcely inside before she felt herself bombarded on all sides. The noise was deafening. The sound of piano music and boisterous laughter seemed to bounce off the walls and ceiling. The stench of male sweat, whiskey and smoke was overpowering; she felt as if her nostrils were burning.

Swallowing her distaste, she inspected her surroundings more closely and found she was standing alongside a wide walnut bar with a brass footrail. Hanging on the wall for all to see was a huge painting of a smiling nude woman sprawled out on a sofa. Abby bit her lip—now *there* was a woman bare as a baby's behind.

A man jostled her arm. His eyes lit up when he saw her; the grin he gave her was leering. "Say, gal," he said on a ninety-proof breath of air, "how about a little dance, just me and you?"

Abby lurched sideways to evade his groping hands. She opened her mouth to deliver a stinging rebuff but she never got the chance.

The barkeep stabbed a finger at her. "You there," he barked. He slapped a tray on the bar and jammed a tall bottle and a small glass on it. "Take this to the fella in the corner."

There was no chance to refuse. The barkeep thrust the tray into her hands. And then refusal was the last thing on Abby's mind . . .

Her mind spun wildly. The man in the corner . . . it was him. *Kane.*

Her feet carried her blindly forward. When she finally stopped at the edge of his table, her heart was thudding so, all she could hear was the blood pounding through her ears.

He looked up.

For what was surely the longest moment of her life, Abby stood paralyzed, staring at the man in the corner. His eyes left her totally unprepared. It was just as Grady said, she thought vaguely. Startlingly light in a starkly masculine face, it was as if he looked not at her, but *through* her, scalding her, burning her inside and out. Not at all comfortable with such relentless regard, Abby felt her throat tighten oddly. It took every ounce of willpower she possessed to banish the unaccustomed impulse to turn and run—as fast and as far as she could.

Her confidence shaky at best, she eased the tray onto the table. "Here's your bottle," she murmured quickly.

If Kane heard, there was no sign of it. This girl . . . he hadn't seen her last night. And she was pretty, he realized suddenly. He was drunker than a man had a right to be, but it wasn't enough to dim her beauty. Her hair was caught up in a velvet ribbon on her crown. He stared at it, momentarily fascinated. The dull, dismal surroundings did nothing to hide the rich, vibrant color. Deep chestnut strands shone with tiny glimmers of gold.

A profusion of curls fell over her shoulder as she bent forward. Unable to stop himself, Kane reached out and tangled his fingers in her hair; the long, chestnut tendril clung greedily, displaying a life of its own. He rubbed the strands between his fingertips, marveling at the silken texture. He found himself battling the urge to crush the lock of hair in his fist and carry it to his nose and mouth, knowing it would smell like a soft scented breeze on a warm spring day.

Caught like a fly in a spider's web, Abby inhaled sharply. Uncertain of his next move, she could only wait for what the moment would bring . . .

She was pretty, he thought again. The ugliness and sterility of his life suddenly mocked him with a vengeance. Indeed, she possessed the face of an angel . . . Despite the fact that she worked in this hellhole, she looked as if she'd never suffered a hardship in her life.

The observation triggered a gut-twisting resentment. He'd seen things—done things—that would drive a sane man to the brink of madness. A bitter ache gnawed at his belly as he recalled all the horrors he'd witnessed . . . Dammit, he thought violently. She had no right to look so—so goddamned angelic! She reminded him of all that had gone wrong in his life . . . and the little that had gone right.

He dropped the lock of hair as if he'd been burned and leaned back in his chair, boldly meeting her gaze. He nodded at the bottle. "Pour," was all he said.

His voice was low—dry and slightly raspy from drink, she guessed . . . Oddly, it was not unpleasant. But he still hadn't relieved her of that unnerving silvery stare. Abby endured it as best she could, flustered but determined not to show it. She lifted the bottle and set it on the table, then poured the glass full of whiskey almost to the brim. The task complete, she wet her lips and began to straighten.

Kane's eyes followed the movement of that pink-tipped tongue around her lips with a scowl. But when it appeared she would withdraw, his hand shot out and clamped around her wrist.

"Sit," he ordered on a grating breath of air.

Abby didn't move. Her thoughts were disjointed and tinged with panic. She couldn't seem to control them any more than she could tear her eyes from where Kane's fingers curled around the fragile span of her wrist. His hold was firm and unyielding, yet not hurtful. His fingers were lean and dark and not the least bit fleshy or dirty. She stared as if in fascination. So these were the hands of an outlaw . . . the hands of a killer. Why wasn't she repulsed by him? she thought wildly. His merest touch should have made her skin crawl, yet she felt all shivery inside. He smoothed his thumb across the fleshy skin of her palm in what was almost a caress . . . Bemused and dismayed by her unpredictable reaction, she tore her eyes back to his face.

"Wh-what do you want?" Her voice came out high and tight; it sounded nothing at all like her own.

For a moment Kane said nothing. He'd startled her, he realized, although why, he couldn't fathom. Surely she was used to it. But her eyes were wide and uncertain and very blue, filled with pinpoints of lights that glittered like tiny jewels. He realized vaguely that he couldn't remember the last time he'd noticed the color of someone's eyes . . .

His lips curled abruptly. Did she know who he was? Undoubtedly. All at once he had no trouble deciphering her expression. She was afraid and trying hard not to show it.

His eyes glinted as he tipped the chair back on two legs. Shoving his thumbs into his belt, he regarded her through half-closed eyelids. "I don't like to play games, sweetheart," he drawled with a lazy half-smile. "Try to keep that in mind."

It was his tone more than the words themselves that rattled Abby from her daze. Why, of all the arrogant . . . A swell of indignant outrage swept through her as he proceeded to inspect her from head to toe. His eyes took liberties no other man had dared, lingering with brazen interest on the tempting swell of her breasts and hips.

Well, she thought half-angrily, half-desperately, at least she had his attention, which was what she'd wanted in the first place. But her fingers fairly itched to slap that insolent smirk from his lips.

The chair came down with a resounding thump. "You gonna sit or not?" he demanded.

Abby clenched her jaw so hard her teeth hurt. She dropped down into the chair unceremoniously. Her lips smiled; her eyes did not as she lifted her chin and returned his bold regard.

She said nothing as he turned and signalled the barkeep for another glass. She kept her head down and averted her eyes when the barkeep delivered it a moment later, praying he wouldn't realize that she didn't belong here. She caught a telltale odor when he shuffled past her and experienced a sliver of relief; apparently the customers weren't the only ones who freely imbibed. That was undoubtedly why he hadn't thrown her out on her ear.

Kane leaned forward and tipped the neck of the bottle into the clean glass. He poured it nearly half full, then set it aside, staring at her straight in the eye, almost as if he expected her to dare or challenge him. "My name's Kane."

"I'm . . . Abigail." She hated the breathless quality of her voice but she couldn't seem to help it.

His laugh got her dander up further. "Abigail, eh? Somehow that doesn't suit you. Sounds too damned prim and proper, for one thing. Maybe I should call you Susannah or Polly or something like that." The brash sweep of his gaze made her grow hot all over.

Abby beat down the fury simmering in her veins. It wouldn't do to anger him, she reminded herself.

She conjured up what she hoped was a convincing smile. "I really prefer Abigail," she murmured.

Kane made no reply. There was a faint, nagging

feeling tugging away inside him. He couldn't dismiss the notion that something wasn't quite right. Abigail—Lord, but it was hard to call her that!—was unlike any whore he'd ever met. Her skin looked fresh and natural, void of any rice powder; nor were her lips rouged like Daisy's. Those incredibly blue eyes were wide and unerringly direct; she didn't reek of cheap perfume. The air of purity which surrounded her was puzzling. He had to remind himself that she was no innocent or she wouldn't be here.

Abby curled her fingers around the glass and brought it closer. She glanced at him with a faint smile. "I . . . I haven't seen you in town before."

He gave a negligent shrug. "I just got in yesterday."

Abby's nerves were jumping. Simply to have something to do, she brought the glass to her lips and took a small sip.

She wasn't prepared for the taste. The liquid burned her throat all the way down so that she coughed and sputtered. Her eyes began to water. When she finally raised her head, she was totally disconcerted to discover Kane watching her with a mocking light in his eyes.

"It's a little strong for my taste," she defended herself weakly.

I'll bet, Kane thought with cynical amusement.

He reached out and caught hold of her hand. "Tell me something, sweetheart." Damn, but he just couldn't bring himself to call her Abigail. "How'd a girl like you get into this line of work?"

He began toying idly with her fingers.

Darn! Abby thought frantically. Did he have to—

to touch her? If she could have pulled away, she would have. Why, just looking at him made it hard to swallow. She was so close she could see each thick dark hair of those devilishly slanted brows. She guessed he had shaved earlier, but already a dark shadow lined his cheeks and jaw. The curl of his lips was thin, maybe even a little harsh. He didn't seem brutal, but she sensed a knife-edged hardness in him. No doubt it came from years of living on the fringes of the law, but the realization did little to quell her uneasiness.

"I suppose you could say I came here . . . out of necessity." Her answer was more instinct than conscious thought. "You see, my father died recently and left me alone with no money." Abby took a deep breath and prayed he wouldn't think she was babbling. "This is my first day, you see. I'm here because I—I had nowhere else to go. No one to turn to—"

Nowhere to run, Kane finished silently . . . and nowhere to hide. Unbidden—unwanted—the thought came out of nowhere, bringing a wealth of bitter remembrance . . . a wealth of aching pain.

Something inside Kane seemed to shrivel up and freeze. "Amen to that," he said heavily. He stared into the cloudy contents of his glass, a bitter twist to his mouth.

A flicker of panic shot through Abby. He looked as if he were a million miles away—and he acted as if he'd completely forgotten her existence. She couldn't let that happen, not when she'd come this far!

"What about you?" she ventured tentatively. "Are you just passing through?"

She breathed a sigh of relief when his gaze lifted, reclaiming hers.

"I've been drifting for quite a while," he said with a shrug. "Thought I'd stick around for a few days and see if any of the ranchers around here could use another hand."

She tipped her head to the side in what she hoped was an inviting pose. Womanly wiles were totally alien to her, but maybe if he were to fall under her spell, he wouldn't refuse her. "In that case," she murmured, "welcome to town." Summoning her courage, ignoring her trepidation, she boldly laid her hand on his where it rested on the tabletop. At the contact, her nerves seemed to quiver. His, she couldn't help but notice, was much wider and bigger than her own.

He focused where her hand lay atop his, seemingly as captivated as she. She held her breath when his gaze trickled slowly up her bare arm toward her face. It rested for a disturbingly long moment on her mouth.

The next thing Abby knew a muscled arm shot out. She felt herself bodily lifted and pulled onto his lap. Struggling for balance, she was forced to twist her fingers in the front of his leather vest.

A searing heat rose within him; he felt as if a fever had entered his blood. Strange, he thought. Tonight with Daisy, he hadn't been able to summon any semblance of desire at all. But with Abigail . . . This potent surge of yearning was suddenly all he could feel . . . and no doubt she could, too.

She wasn't a scrawny little chicken, that's for sure, Kane decided. Her features were delicately molded, yet there was strength in the set of her jaw.

Though she might look—and feel—as fine-boned and breakable as china, she wasn't. As slender as she was, the feel of her flesh beneath his fingers was firm and resilient.

His gaze slid down the ivory column of her neck. Her breasts rose and fell with every breath she took, fanning the burning ache inside him. If they had been alone, he wouldn't delay sampling such tempting bounty with lips and hands and mouth.

No, he thought again, she was no innocent.

"You want to dance?" His whisper was hot and breathy in her ear.

Speech was impossible. Abby's pulse fluttered like a wild bird. The single thought dominating her mind was that he must have been a giant. Even sitting on his lap, she had to tilt her chin slightly to meet his eyes. The hungry way he looked at her did nothing to alleviate her apprehension. His hand scaling up and down the length of her spine left a trail of burning heat wherever he touched. She wanted to scream at him to stop, but she could hardly take in enough air to breathe, let alone speak.

Finally she looked away in confusion. "I'm not really in the mood for dancing," she heard herself say.

"Good," he said thickly. "Because neither am I." Kane couldn't control his response to her nearness. He was only a man, and not a very upright one at that. She felt so warm, so alive, while he felt a part of him had died inside. Maybe it was selfish, but right now he wanted to claim some of that vibrant warmth for his own.

To hell with the ache in his head, he thought suddenly. It had settled in his nether regions.

One hand came up to tangle in her hair. With the other he guided her chin upward and fused his lips to hers. In the back of his mind he expected her to taste of sour whiskey, like Daisy. But her lips had the lush redness of ripe strawberries—and tasted just as sweet.

Abby had one terrifying glimpse of fiercely glowing eyes just before his mouth came down on hers. Her heart lurched. Her mind—her entire being— spun crazily. Her only thought was how she'd been sweet on Marcus Connors for ages. He'd given her her first—her only—real kiss. But it wasn't long before she realized it was nothing like this!

Shock and panic kept her motionless in his arms; his kiss was far beyond Abby's experience. His mouth was hot and hard against hers; she had no choice but to part her lips against the demanding pressure of his. When she did, his tongue dove swift and sure, ruthlessly stroking the honeyed depths of her mouth. She inhaled sharply, scandalized that he would invade her this way. Part of her wanted to struggle, to push him back and demand that he apologize for his brazenness. Yet it wasn't so very unpleasant after all. She felt her fingers curl helplessly into his shoulders. Everything inside her seemed to melt and go weak. She gave a silent prayer of thanks that she was sitting, for if she'd been standing, she'd surely have fallen into a graceless heap.

By the time he lifted his head she was panting softly.

His arm was tight about her waist. He nuzzled the velvety skin of her temple. "There's a better place for this, sweetheart."

His words were a husky whisper directly in her ear. Abby dragged in a startled, half-frightened breath. "What?" she gasped.

"Let's go upstairs. To my room."

Her mind worked frantically. His breathing was jagged and heavy against her cheek. Surely he wasn't saying that he . . . that they . . . Abby didn't know exactly what went on in those rooms upstairs, but she had a pretty good idea. She also suspected that Kane—if she let him—was about to further her education.

The problem was that she didn't have a plan beyond demanding that he help her. Mute frustration welled up inside her. Maybe she should have dragged him out of the saloon, tied him up and kidnapped him . . . The thought never evolved beyond that.

Because it seemed she had a plan after all.

The quick hard pounding of her heart seemed to jolt her entire body. "Whatever you say," she whispered.

With a surge of power he was on his feet. Abby allowed him lead her upstairs, caught squarely between excitement and fear. There would be no turning back now, she acknowledged. Up until this moment, she could have bolted and ran if the going got too rough. But once she was alone with Kane upstairs, that might prove far more difficult.

In his room, Abby stood near the door and rubbed her hands together while Kane lit a lamp. She glanced around as hazy yellow light began to fill the corner. There was a wide bed pushed against one wall, covered with a faded blue quilt. A cracked, yellowed washbasin that had once been white stood atop a small table on the opposite wall. A worn leather saddlebag slumped on the room's only chair.

A crash from the piano downstairs made her jump. How on earth could anyone sleep here, Abby wondered in annoyance . . . All at once she felt like a fool. *You idiot!* she berated herself fiercely. Sleeping obviously wasn't what they came here for.

Trying not to think about the blush that was surely staining her cheeks, her eyes sought Kane's. It didn't help to discover he was standing near the foot of the bed, watching her with those strange silver eyes.

"Come here."

Abby didn't move. She wondered wildly if she hadn't just made the biggest mistake of her life. Kane was so much taller than she. It was a certainty he was stronger . . .

"The night's not gettin' any longer," he drawled. "What are you waiting for?" His smile was slow and lazy, almost taunting.

Feeling like a man on his way to the hangman's noose, Abby moved forward on wooden legs.

Kane's smile waned as she came nearer. In some far distant corner of his mind, he wondered again why she was here at the Silver Spur. A woman like her deserved far more than the little she had.

No, he wasn't so drunk that he couldn't appreciate her beauty. Just the sight of her made his mouth go dry; his blood pooled thickly in his loins. For all her slenderness, her breasts were lush and delectably shaped; he'd have bet his last dollar her rounded fullness would fit his hands perfectly.

The thought made him grit his teeth with need.

He ached with the need to strip the clothes from her body and explore every sweet, enticing inch of her. And he promised himself that soon he would . . . very soon.

His eyes never left hers as he pulled off his gun belt, walked across the rough plank floor and draped it over the chair. A moment later he caught her hand and pulled her against him. He wasted no time feasting on the sweetness of her mouth.

Abby had no choice but to endure his embrace. He held her so tightly she could scarcely move. Her breasts were flattened against the granite plane of his chest. And her tummy was nestled intimately against his . . . why, she couldn't even think it!

But there was more to come. Abby didn't realize he was nudging her backward until it was too late. She felt something behind her knees and then she was tumbling back, the weight of his body guiding her fall against the mattress.

She jammed her fists instinctively against his shoulders, but he paid no heed. His body was anchored to her own, his mouth on the sweeping arch of her throat. "Relax," he muttered. "I'm not worried about the price. We'll settle up later."

He trapped her mouth beneath his again. His hand swept aside a strap and trespassed beneath the red silk bodice, laying claim to the arching curve of her breast. To Abby, his hand was like a brand, touching flesh that no man had ever touched. As if that weren't enough, she felt the graze of roughened fingertips across her nipple. Once. Twice . . . again. Shocked by such blatant intimacy, Abby lay motionless for a moment . . . but only for a moment.

Somehow she succeeded in twisting her head away. "Wait!" she cried.

Her plea emerged in a strangled gasp. Kane's head lifted slowly. He still lay atop her, his legs tangled with her own. His eyes were glittering shards of light. "Christ! Don't tell me you've changed your mind."

The edge in his voice was just a little frightening. Abby drew a deep, tremulous breath. For just a moment, uncertainty eroded her determination.

But she had come this far. And now she was so close! She forced herself to concentrate on her purpose for coming here. Dillon's life depended on her. And she would do whatever she must to save him.

"No," she denied quickly. "It's just that . . ." She broke off, grappling for an excuse, but nothing came to mind. And all the while Kane stared at her—through her. His hand deserted her breast, yet still Abby felt curiously exposed and naked. The only sound in the room was the ragged trickle of her breathing.

"Wait a minute," he said finally. "You said your father just died . . . Don't tell me you've never been with a man . . . that this is the first time you've ever . . ."

A betraying flush crept into her cheeks. Her eyes flitted away from the relentless demand in his. She couldn't look at him—she just couldn't.

She acknowledged his assumption with a tiny nod.

Kane swore with blunt profanity. His body felt like a spring about to uncoil; his desire for her was a twisting ache in his gut. It was that part of him that urged him to be kind to his body and soothe the raging fire inside. Yet he'd never lain with a virgin. Not even Lorelei . . .

He rolled off her and got to his feet. Disgust marked every taut line of his body. "Thanks, honey," he said tightly, "but I'm afraid I'll have to pass."

His statement brought her upright in a flash. "Please, I—it's all right, really. I mean, if it's not you, it'll just be someone else." She was floundering and prayed he didn't know it. She reached for him, keeping her hands anchored to his shoulders. "And I'd really rather it was you, Kane."

She was a little shocked that she could be so bold, but hoping to add credence to her words, she levered herself on tiptoe and placed her lips on his.

Kane inhaled sharply, suddenly disinclined to argue. Knowing she wanted him only inflamed him further, and the shy, tentative way she moved her lips against his added fuel to the fire. Later, he decided dimly, he'd show her how to kiss properly.

Her kiss couldn't have lasted more than a few seconds, but her breathing was quick and shallow when she lowered her heels to the floor once more. The fierce glow in Kane's eyes sent a flutter of alarm through her.

His hands caught at her waist. She felt their warmth burning through the thin cloth of her dress. "You sure about this?" he asked thickly.

As drunk as he was, it didn't take much to push him back on the bed. "I'm sure," she said with a catch in her voice. "Just . . . give me a minute."

There would be no talking with him, no reasoning or persuading, she realized. She'd once heard Dillon laughingly comment to one of the ranch hands about a man whose "brains were between his legs." She hadn't truly understood then, but the hunger in Kane's eyes had broadened her understanding rather quickly—and so had that strange hardness she'd felt pressed against the softness of her belly.

She lowered her lashes and backed away. Kane evidently thought she was being coy; a half-smile of satisfaction curled his lips. One strap of her gown slipped down her arm; she made no effort to retrieve it. All the while she retreated, she prayed she wouldn't give herself away. Kane was not a man to toy with, and what she was about to do was unthinkable.

When she reached the chair in the corner, she turned and presented him with her back. Her palms grew damp as she extended her hand toward the chair. She could feel his stare digging like tiny needles into her and knew he watched her still.

And indeed Kane could scarcely take his eyes off her. He hadn't realized it until now, but her insistence on staying was a soothing balm to his ego. Lord knew he'd been feeling lower than a snake's belly lately. His eyes riveted on the tempting view she presented him. His mind began to run rampant with fantasies. First he intended to find out if those luscious breasts of hers fit his palms the way he hoped. Then he would fill his hands with that enticing little behind . . .

He got up and walked to the window, thinking she meant to undress and willing to give her what little privacy was available. The thought of the hours to come made him shift a little, an uncomfortable fullness straining beneath his pants. A crooked little smile on his lips, he promised himself that little problem would soon be taken care of . . .

"Kane."

He turned, thinking to find her naked and eager and waiting . . .

Instead he found a revolver—*his* revolver—leveled at his stomach.

"Son of a bitch."

Even while he mouthed the curse, he was sorely tempted to laugh. This—this *girl*—had done what every lawman in New Mexico and half the West hadn't been able to do.

His head had begun to ache again. For the first time, Kane wished he hadn't consumed so much of that damned rotgut. In the cobwebbed recesses of his mind, he tried to gauge the distance between them. It wasn't more than a couple of yards. If he edged forward just a little, he might be able to grab the gun . . .

"I wouldn't do that if I were you." Her voice cracked sharp as a bullet. "Take my word for it, Kane. I know how to use this."

The glint in her eyes carried a warning he wasn't inclined to ignore. Besides, the revolver was loaded, and drunk as he was, he could see that she handled it with an ease that spoke of long familiarity.

"What the hell is this?" he asked hoarsely.

Her chin lifted. "We're taking a little trip, you and I, Kane. And since I've wasted enough time as it is, I think it's time we got moving." With one hand she nudged his saddlebag from the chair, then shoved it toward him with the toe of her slipper.

"Pick it up," she ordered.

Kane did as she said, gritting his teeth a-gainst the pounding in his head as he bent and slowly straightened, then looped the bag over his shoulder.

"Very good, Kane." She nodded her satisfaction. "Now open the window. We're going out that way."

He blinked. His gaze slid reflexively toward the window, where a small overhang jutted out over the alley. From there it was perhaps ten feet to the ground below.

He didn't move. "What the hell's wrong with going out the front door?"

"So you can get lost in that crowd?" Her voice reflected her scorn. "Oh, no, Kane. I want you where I can see you." She gestured toward the window. "Open it," she repeated curtly. "Then get yourself outside before I decide to help you along."

An eerie chill ran down his spine. The revolver swung back, and this time it was level with his heart. He shoved the window up, thrust his legs through, and did the same thing any other drunken idiot facing down the barrel of a gun would do.

He jumped.

shoved it toward him with the toe of her slipper. "Pick it up," she ordered.

Kane did as she said, getting up with a grimace, the pounding in his head as he bent and slowly straightened, then draped the bag over his shoulder.

"Very good, Kane," she mocked. "Now open the window. We're going out that way."

He paused. His gaze slid reluctantly toward the window, where a small overhang jutted out over the alley. From there it was perhaps ten feet to the ground below.

He didn't move. "What the hell's wrong with going out the front door?"

"So you can get lost in Fort Crown?" Her voice reflected her scorn. "Oh no, Kane, I want you where I can see you." She gestured toward the window. "Open it," she repeated curtly. "Then get yourself outside before I decide to keep you along."

An icy chill ran down his spine. The pistol swung back, and this time it was level with his heart. He shoved the window up, thrust his legs through, and did the same thing anybody else drunken enough staring down the barrel of a gun would do.

He jumped.

Chapter 3

He hurtled through the air, landing with a dull thud. His legs gave out beneath him and he sprawled forward in the dirt. He lay stunned, the breath ripped from his lungs. Blackness shrouded his vision, then began to recede. It took a moment before he realized Abigail had landed beside him.

It galled him that she was the first to scramble up. Her hair had fallen down around her shoulders, but other than that, she looked none the worse. He, on the other hand, felt as if he'd been run over by a stagecoach. He lumbered to his feet, dizzy and disoriented.

It irritated him further that she'd managed to retain her hold on *his* gun. And sure enough, it was pointed straight at him again.

He glared at her. "What the *hell* is this about?"

"I know who you are, Kane." Her tone was cool and precise. "I know you used to ride with Stringer Sam."

Too late she realized her mistake. She meant the words as an explanation, not a challenge. But Kane had gone utterly still, his features stripped of all expression.

He smiled slowly. "If you're aiming to take me in to the law, I think I should warn you—I wouldn't.

I'm not a wanted man in this territory, sister. I made sure of that before I came here."

His smile was chilling, his voice deadly soft. It passed through Abby's mind that drunk or not, Kane was a dangerous man. And it wouldn't be wise to underestimate him . . . not wise at all. For the first time that evening, she knew a glimmer of true fear.

But there was no sign of it as she raised her chin. "That's not it," she denied sharply. "Unfortunately, I happen to be in need of your services."

There was a flash of white teeth in that dark face. "Sweetheart," he drawled, "if you remember, I was more than willing to oblige you. You didn't have to force me at gunpoint."

Abby despised the betraying color which rose to her cheeks—her only redemption was that her temper flared along with it. More than anything, she longed to wipe that smirk off those ruggedly defined features. The glitter in his eyes was the only thing that stopped her.

Her lips were drawn in a mutinous line. "There's only one thing I want from you, Kane," she informed him tightly. "And that's for you to take me to Stringer Sam's hideout."

She had startled him; she sensed it by the stunned silence which followed.

He scowled at her. "What the hell does a woman like you want with Stringer Sam?"

Abby took a deep breath. "Don't you know what happened last night at the jail?"

A suggestive leer curled those harshly carved lips. "Lady," he said with soft deliberation, "String-er Sam was the last thing on my mind last night.

And I didn't set foot outside my room until well after noon today, thanks to the attentions of a fine piece of—"

"Spare me the details!" She sent him a fulminating glance. Unfortunately, her mind had already conjured up a rather vivid picture of Kane and one of those scandalously painted ladies at the saloon, their mouths fused, limbs naked and entwined . . .

She relinquished the image quickly, hating the flush that still tinged her cheeks; it angered her further when Kane's mocking smile widened.

"While you were having your fun," she snapped, "Stringer Sam broke into the jail. He killed two deputies and a prisoner named Rowdy Roy, a man who happened to be part of his own gang."

Kane's smile withered. He didn't know Rowdy Roy, but it chilled his blood to think of Sam that close.

Abby went on. "You probably haven't heard of the Diamondback ranch. But it's one of the biggest spreads around—my father owns it—or he did until today! Now it's mine—mine and Dillon's." Her voice quavered slightly; somehow she managed to bring it under control. "Stringer Sam came to the ranch looking for Dillon, but he killed Pa instead!"

Kane stared at her; Abby was too distressed to notice that his eyes had gone vague and glassy. "Dillon," he repeated slowly. "Who the hell is Dillon?"

Abby blew out a sigh of sheer frustration. "Dillon MacKenzie! He has this—this vendetta against Stringer Sam. Dillon found out from Rowdy Roy where Sam's hideout is—he left last night to try to find Stringer Sam." In the back of her mind, she wondered if she were babbling. But once started, the words tumbled out in a rush, one after another. "Only Dillon didn't know Sam was anywhere near here—and now that Stringer Sam knows Dillon is headed for his hideout, he's gone after him!"

By the time she finished, Kane's head was buzzing so that he could scarcely think. He had the feeling he was missing something, but he couldn't quite figure out what it was . . . The edges of his vision began to blur. It was almost more than he could handle to remain standing upright.

"That's why I have to reach Dillon before Sam does. I'll pay you—enough that you won't ever have to worry about money again." She paused, peering over at him to gauge his reaction. His features were shadowed, but he wasn't saying anything; he merely regarded her with that strange unblinking stare. She decided to take his silence for concurrence.

She gingerly lowered the revolver to her side. "Your horse," she said slowly. "Is it stabled in the livery?"

He nodded, his gaze heavy-lidded and unfocused. For the first time, Abby realized his drunken state might be a boon. Directing a fervent prayer heavenward, she grabbed Sonny's reins, then slipped an arm around Kane's waist. "We'd better get moving," she told him, her tone deliberately offhand.

The livery was situated on the edge of town, next to the railroad station. Abby hurried as fast as she could, but their progress was rather awkward. Kane staggered alongside her, leaning so heavily on her shoulder that several times she nearly collapsed beneath his weight. By the time they reached the livery she was gasping and winded. But she paid no heed as she skirted the front entrance and led the way to the rear of the livery. Oddly, it was she who stumbled as they rounded the corner. Lean fingers caught at the soft flesh just below her waist. A strange little quiver shot through her—Abby felt their imprint like a fiery brand. She fleetingly wondered what it was about him that made her feel so threatened and exposed. It wasn't just that he was an outlaw—no, it was something more—something she couldn't quite put her finger on . . .

She jerked away, cursing both herself and Kane. "I'm not about to let anyone else see me in this disgraceful dress," she informed him stiffly. "I'll thank you to turn your back so I can change."

He didn't. Instead he looped his thumbs in his belt, his stance none too steady. "And if I don't, what will you do? Shoot me?" Slurred though his speech was, the taunting mockery was still there.

Abby let out a breath of sheer exasperation. "Believe me, I'm coming closer all the time. Now turn around before I decide it's not a half-bad idea after all!"

He did, but not before those glittering eyes swept the length of her. His frankly lecherous regard riled her temper further. "Drunken imbecile," she charged hotly under her breath. "I hope you fall flat on your face!"

She snatched the clothes she'd worn earlier from her saddlebag and stepped behind the sheltering protection of her horse. Despite the darkness, she felt her face heat up. It didn't matter that he wasn't actually *looking*—she was actually undressing with a man present! But not once did she relieve that broad masculine back of her accusatory stare as she jerked on her own clothing. Why, she wouldn't put it past him to bolt at the first chance that presented itself. Her lips tightened. Not that he'd get far in his present state.

Tucking her blouse into her riding skirt, she didn't give a second glance to the scandalous red dress that lay in a heap at her feet. She'd certainly have no use for it again. She hesitated, then tucked Kane's revolver into the waistband of her skirt, concealing it beneath her vest. "All right," she muttered when she'd finished. "You can turn around now." She nodded for Kane to precede her toward the entrance.

A youth of perhaps fifteen sauntered out, smothering a yawn. He stopped short at the sight of the pair advancing toward him. Abby summoned a smile, feeling as if her face were about to crack. "Hello, Todd." Todd Jenkins's uncle owned the livery, and Todd worked for him. He was a little dull-witted, but good with the animals. "My friend here stabled his horse yesterday. We'll be needing him now, if you don't mind."

Todd's eyes lit up. "I know the one. Big shiny black named Midnight."

"That's the one, son." Kane reached out and clapped the boy on the shoulder. One corner of his mouth curved up in a wicked smile. "Since I'm leaving at the lady's summons, I guess it's up to her to take care of the bill. I'll just go on back and get Midnight saddled up."

"Sure thing, mister. He's in the last stall on the right."

Abby's eyes tracked his weaving gait to the rear of the barn. Kane was certainly no gentleman, that was for certain! Her lips compressed. She wondered scathingly if he was always so inclined to tip the bottle—if that was the case, he'd soon learn she wouldn't stand for it.

It didn't take long to take care of the charges. Abby began to pace restlessly, anxious to be on the way. She wasn't sure if it would be possible for them to travel the night through, but she planned to ride as long as they could. Five minutes later found her chafing and fuming. What the devil was taking Kane so long?

Todd sensed her impatience. He sent her an uneasy glance. "I'll just go see if he needs a hand," he muttered.

Abby followed right behind. Had Kane run out on her? There was only one entrance, so she knew his horse was still here. But what if there were a back window and he'd slipped out that way?

She was on Todd's heels all the way, fury marking every determined step. At the last stall, he swung open the gate and started to step inside. Then he stopped so abruptly Abby barreled into his back with a very unladylike grunt. She recovered quickly and stepped out from behind him.

A horse whinnied softly, raising his long graceful neck from where he'd been munching oats to regard them with wary curiosity. He was sleek and muscled, his coat a glossy black, his eyes keen and intelligent. In a far corner of her mind, Abby knew a distant flicker of appreciation for such a prime piece of horseflesh. But the stallion didn't capture her attention for long . . . With a sharp inhalation, she followed Todd's stunned gaze.

Kane was sprawled face-down on the hay, passed out cold.

Kane was dreaming. Of warm, feminine hands stroking over his shoulders and arms, smooth and soothing. Of long, ebony tresses teasing his chest, scented like roses and soft as velvety petals, brushing over skin that was taut and acutely sensitized. A low melodious voice poured over him like liquid honey; breasts full and vibrantly lush pressed against him, softness melting into hardness. Snug in the arms of his dream lover, he sighed, eager to retreat into such a pleasant netherworld once again.

But something abrasive and prickly poked at his cheek. The pungent aroma of straw—and something else, something infinitely less pleasant—assailed his nostrils. As if that weren't enough, a hand like a claw roughly grasped his shoulder. He testily batted it away like a pesky fly, his subconscious rebelling at such a rude awakening.

The sudden movement was a mistake. He promptly discovered his entire body ached as though he'd been kicked from one end of a corral to the other. There was a blacksmith hammering away inside his brain that wouldn't go away. He tried to swallow, but his tongue felt thick and clumsy, as if a wad of cotton had been shoved in his mouth. Belatedly he recognized the source of his misery. He rolled over with a groan. Why, he hadn't been this drunk since the night he'd come home and found Lorelei . . .

Lorelei. His woman. His wife. The only thing in his whole miserable life that had ever had any meaning. The only person on earth he had ever really loved . . . and who had loved him. When he'd met her, he'd thought he could finally make something of his life. For the first time ever he'd been . . . truly content, even happy. But then she had died . . .

She didn't just die, a voice inside mocked. *She was murdered.* And that was when it all started . . .

The pain that scored his gut was agony, fiery and burning like acid, clear to his soul.

"Kane," sniped a voice that sounded nothing at all like the dulcet tones in his dream. "If you know what's good for you, you'll get up right now!"

He winced. "Be a good girl, sweetheart," he mumbled. "Keep it down, all right?"

"I am not your sweetheart, nor am I ever likely to be! And I'll thank you to stop calling me that!"

He dragged his eyelids open, first one and then the other. A woman stood over him, looking for all the world like an enraged virago. A lantern dangled from one slim hand. Jesus! he thought incredulously. What on earth had possessed him to bring a woman to a smelly barn when there was a perfectly good bed at the hotel?

The light from the lantern trapped him in its center. He flung back an arm and shielded his eyes from the yellow glare. Inky-dark sky was reflected in the window behind her head. "Get up?" His voice was a hoarse croak. His throat felt as if it had been stripped raw. "Cripes, what the hell for? It's not even daylight!"

"It will be by the time we leave!"

Abby's mood was anything but tame. She had just spent what was probably the longest night of her life. She'd tried for nearly an hour to wake Kane but he was dead to the world. Adding insult to injury was the fact that it had cost her another five-dollar gold piece before Todd agreed to let them spend the night here. By now, she was frustrated and angry, but most of all disgusted—Kane was tousled and bleary-eyed. He smelled like a brewery and needed a shave. God knew she'd expected neither a hero nor a gentleman, but she hadn't expected a drunk either.

"We'd better get started," she said sharply. "Thanks to you, Stringer Sam is a good twelve hours ahead of us—and so is Dillon!"

Dead silence met her pronouncement.

Kane had risen on one elbow to stare at her. One lean hand came up to absently rub his whiskered jaw. Beneath the lock of black hair that tumbled on his forehead, his brow was furrowed in concentration . . . or was it puzzlement?

She slapped her riding gloves against her thigh; not sure whether to laugh or cry. "My God," she said numbly. "Don't tell me you don't remember!"

It was less a question than an accusation. Snatches of memory invaded Kane's brain. He recalled her turning his gun on him—that, he decided grimly, was unforgettable. But most of what he remembered was *her*—the lush feel of her body against his. And he remembered the taste of her mouth trapped beneath his—her lips were like crushed fruit, damp and moist and dewy.

But Stringer Sam . . . all at once the name jarred something inside him. He sucked in a harsh breath.

It came back in a flash—she wanted him to take her to Sam's hideout.

He lumbered to his feet none too steadily. "Lady," he said very deliberately, "who said I was going anywhere with you?"

Abby gritted her teeth. "My name is Abigail— Abigail MacKenzie. And we had a deal, Kane, so don't try to weasel your way out of it now."

"A deal?" His harsh laugh set her on edge. "That's not the way I remember it."

"Then think of it this way." Abby was too desperate to heed her words. "You'll be saving a man's life—maybe it'll ease your conscience a little."

His conscience! A fiery mist of rage swam before his eyes. Who the hell was she to judge him anyway? Kane thought furiously. Why, she was an uppity little brat who'd probably never wanted for a single thing in her life! She didn't know a damn thing about him—who he really was ... the reasons behind all that he'd done ... Oh, he knew her kind, people who had their noses in the air, who'd convinced themselves they were so much better than their fellow man—they thought they could push everyone else aside and no one would be the wiser. Well, to hell with people like her, he thought savagely. To hell with *her!*

He stared at her coldly. "You're a fool if you think I'll take you to Sam," he stated flatly. "Good Lord, woman, I don't think you realize what kind of man Stringer Sam is!"

"Oh, but I do! I told you last night, Kane. He came to the Diamondback after Dillon—but he killed my father instead." For just an instant, pain gouged a gaping wound in her breast. Tears stung her eyes,

but she blinked them back, not wanting this man
to see her cry.

But Kane didn't see. His mouth compressed into a
thin line. Dillon again, he thought scathingly. She'd
talked about someone named Dillon last night—
Dillon and some kind of vendetta.

His lip curled; he spoke in a flat, staccato rhythm.
"Listen, *Abigail*, and listen good. A woman with
your looks shouldn't have to look far to find another man primed and ready to warm that sweet little
behind. Just because you don't like sleeping alone
doesn't mean I'm willing to risk my hide to save
his."

Abby gaped. What was he saying? Why, it didn't
bear thinking about! But all at once her spine went
ramrod straight. It was just like a man, she thought
furiously—just like *him!*—to think with that part of
his anatomy.

"No, Kane," she began heatedly. "*You* listen. It's
not like that at all, do you hear? I don't know what
hole you crawled out of—I don't care to know! But
I'll thank you to keep your crude little judgments to
yourself. I'll do whatever I have to in order to save
Dillon, is that understood? Furthermore, any other
woman would do exactly the same if Stringer Sam
were after her—"

She never knew exactly what halted her speech.
Perhaps it had something—everything?—to do with
the knowledge that Kane was under a grave miscon-
ception about her and Dillon.

"Her what?" Kane's eyes had narrowed suspiciously. "Exactly what is this Dillon to you anyway?" His hand shot out and wrapped around her
arm, jerking her close.

Abby bit her lip. She'd told Kane last night that Dillon was her brother, hadn't she? *Hadn't she?* Maybe not, or he wouldn't be making such outrageous insinuations . . .

Her breath came jerkily. He frightened her, she realized dazedly. Oh, not because he was an outlaw. Simply because he was so—so overwhelmingly male! So close to him, trapped against the heat of his body, her mind displayed a vivid recall. She remembered the way he had looked at her last night, his eyes glittering with heat. She remembered the intimate glide of his tongue against hers, the shocking sensation of lean, plundering fingers shaping themselves to her breast.

She swallowed, unable to tear her gaze from those dark features that hovered so closely above her own. A bristly shadow hazed the hollow of his cheeks and jaw. His lips were thin and cruel. She was tall for a woman, her body sleek and toned and far from weak, but Kane made her feel that way. And it was then that the craziest notion spun through her mind . . . If Kane helped her find Dillon, they might be alone for days on end . . . somehow she had to protect herself.

"Well?" His voice was rough with demand. His lips twisted into a sneer. "I admit, I'm curious now. What the hell is so goddamned special about your precious Dillon? What's he got that every other man doesn't have?"

Abby's heart was thudding with thick, heavy strokes. She felt her lips move, though she'd have sworn she spoke not a word.

"He's my husband," she blurted.

Chapter 4

Her husband. Her *husband*. Kane stared at her, stunned, dumbfounded and then deeply, furiously angry, not only with himself but with her.

His blistering curse scalded her ears and made her jump. She struggled to free herself. He let her go only to snatch back her left hand at the last instant. "Where's your ring?"

Abby prayed he wouldn't feel her quaking. As a child, she'd discovered she was a horrible liar. When Pa and Dillon had laughed at her display of the bonnet Emily Dawson had given her, she'd promptly thrown it into the horse trough. When Pa found it, she'd lied and told him she didn't know how it got there. Pa hadn't scolded or thrashed her, but Abby was aware that he knew she'd lied. She'd felt so utterly guilty that she'd never lied to him again.

But Kane wasn't Pa. If his forbidding expression were anything to go by, bodily harm was a definite possibility.

"I—I had to get you out of the Silver Spur somehow. I didn't think you'd go upstairs with me if you knew I was married. I took it off last night so you wouldn't see it!" Her cry was wild. She tugged furiously at her hand.

He let her go so suddenly that she stumbled and fell to her knees. "You scheming little bitch," he said through clenched teeth. Her half-shy, tentative manner last night—it was all an act! Fire blazed within him. What a fool he'd been! He'd actually believed the story she'd concocted—that her father had died and she was alone in the world, with no one to turn to, nowhere to go. He had believed and sympathized. He was convinced she was an innocent—a virgin!—brought low by life's vengeance.

Two long strides took him past her into the stall. He spared her no glance as he heaved his saddle onto Midnight's back.

Abby lurched to her feet. "Kane! Wh—what are you doing? Where are you going?"

"Ought to be pretty damn obvious, even to you, *Abigail*. I'm leaving, something I should have done the minute I set eyes on you."

His tone was icily distant. She interpreted all too accurately the iron cast of his profile, the rigid set of his shoulders.

Inwardly Abby was devastated; outwardly she was as determined as ever. "You can't!" She clutched at his arm, as if that alone could keep him there.

He shook her off easily, pausing only to slant her an infuriatingly superior smile. "Lady," he drawled, "you can't stop me."

Later she would wonder what possessed her. Later she was aghast at her own daring. But one second her hand trembled slightly at the waist of her riding skirt. The next her delicate little chin came up . . . and so did the barrel of his Colt.

"That's where you're wrong, Kane." She raised

the gun praying he wouldn't test her. He might be an outlaw—he might be the scum of the earth!—but God alone knew she couldn't shoot him in cold blood.

He half-turned. The flicker in his eyes told her he'd spotted the gun but his arrogant smile never wavered. "Go ahead, sweetheart. If you're so god-damned anxious to show me how well you shoot, here's your chance."

Grabbing Midnight's reins, he jammed his hat on his head and walked past her, bold as you please.

It was a moment before Abby's sagging jaw clamped shut. She followed him outside where dawn's shimmering sunshine heralded another glorious day. Abby alternately cursed and prayed as Kane mounted his horse and set off down the deserted street. The blast of gunfire shattered the early-morning air, whizzing over his left shoulder.

Horse and rider never slowed their pace.

The next shot took the hat right off his head.

The pair stopped. Kane flung his leg over the pommel and leaped to the ground. His long legs breached the distance between them. Hands on his hips, he ground to a halt with the gun mere inches away from his chest. A fierce scowl blackened his expression. "Do you really think that's going to make me change my mind?" he demanded.

Abby stared up into those dark, hard features, quaking from head to toe. In that instant, she cast pride and dignity to the wind. Later there might be regrets—for now, there were none.

She swallowed painfully, her throat clogged tight with fear and desperation. When she spoke, her voice was little more than a thread of sound. "I—I need you, Kane. You're the only one who can help me find Dillon, the only one." The barrel of the gun wavered. "I'll give you anything, Kane, anything you want. Please help me," she whispered. *"Please."*

That one word was his undoing. Kane went utterly still, his gaze locked on the glitter of tears she tried to hide but couldn't. Her eyes were huge, her soft mouth tremulous. The hopelessness of that look clamped tight around his heart and doggedly refused to let go.

He swore silently, disgusted with both himself and her. He'd thought himself immune to all that was decent and caring—that he was so hardened and embittered that not even tears could sway him.

He was wrong.

A bitter ache scored his gut. All at once he couldn't forget the words she had flung at him earlier. *You'll be saving a man's life. Maybe it'll ease your conscience a little.*

Kane had long ago convinced himself his conscience had died along with Lorelei—yet wasn't his damnable conscience why he'd come here in the first place? Why he'd decided to leave his life of lawlessness behind and start over?

Hell, he thought disgustedly. He was a fool, even contemplating something as foolish as this . . . If he had any brains, he'd turn around, ride out of town and forget he'd ever set eyes on this stubborn little beauty.

He couldn't. Damn her blasted angelic face and helpless feminine ploys to hell and back, but he couldn't.

In one fluid motion he knocked the gun from

her grasp and hauled her up against him. "You're pretty damned determined to shoot me," he said tightly. "But tell me this, *Abigail*. Who the hell's gonna take you to Stringer Sam if you do?"

At first Abby didn't comprehend, but then she realized . . . she'd won. She didn't know how she knew, but somehow she did.

She stared up into that rough, lean face. His mouth was a grim slash, his jaw prickly and dark with a day's growth of beard. At that moment, no one had ever looked dearer. "You—you'll help me?"

His gaze scoured her from head to toe. "It's no trip for a woman," he stated. "You'd be better off staying here and letting me go find your precious Dillon."

And take the chance he'd ride off and never come back? "No!" Her objection was immediate and strenuous.

His tone was as harsh as his expression. "I don't have time to coddle a spoiled brat who can't stand the thought of not having her way. You're better off staying here."

His insult slipped right by her. Panic leaped riotously within her; he looked and sounded utterly unyielding.

Her protest was as vehement as his. "You've never even seen Dillon! How could you possibly find him?"

"I can handle it, don't worry. If you tell me what he looks like—I'll find him. Besides, you said Sam's almost a day ahead of us. Having you along will just slow me down."

Abby bristled at his high-handed arrogance. It

was just like a man to think that simply by virtue of his sex, he was both mentally and physically superior. She had grown up with a brother who treated her like she was a fragile porcelain doll, and she certainly didn't need it from this man. Just like Dillon, he was overbearing and overconfident.

"I'll have you know," she began stiffly, her spine poker-iron straight, "I've been riding since I was three years old. I can rope and brand and track a lost calf as well as any ranch hand—and I shoot better than most, something that might come in handy. I don't think you'll find me a liability."

A liability? Kane snorted. What he found her was a pain in the . . .

Her chin lifted. She faced him with a bravado that was more than a little feigned. "I have no intention of letting you go after Dillon without me. Like it or not, we're stuck with each other."

He glared at her. "I don't like it," he told her, his tone downright nasty. "I don't like it one damn bit, so let's get things straight right now—I won't play nursemaid. The sooner we find your precious husband, the sooner I can be rid of you. And believe me, sweetheart, that can't happen too soon."

He stalked to where his hat lay on the dusty earth. He grabbed it and jammed it on his head, then retraced his steps back to his horse—but not before he'd bent to retrieve his gun where it lay near a clump of dry grass.

The stinging retort she'd been about to deliver died on her lips. Sunlight glinted off the eight-inch barrel of the Colt as he turned to face her. Her ire forgotten, she watched as he slid it into the holster tied to his thigh. Rampant challenge glowed in the burning gray gaze that met hers, as if he expected her protest.

But Abby wasn't about to protest, either vocally or otherwise. Oh, no, she hadn't mistaken the glittering challenge in his eyes . . .

She'd managed to sneak his gun out from beneath his nose once.

She wouldn't be so lucky again.

Without a word she turned and headed into the stable. She knew Kane watched as she saddled Sonny. She tried hard not to think about the fact that she was about to ride off with a man who might be every bit as unsavory and dangerous as Stringer Sam . . .

He'd said he would help her. She had no choice but to trust him—trust him and pray he wouldn't shoot her in the back the instant her back was turned . . .

The thought was scarcely comforting.

"Where are we headed?"

It was several hours later. The question earned her nothing but a dark, impatient look. "Well?" she demanded when he said nothing. "Since I'm paying you, don't you think I have a right to know?"

His lips thinned in impatience, which made Abby feel like a fly in his soup and spurred her indignation. "North," came his barely discernible grunt.

She felt like gnashing her teeth. "I'm quite aware of that," she said with false pleasantness. "Would you mind telling me how far north?"

Obviously he did mind, but he obliged nonetheless. "A couple of hundred miles," he said brusquely.

Abby gasped. "That's clear across the Territory! Why, that'll take us a—a good week to get there!"

"If we're lucky," he said curtly. "And that's all I'm going to say. Believe me, sister, the less you know about Sam's hideout, the better. I don't think I need to remind you Rowdy Roy was killed for knowing."

Those words chilled her to the bone. It was little wonder Abby was disinclined to engage in further conversation.

They continued westward, traveling along the flank of the Laramie Mountains. To the east, rugged peaks timbered with alpine fir and pine stretched skyward. She and Kane did their best to ignore each other, keeping their eyes trained anywhere but on the other.

Although Abby was used to spending long hours in the saddle, the hours without sleep last night had taken their toll. By late afternoon she was convinced the day would never end.

Not long after, her eyelids began to droop. She must have dozed, for she jerked awake with a start. Her gaze swung almost guiltily to Kane, only to find knowing eyes already fixed upon her. His mouth was slanted in a sardonic smile, if the twisting of his lips could be called that.

Kane reined in his horse and glanced around. The terrain sloped into a gentle valley a hundred yards distant. Late-afternoon sunlight mirrored the waters of a small lake surrounded by tall cottonwoods. Beyond, sun-baked plains rolled and dipped endlessly. He inclined his head and gave a terse nod. "We'll stop there for the night."

She immediately straightened. "But it's still light

out," she protested. "We can go on for another hour—"

"You won't last another hour and we both damn well know it."

Abby gritted her teeth. She'd thought Dillon's language was bad, but she had the feeling Kane could teach him a lesson or two. It was on the tip of her tongue to retort that, unlike him, there had been no alcohol-induced sleep last night, but something held her back. "I'm just a little tired," she said stiffly.

"So am I, sweetheart. So like I said, we'll camp there for the night." He gave a tug on the reins and nudged his horse into a trot. Not once did he look back to see that Abby followed; Abby wasn't sure if she should be indignant or relieved.

He led the way to a small clearing near the lake. Grass and shrubs grew thick and green near the water. Tall, stately trees crowded the shoreline. Abby reined in when Kane dropped to the ground. He began to stride back toward her but Abby quickly dismounted on her own, declining his help even before he could offer it. Kane stopped short; she didn't glimpse the tightening of his mouth.

He lifted his chin toward her saddlebags. "Got anything to eat in there?"

Abby nodded. Before she left the ranch last night, she had Dorothy pack some provisions. "I've got biscuits and beans and enough dried meat for three days or so," she told him. "After that, we'll either have to hunt or stop somewhere to buy more provisions."

He took charge of unsaddling the horses and settling them in for the night. Abby busied herself with gathering branches for a fire, but her gaze strayed to Kane again and again. She watched him heave the saddle from Sonny's back.

An undeniable air of danger surrounded him, she thought with a shiver. *What did you expect?* chided a voice in her head. *He's an outlaw, a renegade.* It was strange, though—she wasn't precisely frightened, yet she was distinctly uneasy.

She began digging in her saddlebags for the food, acutely aware of his presence behind her. She knew the exact instant he finished with the horses; a tremor slid down her spine. She sensed his eyes on her back like the prick of a needle. Clenching her fingers, she sensed rather than saw him move soundlessly past her. With an effort, she raised her head. Kane had settled himself across from the fire, his back propped against a stately pine tree. His eyes were closed, his head tipped back.

Her gaze roved slowly over his face, as if she were searching for . . . what? A flaw, perhaps? Some hint of ugliness or imperfection? Despite the heavy stubble that darkened his cheek and jaw, his features were not at all displeasing. Clean-shaven, he might even have been quite handsome . . . His nose was straight and thin, if a bit arrogant, his jaw square and hard. But his mouth was no longer set in harsh, implacable lines . . . It struck her then—he looked tired. At the thought, she felt the tight knot of uneasiness slip away.

It wasn't long before the beans were bubbling in the one and only pot she'd brought. She dropped a handful of dried ham into it and stirred, ignoring the man behind her.

It was the aroma of coffee brewing that eventually roused Kane. Abby dished up a tinful of beans and glanced over her shoulder at Kane; his eyes were open and fixed on her. Wordlessly she handed him the plate, then turned to fill another for herself. She sat down a short distance away from him, using a small boulder as a stool.

The sky turned half a dozen shades of purple and gold while they ate. Behind them rose the jutting ridges of the mountains, sharp as a saw blade. To the east the lake sparkled with the waning sunlight. Evening's silence crept across the earth; the only sound was that of the fire hungrily licking at the dry tree branches.

Abby was the first to finish; Kane had helped himself to another plateful of beans. She rose to fill two tin cups with coffee from the pot, handing one to him on her way back to the tree. He grimaced.

"I don't suppose you've got anything stronger?"

Abby straightened. A slender hand came to her hip and she glared down at him. She didn't have to say a word—her disapproval came through loud and clear.

"You haven't had a blacksmith hammering away inside your head the whole damned day," he grumbled. "And riding like the devil himself hasn't helped any."

A well-shaped brow rose. "And whose fault is that?" she retorted sweetly. "As I recall, it wasn't me who poured that whiskey down your throat." She turned and, with a swish of her riding skirt, resumed her place on the boulder—and her glare along with it.

Kane rolled his eyes. Christ, he thought disgustedly. She was undoubtedly a do-gooder, about to deliver a fire-and-brimstone speech on the sins of imbibing too freely. He found himself possessed of a dark, sudden urge to take her down a peg.

"Oh, well," he said with a shrug. "Maybe you're right. Maybe I don't need a good healthy shot of whiskey," he added conversationally. "In fact, right about now I think a good, experienced woman just might be able to take my mind off my aches and pains." He propped his elbows on his knees and nodded toward the now-empty pot of beans. "I have to admit, sweetheart, those were mighty tasty. Do you have any other hidden talents?"

A purely suggestive smile curved his lips. Abby gasped. Surely he wasn't suggesting that she . . . that they . . . The heat of a blush crept up her neck, clear to her hairline. Closer scrutiny revealed his lips now twisted in a smirk.

Abby wasn't sure if she was more angry or embarrassed. Nor did it help that she suspected he deliberately wanted to shock her.

"Oh, yeah," he said softly. "Why don't you show me what those lips and hands can do, sweetheart? I admit, after the taste you gave me last night, I'm mighty curious."

Abby didn't stop to think. She simply reacted, leaping to her feet, wishing she dared overturn his hot coffee on his head. She heard him laughing softly when she skirted him and marched toward her saddlebags.

A moment later she stepped up behind him.

"Kane?" Her tone was dulcet as a softly strummed melody. "I have just the remedy for your head-ache."

"What?" He twisted around to stare up at her.

She dumped the contents of her canteen over his head.

Kane surged to his feet with a curse that blistered her ears. Too late Abby realized her folly; his face was black as a thundercloud. She instinctively turned to flee but she didn't get more than two steps. He was upon her like a bolt of lightning; she felt herself bodily seized and spun around. The next thing she knew he'd flexed his knees. An arm that felt like steel slid beneath her knees. The world tilted crazily as her feet left the ground. She felt herself borne upward in a surge of power.

He began to walk, his stride sure-footed and determined.

"Dear God, st-stop!"

"God isn't going to help you this time, honey." He spoke through gritted teeth.

She flung an arm around his shoulders for balance. "Kane . . . what are you doing?"

"Sweetheart," he mocked, "I have just the remedy to cool your temper."

He was heading toward the lake. Abby gleaned his intention in a flash—he was going to dump her in the water. The knowledge only fueled her desperation to escape. "Kane, no! I—I have my boots on!" She began to struggle in earnest.

A vile oath rushed past her ear, but he didn't stop, merely tightened his arms around her like a clamp. "Then, sweetheart, you sure as hell better kick the damned things off."

"I am not your sweetheart—stop calling me that!"

"Anything you say, Abigail."

"And don't call me that, either! No one's ever called me Abigail except Pa." *Pa*. His name had no sooner passed her lips than her heart squeezed.

"Well, you don't need to worry," he sneered above her head. "You'll be back in Papa's lap soon enough."

His voice stabbed at her like a rusty blade. She pounded her fists against him. "I told you before, Kane, he—he's dead!" Pain as dark as the bloodstain on Pa's chest crowded her heart as she thought of him, now cold and alone in his grave. God, but it hurt to think of him—it hurt even more knowing that he was dead!

A hot ache scalded her throat. She ducked her head. Her hand slowly uncurled on his chest.

They'd reached the shoreline, but that wasn't why Kane halted. He instinctively knew the instant something changed, even before her struggles ceased. She lay limply against him, all resistance gone.

Kane's gaze sharpened. Her head was bent, her expression hidden. But he could see the spiky dampness of her lashes, the tremulous way she tried to steady her mouth. A fleeting voice intruded in his consciousness. *Stringer Sam came to the ranch looking for Dillon, but he killed Pa instead.*

He lowered her slowly to the ground, allowing her to stand on her own but not releasing her completely. He kept her anchored before him with the weight of his hands on her shoulders.

"Stringer Sam?" Even to his own ears, his voice was gritty.

She nodded; he heard as well as felt her ragged inhalation. Low as she spoke, he didn't miss the faint accusation in her tone. "I—I told you this morning. Didn't you believe me?"

He hadn't, but he couldn't tell her that—not now. Something dangerous, something wholly threatening, something he didn't understand, slipped over him. He battled the urge to pull her close and let her cry her heart out, if that was what she wanted.

He cursed himself viciously for his uncertainty. Why the hell should he care if she was hurting? He didn't know her, and furthermore, he didn't want to know her. She was prickly and uppity, the most difficult female he'd ever had the misfortune to encounter. And yet he couldn't deny the tremulous appeal in those wounded blue eyes, those soft, trembling lips . . . or was it just a ploy, a ploy to see that she got what she wanted?

Twice now, he thought furiously, twice now she'd made him feel this way—twice in the same day! He'd be damned if he'd dance to her tune again—and he sure as hell would never let her pull his gun on him again!

He released her, his features hardening. "You'd better turn in for the night if you want to get an early start in the morning." The words were as coolly dismissive as his tone. When she said nothing, he quirked a dark brow. "Unless you intend to do the smart thing and head back the way we came, that is."

Abby's eyes flashed. His sarcasm was almost welcome. For a minute there, she'd had the strangest urge to bury her face in the hard curve of his neck and give way to the bitter tears burning her eyes, uncaring that he witnessed such weakness.

She squared her shoulders and lifted her chin. She didn't know what was behind his abrupt turnabout, but it was foolish to expect compassion from a man like Kane. He couldn't possibly know how deeply Pa's loss wounded her. No, what feelings he had were surely only for himself. If he was helping her, it was only for what money it would bring him in the end.

Back at the camp, she unrolled her bedroll and lay down, watching as night slipped its murky veil over the earth. It wasn't long before she heard Kane return. Neither of them said a word while he spread his bedroll across the fire from her, but the air between them was charged once again.

She rolled, presenting him with her back. Despite her awareness of the man across from her, the buzz of insects and the sigh of the wind through the trees began to work their magic spell. Her limbs grew heavy. She began to drift, her exhaustion blotting her mind of all thought.

Chapter 5

Yellow sunlight dancing against the back of her eyelids roused Abby the next morning. She pried an eyelid open, wincing against the gleaming rays pouring through a gauzy layer of clouds. The events of the last few days poured through her mind like water through a sieve. Had Pa been given a decent funeral? Of course he had. Dorothy and Lucas would have seen to it. Still, Abby couldn't help the niggling twinge of guilt that knifed through her. She should have been there—Dillon should have been there to see him laid to rest. Abby couldn't help the spurt of anger that shot through her. Instead, Dillon was off chasing outlaws . . . and she was off chasing him . . . and she couldn't help but be resentful of her brother for putting her in this predicament in the first place.

Squeezing her eyes shut, she prayed for his safety—prayed that Stringer Sam was not yet hot on Dillon's trail . . . and prayed that she and Kane *were*.

With a sigh that seemed pulled from some hollow, beaten place deep within her breast, she pushed off the rumpled blanket that covered her. Only then did she note that Kane's bedroll wasn't where he'd left it last night. In fact, the bedroll, like the man himself, was nowhere in sight.

Her first thought was that he'd deserted her, the beast! She leaped to her feet and nearly tripped over something—his bedroll, she realized, neatly rolled and tied, placed just a few inches from where her head had rested.

Her insides tightened oddly. It was downright disconcerting knowing that Kane had stood over her while she'd slept, unaware that he was so near . . .

His horse was gone, and his saddle along with it. Where on earth was he?

Ten minutes later she was fuming, wondering if she'd been right after all—maybe he *had* deserted her. Determined not to waste another idle minute, she fumbled around in her saddlebag for the cake of lavender-scented soap she'd brought. She'd been hot and sweaty when they stopped to make camp last night. Though she hated to waste the time, she couldn't resist the thought of a quick wash in the lake. Besides, who knew when they'd be able to camp near fresh water again?

Her steps quick and purposeful, she strode away from camp. Her gaze trained relentlessly forward, she headed toward the trees that stood sentry along the nearest finger of shoreline. So intent was she on her destination that she nearly ran smack into the side of Kane's horse. The glossy black merely raised his head and glanced at her in lazy speculation, then resumed his grazing of the lush grasses near the shore. She wasn't left long to wonder why the horse was here. A flicker of movement through the trees caught her eye. She glanced up in time to see Kane walk calmly into the water.

He wore not a single stitch of clothing.

Abby's heart leaped like a jackrabbit. Oblivious to her presence, Kane waded out further, then cut cleanly through the mirrored surface in a shallow dive. He came up an instant later and stood upright, walking forward several steps until the water lapped at his thighs.

Water shimmied down his body like a rushing waterfall. He shook his head like a great beast, sending a spray of water everywhere. In some shadowy corner of her mind, she told herself it was curiosity that held her there—not pleasure or awe. Yet she was conscious of only one thought. She couldn't deny that when she looked at him, there was power and strength and proud, blatant beauty she'd never thought to find in any man, most certainly not *this* man . . .

He was all sculpted, rippling muscle sheathed in gleaming, coppery skin. His chest was wide, his abdomen ridged with taut muscles. His hips were narrow, his buttocks hard and round and tight-looking.

He turned, providing her a startling, unrestricted view of all that made him so different from her . . . all that made him a man.

Abby's throat constricted. Her muscles froze. She wanted to look away but she couldn't. Was that what she'd felt pressed against her belly the night he'd kissed her? Unconsciously she silently gauged and measured . . . No. Surely not. Because while the sight was impressive enough to make her eyes widen, the memory of that night was vividly etched in her mind. And that boldly masculine part of him had seemed so much bigger, so much harder and rigid . . .

There was a burst of low, vibrating laughter.

"Why, Miss Abby, don't tell me you like what you see." With a gasp her gaze veered up to his face. His lips were twisted in that arrogant smile she'd begun to associate solely with him, a smile she'd begun to hate.

Her cheeks flamed. She was mortified beyond belief at having been caught staring at him—staring at him naked yet! She found herself floundering.

"I—I didn't know where you were. Your horse was gone, so I thought I'd come down and wash up while I waited . . ."

Kane laughed, a genuine, if rusty sound that somehow surprised him. Even from this distance, he could see the telltale color creeping down her neck. He wondered if she was blushing all over. It was an interesting possibility, one he wouldn't have minded investigating further . . . but only if the lady was willing. Unfortunately, that was hardly the case.

"I thought I'd scout around for any sign of footprints." He placed a jaunty hand on the ridge of one naked hip. "Do I dare hope that's soap you have in your hand? In my haste to leave Laramie, I seem to have left without any."

His sarcasm was lost on her. He was moving forward again as he spoke. When Abby realized it, she flung the bar of soap at him, the action both instinctive and defensive.

He caught it neatly, still unabashedly naked and uncaring that he was. "For a married lady, you sure are a shy one," he drawled. "Why, if I didn't know better, I might even think you've never seen a naked man before."

Abby nearly blurted that she hadn't. Oh, she'd seen Dillon and Pa bare from the waist up, but that was all. In horror she realized she was still staring. Belatedly she spun and darted back the way she'd come.

"No need to hurry off," he called after her. "This lake's plenty big for the two of us."

Soft, mocking laughter echoed behind her. Her irritation mounted along with the pace of her steps. Lord, but he was infuriating! And he was crazy if he thought she'd remove so much as a stocking in front of him. She didn't trust him any further than she could see him!

Her opinion of him sank even further when he returned to camp, with his shirt unbuttoned and hanging outside his pants. His manner casually offhand, he proceeded to tuck his shirt in and button his pants, with Abby standing not two feet away. Abby gaped. Why, the man had no decency—no manners whatsoever! She had the feeling he was deliberately trying to embarrass her, but this time she wasn't about to give him the satisfaction. Oh, no.

Kane took one look at the mutinous droop of her mouth and dismissed the notion to ask her assistance in shaving. He didn't like shaving without a mirror, but he wasn't about to put a razor in the lady's hands. She'd likely cut his throat with a great deal of pleasure right about now!

He rubbed the raspy hardness of his cheek, then let it fall to his side. Oh, well, he thought with a twist of his lips. While Abigail MacKenzie certainly was lovely, likable was something she was *not*. Still, he much preferred her contrary and disagreeable behavior to the way she'd been last night. Her vulnerability stabbed at him. He'd lain awake for hours, guilt gnawing at his gut. He'd felt like dirt that he hadn't said he was sorry about her father, but the words stuck in his craw like a chicken bone.

Yet why should he show her any kindness? he wondered harshly. She sure as hell didn't expect it from him; clearly she thought him less than human. He felt like a fool for feeling any softness toward her—for feeling anything at all!

"As soon as you've eaten—" Her voice was cool as frost. "—I'd like to be on our way."

His tone matched hers. "That's fine by me."

Not a word was said while they downed cold biscuits and coffee. They set out again, the atmosphere as frigid as a winter wind blowing across the plains.

Just as they had yesterday, they rode hard in a northerly direction. Kane slowed every so often, looking for signs of another rider having passed through recently. She was disappointed that he had no more luck than he had that morning.

The day grew hotter as the sun climbed toward its zenith. The sky was an endless, dazzling blue unbroken by clouds. No hint of breeze stirred the air. Tugging at the bandana around her neck, Abby dabbed the sweat from her brow. More than ever, she longed for a bath.

It was early afternoon when they stopped to water the horses at a stream. Watching Kane guide his horse to the edge of the water, Abby admitted to a twinge of admiration. She didn't like the man, but he rode like a centaur, as much at home on the back of the animal as a seasoned cowhand. When Kane dismounted, Abby did the same, leading Sonny over to the clear rushing waters where the gelding guzzled noisily.

From the corner of her eye, she watched Kane walk his horse alongside hers. A tingle of some nameless emotion seemed to curl her insides. Both man and beast towered over her and Sonny. Midnight was at least seventeen hands high; he appeared as dangerously fierce as his master, big and black and heavily muscled. As Kane absently stroked his mount's neck, Abby's gaze was drawn to his hands. They were intensely masculine and strong-looking, long and lean and dark. She couldn't help but remember that night at the Silver Spur, the shocking way those very same hands had explored her breasts, oddly gentle for all their strength, cupping her rounded shape and grazing the sensitive peak with the wispiest caress, like the touch of a feather . . .

Her nipples tingled. She resisted the urge to clamp her arms over her breasts. What was wrong with her? The memory was totally at odds with what she knew him to be—tough as dried leather. Wholly dismayed at the treacherous path her mind had taken, Abby sought shelter beneath a huge cottonwood tree.

Kane was hunkered down at the stream, refilling his canteen. He straightened and glanced around at her. Abby remained silent as he approached. He dropped his hat on the ground and eased down beside it. Pulling the cap from the canteen, he took a long pull. He wiped his mouth, then offered it to her.

Abby hesitated. Although she was thirsty, she was unwilling to put her lips where his had been. To do so seemed somehow . . . intimate.

And intimate was the last thing she wanted to be with this man.

Slowly she shook her head. He recapped the canteen, his keen silver eyes fastened on her. "How long have you and your beloved Dillon been hitched?"

His sarcasm penetrated first, the words second. For an instant, Abby's mind went blank—it took a moment before she recalled she'd told him Dillon was her husband. She averted her gaze quickly, uttering a fervent prayer he hadn't glimpsed her confusion.

She said the first thing that popped into her head. "A week."

Kane couldn't withhold the slow grin that curled his mouth. "That's mighty soon to be strainin' at the bit."

"Straining at the bit," she repeated. Her eyes narrowed. "Maybe you'd like to explain that."

Broad shoulders lifted in a lazy shrug. "No need to be so prickly. But it seems like a man just married wouldn't want to leave his wife's side—" He cast a sidelong glance at her. "—let alone her bed. Unless, of course, he found himself chilled to the bone."

Abby's jaw dropped. He was so matter-of-fact she had difficulty believing she'd heard right. Was he trying to shock her again? She didn't know why, but they struck sparks off each other like tinder and flint. It might not have been so bad, except she had the feeling he was going to needle her whenever he could.

She confronted him with a brittle stare. "There's no need to be so crude."

"Crude?" He snorted. "Strange is what it is, lady. I can't think why a man would leave his bride of a week to go chasing after some outlaw. That's no way to start a marriage. He's liable to get his ass killed!"

Fear grabbed hold of Abby's heart. Dillon . . . dead. Dear God, she couldn't even think it.

"In fact, I'd say it's pretty damn foolish of your precious old Dillon to have left you alone with the likes of Stringer Sam around. Look what happened to your father."

"Dillon had no way of knowing Stringer Sam was anywhere near Laramie." Abby defended Dillon staunchly. "And he has his reasons for going after Stringer Sam—good ones, too, I might add. He— he's only doing what he has to do." Lord, was that the truth. "And I'll thank you not to criticize Dillon. I've known Dillon for . . . quite some time and—and he's not at all reckless and irresponsible!"

The smirk hadn't left Kane's face. "Quite some time, eh? Let me guess. Childhood sweethearts?"

"We've known each other since childhood, yes." The conversation was circling back in a direction Abby hadn't counted on. She was beginning to question her wisdom in telling him Dillon was her husband.

"Besides," she went on, "what makes you such an authority? Frankly, I don't know how a man like you could know anything about marriage."

Kane felt as if he'd been backhanded. He couldn't help the vile blackness that flooded him. He swept his hat off the ground and stood, his jaw locked tight.

"You've got that right," he said through clenched teeth. "You sure as hell don't know."

The fierceness of his gaze robbed Abby of all defiance. She rose as well, both puzzled and disturbed. For all that Kane was clearly angry, she couldn't banish the uneasy sensation she'd just said something terribly, terribly wrong.

Abby found herself plagued by a nagging guilt throughout the afternoon. Yesterday morning's claim that Dillon was her husband had been pure instinct; she certainly hadn't considered the consequences. Kane's questions about their "marriage" had caught her off guard, and complicated the situation immensely. She hoped he'd been satisfied with her answers; she prayed he'd ask no more questions.

But while she wasn't proud of the lie, she was just as worried about what she *hadn't* told him. How would Kane react if he knew Dillon was Laramie's marshal? He'd claimed he wasn't a wanted man in Wyoming Territory. But maybe that was because he figured she'd turn him in to the law . . . No, she decided. For now that little secret was best kept to herself.

Jagged mountaintops reared high to the east, silent sentinels. To the north and west, the high rolling plateau seemed to extend forever. The heat was scorching and seemed to undulate in wave after wave on the horizon. Late that afternoon they crested a knobby rise. Not too far distant, a small town squatted at the base of the mountains.

Abby reined in Sonny. Kane had pulled in Midnight as well; he sat with one dark hand resting on the saddle horn, staring intently down at the cluster of buildings below.

Her voice broke the silence. "Crystal Springs?"

He nodded, but not before she glimpsed a brief flare of something akin to accusation in his eyes. Her chin lifted; apparently he hadn't expected her to know where they were. But Pa hadn't raised her to be a simpering, helpless female, she thought stubbornly, and she wasn't about to apologize.

Nor could she resist a cautious excitement. "I thought you said the hideout was a couple of hundred miles north. Are we getting close?"

"Close? Honey, we've got at least another four days of riding ahead of us." He looked at her then, his features harsh, almost brooding. " 'Course, you know you may just be setting yourself up for a big fall. I haven't ridden with Sam for nearly a year. He may have moved the hideout."

Abby's heart squeezed. She couldn't dare consider that—she wouldn't!

With an effort she faced him calmly. "Now who's the one being prickly? I told you before, Kane. I don't expect you to help me for nothing. I'll pay you."

"Who says I'm interested in your money?" With his knuckle he shoved back the brim of his hat. He gave her a leering once-over, his gaze an insult.

Abby felt stripped to the bone. She colored and glanced away. "All you have to do is name your price." Her voice was scarcely audible. "I told you that before."

Her gaze flitted back to his. His eyes were riveted on her face, his scrutiny so unwavering and piercing it gave her a jolt; she felt she'd been struck by lightning. His expression was dark and hard. Yet oddly, he was the first to drag his eyes away. "We'll settle up later," she heard him mutter. "You can count on it, sweetheart."

He spurred Midnight into a gallop. Abby did the same, keeping abreast with the pair although she soon speculated dryly that Kane might be trying to lose them. He didn't slow until they reached the outskirts of the town.

Abby glanced around curiously. Most of the buildings were small and squat, bleached gray by the unrelenting sunshine. They trotted past a bank and a schoolhouse; Kane surprised her by turning down a side street and reining to a halt.

She soon discovered why.

They had stopped before the general store. He dismounted and turned to her, brashly setting his hands around her waist and swinging her down from Sonny's back. He hobbled their horses to the railing, then turned to her.

"Why don't you go inside and get those supplies you said we needed?"

A slender brow rose. "Where will you be?"

He jerked his thumb toward a small building at the end of the street.

The soft line of her lips compressed as she peered over his shoulder. Oh, she should have known—it was the saloon! Before she could say a word, Kane turned and walked away.

Abby was only a step behind him. He spun around and glared. "What the hell do you think you're doing?"

She matched his stare bravely. "You're not going anywhere without me, Kane."

Again those strange silver eyes gave her a perusal that was far too thorough for her peace of mind . . . "Why, sweetheart, I'm flattered."

"Don't be," she said shortly. "I wouldn't put it past you to sneak out the back door."

At his side, those long fingers curled hard into his palm. Abby had the distinct sensation he wished her neck were between them. "As I recall, sweetheart, that's your trick, not mine. But you're welcome to come if you want. I thought I might ask a few questions, maybe see if your husband or Sam passed through here. 'Course I doubt if anyone will be inclined toward talk once a lady like you walks through the door. I'd have thought you might know by now what men expect of females who like to frequent saloons." Each word was like the prick of a knife. "But if you don't mind everyone thinking you're a whore, hell—why should I?"

He seized her wrist and hauled her up against his side. By now Abby's suspicion had distilled; his point, she realized rather sheepishly, was a valid one. But she wouldn't say she was sorry, not when he was being so deliberately hurtful.

He'd called her bluff . . . and won.

He would have strode away with her in tow if she hadn't resisted. But she did and he turned on her, his features as black as a thunderhead.

"You go on. I—I'll wait for you here." Her head was down, her voice low and not entirely steady.

She couldn't look at him—she just couldn't. His grip on her wrist started to tighten; he abruptly checked himself when he realized her change of heart. He released her with a scowl.

"Don't stand around here in the street," he said curtly. "Why don't you wait in that restaurant there." He pointed to a window next to the general store. "I'll be back as soon as I can."

Abby didn't linger after he left. In the general store, she replenished what supplies they'd used, chatted briefly with the storekeeper and left. In the restaurant, she ordered coffee. After nearly half an hour passed, she decided she'd better order a meal before they sent her on her way. The ham and biscuits smelled delicious, but when they finally arrived Abby found she was too on edge to eat more than a few bites. More than an hour passed before Kane finally showed up to collect her.

She jumped up from the table. "Did you find out anything?"

He shook his head. Abby's shoulders sagged but she refused to let her spirits sag. There was enough daylight left to ride a little longer; the western sky was aglow with the purple blush of twilight when they decided to make camp for the night. Kane chose a tree-sheltered clearing near the stream they'd been following.

Kane unsaddled his horse, promptly settled his back against a tree trunk and stretched his legs out. He covered his face with his hat and laced his fingers across his abdomen. Ten minutes later when Abby returned from rinsing her hands and face in the stream, he hadn't moved so much as an inch.

She walked by and caught the distinct odor of smoke and strong drink. Squaring her hands on her hips, she fixed him with a glare. She was both disappointed and frustrated that he had nothing to report about Stringer Sam or Dillon, especially after the fuss he'd made about her going with him. Thinking he was asleep, she spoke her mind.

"I have to wonder, mister, if it was really information you were after in that saloon." She muttered her indignation. "Maybe it was just a good excuse for a chance to tip a whiskey bottle again."

She'd scarcely turned her back when she felt the hair on the back of her neck prickle, as if in warning.

"Maybe," intruded a quiet male voice into the silence, "you'd like to repeat that."

Abby turned slowly to face him. The air between them was suddenly crackling. "Obviously you heard me quite well," she said stiffly. "But if that's what you want, I'll say it again. I think you're awfully fond of your bottle, Kane."

His mouth twisted. Lord knew he had enough reason to seek comfort in drink. But he'd learned long ago that whiskey didn't change what he was— and what he had done. It only made him forget . . . but only for a while.

Bitter fury seeped through him, like a cloud creeping across the sun. No, he thought. There was no ease to be found in the bottom of a bottle.

There was none to be found anywhere.

But she had no right to preach to him, this woman who'd no doubt never known a day of hardship in her life—no right at all.

He rose slowly to his full, considerable height. "You just won't do it, will you? You just won't give an inch. You think I'm the scum of the earth and you're determined I'll know it. Who the hell are you to judge me?"

"I—I wasn't." Praying he wouldn't guess her sudden nervousness, she watched him warily. She tried to step back, only to find her way blocked by a massive tree trunk. "I was just trying to—"

"The hell you weren't. You thought I was good enough to help you save your husband's hide. Ah, but you forget that when it's convenient, don't you? Well, I haven't forgotten, sweetheart. And you know what? I think it's time for the payoff."

Abby's throat seemed to close off. "Wh-what do you mean?"

His smile was not a nice one. "You said all I had to do was name my price. Well, it's time we settled up, sweetheart, and what I want is you."

You. Alarm bells went off in her head. Her heart began to pound so hard she was certain he must surely hear it. "Wait," she began. "I think maybe we should resolve this once and for all—"

He took off his gunbelt and dropped it on the ground. "I quite agree, Abigail."

His easy tone belied the savage light in his eyes. He caught her just above her elbows and stepped forward. There was no mistaking his anger. His eyes were dark gray and depthless, as turbulent as a summer storm.

Abby's mouth went dry. Her breath came fast, then slow, then fast again. "You misunderstood," she said quickly. "I—I promised you money!"

He shook his head. "As I recall, yesterday morning in Laramie you said, 'I'll give you anything, Kane, anything you want.' That's another thing I haven't forgotten."

"No!" she cried. "I—I won't let you do this, Kane. Do you hear? I won't let you!"

"Sweetheart—" That hard smile still hadn't left his mouth. "—you can't stop me."

The softness in his tone was deceptive . . . Arms like iron bands came around her, dragging her against him. Tension and anger radiated from him, snaring her in a web from which there was no escape. She was trapped, not only by all she sensed in him, but in the steely binding of arms tight and hard about her back.

She had one shattering glimpse of his eyes, filled with fury and a glittering heat, a heat that was far more frightening than his anger. She would have cried out but his mouth came down, sealing hers like a hot brand. For one shocked, frozen moment, Abby remained passive, but only for an instant. She sought to twist away, but Kane allowed no room for struggle. His arms tightened; they were fused together from chest to knee, so close her feet were jammed between his, her breasts crushed against the unyielding breadth of his chest.

She tried to bring her hands up but it was no use. His lips plundered the softness of hers, raw and hungry and ruthlessly demanding. Abby despised her helplessness, but she was wise enough to recognize that Kane's size gave him an unfair but unremitting advantage over her. She was no match for his strength.

But Abby wasn't about to concede victory—and damn his hide, she didn't care if he knew it. She held herself rigid in his arms and when his tongue came out to trace the seam of her lips, she clamped her lips together and barred him entrance.

His head came up. His hold on her eased though he didn't release her. "What!" he mocked. "Hasn't your husband taught you how to kiss yet?" An arrogant smile curled those hard lips. "Sweetheart, if you gave him this kind of reception seven nights in a row, no wonder he headed for parts unknown."

Though Abby's face burned scarlet, she didn't back down from his sneer. "You're not half the man Dillon is," she said levelly.

"Is that a fact? Well, let me tell you something, sweetheart. I'm beginning to wonder if there's really a flesh-and-blood woman under all those clothes. Let's just see, shall we?"

He moved before she could stop him. His hands came up and flicked open her vest, closing unerringly over the mounds of her breasts. Even as their eyes locked, challenging gray slate with startled blue, he raked his thumbs across her nipples, intimately acquainting himself with her swelling softness.

A red-hot anger choked her. Lord, but he was a snake to touch her so—to handle her so . . . when he thought she was married yet! Fury lent her courage—and strength.

She wrenched free of his hold. Drawing back her arm, she dealt a stinging, open-palmed blow to his cheek. "You don't have a shred of decency in you," she hissed. "You're an animal, Kane. And don't ever—ever!—touch me like that again."

Kane's eyes blazed fire and ice. Like hell, he thought fiercely. I'll touch you any damn way I want.

But the thought had no more than crossed his mind when a burst of wheezing male laughter sounded from behind them.

"Well, well, looky here. Looks like you got yourself a stray on your hands, doesn't it now!"

Chapter 6

～～∽∽⌒∽∽～～

Son of a bitch.

The curse resounded in the chambers of Kane's mind. He stiffened, his hands falling away from Abby. Slowly he turned to face the owner of that gritty male voice, cursing himself for letting his guard down. If he hadn't been so determined to rile Abby the way she riled him, the keenly honed instincts that had served him so well over the years would never have failed him now.

Not ten feet away were two men on horseback, one lean and stringy-looking, the other heavy-jowled with small, beady eyes that would have looked right at home on a wily coyote. Kane's eyes slid to his gun belt, lying on the dirt six feet away. *Shit*. If only he hadn't been so goddamned eager to discard it.

"Havin' trouble with the little lady, mister?"

"Nothing I can't handle." Kane's easy tone didn't fool Abby. He was as tense as a metal wire. She instinctively eased closer.

"Didn't sound that way, the way we heard it." The heavy-set one gave a wheezing laugh. "Say, Jake, I think this boy could use a lesson or two. What d'ya say?"

"I'd say that's the best idea you've had all year,

105

Chester. And you know what they say—no time like the present." Jake gave a grating chuckle, a sound that chilled Abby's blood. Both were unshaven and unkempt. An air of menace clung to the pair, as thick as stale smoke. Her heart began to pound.

The one called Chester spit out a greasy wad of tobacco and hitched his chin toward Kane. "You there, put your hands on your head real slow-like and move away from the lady."

Kane remained where he was, arms taut, fingers flexed. The two were eyeing Abby like a child might eye a sweet treat behind the counter.

He didn't like it—he didn't like it at all.

Rage splintered across Chester's face as he nudged his horse forward. "If you're smart, mister, you'll do what I say." Without warning he drew back his boot, then thrust his heel out against Kane's chest. On horseback, his added height gave him the momentum he needed to knock Kane off-balance.

By the time Kane recovered, whirling on him with teeth bared, Chester had hoisted a rifle to his shoulder. It was aimed dead-center at his heart. He motioned with the barrel.

"Git yourself over to that boulder and kneel down . . . no, not that way. We want ya where you can see how much your little gal there likes a *real* man." He grinned, displaying a mouthful of stained, yellowed stumps. "That's good, right there. Now put your hands behind your back and keep 'em there."

Jake swung down off his horse. He crooked a finger at Abby.

Abby stood like a trapped doe.

Jake let out a foul curse and strode toward her.

"You two don't hear so good, do ya?" He grabbed her arm in a bruising grip and twisted his hand in her hair, jerking her face up to his. "We can do this nice and easy-like, or we can have some fun. Which is it gonna be, sister?"

Lank, greasy hair stuck out from beneath his hat. Fetid breath struck her face, as sour as the odor of his unwashed flesh. Abby's stomach heaved.

Terrified, praying it didn't show, she spit in his face. Jake's features contorted into an ugly mask. He grabbed a fistful of her shirt, then shoved her with all his might, sending her tumbling to the ground. Though she tried to stifle it, a half-sob of pain ripped from her throat.

Her cry went through Kane like a knife ripping through paper. He sprang up on the balls of his feet, his body coiled and ready to spring. The chill of cold metal rammed against his temple was the only thing that stopped him.

Chester leered at him. "I wouldn't if I was you, mister, less you want your little gal to see your brains splattered from here to the Sweetwater."

Earth and sky spun by in a sickening whirl. Dazed by her fall, Abby cried out when ruthless hands yanked at her wrists, jerking them behind her back. Jake cinched her wrists tight with a strip of rawhide. She winced when he gave a last vicious tug. The rawhide bit deeply into her flesh.

He flipped her over and hauled her to her feet. Grating laughter filled the air when she stumbled.

"You bastard!" she cried. "I'll die before I'd let a filthy beast like you lay a hand on me!" Sheer bravado prompted her outburst. Jake retaliated by ripping open her shirt, sending buttons flying in all directions. She jerked when he wrenched the material from her shoulders down to her elbows, exposing her white cotton chemise.

He chortled. "Hooeee, Chester, looky what we got here!" Gleaming black eyes devoured the sight of her full breasts straining against the thin cloth. Abby paled when he whipped out a knife. In a horrified frenzy, she thrashed wildly, trying to slam her knee into his groin. He twisted, easily deflecting the blow.

"You wanna fight? Hey, that's all right by me, sweet thing. Hard and fast and rough is just the way I like it."

With one stroke he slit the flimsy pink ribbons of her chemise from her waist upward. Freed from their restraint, her breasts spilled out, white and round and bare. Sheer lust flamed in his eyes.

Next to Kane, Chester's attention wavered. His eyes nearly bulged out of his head.

Jake grabbed Abby. He squeezed her so tight she feared her ribs would snap, then jammed his knee between her thighs. Terror like ice clogged her veins. Abby tried desperately to strain away but succeeded only in chafing her wrists. Hot, wet lips opened hers; his tongue gouged deep. Abby turned her face away and gagged. She moaned as hot hands roamed her breasts, squeezing roughly, pinching her nipples and making her gasp in pain.

"I'm ready," he panted. "Oh, yeah, wait till you see what I got for you, sweet thing." In horror she saw him fumbling with his pants. She wrenched away with a cry.

Exactly what happened next, Abby couldn't say. She heard a man scream with pain—Chester—

and then a deafening explosion. A burning smell
assailed her nostrils. She felt more than saw Jake's
body jerk. He staggered back, his expression dumbfounded. Blood like a crimson flower blossomed on
his chest. He slumped to the ground.

Smoke drifted in the silence. When it cleared
Abby saw that Kane had Chester pinned to the
ground, a knee on his chest, the gleaming tip of a
knife laid against his whiskered throat. "Say your
prayers, you bastard. 'Cause you're on your way to
hell just like your friend."

Chester began to blubber. "Don't kill me, mister!
It was all Jake's idea, I swear. I didn't want to kill
ya, honest, but Jake wanted to hump the girl!"

Kane smiled tightly. "Tell that to some other
sucker, fella."

Abby dragged in a searing breath. "No!" she
cried. "Kane, you—you can't kill him!"

"Why the hell not?" His tone was flat and emotionless.

"Because if you do, you—you'll be no better than
the two of them!"

Their eyes collided, his fierce and burning, hers
mutely pleading. She glimpsed in his a venomous
glitter, and sensed his rage was directed not only
at the man held hostage on the ground, but her as
well for attempting to stop him.

An air of utter ruthlessness surrounded him, an
air that frightened her. The cords in his wrist grew
taut, the tension in his chiseled features terrible to
behold. His knuckles turned white on the hilt of the
knife as he battled the urge to finish the murder in
his heart. Seconds passed, seconds that stretched to
an eternity.

With a snarl he leaped to his feet. "Get your hide in gear and take your buddy with you. And you sure as hell better hope you never cross my path—because if I ever see you again, the lady here won't be with me to save your worthless ass."

He meant what he said; every one of them knew it. Chester scrambled up as fast as his girth and the wound in his shoulder would allow. He dumped the other man's body across his horse and gave it a sharp slap on the rump. Whether Jake was dead or alive, Kane didn't know—he didn't care. He watched Chester mount and spur his horse forward. Then he turned to look at Abby. His eyes found hers through the twilight gloom.

"Dear God," she said numbly. "You—you stabbed him." The words were more breath than sound. Her gaze followed Chester's rapidly disappearing figure.

"I had to find some way to get him to drop the gun. Lucky for you that I did, or that bastard Jake would be rutting between your thighs right now!"

Abby flushed, both at his crudity and the stabbing condemnation in his tone. "I suppose you think I should have slapped their hands and asked them to leave," he went on harshly. "Honey, those two deserved everything they got. Do you have any idea what they'd have done to you? A lady who looks like you do would fetch one hell of a price in a whorehouse—after they got through with you, that is. We were goddamn lucky—*you* were goddamn lucky. I just hope to hell I don't regret letting them live."

Abby didn't answer, not because she didn't want to, but because she couldn't. Kane's words painted a stark picture in her mind. The enormity of what had happened began to seep in. She shuddered with revulsion. Her vision blurred; spots danced in front of her eyes. For an instant she feared she would faint—she, Abigail MacKenzie, who had never fainted in her life! She shuddered again, recalling the way that horrid man Jake had touched her—what he'd been about to do! Though she tried, she couldn't control the weakness that rushed through her, making her legs feel like mush.

The hands that plucked at the torn ribbons of her chemise were none too steady. From where he stood Kane could see the telltale imprint of that bastard Jake's hands on the swelling flesh of her breasts. He swore softly; she'd bear those bruises for a while. He crossed to her, his mouth a tight line in his face. She was struggling to hold the gaping edges of her chemise closed with one hand and pull her shirt back over her shoulders with the other.

"Wait."

His voice was gritty. She stopped, her eyes lifting slowly to his. That she didn't argue was a sign of just how shaken she was, he decided grimly.

"Hold still. I want to check those ribs."

He left no room for protest. She froze, the back of her arm pressed against her chest. Kane tried hard not to look, but bloody hell!—he was only a man, and not a very upright one at that. He bit back a groan. Her chemise was nearly transparent. He had no trouble discerning the shape of her breasts, trembling and soft and full; the darker, dusky outlines of her nipples visible through the sheer cloth. He wondered if she knew the pressure of her arm merely made the round, cushioned fullness swell still further.

She flushed when he slid his hands inside her chemise, engulfing her rib cage. At his touch, Abby inhaled sharply. His gaze cut immediately to hers. "Sore?"

She hesitated. "A little," she admitted.

That no-good son of a bitch. Aloud he muttered, "I thought for sure that bastard was going to snap you in two."

Abby wet her lips, her eyes clinging to his. His expression, she noticed vaguely, had lost some of its harshness. She struggled to form a smile. "So did I." Her voice emerged feathery and weak, totally unlike her own.

Kane said nothing. He had stepped close, so close she could see the dark gray specks in his irises, the shadow cast on his cheekbones by half-lowered lashes; so close she could feel the warm heat of his body, warm against the chill night air.

She flushed when his gaze once again lowered. Modesty dictated she avert her head, but his scrutiny of her near-naked breasts didn't make her feel soiled and dirty, as Jake's had—she knew he was only checking for injuries. Still, she was sharply aware of the way his fingers slid along her skin, grazing her ribs, probing slowly, gently gauging. His fingertips were faintly callused, but the sensation was not at all unpleasant. She felt an odd, unfamiliar quiver low in her belly. In fact, she thought with the faintest tinge of panic, it was all too pleasant.

They were both holding their breath when at last he withdrew his hands. But while both were achingly aware of her state of undress, neither was aware of the chaos going on inside the other.

Abby awkwardly tugged her shirt back over her shoulders, all at once feeling naked and exposed. Kane presented her with his back. By the time she'd finished, the sudden onset of night fell upon the earth like a smothering cloak. She bit her lip, staring at the rigid lines of his back. He seemed to sense she was finished and turned back. Their eyes locked. A strange, palpitating tension sprang up between them.

Abby was the first to tear her eyes away. "Do you think he's dead?"

Kane didn't need to ask who. His gaze bounced upon her, then swung off to search the inky darkness. Woodenly he answered, "My aim's not what it used to be if he isn't."

A part of her was appalled at such callousness; still another whispered he'd had no choice. Abby shivered as the shadows seemed to move closer. "We'd better start a fire before it gets any later—"

"No. No fire. Not tonight."

Her breath caught. A flurry of fear gripped her mind. Kane could have kicked himself when he saw it.

"You don't think he'll come back, do you?" Though she tried, Abby couldn't quite keep the tremor from her voice.

Kane despised the surge of longing that rose up inside him. He wanted to drag her in his arms, kiss away the puckered frown between her brows, soothe her fears . . . Christ! What the hell was the matter with him?

"I doubt it," he said at last. "But I'll keep watch just the same. You might as well try and get some sleep."

It was a dismissal, abrupt and somehow almost cutting. To her horror, she felt a stinging rush of tears behind her eyelids. Feeling wounded without knowing quite why, she pulled in a long, uneven breath, battling the urge to cry.

But Kane had heard the deep, shuddering breath she drew. His head whipped around. He regarded her suspiciously.

"What's wrong?"

She just shook her head, unwilling to say anything for fear her voice would betray her tremulous feelings right now. Her emotions lay scattered in every direction, but she couldn't seem to help it. She would have turned away, but all at once he was there before her.

"I may be a lot of things, sweetheart, but I'm not stupid. And I'm not blind." He caught her chin between thumb and forefinger, turning her face up to his. "Now tell me what's wrong."

Though his voice was still gruff, some of the fierceness had left his face.

"I just—I just don't know why you're so angry with me," she heard herself say haltingly. She shuddered. "I know those men probably followed us from Crystal Springs. But it's not my fault . . . I didn't do anything to make them try to do—" She flushed painfully. "—what they did."

No, he thought vaguely, she hadn't. There was no need to. His insides twisted with guilt . . . and something else. It wasn't just her chestnut-haired beauty that beckoned to a man—it was her pride and fiery spirit that made a man long to tame it, yearn to make her surrender. No man was immune from it, including him . . . especially him.

For just an instant, the plane of his jaw hardened. He hated the betraying moisture in her eyes, hated himself for putting it there. He was only half-aware of reaching for her, tugging her close.

"No," he agreed, his voice very low. "You didn't do anything wrong. If anything, it's my fault for letting them sneak up on us."

Their eyes locked. For a mind-splitting moment, there was no doubt both were locked fast in the remembrance of what they'd been doing.

"It wasn't your fault. You couldn't have known what they intended to do." Her arms slid around his waist. She shivered; his arms tightened.

Slowly she raised her head. "Kane," she whispered. "I . . . don't blame you for shooting Jake. I know you did it because . . . you had no choice."

Kane clenched his jaw. He wasn't about to divulge the burning rage he'd felt at the sight of Jake's hands on her. Nor could he divulge the fear that had gripped his mind while Jake stood over Abby. He'd been afraid, not for himself, but for Abby. He'd known she wouldn't meekly submit—and she hadn't.

He'd shot Jake because it was either that or tear him apart with his bare hands.

"You were a fool to try to fight him," he heard himself mutter. "You could have been hurt a lot worse. Christ, when I think what he might have done . . . !"

"But he didn't."

She turned her head against his shoulder, rubbing her cheek against the soft cotton of his shirt. It spun through her mind that his arms were a strange place to find comfort, but he felt so good, all warm, solid strength.

Her breath, warm and moist, trickled across the hollow of his throat. His voice drifted above her head. "You sure you're all right?"

Abby nodded. Her mouth went dry. Slowly, as if he were giving her the chance to move away if she wanted, he threaded his fingers through her hair and tilted her head back so he could see her. His eyes darkened when she made no move to stop him. And she knew, with stark, shattering clarity, that he was going to kiss her again . . .

Her hands came up to clutch at his shoulders, as if in protest. Instead she found her fingers clinging, the muscle beneath her fingertips startlingly hard. Her breath fluttered, like a leaf caught in the wind; he trapped it between his lips and caught it in the back of his throat.

The kiss was not what she expected. It started off deep and slow and rousing, melting all through her like warm honey. His mouth slanted first one way and then the other. She wondered how it might feel on other places . . . She gave a tiny little sigh, helplessly twisting her head to accommodate him.

The sound was like a dam breaking inside him. "Open your mouth," he said against her lips. "Just . . . do it," he urged. "*Please.*"

She did, and was rewarded by the sweeping entrance of his tongue against hers, as bold and fearless as the man himself. Her stomach quivered. Her heart beat the pounding rhythm of a drum as the seductive persuasion of his mouth grew blatantly erotic. He tugged her lower lip between his before dipping within to trace the bottom edge of her teeth. Abby felt a melting curl of heat unfurl low in her belly.

Darkness engulfed them; the sounds of the night slipped away. Abby was conscious only of the dark, sweet pleasure of his kiss. His mouth slid with slow heat down the fragile arch of her throat. She'd forgotten her state of undress, but Kane hadn't. Impatient hands flicked aside the tattered edges of her chemise, baring her breasts to him.

She anticipated his touch even before it came. Her breasts seemed to tingle and swell. Her nipples grew tight and peaked. When his thumbs raked across both aching summits, a white-hot current stabbed through her, from her belly to the secret place between her thighs. Her fingers dug into the binding hardness of his arms. Her mind groped fuzzily. There was a reason this shouldn't be happening, but dear Lord, it was so hard to think . . .

Kane gritted his teeth. Hunger as sharp as a blade cut through him. His manhood swelled stiff and rigid; he felt he was going to burst his britches. He wanted to push her down, feel her tight and wet and hot around him, and drive deep inside her until there was only mindless, pulsing ecstasy.

If you do this you'll be no better than the two of them . . . The stricken little cry reverberated in his head, over and over.

He tried to close his mind to it. He covered her mouth with his, his kiss rough, almost bruising. He filled his palms with her buttocks and lifted her, grinding her against the part of him that ached for her the most.

You'll be no better than they are . . .

The taunt tore through his mind again. Chester

and Jake. Sweet Jesus. He was *already* no better than those two scoundrels. He was worse . . . *worse*.

She just didn't know it yet.

Slowly he lifted his head. His breathing was harsh and scraping. "If you don't want this to go any farther, now's the time to say the word."

His expression was dark and tense. She'd felt the explosion of violence in his kiss, as if he'd suddenly wanted something more from her, something she didn't wholly understand. Sensing the sudden darkness of his mood, she drew a deep, shaky breath. Her fingers clutched at the pink ribbons on her chemise.

It was all the answer Kane needed.

"You'd better get some sleep."

She stared at him, confused by his curtness, confused by her body's wanton response to his kiss. Her tongue came out to touch her lips, swollen and moist from his mouth. "Kane—"

He clenched his teeth. If he didn't know better, he'd think she was teasing him! "*Now*, Abby."

"But—"

"*Now*. Before I change my mind!"

His features were closed and inscrutable, somehow fierce. He picked up Chester's rifle and stalked to the edge of the camp.

For the second night in a row, she fell asleep struggling against tears . . . and not knowing why.

Abby opened her eyes to brilliant, sun-washed sky the next morning. She lay motionless, aware of an unaccustomed ache in her muscles; the events of the night before flooded back in rampant remembrance. She turned her head slightly and spied Kane.

He must have started a fire this morning, for he was crouched before it, a cup of coffee cradled in his palms. He must have sensed her scrutiny, for he chose that moment to raise his head.

Their eyes collided.

The silence was stifling. The entire world seemed to be holding its breath as time raged on. Staring at him in the cold light of day, Abby found it difficult to believe this was the man who had held and comforted her, then kissed her with such fire and passion. His expression was coolly remote. He appeared dangerous and unapproachable, his jaw shadowed with a bristly growth of beard. Apparently he'd just come from the stream; his hair was wet. His shirt hung open, revealing the dense mat of hair on his chest. All at once she could scarcely draw in enough air to breathe.

Abby was the first to drag her gaze away. Kane stared at the fire while she rose, her movements rather stiff. The morning air was chill, though the blaze of the sun promised another scorching day. She kept the blanket draped around her shoulders for modesty's sake. It had been too dark last night to search her saddlebags for a clean shirt and chemise. Her steps carried her without volition to the fire. She shivered a little and stretched out her hands toward the crackling flames, feeling awkward and unsure of herself.

"Coffee?" Kane didn't look at her as he spoke.

"No, thank you. I think I'll just go wash up." Her tone was carefully neutral.

At the stream, she dropped her clean clothes on a

rock and sat down to pull off her boots. She wasted no time pulling off her ruined shirt and chemise. She started to reach for her clean chemise, then stopped, her gaze riveted longingly on the stream. She'd meant to merely rinse her face and hands, but the heat and two days of travel had left her feeling dusty and sweaty—she couldn't remember when she'd been so dirty! The water lapped her toes, clear and cool and inviting. On impulse she stripped completely, grabbed her soap and waded into the stream.

At first the bite made her gasp, but she ventured further, until the water nearly reached her shoulders. She ducked under, immersing herself completely. She worked the soap into a lather and quickly washed her hair and her body. Although it felt heavenly, she resisted the impulse to linger. Using her torn chemise as a washcloth, she hurriedly scrubbed herself. She left the stream regretfully a few minutes later.

She'd just struggled into her chemise and drawers when a prickly unease tickled her spine. She whirled, some sixth sense warning her she wasn't alone.

Kane sat on the bank, some twenty feet distant, a rifle propped on his knees.

Disbelief warred with dismay; a ready anger surged to the fore.

She snatched up her shirt and clutched it to her breast, glaring her displeasure. "If you were a gentleman, you wouldn't stand there gawking."

Kane met her regard calmly. He'd have turned his back if she'd asked, but as usual her tartness got his dander up. He didn't bother to tell her he wasn't about to leave her alone after what happened last night—he knew she'd never believe him.

His insolent gaze wandered slowly down the slender length of her legs and back to her face. A derisive smile touched his lips. "As I recall, it seems to me I *did* act the gentleman last night."

At his pointed reminder, Abby's cheeks began to burn. He was right, but did he have to be so—so arrogant about it? "A gentleman wouldn't remind me of that!"

"I never claimed to be a gentleman, which reminds me . . . Seems to me that for a married lady, you were pretty damned eager to cozy up to me last night."

Abby blanched. Heaven help her, she had liked it when he kissed her. She'd loved the way he'd made her feel, all tight and tingly inside, yet at the same time all hot and liquid; she'd loved the feel of his hands on her breasts, teasing her nipples to tingling erectness. She'd even found herself wondering what his mouth would feel like there . . .

Deep inside she was appalled. She hadn't thought a lady was capable of such wanton thoughts. Dear Lord! What was wrong with her?

But she didn't want to think about that right now—she didn't want to think about *him*.

"I—I wasn't myself last night, Kane," she defended herself weakly. "And I don't appreciate you making it sound as if it was all my fault!"

"I didn't see you trying to stop me," he drawled. "But I guess I can understand your predicament, being without your husband and all." His insolent gaze settled on her breasts, reminding her of all he'd seen . . . and touched. "Just let me know if you change your mind. I'll be happy to stand in for him any time, sweetheart, any time."

Abby was too shocked to say a word. Oh, but he was cruel and jaded, rude and abrasive. God, how she hated him!

Chapter 7

⟋⟍ ◯◯ ⟋⟍

They left the shadow of the mountains behind that very morning. On either side of the trail they followed, sun-baked plains rolled and dipped clear to the horizon, blending with the sky. The air was laden with the scent of summer grass, undulating wildly beneath the ceaseless caress of the wind. Even while Abby acknowledged a strange, awesome beauty to the scene spread out before her, a yawning hollowness swelled inside her—it seemed as if the edge of forever stretched endlessly before them, empty and forlorn.

Late afternoon they came upon a modest farmhouse nestled in a small basin, faded and weather-beaten. Texas bluebonnets sprouted next to the house. Several shirts flapped lazily on a clothesline. Nearby was a small corral. Between the house and the barn was a well-tended garden.

A wiry, middle-aged man stood just inside the corral, watching their approach. Kane tipped his hat.

"Afternoon," he called out. "Mind if we water our horses?"

"Help yourself." The man stepped through the gate and gestured toward a trough filled with water. He shut the gate and ventured toward them.

Kane swung down from Midnight. He turned toward Abby but she had already swung her leg over the pommel and leaped lightly from Sonny's back. For the space of a heartbeat, their eyes clashed.

Abby lifted her chin and turned to the man. "We appreciate your hospitality, Mr. . . ."

"Willis. Amos Willis." He shook the hand she extended.

"I'm Abigail, and this is Kane." Abby smiled warmly. "I hate to trouble you further, Mr. Willis, but is there a well where I could get a drink?"

"Sure 'nough is, ma'am, right around the side of the house. Just help yourself."

She pulled Sonny to the trough, then walked toward the spot he'd indicated. It didn't take long to pull up a bucket of water from the well. Abby filled the dipper with fresh, cool water and drank thirstily. The top few buttons of her shirt were undone against the heat, so she dipped her neckerchief into the water and wiped her face and neck. She sighed; the damp coolness felt deliciously refreshing.

The two men were busy talking when she rejoined them. Kane paid her no heed. Feeling piqued and determined not to let him get the better of her, she focused her attention on Amos, who hitched his thumbs in his suspenders and shook his head.

"Like I said, only man's been through here rode out before dawn. Spent the night in my barn, he did. Real pleasant fella—from Laramie I believe he said. I saw a badge in his saddlebag, so I 'spect he was a deputy or some such."

Abby felt as if all the wind had been knocked

from her lungs. For one paralyzing moment she could neither move nor breathe.

She heard Kane's voice as if from a very great distance. "A deputy from Laramie, eh? Pretty far from home, I'd say."

"That's what I thought, too. I thought he was headin' home, but when he left, he rode out to the north."

There was a horrible constriction in Abby's throat. Her mind was racing in tandem with her heart. Kane couldn't possibly fail to make the connection—he would *know* Dillon was an officer of the law . . .

The two talked for a few minutes more. Abby longed to sink beneath the earth, never to be seen again. In a daze she heard Kane thanking Amos. He turned to Abby.

"I think it's time we moved on, don't you, Abigail?"

Strong fingers dug into her waist. She was bodily lifted and set on Sonny's back. She caught a glimpse of his profile as he swung away; his features bore no trace of emotion, but Abby wasn't fooled. His steely calm masked a seething tension—she'd felt it when he lifted her into the saddle.

He slapped Sonny sharply on the rump and they were off.

Apprehension tightened every muscle in her body. She half-expected Kane to whirl on her the minute they were out of earshot. But they rode hard for nearly half an hour, so long she began to think perhaps she'd misjudged Kane. She began to relax, a subtle softening within her. Maybe, she decided cautiously, it had been silly to dread Kane discovering that Dillon was Laramie's marshal. Maybe he wasn't as heartless and insensitive as she'd thought. In fact, maybe it was time she gave him credit for . . .

A strong brown hand shot out and grabbed Sonny's bridle. They halted so abruptly she nearly pitched over the gelding's head. By the time she'd gathered her wits about her, Kane was off Midnight's back and standing before her.

Her heart lurched sickeningly. Kane said nothing, merely pinned her with the relentless glitter of his eyes. It vaulted through her mind that this was the calm before the storm . . . She wanted to plead with him that she'd had no choice—she'd been afraid he wouldn't help her if she told him the truth! But his grim countenance robbed her of the inclination.

Oddly, he made no move to touch her. His stance was supremely arrogant, his legs planted wide apart, his shoulders as wide as the mountains they'd left behind.

"Off," was all he said.

Abby's mouth went dry as dust. His tone was deceptively soft. Dismay shot through her. She was distinctly wary of the predatory air that lurked about him.

"If you're smart," he said in that same deadly soft tone, "you'll do what I say, Abigail."

A low-grade panic touched her spine. Abby clutched the reins more tightly. Sonny began to back away.

"We can't stop now, Kane." She tried to reason with him. "Didn't you hear Mr. Willis? Dillon stayed in his barn last night! We're less than a day behind him—we can't afford to waste any time!"

The next thing she knew she'd been yanked off Sonny's back. Her head swam dizzily.

Kane's hands came down on her shoulders like iron clamps. "Seems to me Dillon can take care of himself." He spoke through clenched teeth. "Especially considering he's a goddamned deputy!"

Abby blanched. The very air seemed to thunder with his rage. "No," she gasped. "He's not! He's—"

He shook her so hard her head snapped back. "Don't lie to me, dammit!"

She closed her eyes to shut out the sight of his face. It did no good; she could feel the force of his wrath in every pore of his body. Her eyes opened, huge and uncertain. He looked ready to explode.

"Answer me! Is he a lawman?"

She nodded, struggling to squeeze sound past the tightness in her throat. "Dillon is . . . he's Laramie's marshal."

A vile curse rent the air. Hard fingers dug into the soft flesh of her arms. Abby gasped. Kane towered over her by half a head. He was so tall, so much stronger than she was . . . Fear winged through her as she sensed the violence within him, as fiercely raging as a storm.

He flung her away from him, and she fell to her knees. "You're crazy if you think I'll take you straight to a lawman. God, what a fool I was! I believed all that talk about his vendetta against Sam—and all the while he's the law! If he finds out who I am, he'll throw my hide in jail . . . if he doesn't blow my head off first!"

"No," she said faintly. "I—I won't let him, I swear."

"You expect me to believe a word you say? Christ, and I thought I was bad!" He gave a harsh laugh. "Honey, most lawmen shoot first and ask questions later."

"I'll make certain he doesn't—I promise you! For heaven's sake, think about it! It's not you Dillon wants. It's Stringer Sam, I swear! I told you the truth—he has a vendetta against Stringer Sam because he left him for dead once!"

He made no effort to veil his contempt. "I'm through listening to you, sweetheart. Maybe it's time you found some other fool to take you to Stringer Sam, because I've had it with you! I've had it with the way you treat me like dirt—the way you think you're better than me—"

He was so hard, so utterly unyielding. Abby refused to give in to the tears burning just behind her eyelids. She surged to her feet, consumed by a reckless anger.

"You're right, Kane, you are a fool! And it sure as hell doesn't take much to be a better man than you!"

His spine went rigid. At his side, his hands clenched into fists. He took a step forward, then abruptly checked himself, his eyes burning like the fiery pits of hell. Too late Abby realized she'd gone too far.

"I don't have to take this, sweetheart." His voice was gritty with suppressed anger. "And by God, I won't. Not from you or anyone else—"

"Fine!" she shouted. "I don't need you, Kane. I don't need any man. I—I'll find the hideout myself!"

He sneered. "Oh, that's good, real good. Just how

the hell do you think you're gonna do that?"

She snatched Sonny's reins, leaped on his back. "You said Sam's hideout was north of here. Mister, that's all I need to know."

She left him standing in a choking cloud of dust.

Kane told himself over and over he didn't give a damn what she did . . . where she went . . . what did or didn't happen to her . . .

It was a lie, through and through.

But she was right about one thing—he *was* a fool. Abigail MacKenzie had been nothing but trouble since the moment they'd met. This was the perfect chance to walk away and turn his back on her for good—to say to hell with her noble effort to save her husband. Likely as not, Sam had already caught up with her precious Dillon and the poor sucker was dead, so what was the use in sticking around?

She'd already lost her father, an unwelcome little voice needled him. What if Dillon *was* dead? She might need someone . . .

Not him, jeered another voice in his head. After all, she'd made her feelings toward him perfectly plain—she was convinced he was scum—that he was no damn good. *It doesn't take much to be a better man than you.* He stiffened, his gaze alert for the telltale signs of her trail he'd been following since she'd ridden off. Even now, hours later, the taunt still rankled.

Maybe because she was right.

Still, he didn't need anyone—especially spoiled baggage like Abigail MacKenzie—rubbing his face in it.

It was inevitable, perhaps . . . there was a sharp,

knifelike twinge in his chest as he thought of Lorelei. Why it was so, he didn't know. Abby was nothing like Lorelei, nothing at all. Abby was sassy and infuriating. She made him mad nearly every time she opened that pretty little mouth of hers. Lorelei had been sweet-natured and serene, even-tempered and calm. Always a lady, she hadn't minded depending on him, looking to him for advice.

He'd been surprised the first time she'd asked his advice. He was, after all, just a hired hand on the ranch she'd inherited on her husband's death. She'd made him feel worthwhile, as if he were someone who really counted . . . It was a new experience for Kane, who'd grown up in Georgia fending for himself. But Lorelei had made him feel needed, as no one had ever needed him before . . .

Pain burned his heart, raw and searing. Christ, it seemed as if a lifetime had passed since then.

A lifetime of hell.

No, he thought again, Abby was nothing like Lorelei. She was fiery and rash and determined, the stubborn little fool! But even while he damned her for being so foolhardy, he admitted to a twinge of admiration. He didn't know of any other woman with the guts . . . . No. No, that wasn't right . . . with the *courage* to ride off on her own as she had.

If he was smart, he'd run . . . run and hide as never before. He was good at that. But Kane knew he wasn't going to be smart about this, not smart at all.

You said Sam's hideout was north of here. Mister, that's all I need to know.

At first he hadn't been convinced she meant what she said. But he was now . . .

And that scared the living hell out of him.

* * *

Abby was feeling anything but courageous when she finally laid out her bedroll for the night. It was lonesome traveling without Kane; why it was so, she couldn't say—she assured herself staunchly it certainly wasn't because she missed his companionship! Several times she'd been overcome by the strangest sensation, as if she had only to turn around to find him trotting behind her. Several times she did actually twist around.

But there was nothing there. Nothing but the keening of the wind, and rippling grassland.

The day had left her physically as well as emotionally drained. She'd felt limp as a wet noodle when she dropped from the saddle. But Sonny had to be fed and brushed down, there was a fire to be kindled and a meal to be fixed. Kane had been seeing to their horses in the evenings; Abby hadn't realized how much she'd come to rely on his help. Her footsteps were dragging by the time she sat down to a supper of beans. She forced herself to eat, knowing she would need her strength.

Night descended, heavy and thick. She shivered, for along with the enveloping mantle of darkness came the awful sensation of being the only person in a vast, terrifying wilderness. In that timeless instant when day became night, the wind ceased its restless prowling of the earth. For the span of a heartbeat—then another and another—the world lay still and silent, as if the entire universe held its breath. A sudden pop from the fire made her jump.

She hugged her arms around herself, succumbing to a stark loneliness, and all because of Kane, blast his fickle, outlaw hide! Maybe it hadn't been wise to strike out on her own, but what choice did she have? Kane had been about to abandon her—he'd as much as said so!

And abandoned was suddenly exactly how she felt. She despaired the hot ache that crowded her throat. Struggling to overcome it, she told herself she was better off alone. She began to list every little grievance she had against him. He was coarse and crude. Rude and arrogant. He'd said things to her that no gentleman would say to a lady, things that were unforgivable—

Unforgivable.

She cringed inside. That word might well describe how she had treated Kane. She'd been angry, and so she had struck out . . . Pa had often said her tongue could cut deep as a whip and now she was ashamed and guilty and so afraid it was too late . . .

Pa, she thought bleakly. Oh, if only she'd been able to make Kane see she had to find Dillon. She couldn't lose him, too . . .

The hair on the back of her neck prickled eerily—she had the strangest sensation she was being watched. Somewhere behind her there was a rustle. Her head came sharply around. Her ears strained. She sought to see into the gloom, fighting against a rising panic. But beyond the glow of the fire, the world was laden with shadows.

Her hand slid along the ground, in search of the Colt she'd laid alongside her bedroll. Sonny raised his head from where he'd been contentedly munching grass, as if he, too, sensed another presence. The wind began to rise, a low, eerie wail.

Abby's mouth was bone-dry. There was a crackling sound just behind her, like the trampling of grass ... Footsteps! Someone was coming! Who? She thought of Chester and shuddered. Her fingers closed around the barrel of the gun; she lifted it into her lap and rose slowly to her feet. She couldn't have forced a sound past the lump of fear clogging her throat, but her nerves were screaming. Poised in a half-crouch, she stood still as a statue, her heart pounding so hard her chest hurt. Just when she thought she couldn't stand it any more, she spied a giant shadow gliding toward her.

"You there." The sound came out high and thin and quavery. "Don't come any further." She raised the barrel of the revolver and prayed the visitor couldn't hear the fear in her voice.

The figure halted. Abby caught just a glimpse of cold, pale eyes glittering beneath the brim of his hat.

There was the unmistakable rumble of swear words.

Kane. A rush of blind, sweet relief swept through her.

Two steps brought them toe-to-toe. He scowled blackly. "I'm getting tired of having you wave a gun in my face!" He wrested it from her and stuck it in his belt.

Bravely she raised her chin. She was secretly glad to see him, but pride wouldn't let her admit it, especially to him. "What are you doing here?"

He laughed bitterly. "Honey, you just proved what I've known all along—you've got no business being out here on your own. Christ, you didn't even know I was trailing you!"

Hot color flooded her cheeks. Abby recalled the tingle of unease she'd felt several times today. He was right—she should have known he was following her. But she didn't say so. Oh, no.

"I did, too!" she lied. "Although for the life of me, I don't know why you would bother—unless you intended to shoot me in the back—and steal my horse and my money!"

Hard hands seized her by the shoulders. He hauled her close. "Let's get one thing straight," he hissed. "I never shot anyone—anyone!—in the back, least of all a woman. I know you find it hard to believe, but I do have scruples—not many—but I do have a few. I told you I'd help you find Sam's hideout—and by God, I will."

Her lips pressed together mutinously. "No, you won't. I told you, Kane. I don't need your help. Furthermore, I don't want it!"

Her loftiness made his blood boil. He was thoroughly disgusted at his spate of conscience. "God, but you just can't stand not to have your way, can you? You, lady, are spoiled rotten." His hands fell away as if he could no longer stand to touch her. He gave a low whistle. Midnight came trotting forward.

Abby watched as he heaved the saddle from the stallion's back. "You think you know so much about me," she said stiffly. "But you don't know a thing about me, Kane, nothing at all."

Midnight's bridle in hand, he turned to face her. His stance was supremely arrogant, a hand on his hip, his knee thrust forward.

The smile he slanted her was rimmed with hardness. "Don't I? Honey, I haven't forgotten you told me your daddy owned one of the biggest spreads in Wyoming. That told me a lot, that and your high-and-mighty attitude. But tell me something, sugar. I'll bet Daddy gave you the best of everything, didn't he? Anything sweet li'l ole Abigail wanted, she got."

Abby was stung. His jeer was no less than a conviction. "You're wrong," she began.

"Am I? Honey, I've seen your horse, your saddle, those butter-soft leather boots you wear. Why, I'll bet Daddy even packed you off to some fancy Eastern school for ladies, didn't he?"

It was on the tip of Abby's tongue to blurt out the truth—that Mrs. Rutherford had kicked her out of her school for ladies. She kept quiet only because Kane would have taken great pleasure in her humiliation. Still, she couldn't help the betraying tide of color that crept up her neck.

Kane shook his head disgustedly. "Christ, I knew it!" In some far distant plane, Kane was appalled at his behavior. For the life of him, he didn't know why he baited her so. Maybe it was the ugliness inside him.

Or maybe because it was easier to keep her distant than let her close.

"You're a spoiled little daddy's girl, all right," he accused harshly. "Other people might be impressed by Daddy's money, sugar, but not me. You might think everything has to go your way, but I don't see it that way—I don't see it that way at all. You're stubborn and reckless and pigheaded. You don't think of anyone but yourself!" His tone was scalding.

Stunned by his outburst, Abby tipped her chin.

"If that's what you think, then why are you here?" she asked quietly.

In all honesty, he didn't know. He didn't understand his feelings toward her. He owed her nothing. He wanted nothing from her!

Damn her, he thought fiercely. Damn her for being so young and defenseless and scared. Oh, she tried to hide it. But for an instant she had looked utterly stricken. He steeled himself against the hurt vulnerability he had seen there.

"I'll be goddamned if I know," he said almost savagely. "Oh, you don't need to worry, though. I'll find your precious Dillon for you, but this time we're playing by my rules, sweetheart. We do things my way or not at all."

Abby had gone very pale. "I see. And what if I choose not to abide by your rules?"

He smiled nastily. "I don't see as how you've got a choice, not if you want to find Dillon."

A helpless fury burned inside her. It was galling to admit that he was right, but she could no longer delude herself. If she were to ever find Dillon, she would have to accept his help.

From somewhere she dredged up the courage to look him straight in the eye. "Fine," she said with all the dignity she could muster. "But this only confirms my opinion of you. You are rude and arrogant—you're a bully! You are without a doubt the most thoroughly detestable man I've ever had the misfortune to encounter!"

He dropped his bedroll on the ground beside hers, his expression grim. "Then it sure as hell looks like we deserve each other, doesn't it?"

Chapter 8

They were reluctant partners indeed.

Kane said no more than half a dozen words to her the entire day. The strain was almost more than Abby could bear. He was still angry with her, that much was clear.

In all honesty, she couldn't blame him. At first, she'd tried to excuse herself. She reminded herself she hadn't told an out-and-out lie; she had simply neglected to tell him that Dillon was an officer of the law.

She had deliberately deceived him—and wasn't that as bad as a lie?

But that wasn't the worst of it.

A gnawing guilt nagged at her incessantly. It preyed on her mind that Kane didn't know that her so-called husband wasn't her husband at all . . . but her brother. More than ever, she regretted her deception, yet how was she to tell him?

Some inner voice warned her that he wouldn't take such news lightly . . . She was almost afraid what might happen if and when they did meet up with Dillon. Good, what a fool she'd been! If only that sense of stark, raw virility hadn't frightened her so . . . It *still* frightened her.

Her breath came unevenly whenever he was near.

She'd grown up around more men than women, but never had she been so overwhelmingly conscious of one man's body. Her gaze strayed to Kane again and again. She noticed the way his shoulders stretched the worn cotton of his shirt, awesomely wide and powerful; the sinuous flex of his buttocks whenever he shifted in the saddle. She was secretly mortified that she could entertain such improper thoughts; she was even more shocked that she could be so aware of a man in such a scandalous, indecent way.

Especially *this* man.

He'd kissed her three times now—and three times now her body had displayed a shocking will of its own. It made no sense that she should find pleasure in his arms. She should have experienced disgust and revulsion . . . as she had with Jake. Kane was, after all, an outlaw. It struck her then . . . She'd expected him to be clumsy and lewd, dirty and evil.

He wasn't. Oh, he made no secret of his feelings—he was unfailingly blunt, but Abby was honest enough to admit she'd been rashly provoking more than once.

Her gaze stole to his grim-lipped profile. His lips were drawn in a relentless line. There was an odd tightening in her middle. She recalled exactly what it felt like to have that hard mouth fused against hers, impassioned and demanding . . . The thought progressed. She imagined him kissing her with eager, gentle tenderness . . . Gentle? Tenderness? No, not Kane. Dear Lord, she must be mad. The man was tough to the bone!

They passed through a small town that evening.

More than ever, Abby longed for a bath. She had never felt so dirty in her life. Dust sifted like flour over her clothes. Even her mouth felt gritty.

A weathered sign snagged Abby's attention as they moved down the dusty, sun-baked street—it was the local hotel. She reined in Sonny.

"Wait," she called to Kane. He turned with a lift of those devilishly arched brows. She held his gaze levelly. "We're going to have to stop soon for the night." She nodded at the hotel. The idea of a soft mattress and a bath sounded too heavenly to pass up. "We might as well be comfortable."

A gleam appeared in his eyes. "Why, Abigail," he drawled, "are you askin' what I think you are? Why, what would dear old Dillon think?"

Abby shot him a withering glance and nudged Sonny forward.

In front of the hotel, she dismounted and hitched Sonny to the rail. Kane followed right behind her; Abby did her best to ignore him.

Thankfully, the hotel had two rooms available. She caught just a glimpse of a small dining area where they could eat. She paid for a room for herself and for Kane, aware of the clerk's puzzled glance traveling between herself and Kane as she handed over two crisp bills; she knew he thought it odd that she paid for both rooms, but he said nothing. Kane lounged against the counter, as unperturbed as ever.

Kane carried their gear upstairs. The soft line of her lips tightened slightly as she saw that he had the room directly across from hers. She took her saddlebag and pointedly turned her back.

A few minutes later there was a knock on the

door. Two young boys stood there with the small wooden tub she'd requested. They brought buckets of hot water next; Abby rewarded them with a generous tip when the last had been emptied. She shed her dusty clothes impatiently, leaving them in a heap on the floor. She stepped into the water, leaned back and let the heat soothe the ache from her tired muscles. The tub was rather cramped, but Abby couldn't remember when a bath had felt so wonderful. Not even the thought of Kane, disturbing though it was, could dim her pleasure. She soaked for a long time, then washed and rinsed her hair and climbed from the tub.

She changed quickly, wryly noting it was her last clean change of clothing. Hunger cramped her stomach as she brushed her hair and twisted it into a braid, reminding her she hadn't eaten since this morning. She descended the stairs, suddenly aware of boisterous laughter filtering from the dining room. She paused uncertainly at the edge of the rough, planked floor and glanced inside. She hadn't noticed it earlier, but a bar ran the length of the far wall. The evening hour had attracted a number of patrons. Although the crowd was noisy, they didn't seem particularly rowdy. Still, Abby was just a little ill at ease at the thought of entering the room unescorted.

"Say, you're new in town, ain't ya? How 'bout I buy your dinner and we'll git acquainted?"

A whiskered cowboy stepped up before her, an undisguised gleam of appreciation in his eyes. Though the man's demeanor was more friendly than threatening, Jake's leering image flashed in her mind. She shuddered.

Steely fingers curled around her arm. She was drawn close to a hard, masculine form. "Sorry, fella," said a familiar, grating voice near her ear. "The lady's spoken for."

The cowboy's gaze traveled from Kane's possessive hold on her waist to the warning glint in his flinty gray eyes. He gulped and tipped his hat, all apologies. "Didn't mean to trespass, mister. No sirree." He held up his hands in a conciliatory gesture and backed away.

"No harm done."

Kane steered her toward a table in the far corner and saw her seated. Abby's chin lifted as he took the seat across from her. "I'm hardly spoken for," she said stiffly. "Furthermore, I hired you as a guide—not a guardian. And that man seemed very nice—what if I'd wanted to have dinner with him?"

"Excuse me for doing you a favor—or rather, doing *Dillon* a favor. And you sure as hell *are* spoken for, lady—though it's beyond me why the hell I should be the one to have to remind you. But if that's the way you want it—" His chair scraped against the floor, as abrasive as his tone. "—you're the boss."

She was on her feet even as he was. When he would have stepped past her, she reacted unthinkingly. Her fingers unconsciously caught his arm.

"Kane . . . wait!"

He froze. Her voice was strangely breathless. Beneath her fingertips, the muscles of his forearm were rigid. Her fingers moved, an involuntary exploration. She swallowed, her eyes fixed on the wild tangle of hairs at the base of his throat. The scent of soap and man assailed her—it gave her a start to see that he, too, had bathed. His clean-shaven cheeks revealed a sternly set jaw. Though he was unsmiling, his lips were beautifully chiseled. The muscles of her belly tightened oddly. He wasn't handsome, not in the classic sense, but in some raw, elemental way she couldn't define.

All at once her heart was pounding almost painfully. The pink tip of her tongue came out to moisten her lips. "I—I'm sorry," she said haltingly, her voice scarcely more than a wisp of sound. "I shouldn't have said . . . what I did."

She stopped short of admitting she was wrong, though the reason why eluded her. Normally she wasn't so—so stubbornly unreasonable. But Kane seemed to bring out the worst in her.

She swallowed painfully. "Don't go." Her voice went lower still. "Please."

His eyes caught hers, dark and relentlessly piercing. If anything, the muscles beneath her fingers seemed to turn to stone. Abby was sorely tempted to snatch her hand away, yet some force beyond her control compelled otherwise.

Wordlessly he held out her chair for her once again. Abby sat, her breath tumbling out in a rush. She hadn't even realized she'd been holding it.

As hungry as she'd been, she couldn't have said what food she ate. When the waitress removed their plates, he leaned back in his chair.

"Mind if I fetch myself a drink?"

It was on the tip of her tongue to retort that she did indeed. She bit it back just in time. "Not at all." The coolness of her tone matched his. As he crossed the room to the bar, she couldn't help but admire his long, loose-limbed grace. He had nearly reached the bar when a voluptuous brunette clad in a low-cut gown of crimson velvet and lace halted him mid-stride.

Abby couldn't help but overhear. "Kane?" the woman exclaimed loudly. "Kane, honey, is that really you?"

He turned. Moist, heavily rouged lips smiled up at him. Abby's eyes narrowed as he took the woman's hand and brought it to his lips. Though she strained to hear, Abby couldn't quite catch his low murmur.

The woman gave a low, husky laugh. Her dress was cut so low over her bosom it was positively indecent. The material hugged her torso like a second skin, so tight her nipples were clearly outlined. Kane took a bottle of whiskey from the bartender, then glanced over at Abby, a decidedly challenging gleam in his eyes. Abby stiffened when he began to lead the woman over to their table.

He stopped alongside her, an arrogant smile on his lips. "Fanny," he said easily, "this is my boss, Abigail Mackenzie. Abby, meet Fanny O'Hara."

The woman let out a titter. "Your boss!" she exclaimed. "Why, Kane, I do believe you're serious!"

Kane glanced at Abby. His smile didn't falter. "You might say I'm on the straight and narrow."

"So you're not with Sam anymore?"

He shook his head and pulled out a chair for her. The woman sat boldly as Kane resumed his seat.

"Sam's a cold-jawed bastard if ever there was

one." Such bluntness from a female made Abby gape. "Why," the woman went on, angling herself toward Kane, "you were never in the same league as Sam and we both know it."

Kane shrugged. His gaze wandered down her form. The sheer lace did little to conceal the twin white globes of her breasts, and it was there Kane's attention lingered.

"You look downright respectable, Fanny. Tell me, how've you been?"

Respectable? Abby began to fume. If Fanny leaned over any further, those mountainous breasts would pop out of her dress right into Kane's lap—not that it appeared Kane would mind.

Fanny gave a sultry laugh. "Respectable? Lord, I hope not! But I sold the Pleasure Palace for a tidy little sum and bought myself a ranch about a mile west of town." She paused. "Gets downright lonely sometimes." As she spoke, her hand trailed up and down Kane's sleeve. She smiled with sultry invitation directly into his eyes.

A sharp stab of some unknown, not very pleasant emotion pierced Abby's chest.

Fanny rose and placed a hand on Kane's shoulder. Abby didn't miss the way her fingers slid beneath the neckline of his shirt.

"If you're not busy this evening, why don't you come on out to the ranch for a while and have a drink with me?"

Kane's eyes flickered to Abby. "The boss lady here tends to keep a pretty tight rein on me."

"Oh, surely not that tight. And you don't mind if I borrow him for a while, do you, dear?"

Abby bristled silently. The woman didn't even

have the decency to look at her! "Be my guest," she replied frigidly.

"Then I'll see you later, won't I, Kane?" She framed Kane's cheeks with her fingers. In full view of anyone who cared to look on, she lowered her head and kissed him full on the mouth, a long, leisurely kiss that seemed to go on forever. Abby averted her head, certain her face flamed scarlet.

Fanny twirled away, her skirts swirling with the sway of her hips. His glass in hand, long legs sprawled under the table, Kane's scrutiny never wavered from her retreat. Abby felt like kicking him——if only she dared!

At last he turned back, contemplating the amber liquid in his glass.

Abby spoke, her voice low and controlled. "You two seem rather well acquainted."

A slow, suggestive smile curled those hard lips. "Fanny's an old friend."

A friend? Abby sniffed. She would gladly bet her half of the Diamondback that those two had shared a lot more than friendship.

"I see." She glared at him.

Her disapproval raked through Kane like claws. He let out a laugh, feeling suddenly almost brutal. "Fact is," he drawled, "Fanny and I go way back. You heard her mention the Pleasure Palace? Well, the Pleasure Palace was the best damn whorehouse this side of the Rockies. Those girls knew every trick there was to turn a man inside out."

Abby went white. She knew what he was doing—— his crudity was just another calculated move to humiliate her.

"Must you always be so insulting?" Her lips scarcely moved as she spoke.

He shrugged. "You did ask," he said mildly.

She got to her feet. "I think I'll say good night now."

He rose as well. "I'll see you to your room."

"Don't bother," she said coldly. "I'm quite capable of finding it myself."

"Nonetheless, I insist."

Abby's lips tightened. She wrenched her arm away when he would have taken hold of her elbow. He made no move to touch her again as they ascended the stairs and moved down the hallway.

At the door to her room she turned to face him. "I'd like to get an early start in the morning," she said shortly.

He gave a silent, mocking salute. Abby stood for a moment, tensing as he started to retrace his steps back down the stairs . . .

Her dignity was lost beneath cold, biting fury. "You're going to see her, aren't you?"

Kane pivoted slowly. "Who?"

"You know who." She had to fight to find the courage to meet his eyes. "Your friend Fanny!"

His eyes flickered, as dangerous as a summer storm.

"You object?"

"Of course I do! I—I know what she is, Kane— what she was. She's the kind of woman who—who can be bought!"

His laughter held no mirth. "And I'm the kind of man who can be bought. The way I see it, there's not much difference between her and me."

"It's not the same thing and you know it!"

"Why, sweetheart, don't tell me your opinion of me has improved. Frankly, I can't see why you give a damn what the hell I do—or who I do it with, as long as it isn't you."

Abby flushed painfully. His mockery cut bone-deep. She steeled herself against an elusive hurt. "Must you always be so difficult?" Her voice was very low.

"Seems to me I'm not the one being difficult here. I just don't like being judged—and I know Fanny doesn't either."

"She—she's a harlot, Kane, and don't you dare say she isn't!"

His jaw clenched. "She sure as hell doesn't pretend to be something she isn't," he said tautly. "Fact is, sweetheart, she could probably teach you a thing or two about being a woman."

He whirled and left her standing there.

Kane was in trouble. He'd known it the instant he walked into Fanny's parlor. The truth was that he'd had no intention of coming here. But Abby, blast her pretty little hide, had goaded him, making him feel lower than low. Who the hell did she think she was to preach to him?

Fanny was on her knees before him, clad in a frothy white nightgown that revealed far more than it concealed. The silk was so sheer he had no trouble discerning the deep brown color of huge, dark nipples, or the black thatch of hair at the juncture of her thighs. Kane found the display far less arousing and appealing than he should have. He discovered himself thinking her breasts were much too big and heavy; they jutted almost obscenely from her chest.

His mind was fuzzy from drink. Abby was right, he decided hazily. He did drink too much . . .

Abby.

Some strange emotion coiled in his gut. He thought about what she was doing right now. No doubt she'd undressed and gone straight to bed. The thought of her undressing nearly wrung a groan from him. He recalled all too vividly what she'd looked like the morning he'd caught her bathing. Her chemise had been simply cut, unadorned except for a small white ribbon of lace across the top of the bodice. Her skin had been damp and golden, glistening like warm honey. Her nipples were small and peaked, prickled against the cool morning air. The sight of her had been like a closed fist rammed hard in his gut.

It was odd—damned odd, Kane decided in some muddled, whiskey-laden corner of his mind. But the thought of Abby dressed in soft white cotton was a hundred times more exciting than the near-naked woman before him.

Fanny tugged one side of his shirt from his shoulder. Kane looked on as sleek, feminine fingers pursued a relentless pathway down the furry darkness of his chest, clear to the waistline of his pants . . . and below. He felt the delicious shiver that racked her as her fingertips delicately traced the outline of his maleness. A part of him reveled in it—at least *she* wanted him—even as another part of him remained curiously indifferent, a million miles away. His body remained distinctly unaffected by that bold, feminine caress.

Slowly she drew back, tipping her head to the side. "What's wrong, Kane?"

"Nothing." He set aside his glass and pulled her into his arms. But Fanny's lips, hot and experienced, were almost cloyingly eager, her arms too clinging. Kane fought the unwelcome reminder of how the sweet, captivating innocence of another kiss had inflamed him far more . . . He ground his mouth against hers almost angrily.

She drew back, breaking the encircling hold of his arms. "Kane," she said softly, "you don't have to pretend to something that isn't there." When he merely scowled, she smiled almost sadly. "I know the difference, remember?"

Kane said nothing, merely stared at her. *Harlot*, Abby had called her, and all at once Kane understood why. She looked cheap and tawdry, her chest thrust forward to reveal those gargantuan breasts. The rouge on her lips and cheeks was overly bright and garish. *Harlot*. A twist of bitter amusement pulled at his lips. No one but Abby would have put it so tactfully. Abby, no matter that she was fiery and outspoken, was still very much a lady.

It didn't stop him from wanting her . . . wanting her with a hunger that seared like fire in his gut.

And that was the whole damn problem.

Kane was suddenly furious, both with himself and with Abby. Fanny was lush, willing and eager. Since he'd lost Lorelei, women like Fanny had been his only salvation—vessels in which he could find forgetfulness, and a measure of pleasure, no matter how fleeting. His insides were suddenly screaming. Didn't he deserve that? Hadn't he suffered enough? Was it so wrong to lose himself in the warm embrace of a woman for the night—to seek comfort the only way he knew how? And why did

Fanny leave him so cold? Why was tonight so different from all those other nights?

He jerked at the touch on his arm. Fanny gazed up at him, her expression understanding. "It's her, isn't it? That woman who was with you at dinner tonight."

But Kane didn't want understanding just now. He wanted . . . her. Abby . . .

He wanted what he could never have.

"She's my boss, Fanny. She's paying me to do a job for her, no more, no less." He stood abruptly. "I'm sorry," he said with genuine regret. More quietly he added, "I guess I'm just not in the mood."

Fanny sighed and went to retrieve his hat. Together they walked to the front door. There he whistled for Midnight. "If you decide otherwise," she said softly, "I'll still be here."

He stepped outside and touched the brim of his hat. "I'll keep that in mind."

Fanny closed the door slowly after he'd gone. He wouldn't be back, and they both knew it.

Chapter 9

Where was he?

Even as the question rampaged through her brain, Abby turned and pounded her pillow as she had a hundred times tonight. Her ears strained to hear the slightest sound from outside the door, as they had for hours.

Was he still with Fanny? Her mind conjured up a vivid image, an image she tried to will away but could not. Even when she closed her eyes, she imagined she could see him, his big body naked and hard, poised over Fanny, his hips churning and flexing . . . She flounced over once again, cursing herself for allowing him to so disrupt her sleep . . . and her life! Why should she care what he did—or with whom? He was a womanizing rogue, a cad, and she was the world's biggest fool to even think twice about him!

There was a thump on the door. The sound was so unexpected she jumped. She scanned the darkness, staring at the door as if she could see right through it.

The second thump was twice as loud as the first. Abby bolted upright, clutching the sheet to her breast. Her pulse began to pump frantically.

"Open up this goddamned door."

Kane. Relief rushed through her, followed by a rush of irritation. By now the night was surely half over. What on earth was he doing? She slid from the bed, lit the bedside candle and turned the lock. Using the door as a shield, she peered out at Kane.

"What?" She unloosed all her vexation into that one word.

Kane shoved his booted foot into the narrow opening. Her eyes were wary and suspicious, that elegant little nose tipped high in the air.

"Let me in."

"Whatever for? It's the middle of the night and—"

She got no further. Kane pushed the door inward. Caught off guard, Abby stumbled backward. She grabbed the bedpost to steady herself.

"Kane! For heaven's sake, can't this wait?"

"No. Goddammit, it can't."

His voice was a low rumble of sound. Abby's heart slammed to a halt. His shirt was unbuttoned nearly to his waist, revealing a slice of broad, darkly matted chest. His belly was flat as a washboard, covered with the same, intriguingly dark mat of hair. He stood there, completely filling the doorway, powerful and imposing and starkly male.

"Kane, please! I—I'm not dressed!"

Very deliberately he closed the door. Two steps brought him within inches of her. One hand was at her throat, her eyes huge and dark and wary.

His drink-induced haze cleared like dew beneath a blazing sun. His gaze devoured her, a veritable feast to a man dying of starvation. She'd been sleeping in her chemise and drawers, certainly not a sight to send a man into the throes of passion. He'd never seen Abby with her hair down; it was glorious, falling in rich, thick waves of sunburst glory clear to her hips.

Her tongue slid over her lips. Desire tightened his gut like a white-hot brand, the desire that had so eluded him with Fanny.

He moved closer, staggering slightly.

Abby's eyes widened. "Oh, you—you stupid fool! You're drunk!"

"Not drunk enough," he muttered. He felt light-headed and giddy, but not from the drink he'd consumed. He reached out and snared her by the waist.

Abby went rigid. Although the odor of whiskey was strong, it was the unmistakable scent of perfume that sent her temper skyrocketing. "God, you are unbelievable! How dare you come here after being with that harlot!"

He sneered. "And what if I was? You may have hired me, but you don't own me. Who I choose to spend my nights with is no business of yours."

"And who are you to come barging into my room like this?" she cried. "Get out—now!"

He didn't move.

Abby shoved at his chest, but he was as immovable as a rock. "Get out, Kane! You're disgusting—"

"Disgusting, am I?" His bitter laugh was directed solely at himself. "You know, you're right. I *am* disgusting. Because you managed to make me feel guilty as hell—and damned if I can figure out why!"

Her chin swept up in disdain. "Forgive me if

I don't care to hear the intimate details of your evening with Fanny."

"Intimate? God, that's rich!" He threw back his head, the cords in his neck standing out tautly. He didn't know why he let her get to him. He already knew she felt he had no scruples. Hell, she'd as much as told him so.

"Sugar, you and I have been a hell of a lot more *intimate* than Fanny and I were tonight."

His revelation left her stunned. "What?" she asked faintly. "You mean that you . . . that she and you . . ." She faltered, unable to go on. Her cheeks burned.

"That's right." Kane's expression was savage, his tone just as fierce. "We *didn't*—not that the lady wasn't willing."

Abby was stunned. She found his statement difficult to believe, yet he was so adamant she had no choice. But why was he so angry? She gasped when his hands clamped around her waist and dragged her against him.

"That's hardly my fault," she cried shakily. "Go back to her, then, if that's what you want. Just go back and—"

"That's mighty generous of you. But the truth is, sweetheart, I don't want her! In fact, I couldn't lay a goddamned hand on her!"

Abby tried to pull away; he wouldn't let her. "Kane," she said desperately. "I don't understand what this has to do with me . . . why you're so angry—"

He let loose a curse that blistered her ears. "It has everything to do with you, don't you see?"

Shocked, she inhaled sharply, uncertain of all she sensed in him.

"Kane," she said desperately, "you—you shouldn't be here. No gentleman—"

"How many times do I have to tell you, sugar, I'm no gentleman. And you can pretend all you want, but you're no lady."

Shocked, Abby couldn't do anything but endure the ruthless heat of his gaze.

"Don't give me that hurt, wounded look," he sneered. "I fell for it once, but not again. You can play the prim, proper bride all you want, but you don't fool me."

She drew an unsteady breath. "Kane, I—I don't know what you're talking about!"

"If you wanted to ruin my night with Fanny, you did a real fine job. Because all I could think of was you." He laughed harshly. "Oh, yes, sweetheart, *you*. And you couldn't have done better if you'd planned it that way—Jesus, maybe you did! Maybe you're the kind of woman who can't be satisfied with just one man—hell, I don't know. But for a while there tonight, why . . . I could have sworn you were jealous."

Jealous! Why, of all the . . . ! She'd managed to wedge her hands between their bodies. She opened her mouth to inform him his charge was utterly ridiculous . . .

She never got the chance.

Her hands had come up between them, but when she would have pushed indignantly at his chest, he snared her wrists and dragged her close . . . so close she could feel the rampant thunder of his heart. And all at once her own was doing funny things in her chest, her pulse clamoring.

Dark, fathomless eyes pinned hers. "You're a

tease," he accused almost fiercely, "whether you admit it or not. It doesn't matter that you're married. You like it when I touch you, don't you, *Abigail*? You like it when I kiss you."

"No." She shook her head, the word hardly more than a wisp of air. "*No* . . ." But it was more a denial of herself than the truth.

And Kane knew it.

He was so close, she thought in panic, too close . . . The very air around him seemed to pulse with a force that was purely raw, purely masculine. She felt impaled, consumed, swallowed up by something dark and desperate, something she didn't understand . . .

Something she couldn't fight.

His head lowered. His mouth hovered dangerously near hers. "Remember that night with Chester and Jake? I kissed you. And I held you—and I touched you . . . here." With his thumbs he slowly, deliberately, circled the dusky crowns of both breasts. Immediately her nipples thrust impudently, hard and pointed against the sheer cotton of her chemise.

His fingers slid to the dainty pink ribbon which held the garment closed. He tugged. A vile curse filled the air when the ribbon knotted. He raised both hands to the scalloped edge of material. The delicate cloth rent cleanly in half beneath the pressure of his hands.

Abby's entire body jerked. Her mind reeled. She was terrified of the way he made her feel—afraid and breathless and excited all at once.

She jerked when a callused fingertip trespassed boldly down the valley between her breasts and up again—he displayed no hesitation, no faltering whatsoever. Not once did he release her from the relentless probe of his eyes. He smiled thinly, a goading smile of satisfaction. Abby almost hated him for it—hated him for this strange mood he'd fallen into—and into which he'd pulled her as well.

Kane intercepted her glare. He laughed at the mutinous sparks that leaped in her eyes. "So fiery. So defiant," he remarked casually. "Is that your game, sweetheart? Is that how you manage to make men like me go crazy over you? Is that how you got your precious Dillon? Was marriage the price he had to pay to have you?"

His mockery cut deep. Abby couldn't help it. Her gaze faltered. Such an easy surrender was galling, but she couldn't help it. Her mind began to race. Should she try to run? Dear Lord, how could she? She was half-naked! She raised her arms in an attempt to shield her nakedness.

The smile vanished. "Oh, no," he said harshly. "I'm not going to let you hide, sugar. I'm going to look my fill, the way you looked yours that first morning at the lake." He gave a grating laugh as she flushed scarlet.

And look his fill he did. Time dragged endlessly. Mortified that she was standing before a man clad only in her drawers, horrified that Kane would look at her so, she squeezed her eyes shut. It made no difference. Still she could feel the scorching heat of his eyes on her body.

"This is all I've thought about for days," he said thickly. "Did you know that? Seeing you like this. Your breasts in my hands, naked and warm. Your nipples hard against my palm. I've wondered how you would taste—" A fingertip whisked across the peaks of both breasts. "—right here. I've lain awake nights wanting to feel your breath in my mouth, your legs wrapped around mine—" His whisper was stark and wanton. "—while I'm deep and hard inside you."

Abby's throat locked. She couldn't say a word. She could only stand there, battling the urge to open her eyes, not knowing if she dared.

Again he touched her. Boldly. Brazenly. As if he owned her. With a gasp her eyes snapped open, only to widen in shock when he cupped one breast in his hand, as if he were weighing, measuring. She started to wrench her face aside but Kane wouldn't allow it. His arm like an iron band, he swore violently and pulled her even closer.

"Don't test me, Abby. Goddammit, I won't hurt you. Just do what I say. *Look* at me." The demand in his voice was no less fierce, but his grip on her waist eased slightly.

Trying hard not to tremble, Abby swallowed. The roof of her mouth felt like cotton. Helplessly she raised her eyes once more.

He leered his approval. "That's the way. Now look at my hand on your skin." There was a subtle movement of his hand on her cushioned softness, barely grazing. His fingers splayed wide across her breast, deeply tanned against the unblemished creaminess of her flesh. The contrast was riveting.

"Tell me, sugar. Do you see what I see? Dark against fair? Bad against good?"

His fingers moved again, ever so subtly. Now her

nipple lay pink and pouting between his knuckles. Abby held her breath, afraid to move.

His eyes narrowed. "Come on, sweetheart," he taunted. "Tell the truth now. Does it offend you, seeing my hand on your body, my filthy, scummy hand? After all, you're the daughter of the man who owned the biggest spread in the Territory, and who the hell am I but worthless trash?"

He was being deliberately hurtful. And yet—he was right. He was an outlaw. A renegade. She *should* have found his touch revolting . . . disgusting. A stab of irony pierced her. Dear Lord, if only she did—if only she could! Maybe then she wouldn't feel so torn!

And then there was Kane. He sounded so— so bitter! His features were twisted, his jaw tense and rigid. Even as she stared, his lips spasmed, as if in anguish . . . as if he were fighting some gut-wrenching, inner pain. Some nameless emotion speared her heart. Pulled from somewhere deep in her mind was the notion that maybe he was trying to punish not her, but himself.

Totally unaware that she did so, she reached for him. He caught her wrists in one hand, the movement so sudden she cried out, not in pain but in shock. With the other he raked his thumb across the peak of her breast.

"Tell me," he hissed. "Does it make you feel dirty, me touching you like this?"

Shaken by his dark mood, confused by the leashed violence she sensed in him, Abby could only shake her head.

"Oh, don't be shy, Abby. We both know you're

not. Or is it admitting the truth that's so hard? Come on, now. Don't you feel soiled and degraded and unclean? No, wait! Let me think. Oh, yes . . . I believe *detestable* was the word you used . . . That's right. You find me detestable!"

She shook her head. "I—I didn't mean it," she said weakly. "Kane, I—"

"Don't lie to me!"

Lean fingers threaded through her hair. He twisted her face up to his. Abby resisted instinctively but her reprieve was short-lived indeed. The instant she strained away her naked breasts bobbed into view. She had no choice but to angle herself against him.

"Kiss me," he said suddenly.

Abby blinked. He transferred his hands to her waist, his eyes glittering dangerously. He seemed bigger than ever, and while he didn't exactly frighten her, there was a knife-edged hardness in him that made her wary of crossing him.

She took a deep fortifying breath and levered herself on tiptoe, then pressed her lips against the grim slash of his mouth, trying desperately not to think about the pleasantly rough abrasion of his shirt against the tips of her breasts. The kiss lasted only a second, but by the time her heels again rested on the planked floorboards, her heart was skittering wildly.

Kane regarded her unsmilingly. "Again," he ordered.

Not daring to argue, Abby once again complied. For all his fierceness, his lips were smooth and far softer than she would have dreamed. He displayed no reaction whatsoever, but remained still as a statue. Flustered and breathless, she braved a glance at him.

She was dismayed to find him surveying her intently, his gaze thoroughly unsettling. His eyes were the color of steel—and just as unyielding.

He offered a scathing smile. "Not with your lips closed tight as the lid of a casket—" He refused to let her misunderstand. "—but the way I showed you." He laughed as comprehension washed across her features. "That's right," he drawled. "I see you remember, sweetheart. 'Course if you need another lesson, I'll be glad to oblige . . ."

Abby went fiery-hot, then cold. Oh, but he was a beast! She knew what he wanted—her mouth open and avid beneath his, the way it had been the other night when he'd kissed her so ardently. But she couldn't. She *wouldn't*. Not again . . . not willingly!

"I'm still waiting, sweetheart." His tone cracked sharp as a whip.

Her breath came jerkily. "No," she said shakily. "Not again, Kane. I—I can't!"

"Why the hell not?" he taunted her mercilessly. "You want to, Abby—you know you do. You liked it as much as I did."

"I—I didn't!" Yet even as she spoke, hot shame welled inside her. Lord, she was no better than Fanny!

"Tell yourself whatever you want," he said harshly. "But if I were you, I'd do it and get it over with—and make it count, sweetheart, because I'm not leaving here until I'm satisfied."

Satisfied? Abby was half-afraid to speculate on his meaning. But his expression warned there would be no denying him; she realized with a sinking flutter of her heart that she had no choice but to give in.

Slowly her arms crept up and around his neck.
Her eyes drifted closed as she pressed her mouth
to his.

Her senses alone guided her—that and the lim-
ited experience she'd gained in this man's embrace.
Unaware that she did so, her fingers slid through
the midnight hair that grew low on his nape; it was
like rough silk, the texture oddly pleasing. In spite
of herself, she felt her body relax. Her lips softened
and parted. Kane was not inclined to reciprocate.

Her fingers stilled in his hair. His body was rigid
as stone against hers. Abby frowned. This was what
he'd wanted, wasn't it? She cautiously trailed the
tip of her tongue along the seam of his lips, back
and forth with delicate precision, tilting her head
first one way and then the other, as he had done
to her. A bolt of sheer pleasure shot through her,
but Kane remained taut as a bowstring, so taut she
feared she'd done something horribly wrong.

Her heart plummeted. All at once she felt like
crying. But just as she would have wrenched a-
way, his grip on her waist tightened almost convulsively.

His mouth opened on hers. Abby's spine turned
to water. Control was no longer hers, if indeed it had
ever been hers. But it didn't matter. *Nothing* mattered but this moment. She clung to him, her nails
digging into the binding tautness of his shoulders.
He kissed her endlessly—wild, drugging kisses that
lured her ever deeper into a heady realm where
nothing mattered but the searing fusion of his mouth
on hers.

She was breathless and dizzy by the time he

released her lips. "God," he said thickly. "You might not have a lot of experience but you sure as hell learn quick, don't you?" His eyes darkened. "But I wonder . . . are you as warm and willing with your precious Dillon as you are with me?"

He was still angry. The realization had no sooner tumbled through her brain than he hauled her against him. Abby gasped as he pulled her against his hips. She could feel his manhood as she had the other night, swelling hard and thick against the softness of her belly. She was stunned to feel an empty ache spawning deep inside, a desperate yearning very near the place that alien hardness nestled . . .

He raised his head. Abby nearly cried out at the fierceness of his expression. "Is this what you want, Abby? This feeling of power, of always being right, of being in control? Does it make you feel better than me knowing you can make me want you like this?"

His words made no sense; *he* was making no sense. But Abby knew she couldn't fight him, just as she knew there would be no reasoning with him.

Before she could say a word, his mouth smothered hers, hard and relentless. Kane wanted to cheat her of any pleasure, as he had been cheated of all that was good and sweet in his life. He wanted her to feel robbed as he had been robbed . . . afraid as he had been afraid.

Abby had no choice but to endure. She tried to twist away but his arms were like manacles around her back. Dimly she felt her hair ensnared in one huge fist, then wrapped around his hand.

His lips plundered hers with ruthless thorough-
ness. Abby's fingers twisted into the front of his
shirt, not resisting, but not yielding either. If anything, it seemed to incite him further. Her lips felt
swollen and bruised beneath the punishing intensity of his kiss. Determined to show no weakness,
no fear, she tried to check the low whimper that
welled in her throat.

She tried in vain.

As low as that faint, choked sound was, he
heard . . . and froze. He stiffened, his entire body
like an iron wall against hers, his arms so taut she
feared he might crush her.

For the space of a heartbeat, then another and
another, neither moved. Finally, his chest expanded
with a long, inward pull of air into his lungs.

The pressure of his mouth eased subtly. Abby
drew a deep shuddering breath of her own. But
though the tension in his hold remained, the anger
was gone.

His kiss was now almost unbearably sweet,
almost apologetic, soothing the tender flesh he'd
ravaged earlier. Abby couldn't help it. Her lips
parted, like the flowering of a rose. His fingers
tightened on her scalp. This time it was Kane who
groaned, a sound pulled from deep in his chest. All
at once Abby was shaking, not with fear, not with
revulsion . . . but with pleasure.

She had a brief sensation of weightlessness, then
she felt the rumpled covers of the bed at her feet,
the softness of the mattress at her back. The weight
of Kane's body followed her down; not once did he
release the searing fusion of their lips. The contact
was deep and intimate, slow and rousing, as if he

sought to give her back all he'd taken from her earlier. Desire flashed through her, zinging through her bloodstream like fire.

Kane fed on her mouth greedily, savoring the ripe lushness of her mouth. She tasted as good as he remembered—God, even better. He ripped open his shirt, desperate to feel even more of her. Reluctantly he released her mouth. His gaze was dark and burning, devouring the sight of her breasts jutting and bare against the dark fur on his chest. Lord, she was sweet, he thought with a groan. Her mouth was shiny and wet, like fresh, succulent fruit, he noted dimly.

A lean fingertip circled the deep pink circle atop the fullness of her breast, barely grazing the tip. A primitive satisfaction blazed within him as it sprang tight and eager. Her eyes flew open, cloudy and dazed, alight with surprise and wonder. The sight sent his pulse raging and his heart to pounding. The blood settled hot and full in his loins. Slowly he began to ease down her torso, intent on claiming even more delicious bounty for his own.

Abby gasped at the erotic friction of her nipples sliding through the dense mat of hair on his chest. They seemed to tingle and ache, so much so that she squirmed restlessly, wanting something, but not quite sure what . . .

And then she knew.

The sight of Kane's dark head poised above her breasts, bare and round and gleaming, should have shocked her—in some deep, dark corner of her mind, perhaps it did. But once again, it didn't matter. Because suddenly all her senses were alive and screaming with nerve-shattering anticipation. Waiting. Wanting . . .

His hand had slid from her ribs to the cushioned underside of her breast. His breath trickled warm and arousing across her rounded flesh, a divine torment. Even as she watched, he lowered his head.

With his tongue, he touched her nipple.

A bolt of sheer delight shot the length of her spine. This couldn't be wrong. Dear Lord, it couldn't. Never had Abby imagined such sweet, piercing pleasure—but there was more, she realized, as he took full possession of the ripe, tender peak.

The feel of his mouth drawing, pulling, suckling hard, then soothing with the eager lash of his tongue was an exquisite ecstasy. Her neck arched. Her body bowed, as if in offering. In response Kane laved with the same careful attention the other straining peak. Her fingers slid into the midnight darkness of his hair, as if she wanted to keep him there forever.

"Kane!" she cried unthinkingly. "Oh, God, Kane!"

Kane raised his head, his eyes glittering. In the wavering light thrown by the candle, her skin shone like moondust. Her nipples were rouged a deep rose, as shiny and wet as her mouth had been earlier. Her breath was shallow and panting, driving him to a fine frenzy.

Go ahead, his body urged. *Take her. It's what she wants. It's what she's asking for. Christ, she's as ripe and ready as Fanny was, and you're as hard and throbbing for her the way you weren't with Fanny.*

Desire churned through him like a raging tornado. His blood felt as if it were on fire. His shaft was heavy and full, throbbing and painfully rigid.

Primitive urges ruled him: the thought of plunging deep in her shadowed cleft, feeling her hot, feminine warmth clamped tight around his burning flesh. But buried deep in his mind, some last shred of sanity remained, warning him he couldn't surrender to the explosive demands of his body. Only she was so soft ... and never had he been so hard, so desperate and in need ... There had to be a way to quench this fire in his soul. There had to be ...

He rolled to his side, taking her along with him. Her eyes flashed up to his.

"Kane—" His name emerged as a jagged cry.

"Don't," he grated. "Don't say anything." He covered her mouth with his. He fumbled with the buttons on his pants, then released himself into his hand ... and hers.

Abby's breath left her lungs in a scalding rush. He caught at her fingers ... Abby tore her mouth from his, shocked to the core at what he was doing ... what *she* was doing. But even as her eyes widened, his closed. She nearly cried out at the stark agony she glimpsed in the instant before his own squeezed shut.

His hand clamped hers ... and hers was clamped tight against the shape of him, molded around the turgid, ridged plane of bold, masculine flesh, held tightly in place as he sought the motion that would bring an end to this torment ... She thought her heart would burst clear through her chest.

"God," he said raggedly, and then again: "God!"

His breath grew rough and scraping. He cast back his head, his features contorted, the cords in his neck standing out tautly. And then with a heaving cry, he caught her hips against his, binding them together, grinding and circling. Not fully aware of what was happening, but seized by the undeniable notion that she must cling to him or he would be forever lost, she slipped her arms around his neck.

His hands locked tight around her back. A tremendous shudder wracked his body. Abby knew, in some elusive way beyond the bounds of understanding, that it was over—that the passion which had gripped him was spent. Slowly she felt the rigidness seep from his body. Abby smiled slightly, shifting a little to accommodate his heavier weight.

He sprang to his feet.

Abby stared, feeling confused and still rather dazed. She spoke his name, a mere wisp of air: "Kane?"

Three steps took him to the door.

She struggled to sit up. "Kane!"

He walked out without a word, slamming the door shut behind him.

Chapter 10

A rough hand at her shoulder jarred her awake the next morning. Reluctant to forsake the misty layers of sleep in which she was immersed so pleasantly, Abby swatted the offensive intruder and rolled to the other side of the bed. The next thing she knew a firm hand descended sharply on her backside. The sheet and thin blanket did little to ease the sting.

She bolted upright with a gasp, instinctively clutching the covers to her breast.

Kane stood not two paces distant. Her mind recorded a fleeting impression of cold gray eyes and tautly set shoulders. Remembrance flooded her mind like a raging tide, stark and vivid, of all that had happened last night. Dear Lord, what had she done—what had *they* done?

She swallowed nervously. "How—how long have you been there?"

"Long enough to know you'd better get your ass in gear if you want to get an early start." He was already halfway across the room. For the second time in twelve hours, the door slammed shut behind him.

Abby pushed the covers aside. "Well, good morning to you, too," she muttered crossly.

On the washstand was a pitcher that had once been painted with dainty pink flowers but was now faded and cracked. She poured a generous amount of tepid water into the washbasin, grimacing a little as she splashed it onto her face and arms. She nearly tripped on something as she turned to reach for a towel; it was the shredded remnants of her chemise. Beside it were her drawers.

Hot color stole into her cheeks. Abby was heartily glad she was alone. She'd changed after Kane had left last night. She didn't fully understand the significance of the damp, sticky spot that had stained her drawers; she knew only that it had something to do with what had happened between them. Picking them up, she scrubbed them hurriedly in the washbasin. Wringing them out before she stuffed them in her saddlebag, she glanced at the underclothes she wore, wryly concluding they had better find Dillon soon—the ones she wore were her last remaining set.

Kane was already there when she ventured downstairs a few minutes later. Her mind strayed to the room upstairs—and her last sight as she'd closed the door: the tumbled bedclothes were evidence of all that had transpired there last night. Meeting his gaze was the hardest thing she'd ever done. One glance at his black scowl convinced her his disposition hadn't improved. Abby thought longingly of breakfast but decided not to say anything. She suspected neither of them were in the mood for an argument.

It struck her as they left the hotel that he had yet to say a word to her since she'd come downstairs. She raised her chin, resolving to dismiss the memory of last night; it was glaringly apparent Kane already had.

She couldn't. Dear God, it was all she could think about. The memory muddied her thoughts throughout the morning. Her insides tightened every time she recalled their torrid exchange last night.

Kane was right. She could have called a halt to it but she hadn't—and he was convinced she was married to another man yet!

Not that it had stopped him, though. She stared out to where golden plains bowed to the heavens, aware of an odd heaviness in the pit of her stomach. She'd thought no man would dare lay a hand on a married woman.

But Kane had dared. He'd dared much more.

And she hadn't lifted a finger to stop him. No wonder he'd branded her a tease! Indeed, stopping him had been the furthest thing from her mind. She wanted it to go on and on. She wanted to feel his mouth on hers, draining her of strength and will. She wanted to feel his tongue in her mouth, his hands on her breasts, brushing the crests with callused fingertips.

Recalling the feel of his mouth on her breasts made her go weak all over. It wasn't so much the intimacy of his caresses, but what he'd said that had broadened her awareness considerably. Despite the fact she'd secretly yearned for it, she'd been a little shocked when he had so boldly voiced his urges aloud.

He'd called her beautiful . . . and he'd said he wanted *her.* Abby had never thought of herself as either beautiful or desirable. Oh, Pa had always said she was pretty and sweet, but that was different.

She'd been so convinced she hated Kane. But—oh, sweet Lord—she had liked what he'd done. Heat welled up within her as she thought of her hand, trapped against that part of him. Maybe it was shameless . . . maybe God would strike her dead for such sinfulness . . . but she'd liked knowing he wanted her in that way. She'd liked knowing he *needed* her . . .

He'd been vulnerable last night. And to a man like Kane, that was a weakness he couldn't stand.

Something had changed, she realized with a shiver. *Everything* had changed.

He was as short-tempered as ever. The jutting angle of his jaw proclaimed his disinclination for conversation, but he was quick to snap at her the few times she lagged behind. Abby bit her tongue more than once throughout the long morning. His disposition, she decided indignantly, was sour enough to curdle fresh milk.

They soon approached the foothills of the mountains. Her irritation grew with every mile. Kane showed no sign of softening whatsoever.

Mid-afternoon the trail brought them to a tree-sheltered sanctuary. Abby caught her breath in delight. The crystal waters of a mountain stream darted alongside the trail, brightened by a profusion of wildflowers on the opposite bank. A cluster of lofty cottonwood trees stretched high overhead. They beckoned temptingly, like a sweet treat to a child. Abby reined in Sonny.

"Let's stop here."

Kane shifted in his saddle. The creak of leather was his only pronouncement, but his expression conveyed more clearly than words his displeasure.

Abby bravely tilted her chin. "I'm bushed," she announced. "And I can't go another mile without eating." With that she swung down from Sonny, hauled out a handful of beef jerky from her saddlebags and marched over to the canopied world beneath the trees.

The temperature was much cooler beneath the trees. She sighed in sheer delight, casting a half-smug, half-defiant glance toward her nemesis. It would have been heaven indeed—except that Kane was still glaring at her.

He dismounted but made no move to join her. Her lips tightened when he abruptly turned away, as if dismissing her. She popped another piece of jerky into her mouth, determined to enjoy it in spite of him.

She watched as he approached the stream. He bent low for a long cool drink, then straightened. Heedless of her presence, he unbuttoned his shirt and shrugged it from his shoulders, dropping it carelessly on the ground beside him. Abby chewed more slowly. Try though she might, she couldn't drag her gaze away from the sight of his naked torso.

His back was long and lean like the rest of him, cleanly halved by the shallow groove of his spine. His skin was sleek and sun-browned, like oiled leather. He knelt, splashing water on his face and chest. Abby swallowed, unwillingly fascinated by the rippling undulation of muscle beneath his skin.

The jerky now tasted like a lump of cold ash in her mouth.

The muscles in her stomach quivered. All at once she was burning inside, a burning that had nothing to do with the sun blazing down overhead. Oh, she'd managed to keep it at bay throughout the morning, but seeing him like this, she could do so no longer.

Why? screamed a voice in her mind. Why, whenever she looked at him, did she experience this restless ache inside? Why should he be the one to make her feel like this? Why, why, why? Abby didn't understand it.

She didn't understand *him*.

Nor did she understand why he was still so short with her. He'd shown no signs of softening, not once throughout this endless day. He was angry about last night, that was something Abby was almost certain of. Did he blame her because she hadn't stopped him? An awful knot swelled in the pit of her stomach. Did he think she was a tart, allowing him to touch her as he had? The questions swept through her mind like the winds across the plains.

But Kane didn't blame her. He was far too busy blaming himself for what had happened last night.

Guilt gnawed at him. Guilt—and shame. Always before he'd managed to steer clear of married women—it was a hell of a lot safer that way. And it had been different with Lorelei. She'd been married when he'd hired on at her husband's ranch. But within a month her husband was dead—and he hadn't laid a hand on her until long after that.

But his feelings when he was around Abby scared

the living daylights out of him . . . Sure, he'd been drunk last night, but that had only sharpened his desire for her—and robbed him of his restraint. He'd been only a hair away from taking her the way the masculine dictates of his body had urged. He had the sneaking suspicion she wasn't aware of that. Maybe she was no virgin, but she was hardly experienced when it came to men.

She was dangerous, he decided blackly. Dangerous in a way he didn't fully understand.

He'd tried to forget her. He'd tried to empty his mind of all feeling. But with a mouth that promised heaven, and a body that promised the road to hell would be paved with pleasure, how the devil could he ignore her? He snorted, disgusted with himself. Shit, even when they argued, all he could think about was how those soft lips felt trapped beneath his, how it would feel to make love to her—*really* make love to her. And his body had a way of reminding him all too keenly just how much he longed to do exactly that.

His nostrils flared. His fingers curled into his palms. Oh, yes, he'd discovered last night just how very much he wanted the lady. He could almost feel her warm and pliant against him once more, the fresh scent of her hair, the delicious weight of her breasts against his chest, her belly notched against the part of him that needed her the most.

With a muffled curse he flung another handful of water on his face and head, as if to cool his rampaging thoughts.

If he had any sense, he'd leave while he still had the chance. Yet what about Abby? jeered a voice in his head. She was wild and headstrong—

Christ, she'd lied to him again! But despite her fiery stubbornness, she was still a woman—and as much as she deserved it, he could hardly abandon a woman . . .

He shoved himself upright. From the corner of his eye he spied her. She rose from her spot beneath the tree. Her riding skirt hugged the curve of her hips, swirling gently around the tops of her boots.

He stiffened as she strode toward him. His gaze fell to where she'd unbuttoned several buttons of her shirt, revealing a triangular patch of skin that glowed like golden honey. Desire flared hot and bright, stark and primitive. He wanted her all over again—so much it hurt inside.

She halted directly before him. Doing his best to ignore her, Kane bent and picked up his shirt. He didn't miss the way her soft lips compressed.

He slipped his shirt over his shoulders, the movement as lazy as his tone. "Something on your mind?"

Abby straightened her spine. "You are," she said evenly.

He laughed, a sound that held no mirth. "Why, sugar, I'm flattered."

She confronted him with a cool stare. "Really? Is that why you haven't ventured a single word all morning, except to snap at me? Why you've yet to look me full in the face even once?" She drew on a thin thread of courage. "I—I see no reason for it to continue, Kane."

"What! You don't like the way I behave? Honey, you hired me as a guide, remember? I didn't know I was going to have to entertain you."

Abby gave him a long, slow look. "There's no use

in pretending you misunderstand," she said quietly. "We both know why you're acting this way. Pretending you didn't come to my room last night isn't going to make it go away—it won't make either of us forget." There was a small pause. "Maybe," she continued cautiously, "we should talk about it."

But Kane didn't want to talk about it. The very thought of his nocturnal visit to her room made him feel foolish and awkward and exposed. So what if he'd been drunk? That was no excuse for what he'd done—for how he'd used her—and he *had* used her to find the release he hadn't been able to find with Fanny.

Christ! What *did* she think of him?

He didn't want to know. God help him, he didn't.

His mood grew even more vile. He stared at her, wishing like hell the sun wasn't pouring through her hair, weaving through the strands and turning them to sunburst gold. In that instant, he almost hated her. She was so cool, so calm, while he felt like a runaway range fire.

"It's funny," he drawled. "But somehow I thought you'd *want* to forget about it." He rolled his eyes and grimaced. "Instead the lady wants to *talk* about it!"

Abby inhaled sharply. He'd placed one hand on his hip, his stance arrogant and overbearing. So. This was the way it was going to be. Oh, but she should have expected sarcasm from him—she *had* expected it! Lord, but he was infuriating!

She struggled for a calm she was suddenly far from feeling. "You're the one who seems to be having trouble dealing with it, Kane, not me. And you know what? I think you're angry—with yourself, and with me—not because of what you did, but what you felt."

His eyes narrowed. "Is that a fact?"

"It is," she said levelly. "And you know what else? I think you were feeling sorry for yourself last night, Kane. I think you were feeling . . . I'm not sure how to put it. Lost, maybe. And very alone. I'd say that's why you went with Fanny, only . . . only you didn't find what it was you wanted with her."

He scowled. "You don't know the first thing about me!"

Abby didn't retreat from his thunderous glare. "I think I do. I think you came to my room because—" She faltered, praying he wouldn't see how she was quaking. "—because you wanted to feel needed. Because you're tired of being alone, Kane. Because you finally gave in to the urge to reach out to someone—"

"Don't delude yourself, sugar. I came to your room for one reason only—lust is what it's commonly known as—and that's a polite way to put it, at that." He gave her a leering once-over. "You just happened to be available."

Abby drew herself up stiffly. "There's no need to—"

"Don't," Kane said through lips that barely moved. His eyes narrowed. "Don't even *think* of preaching to me—because you sure as hell weren't thinking about your husband last night."

He laughed, the sound cold. "That's right, sugar. I might have been drunk but I wasn't that drunk. It wasn't *his* name you were panting when I was kissing your breasts—it was mine. And it sounded to me like you were begging for a whole lot more."

Abby blanched. *Dillon*. Dear Lord, what would he think if he knew what she'd done? She'd lain almost naked on a bed with a man she hardly knew, a renegade, a criminal. Her heart squeezed. Somehow, it hadn't seemed so wrong . . . until now.

Kane was being unforgivably cruel. He was twisting their encounter into something it hadn't been—sordid and distasteful. And all at once she loathed him for making it sound so—so ugly.

"I can see you forgot all about your dearly beloved." His lip curled. "Seems to me you were awfully quick to forsake honor and fidelity."

A slow burn simmered along Abby's veins. "Honor? Fidelity?" She glared her displeasure. "What would a man like you know about either?"

More than you know. Dear God, Kane thought, *more than you know . . .*

His lips curved into a derisive smile. "Tell me, sugar. Does Dillon know what a hot little number you are the minute his back is turned?"

Her temper sparked like a keg of dynamite. "Oh, you're a fine one," Abby burst out. "First you tell me that I—I drove him off! Now you're telling me I'm—I'm promiscuous!"

"What else would you call it when you let me do what I did last night? Jesus, you're married, but that didn't make any difference to you—you were goddamned eager to have me under your skirts, honey. Fact is, I could have spent the whole damn night rutting between those pretty white thighs of yours and you'd have been crying for more!"

She paled visibly, for an instant her features utterly stricken. Kane despised himself for putting that look on her face, but moral dilemmas were new to him and he hated it. She was fresh and young and natural; he couldn't ignore her beauty. Hell! What man could? She made him ache inside, reminding him of everything he'd always wanted but could never have. And yes, it was selfish!—but he resented her for it, and it was this demon inside that made him taunt her so.

His every word was like a claw sinking into her flesh; the pain was immense. She was grateful when the hurt was replaced by a cold, biting fury. "And I'm a fool, Kane, a fool for ever letting you near me. And yes, that's exactly what it would have been—*rutting*. Because I said it once, and I'm saying it again—you're an animal, Kane, an *animal*."

Her voice trembled with the force of her anger. Her only thought was to hurt him as he had hurt her. "You—you dally with women like Fanny, because no *lady* will have you!"

His lips were ominously thin. Abby paid no heed.

"I'm well aware I shouldn't have let you touch me like you did. But you're just as guilty as I am," she accused, "because you tried to seduce a married woman, and that just proves what kind of man you are—you're rough and unscrupulous and jaded!"

He reached for her. She batted his hand away.

"You have no scruples, no concept of decency whatsoever!"

"Stop it." Though his warning was deadly calm, there was a tempest brewing in his eyes.

"I won't! You—you're no good, Kane. You're coarse and vulgar! I knew it when this whole thing began, but you were my only hope of finding Dillon."

Their eyes locked in fiery combat, hers defiant, his condemning. "You're lying," he said through his teeth, "the way you lied about who he was."

"The hell I am! I've put up with you, I've suffered your pawing and your crudeness so you would help me find Dillon." She plunged on recklessly. "But you were right, Kane, you were right! Every time you laid a hand on me I felt dirty and soiled! It makes me cringe to think how I let you touch me. Do you hear? It makes me sick!"

Kane went rigid. He didn't stop to reason or think, he simply reacted, snagging her by the waist. Abby raised her fists high aloft to pummel his chest but she never got the chance. He seized her wrists and dragged them behind her back, then wrenched her against him.

His mouth crushed hers. His only intent was to silence her, to subdue her in the only way he knew how. Her opinion of him shouldn't have mattered, but it did. Her feelings about him shouldn't have mattered, but they did, God rot her soul! Damn her, he thought bitterly. Damn her for making him sink even lower than he already was. Damn her for her prodding and goading—damn her for punching through the hardened shell he'd built around himself.

Locked in his merciless hold, Abby could only submit. Unlike last night, he demanded no surrender—nor did he allow it. His kiss was devouring and consuming, his teeth raking against hers. Her mind spinning from lack of air, she felt her knees buckle, her limbs weaken as if they were mush.

Kane felt it too. He tore his mouth from hers, his gaze never leaving hers as she shrank away. She pressed shaking fingers to her lips and stared at him as if he were a creature straight from hell.

His insides twisted into a sick, ugly knot. "Christ," he said with a shake of his head. His tone was thick with self-disgust. "You're right. I *am* an animal."

Too late Abby realized she'd made a terrible blunder—she'd pushed him too far. Time stood still as they stood there, both rigidly immobile. The air was suddenly hot and stifling.

Her expression both confused and stunned, she drew a deep, tremulous breath. Her hand moved of its own accord, reaching up toward his cheek. "Kane—" she whispered.

He released her abruptly. "Just leave me the hell alone, do you hear?" His tone was so fierce that Abby stumbled back, retreating instinctively. "Just leave me the hell alone."

He turned his back and strode away.

Never in her life had she been so confused.

One minute Abby was furious at his callousness, the next she was hurt as she'd never been hurt before. It made no sense that he should stir such anger in her. It made no sense that his rejection should wound her so, but Abby couldn't help it. She wanted to run and hide—most of all, forget she'd ever laid eyes on Kane . . .

But Kane was her only hope of finding Dillon. And God help her, she wasn't certain if that was a curse or a blessing.

Once they were back on the trail, Kane rode slightly ahead of her. Abby's nerves were screaming by late that afternoon. So immersed was she in trying to figure a way out of her predicament, it gave her a start when Kane spoke her name, his tone rife with annoyance. Only then did she realize this was the second time he'd called her.

She tipped her chin. Coolly she met his regard, but he said nothing. Instead he gestured toward the north.

Abby followed the direction of his finger. The entire horizon, which should have been dominated by craggy mountains, was a thick, oozing mass of dark storm clouds. Even from this distance, they seemed to swirl and swell ominously. Abby sucked in a harsh, indrawn breath and tugged on Sonny's reins.

"No sense riding into that mess. We might as well stop for the night right here."

His statement brought Abby's head whipping around. She watched as he swung down from Midnight. There was nothing the least bit compromising in the profile he presented to her. He appeared as hard and unyielding as the mountains eclipsed by the clouds. Indeed, she observed with mounting indignation, he looked as if he hadn't given a second thought—no, nary a first!—to everything that had transpired between them.

"It's too early to stop," she disagreed adamantly. "We've got a good four hours of daylight left. No, we keep moving."

Kane's head came up. From where he'd been about to hobble Midnight to a tree, he fixed on her a long, disbelieving look that implied she was clearly less than rational.

He stated the obvious. "Unless I miss my guess, that's one hell of a storm."

Abby saw red. "The wind is from the west." She met his challenge with one of her own. "It'll move on long before we reach it."

Kane said nothing, merely directed her another burning stare.

Abby squared her shoulders. "I'm not afraid of a little rain," she said shortly. "I don't know why it should bother you."

Kane climbed back on Midnight. "Have it your way," he muttered under his breath. "You will anyway." He dug his spurs into Midnight's flanks. He didn't look back to see if Abby followed.

An hour passed, maybe more. Abby couldn't be certain. The tension between them was almost more than she could stand.

In some far distant corner of her mind she realized it couldn't go on . . . *she* couldn't go on like this.

It wasn't long before she realized her mistake. The wind shifted. Now it was blasting in from the north. Anxiously she raised her head, scanning the rapidly approaching cloud bank. The sky was a seething mass of black.

Sonny began to toss his head. He pranced uneasily, then all at once wheeled in a circle. Abby couldn't suppress a startled cry of surprise. Beside her, Kane stretched out a hand to grab Sonny's bridle, but the skittish gelding eluded him. Abby tightened her grip on the reins. With a soft murmur, she leaned forward in an attempt to calm her horse.

Abby was never quite certain how it happened . . . One moment she was running her knuckles up and down Sonny's neck the way he liked; the next thing she knew she was hurtling backwards, earth and sky whirling all around her . . . She hit the ground with a dull thud.

The breath jolted from her lungs, it was an instant before she realized she'd been thrown. Kane's face swam above her, his features a blur. Strong hands pulled her upright until she was sitting. Fleetingly she registered Sonny's hooves pawing the air once more. His doe-soft eyes rolled back in his head. He reared wildly once again, his sides heaving. Belatedly it flashed through Abby's mind that something—she didn't know what—had spooked the gelding. Still in a daze, she saw him bolt madly.

Kane was on his feet, shouting unintelligibly. From the corner of her eye Abby heard him whistle for Midnight. Never in her life would she forget what happened next . . . Sonny raced wildly across the grassy meadow, straight toward a half-dead tree whose naked limbs lifted heavenward in silent supplication.

The gelding halted, beneath the tree now. He screamed, an unearthly sound that raised the hair on the back of Abby's neck. The voice fell eerily silent—it was as if the entire universe held its breath. Beneath the blue-black sky, both tree and horse were outlined in stark silhouette.

There was a tremendous flash of light. A streak of silver ripped through the sky, as if thrown by the hand of God. Abby couldn't move. The air seemed to hum and sizzle. A thunderous explosion shook the ground on which they stood. Abby squeezed her eyes shut, as if by doing so she could drown out the sound.

When she opened them, Sonny lay on the ground

beneath the tree. An acrid odor burned Abby's nostrils; tendrils of smoke wisped skyward. Abby knew instantly something was very, very wrong. Shakily she rose. She took a single step forward, then another and another. Soon she was running blindly forward, only dimly aware of Kane shouting behind her.

Her heart ready to burst, she was almost there when she tripped, falling heavily to her knees. She crawled the last few feet to Sonny, who was still screaming—in pain, she realized belatedly. Her tardy mind at last fit the pieces together—the flash had been lightning striking the tree—and Sonny along with it.

The gelding's legs thrashed wildly. Abby slid her hand over Sonny's shoulder. Her hands were shaking. Beneath her fingertips Sonny's sleek muscles coiled and knotted. A tremendous shudder shook the gelding's body; his legs flailed one last time, then went still. The awful screams fell silent.

A numbing fear took hold of Abby. Tears scalded her eyelids. She blinked them back. If only this was a dream, she thought desperately. If only she would wake up and it was just a bad dream. But Pa was gone, she recalled chokingly. And now Sonny. And they hadn't found Dillon . . . Oh, what if Kane was right? What if Dillon was next? What if he was already *dead* . . .

Her fingers clutched the roughness of Sonny's mane. "No," she whispered brokenly. "*No!*"

Behind her, Kane hesitated, uncertain what to do. Her pain was keenly evident. Hard as he tried, he couldn't ignore it. He had to force himself to harden his heart. He glanced at the churning clouds above and back to her.

"Abby."

He spoke her name, very low. She heard him. He knew it from the way her shoulders stiffened and squared.

"Abby, we have to leave." His tone sharpened. "We can't stay here any longer." He laid a hand on her shoulder.

Her fingers only twined in Sonny's mane all the harder. Kane dropped to his knees beside her. He bit back a curse when he had to pry her fingers loose.

Abby wrenched herself away and surged upright. Small hands fisted at her side, she faced him defiantly. "I can't leave!" she cried. "Sonny's dead! I can't just leave him lying out here. He needs to be buried!"

Rain pelted his head. The sky rumbled a warning. "Abby, we can't! It's dangerous to be out here in the open during a storm!"

"Then go!" she shouted. "But I'm staying right here until I'm finished!"

"For Christ's sake, woman! There's a shack just over the next hill! As soon as the storm breaks, I'll come back and see that he's buried."

Fire blazed in her eyes. "He was my horse, Kane! I'll do it myself!"

"Dammit, Abby, we've got to find shelter—now!" He wrapped steely fingers around her wrist. If he had to tie and gag her, she was leaving with him!

She tried to jerk free. When his grip merely tightened, she gave a little scream of fury. "No! I can't leave him here for the buzzards and wolves . . ." A blustery flurry of wind whipped around them. Abby felt as if she had been caught in it as well.

"Oh, God, don't you see? I—I couldn't stay and see that my pa had a decent burial. I have to see that Sonny has one . . . I have to do this, Kane—I have to!" Her voice cracked—and so did she.

She went wild then, pounding at his chest, clawing at him as she struggled to free herself. Her eyes were glassy, her expression so frenzied he decided grimly she was only half-aware of who he was and what she was doing. He shook her roughly, but that only intensified her efforts. Finally he wrapped his arms around her and squeezed her until her eyes flew wide and she gasped for much-needed air. She went limp against him.

He framed her face in his hands. "Abby," he said urgently, "I'll come back and bury Sonny. Do you hear? I swear I won't let you down." There was no thought of refusal, none whatsoever.

She gave no sign that she heard him. Kane pressed home his advantage and half-dragged, half-led her to where Midnight stood waiting, his ears pricked high and alert. He lifted her into the saddle, then mounted behind her. She sagged forward, like a flower whose stem had been snapped. Kane muttered under his breath and tightened his hold around her. At a word from him, Midnight sprinted ahead.

The heavens opened up then. Rain poured down in wind-driven sheets. They were both drenched by the time they arrived outside the shack. Kane gave a silent prayer of thanks that it still stood— he hadn't been certain it would be there. Only later did he realize he couldn't remember the last time a prayer—of thanksgiving or otherwise—had crossed his lips.

He tethered Midnight near the porch. A moment later, he flung open the door of the shack. He pushed Abby through the opening, then followed her in. He'd figured out the shack was used for hunting; it had never been occupied the few times he'd passed through here. But it was obvious someone stayed here at least several times a year—the interior was just as he remembered. A supply of wood had been laid in, and while the rough plank floor was covered with a layer of dust, it wasn't filthy. The wooden table and chairs were in passable condition, and even the narrow bed in the corner had been neatly made up with a faded brown quilt.

He slammed the door shut and shouldered his way past Abby to the fireplace. The rain had sent the temperatures plunging, and although the air wasn't cold, he and Abby were both drenched to the skin. With determined efficiency, he soon had a fire roaring in the hearth.

Abby still hadn't moved. Her listlessness disturbed him; it wasn't like her to be so passive. He pushed her into the nearest chair. "You'd better get those wet clothes off." He pointed to the wool blanket neatly folded on the end of the bed. "You can dry off with that before you change."

A faint distress crept into her eyes. Kane scowled. "You can do it while I'm gone," he said brusquely. She made no response, but he could see the silent question in her gaze. "I'll be back when I'm through bury—" He broke off as a spasm of pain whitened her lips. "—when I'm through," he finished lamely.

His steps carried him toward the door. Outside, the storm wind howled fiercely. Rain lashed the windows and walls, but Abby made no effort to prevent him from leaving—not that he'd expected she would. No, he decided bitterly, concern for his safety would be the last thing on her mind.

His eyes were watering, his lungs burning when he burst inside a long time later. The storm had abated, but the rain had not. Darkness had invaded the shack. The only light came from where the fire cast its golden halo into the room. His eyes strained to find Abby. She sat on the floor, wrapped in the rough wool blanket, her back propped against the far wall. Her head was bowed low; she appeared to be asleep.

Kane crossed to stand before the fire. His hands ached from digging a hole deep enough to cover Sonny's body. The pads of several fingers were blistered, he noted, raising them to the buttons of his shirt. He stripped quickly, his boots and wet clothing slapping against the floor. Naked, he turned to fumble in his saddlebags. He dragged a shirt over his wet limbs before yanking on another pair of pants. He didn't bother to put on the shirt.

He turned, inhaling harshly as he realized Abby was awake . . . and watching him. She looked like a child, her eyes huge and very blue, her gleaming hair falling softly around her shoulders, small fingers clutching the edge of the blanket as if it were her only link to life itself.

Their eyes locked for a never-ending moment. A guarded tension rose between them. Abby was the first to break the stifling silence, her voice as thin as threadbare cotton.

"It's done?" she whispered.

Kane inclined his head.

She stared at him through eyes that stung painfully. The blessed numbness that had overtaken her had long since slipped away. A burning ache seared her breast. Kane owed her nothing, yet he'd gone back out into this awful storm to bury Sonny. The least she could do was thank him . . . Her mouth opened. Her lips trembled as she struggled to find her voice. And then . . . she did the very thing she was trying so hard not to do . . .

She started to cry.

Chapter 11

K ane felt as if he'd been punched in the gut. Not once. But over, and over, and over.

It seemed odd to see this strong, fiery woman in tears. She'd turned away from him, but beneath the blanket, her shoulders were shaking. The sight completely unnerved him.

Never had she been more vulnerable.

Never had he resented her more.

Because tears were the one thing he hadn't expected from her... the one thing he couldn't deal with.

A voice like a cattle prod reared inside him. *Don't just stand there, you fool. Comfort her.*

His insides wound into a knot, coiled tight and hard. *I can't*, he thought. *She thinks I'm a coldhearted bastard.*

She's right, too, jeered the first nagging voice. *But she needs someone, Kane. She needs someone now.*

Not me. Christ, I'm the one person she doesn't need.

Look around, you horse's ass. Do you see anyone else? She's alone, Kane, alone just like you've always been. Her pa's gone, remember? You're the only one here, Kane, the only one who can help her.

Panic surged within him, panic and some nameless emotion as violent as the storm that raged

193

earlier. He felt like shoving his hand through the
wall. He felt like running out into the night, until
he could run no further. He clenched his fists, over
and over, unable to go to her, unable to leave.

"Abby." Uncertainty made his voice harsher than
he realized. "Abby, stop it."

Seized by a bone-deep despair, Abby merely wept
harder. Utter helplessness welled up in her, a flow
she couldn't stem.

The sound of her weeping tore at Kane's heart,
even as it tore at his sanity. He ground out her
name, the sound as raw as her sobs. He wondered
furiously if this wasn't just another ploy—a woman's trick to get him to knuckle under and do her
bidding.

"Abby . . . Jesus . . . Don't cry. For heaven's sake,
please don't cry."

Bracing himself inwardly, he knelt down beside
her. Laying a hand on her shoulder, he tipped her
chin to his. She made no effort to fight him. Tears
slid unheeded down her cheeks, pale and glistening. She looked utterly defeated, too beaten to even
wipe them away.

Something caught at his heart. Slowly, as if the
movement caused him great pain, he closed his
arms around her. She gave a dry, heartbreaking sob
and clung; the sound pierced his chest like a rusty
blade. All at once Kane found himself struggling
with the unlikely position of having to be strong
for both of them.

He didn't want to be. God, but he didn't! He'd
been on his own for too many years. He'd lived his
life for too long without ties. He didn't want Abby
leaning on him for comfort or support—he didn't

want the responsibility and he sure as hell didn't need it!

But her body nestled against his aroused a flood of sensations he didn't want to feel—a feeling of protectiveness, of possessiveness as foreign to him as he suspected tears were to her.

Scalding tears seeped into the hollow of his throat. "You were right," she wept. "We should have stopped for the night. I shouldn't have insisted we keep going."

She rocked against him. He eased her face into the notch between his neck and shoulder. "You couldn't have known the winds would change. No one could."

"*You* did." Abby hated her foolish tears, but she couldn't seem to help it. "God, I should have listened to you. It's my fault Sonny's dead . . . If I hadn't been so—so stupid, so stubborn and determined to argue with you, Sonny would still be alive . . ."

It wasn't just the horse. Kane was achingly aware of that. No, her weakness right now wasn't solely because of guilt over Sonny. As she'd already revealed, it was all mixed up with guilt over leaving her dead father. He knew what it felt like to lose a loved one—God, when he'd lost Lorelei, it was as if his heart had been ripped out.

"Maybe you're right," he whispered, smoothing the rain-washed cloud of hair that tickled his chin. "Maybe it wouldn't have happened if we hadn't gone on. On the other hand, there's every chance the storm would have caught us anyway, even if we *had* stopped for the night—and maybe Sonny would *still* be dead."

With his thumbs he gently wiped away the dirt and dampness from her cheeks. "We can't go back, Abby. We can't change what happened, and so we have to learn to live with it."

He pulled her onto his lap, settling her against him like a kitten. She melted against him as if she belonged there. He squeezed his eyes closed, aware of a tightness in his chest that was nearly unbearable—part pleasure, part pain.

He offered no more advice, certainly no wisdom—God knew it wasn't his to impart. But his presence seemed to calm her. Her crying soon ceased.

Night descended, heavy and thick, while the roll of thunder grew ever more distant. The fire sizzled and hissed. Sparks showered and crackled, sending a blaze of yellow further into the shadows.

At some point her hands had crept up to his naked chest. The softness of her cheek, still damp with her tears, nestled just above his heart. Her long, ragged sigh stirred the dense mat of hair on his chest.

Every muscle in Kane's body went rigid. The closeness of warm, feminine flesh, the fragrant, womanly scent of her, her yielding pliancy, the fragile weight of her breasts pressing his chest . . . The warning signs were abundantly clear.

He thrust her from his lap.

Abby knew the instant something changed. She'd felt the tension invade his body a fraction of a second before he shoved her away. Caught off guard by his abruptness, she could only stare as he bounded to his feet and strode toward the fire. Once there, he shoved his hands through his hair, his displeasure keenly evident.

Bewildered, she whispered his name.

There was nothing. Even the fire ceased its crackle and hiss.

A pang shot through her. She rose to her feet. Rather awkwardly she moved to stand just behind him, careful not to trip over the trailing ends of her blanket. For a timeless moment she remained huddled there, her arms around her middle, trying desperately not to feel so forlorn, so . . . abandoned.

His withdrawal was complete and absolute. She could see it in the iron cast of his jaw. Why? she cried. What had she done to make him suddenly so—so distant! All at once she felt so hollow, so empty that she wanted to die.

Her shuffling had alerted him to her presence. He whirled, his expression so fearsomely forbidding she stumbled back a step.

His mouth thinned as the blanket slipped, revealing one smooth, bare shoulder.

"Why didn't you change like I told you? You had plenty of time."

Abby flinched. His tone was like a whip. She inclined her head to where her chemise and drawers lay draped over the shack's only two chairs. Her gaze remained riveted to his as she whispered, "My underwear's still wet."

He jerked his head to where he'd dropped her saddlebag in the opposite corner. "I never met a woman traveled with only one set of underwear."

His rudeness made her cheeks burn. Feeling more foolish and uncertain than ever, Abby shook her head. "I only brought two, besides those." She nodded toward the chairs. "Jake ruined one," she went on, her voice very small. "And the other . . ."

Her voice trailed off. They both recalled last night, the way he'd torn her chemise cleanly in two. The memory rose stark and vivid in both their minds, shared but appreciated by neither. Kane jerked his gaze away, muttering under his breath. Knowing she was naked beneath the blanket wreaked havoc with his insides.

Abby directed her gaze to the floor. A shiver tore through her. It had taken her a long time to get warm after Kane had left. All at once she wanted his arms hard and tight around her once more. She wanted it with a yearning that made her ache inside. But what could she say? *Hold me, Kane. Hold me close and don't ever let me go.*

Scarcely daring to breathe, she started toward him.

His lips drew back in a relentless line. He stepped back and flung up his arm. "Don't," he warned.

Abby was not to be deterred. Behind a mask of courage and bravado, she breached the single step that lay between them. Trembling inside, but compelled by some deep-seated need she didn't fully understand, she extended her fingers toward the raspy hardness of his cheek.

His hand snaked out. His fingers wound around her wrist.

She cried out at the fierceness of his clasp. "Kane, please, you—you're hurting me!"

His gut twisted. No more than she was hurting him, he thought. God, only half as much as he was hurting! Sweat beaded on his forehead. He didn't want to be here. He didn't need any more complications in his life. He had problems enough without adding one more, let alone this particular one. Goddammit, he didn't need *her*.

He released her, his breath harsh and scraping. "You heard me." His tone was grating. "Don't touch me. Just—just stay the hell away from me!"

Her wounded expression stabbed like a blade. She shook her head in puzzled confusion. "Why are you doing this? Why are you being so—so deliberately hurtful?"

"You're fine," he told her brusquely. "Tougher than any woman I know—hell, tougher than most men!"

She shook her head wildly. "No, Kane, I—I'm not." Her lips trembled. "Surely you of all people know I'm not!"

Frustration and bitterness warred deep in his heart. "I don't know anything," he said harshly. "I don't know who I am anymore. Christ, Abby, I don't know what the hell you're doing with a man like me!"

Again she shook her head. She spoke the only truth in her mind. "I—I'm not afraid of you, Kane." She wanted very badly to touch him, she realized. But his regard was blistering, his features black with rage, his nostrils pinched and white. And she couldn't stand it if he rejected her yet again . . .

"Maybe you should be," he said fiercely. "Who am I for you to put your trust in? I'm a criminal, wanted by the law. Do you have any idea what men like me do to women like you?" Her face drained of color, but still she didn't retreat.

Kane went a little crazy then. "Jesus, I could be leading you off to God knows where—to do God knows what to you! I could tie you up and rape you—a thousand times, a thousand ways. I could beat you, treat you like the animal you're so fond of calling me. And when it was over, you'd pray for death because a woman like you could never stand the shame of being used by a man like me."

Each word was like an angry, pelting blow. He wanted to seize her, haul her up against him and ravage the soft, sweet innocence of her mouth. He wanted to hurt her as she was hurting him. He wanted to turn her faintly shocked, bemused features white with fear . . . to see her turn from him, make her see him for the black-hearted scoundrel he really was.

But she didn't whirl to run screaming as if he were a monster from hell. She just stood there, huddling beneath that god-awful blanket, her eyes brilliant and blue and unwavering. The purity of that look tore at him like a spear. God! What would she say if she knew he was wanted for murder?

But it was a murder you didn't commit, whispered a voice.

He was a coward, he realized defeatedly. That was why he'd left Sam's gang. It wasn't just because he was tired of being hunted, tired of running . . . He'd left because he was afraid someone would catch up with him. He was afraid some gung-ho sheriff would shoot him. Or see that he hanged. He had nearly felt the rough hemp of a noose scraping his neck once . . . and that was a fear he'd never been able to conquer. He didn't want to die . . .

And he was just as fearful of Abby, because she made him feel things he didn't dare feel again.

Her eyes still hadn't left his face. "You wouldn't—do those things to me." She moved so close he felt her chest expand in a deep, tremulous breath. "You wouldn't hurt me, Kane. I know you wouldn't. I—I trust you."

He felt suddenly savage. "Come on, Abby. You think I'm sinful and corrupt, a piece of worthless scum. And I am. Shit, I—I'm no better than Stringer Sam!"

Her fingers jerked on the edge of the blanket. "Don't say that," she cried. "Sam doesn't have a conscience. He—he doesn't even have a heart."

He laughed, the sound brittle. "And what makes you think I do?"

She gave a stricken little cry. "God, how can you even ask that? Oh, you try to act so cold, so heartless, but you're not—did you think I couldn't feel the difference when you held me tonight? I—I'm not made of stone, and—and neither are you!"

He turned his back on her. Damn you, Abby, he raged inwardly. Don't do this to me. Not here. Not now.

"And what about Sonny? Oh, I know it was silly to be so upset . . . but you—you buried him . . . for me . . . and then you took care of me, Kane . . . and no one as evil as Stringer Sam would do that for someone else . . ."

Her voice wobbled traitorously. "I didn't even realize you'd left, and then when I did . . . I felt so guilty, because you didn't have to do anything for me, but you did . . . And I was so worried with you out in that horrible storm . . . all I could think was . . . what if you were lying out there . . . hurt . . . alone . . ."

Kane swallowed, his jaw clenched tight, trying vainly to shut out the sound of her voice. God, he thought rawly. He'd been so convinced she wouldn't even care——that she hadn't even noticed he was gone . . .

"Oh, damn . . . What's wrong with me? It's starting all over again . . . I'm crying and——" She didn't know her voice had already given her away. "—— and I never cry, at least almost never . . ."

She choked back a sob. It was no use, the sound escaped, tearing Kane's heart to shreds. She lowered her head, unable to see for the tears that blinded her. She stumbled and turned, her only intent started to get away before she shamed herself further. Only suddenly he was there. *Kane*.

And this time he wasn't pushing her away.

Hard arms engulfed her. He crushed her against him. For the second time that night his thumbs grazed her cheeks, skimming the moisture away. With an effort, she willed away the last scalding rush of tears. His hands slid into her hair. Slowly he pulled her head back.

His expression was years beyond her experience. His eyes were fire-bright and glittering, a look that stole her breath and sapped the strength from her legs. *Hungry* was the only word that filled her mind.

He stared at her mouth.

She stared at his.

Time stretched endlessly, gauged only by the ragged rhythm of her heart. Abby knew what it was he wanted . . . . just as she knew, in some distant corner of her being, that this time there would be no turning back, for either of them . . .

But she'd been through too much tonight. She was tired of pretending she was strong, when she wasn't strong at all; she was tired of pretending she wasn't scared, when in reality she was terrified of all that had happened these past days . . . terrified of what *might* happen.

But Kane meant heat and warmth, his arms safety and security. Beyond that, she refused to analyze any further.

His mouth still hovered just above hers. Beautifully firm, beautifully sculpted. An odd dryness settled in her throat. All she had to do was lift her head . . .

Their lips clung.

His fingers tightened on her scalp. The pressure of his mouth was sweetly fierce. It struck her that this kiss was totally different from the others they'd shared. Always before there had been an undercurrent of anger, of sheer male domination. But now she sensed he was fighting some dark, desperate demon inside, that *he* was the one who was scared. The thought made her ache inside. She uttered a low moan. Bare, slender arms crept up to encircle his neck.

The blanket slid to the floor.

Kane was lost. The sweet clinging of her mouth and arms, the press of her body against his, soft and rounded and naked . . . He fought to rein in his runaway emotions, the rampant thunder of desire that raged within him. *He wanted her*. The desperation that drove him was purely selfish, purely greedy. It didn't matter that she was married—God, it was the last thing on his mind right now! He'd wanted her the moment he'd laid eyes on her back in Laramie. It seemed a lifetime had passed since then, which only made this gut-twisting desire all the more intense.

His hands drifted, discovering the tender bounty of her breasts, the curve of her waist, the shape and suppleness of her hips. She didn't stop him. God in heaven, she was so warm, so willing . . . She let him touch her as if he owned her—and suddenly that was exactly how he felt, his chest bursting, as if she belonged to him and no other. He refused to think of her husband, the man who would soon claim her again. He emptied his mind of all but the fevered clamoring inside him, the driving need to possess her at last. His tongue dove far and deep, a provocative prelude of the act soon to follow.

His head was spinning when he finally released her mouth. He withdrew only long enough to shed his pants. Dimly he registered that his hands were shaking. He half-turned, giving Abby a heart-catching veiw of bold, brazen masculinity, unconfined and unrestrained. The glow of the firelight caught the striking perfection of his form in sheer, golden silhouette.

Her gaze flew wide. She couldn't help it. Her mind skipped back to the time she'd seen him in the lake . . . There was a difference, she realized numbly. Now he was thoroughly, wantonly aroused. Her breath slammed to a halt. He was so—so . . . Her mind now rushed forward . . . Dear Lord, how could he ever . . . how could *she* . . .

The thought went no further. She felt herself lifted and borne backward. The soft mattress gave beneath her back. Abby was quiveringly aware of his unyielding breadth atop her. And then even that thought faded to nothingness as his mouth sought hers, his kiss deep and rousing.

His hand slid slowly down her throat. Her pulse began to race. The quick, staccato pounding of her heart was so hard and fast she was certain he could see if not feel it. Her nipples grew tight and tingly, anticipating his touch long before it came.

Slowly he circled the boundary of each breast, first with his fingertips, then with his palm, coming close to the quivering peaks but never quite touching. The elusive torment was almost more than Abby could stand. She moaned when at last he grazed her throbbing nipples, first one and then the other, toying and circling and teasing. And then his mouth trapped one straining summit, tugging, suckling, lapping until she was awash in mindless sensation, turned completely inside out.

Her lips parted eagerly as he reclaimed the moist hollow of her mouth, rimming his tongue along the edges of her teeth until hers met his in timid exploration. He crushed her against him. Abby reveled in the contact. He smelled of earth and wind and rain and all at once it seemed she couldn't touch him enough. She ran her hands over the binding tightness of his shoulders and arms in wordless praise. Growing bolder, she splayed her fingers wide in the hair that grew dark and dense on his chest and belly.

He groaned again, the sound low and vibrating, echoing in the back of her mouth. The heel of his hand skimmed the hollow of her belly, intent on claiming still more tender prey. She stiffened when strong fingers threaded through the springy down that proclaimed her womanhood. Her heart plunged into a frenzy. Surely he wouldn't touch her there . . .

He did. With a brash, intimate caress as daring and undaunted as the man himself.

Her body jerked.

"Kane—" Softly she cried his name. He silenced her with a devouring kiss, soothing, luring her ever deeper into this dizzying world of passion, one boldly invading finger venturing lower still, even inside her . . . She clutched his shoulders. Did people really do things like this? No. Surely not. But she was stunned when a showering current raced through her, straight to the place his hand now claimed with such blatant possessiveness. She began to tremble. Dear Lord. Was this right, or wrong . . .

It was heaven. Centered deep within that secret cleft was a tiny nubbin of flesh, so achingly sensitive his first sweeping pass wrung a gasp of wholly unexpected pleasure from her.

And it was there his fingers now worked, plying with delicate precision, grazing her teasingly, then seeking and delving until at last her hips initiated a tentative, sinuous rhythm of their own. She sensed that pleased him. His groan vibrated against her mouth.

A peculiar heaviness gathered between her thighs; a strange questing gnawed low in her belly. Every nerve within her was screaming, straining for something more, something just beyond her reach. She whimpered helplessly.

The low, pleading sound nearly pushed Kane over the edge. He dragged his mouth from hers, staring down at her exquisite features. Her eyes were closed, her lashes dark and still spiky with tears, her lips moist and parted. Her hands had fallen away to rest on either side of her face. Suppressing a groan, he intensified his efforts, the rhythm of his thumb now wildly erotic. His reward came seconds later; her taut flesh convulsed around his fingers.

A rush of some nameless emotion swept through him. He muttered her name, a touch of ragged harshness to his voice. Kane knew he could hold off no longer. The evidence of her readiness, damp and sleek and lush, still lingered on his fingertips. And he was so achingly full he thought he might burst.

His chest heaving, he stretched out atop her. The swollen tip of his organ, smooth and round and throbbing, grazed damp, dark curls. His entire body jerked in reaction. The very thought of thrusting deep and hard inside her clinging wet heat obliterated his last vestige of control.

He buried his head in the musky hollow of her shoulder. With his knees he spread her wide. Squeezing his eyes shut, he opened his mind and senses to the mindless ecstasy he knew awaited him . . .

One powerful thrust took him clear to the heat and heart of her.

His head jerked up; Abby's eyes snapped open. She couldn't withhold the strangled cry that ripped from her throat and shattered the night. They froze as if they were one—as indeed, they were, both overwhelmingly conscious of his turgid length buried clear to the hilt inside her. Abby lay trembling, her nails digging like talons into the flesh of his shoulders. She prayed desperately that the tearing pain would soon subside.

Above her, Kane lay utterly still, his heartbeat a drumming echo of her own. He was shocked by her body's fragile resistance . . . and what it meant. No, he thought, wholly stunned. How could this be? How could she possibly be a virgin when she was married . . . *married*!

He was afraid to move, just as afraid not to. His mind told him to back away now, to retreat before it was too late—Christ, it was already too late! But while his mind urged one course, his body retained a primitive will of its own.

The cords in his neck stood taut. He braced himself above her, only half-aware as he relieved her of the burden of his weight. But his blood was pounding thickly, surging heavily, there where he lay planted so solidly within her.

God, it felt so good. *She* felt so good. Especially there where her belly pressed his—soft against hard. Passion soared overwhelmingly. He tried to withdraw, only to submit helplessly to the overwhelming demand of his body. He sank into her satin depths once more. Again. And again. And then he was plunging. Driving. Praying the end would come quickly, because he couldn't stop . . . Hating himself because he knew he should have been slow and careful and easy, but he couldn't. Dear Lord, he couldn't. A groan rumbled in his chest, the sound low and anguished. He could only give in to the burning frenzy of hunger and need . . .

He gritted his teeth. Release claimed him, rolling over and through him, wave after scalding wave. The force of it astounded him. He shuddered, collapsing against her.

Only a few seconds passed before he rolled off her.

Abby felt him leave the bed. His recovery was far swifter than her own. Her world was still spinning. Turning her head, she glanced toward the fire just as he stepped into his pants. She sat up slowly, crossing her arms over her breasts, feeling uncertain and naked and exposed as she hadn't earlier. From somewhere she summoned the courage to meet his eyes.

It was a mistake. One glimpse of his rigid features and she longed to sink into the earth, never to be seen again. Her eyes widened when he approached, but he only tossed her clothes into her lap. They were still damp, but Abby no longer cared. Her hands weren't very steady, but through some miracle she managed to struggle into her clothing without assistance.

Not once did he release her from that accusatory glare.

"I think I deserve an explanation." His tone was dangerously low, like the distant rumble of thunder.

Abby stared down at the folds of her riding skirt.

"You were a virgin," he went on flatly.

Her lips compressed. Certainly she could hardly deny it.

The next thing she knew he was hauling her roughly to her feet. A muscle jerked in his jaw. Abby inhaled sharply at the anger leaping in his eyes.

"How?" he demanded, giving her a little shake. "How the hell can that be?" He grabbed her hand, stared at the place where a ring should have circled.

"That night at the Silver Spur, you said you took off your ring because you were afraid I wouldn't go upstairs with you if I knew you were married. But you were *never* married, were you?"

She was stunned. He wasn't just angry, she realized. He was furious . . . She swallowed helplessly, shaking her head.

He released her, as if the touch of her was suddenly abhorrent. "Cripes," he swore. "I'm beginning to wonder if I can believe anything about you, *Miss* Abigail . . . Is that even your real name? And what about this whole damn story you concocted? Oh, you're a fine one to sit in judgment of me, considering you lied to me from the very beginning—"

"Oh, you stubborn fool!" Abby stomped her foot, as angry as he. "Everything I told you was true . . . My father . . . Why we have to find Dillon before Stringer Sam gets to him . . . the only thing I lied about was Dillon—"

Kane's lip curled. "Oh, yes. *Dillon.* So he really exists, eh?"

"Of course he does!"

"And he's Laramie's marshal?"

"Yes!"

Kane was before her, his movement like quiet lightning. With his hand he prodded her chin up. "Then tell me this, Abby. Why are we chasing across the Territory after him if he's not your husband? What the hell is he to you that you're risking your damn fool neck in order to find him?"

Everything inside her seemed to go weak. She closed her eyes in order to shut out the ruthless demand in his features.

"He's my brother," she whispered.

Chapter 12

*H*er brother.

   The revelation bounced off the chambers of Kane's mind, again and again. For the space of a heartbeat, it was as if the wind had been knocked from his lungs. A feeling akin to elation ricocheted through him, but in its wake trailed a ready anger.

   His hands fell away from her shoulders. He didn't dare touch her right now. His temper was anything but tame. "Your brother," he repeated tensely. "Dammit, why couldn't you tell me?"

   "What did you expect me to do? I had to protect myself somehow. I was about to head out alone with a man, a man I didn't know—and what little I did know was hardly reassuring. It was the only thing I could think to do!"

   "It was your choice to go, Abby, not mine. I told you from the start you'd be better off staying home."

   Her eyes darkened. "I couldn't do that, Kane. My God, he's my brother! And after what happened to Pa, I couldn't stay home and wait—I just couldn't! Besides, how did I know you'd really try to find Dillon—that you wouldn't just go your own way and to hell with my brother? You have to admit, your past is hardly lily-white!"

His lips twisted. That was just what he didn't need to hear from her right now.

"And what about later, when I found out he was Laramie's marshal? Why didn't you tell me the truth then? Why keep up the pretense? Last night you said you trusted me," he went on stonily. "Or was that just another lie?"

"No, no, of course not!" She clasped her hands together before her to still their trembling. "But you have to understand, Kane, you—you scared me!"

"You?" His laugh reflected his scorn. "Honey, nothing scares you. You were the one pulled a gun on me, remember? Seems to me a mighty gutsy move for a woman—and you claim you were *afraid*?"

"I wanted to tell you, I swear. But I was afraid you'd be angry—the way you are now. I was afraid you'd leave me and then I'd never find Dillon!"

Kane merely stared at her, the line of his mouth grim and unrelenting.

Abby bit her lip. Oh, how could she explain? "The way you looked at me scared me, too, only in a much different way ... the way you kissed me that very first night scared me!" Unbidden, her gaze slid toward the bed.

"Oh, I get it. You were afraid of doing exactly what we just did. Well, sugar, you sure had me fooled." His eyes raked over her, stopping on the juncture of her thighs. "All that moaning you did had me convinced you wanted it as much as I did. But it seems that was just a treat to keep me panting at your heels, wasn't it—a way to keep me in line— payment in advance, you might say."

Abby caught her breath. His urgent desire had

been thrilling. It had merely heightened her own. But now he made it sound almost dirty!

She was suddenly shaking. She pressed cool fingers to her burning cheeks. "Stop it," she said unsteadily. "It wasn't like that at all, Kane. It wasn't like that and you know it!"

"Do I?" His lip curled. "Did it make you laugh, knowing how gullible I was? God, I should have known you weren't married. The signs were all there—you didn't know how to kiss. You nearly jumped out of your skin when you saw me naked! But no, I was a fool. Not once did it cross my mind you might be lying!"

Abby's chin went up. "I'm the one who's a fool, a fool for caring about you. God, sometimes I think you want me to think the worst of you. But I suppose that's to be expected. You're certainly always ready to believe the worst of me!"

Kane's jaw clenched hard. If he was bitter, he couldn't help it. It made no sense why he should feel so—so betrayed. So used. But that was exactly how he felt right now.

You idiot! bellowed an unwanted voice in his ear. *So what if she lied? She only did it to protect herself. Can you blame her? Besides, didn't you hear what she said? She cares for you, dirty scoundrel that you are. Doesn't that mean anything to you? Or are you going to sit back and ruin the first good thing that's come along in longer than you can remember?*

The emotion that tore through him was painfully sweet . . . just plain painful.

Only now did Kane realize . . . in spite of her temper, in spite of her tongue, Abby was a lady, well-born and gently bred. No doubt he'd ruined her for any other man, ruined her chances of making a good marriage. Guilt seeped through him like acid.

And yet . . . he couldn't regret it. A swell of primitive male pride welled within him. Damn him for the cad he was, but he liked knowing he was the first—the first man to lay with her, to claim her sweet innocence for his own, the one to take her from girlhood to womanhood.

That was something no one could ever take away from him.

He stared at her, becoming slowly aware of the way that her lovely mouth quivered. Her eyes were once again glistening and overbright. His gut twisted.

Though it cost him no little amount of pride, he extended his hand. "Come here," he said roughly.

"No! You're hateful, Kane! Mean and cruel!"

His face tightened. "Come here," he repeated. This time his eyes were no more than a flicker of light. There was no mistaking the threat implicit in his tone if she failed to heed him.

"You expect me to—to crawl back in your arms after what you just said? You make me sound like a—a cold, calculating shrew!" The strain of all that had happened today was suddenly too much. She was half-crying now. "I'm a fool, all right, but not that big a fool!"

Kane reached her with a muffled oath. His hands curled around her upper arms, biting into her flesh as he tried to draw her close. But something snapped inside her. She went a little crazy then, tearing into him with a strength borne of near-hysteria, arms flailing, scratching, kicking wildly, shouting at him to leave her be.

"Abby!" He blocked a well-placed knee aimed squarely at his groin. With a cry of rage she renewed her attack. They were both laboring for breath when at last he succeeded in pinning her arms to her sides. She tried to twist away but Kane was too quick for her. His arm snaked around her waist. He dragged her back against his chest. "For heaven's sake," he began, "will you just listen to me—"

He got no further.

The door burst open. A cold gust of wind and rain preceded a gritty male voice. "Well, well, here I thought I'd have this place all to myself. Guess I was wrong, eh?"

Kane's head shot up. He blinked, convinced his eyes deceived him. Because the man who filled the doorway was a man he'd thought never to see again . . .

Stringer Sam.

Kane's first instinct was to thrust Abby behind him. With an effort he restrained himself. The alarm that kindled along his nerve endings was the one thing he didn't dare let Sam glimpse.

Because Sam liked to prey on weakness. He liked to prey on fear.

Everything changed in the instant between one heartbeat and the next. Every instinct Abby possessed warned her that something was terribly, terribly wrong.

Along with the stranger's intrusion came a tension that charged the air like the sizzling hiss of lightning that had struck Sonny. As if that weren't enough to send warning bells clanging all through her, Kane's arm around her waist was like an iron clamp. Behind her his entire body had gone rigid. But when his voice sounded above her head, his tone was as easy and smooth as velvet.

"It's been a long time, Sam."

Sam. Dear Lord, it couldn't be . . . a sick feeling of dread seized her in its grasp. Abby's legs would have buckled if Kane's arm hadn't tightened ever so slightly around her.

She couldn't tear her eyes from Stringer Sam. *So this is the man who killed Pa.* The thought rampaged through her mind. If she hadn't been so terrified, she'd have taken great pleasure in scratching his eyes out. But there was no doubt that he *was* terrifying to look at.

He was younger than she'd expected, somewhere around thirty, she guessed. He was even taller than Kane, stringy and lean. Nor was he ugly—some, in fact, might even consider him handsome, with angled, hawk-like features. She watched as he flicked off his hat and tossed it aside. His hair was slicked back from his forehead, as sleek and dark as his rain-spattered slicker. His eyes were black and depthless, the slant of his lips cruel, even when he smiled, as he was doing now. But there was an air of menace about him, a stay-the-hell-out-of-my-way look about him that sent ice-cold shivers traveling the length of her spine.

He moved further into the shack. "You and your lady friend don't mind if I bed down for the night, do you? It's mighty wet outside." His voice was as oily-smooth as his smile, she decided with a shudder.

Kane's fingers splayed wide over her belly, the

gesture blatantly possessive. Abby wasn't about to object to his high-handed arrogance. Behind her she felt his shoulders lift in a shrug. "Why not?" he murmured.

Abby bit back a gasp. Was he mad, allowing a man like Sam to stay the night with them? Likely as not, they'd wake up with their throats slit! Sam headed back outside. As soon as he was gone she tore herself free of Kane's hold.

"Are you insane?" she whispered as loudly as she dared. "We can't let him stay the night!"

"We can't say no either," he said grimly. "I may not ride with his gang anymore, but if I send him on his way, he'll be suspicious, and you don't want that." He didn't give her the chance to either agree or disagree.

His hands came down hard on her shoulders. His tone grew fierce. "Listen to me, Abby, and listen good. I want you to follow my lead. Don't question anything I say—anything!—and I mean it. And for God's sake, don't argue with me."

"But—"

He gave her a little shake. "Just do it, Abby. Do you hear me? Just do it!"

He was so tense and wired Abby could only nod, her eyes huge in her pale face. When he told her to get into bed, she scurried across the room without another word.

Sam slammed back into the shack a minute later. He shrugged off his slicker and shook his head like a wet mongrel. He spread his bedroll out before the fire and laid down with a mighty yawn.

The silence was stifling.

Abby lay huddled under the blanket, her back

to the other occupants of the shack. She was afraid to move, to even close her eyes. It seemed forever before there was a touch on her shoulder. "Abby." Warm breath wafted across her cheek.

Kane. She rolled over with a gasp, her gaze darting across the room. "Kane! Is he—"

"Asleep." He stretched out beside her.

She tried to peer over his shoulder. "Are you sure? Maybe he's—"

"I'm sure. I can tell by his breathing. Now hush so we can get some rest."

His tone was stinging. She despised the stupid, foolish tears that threatened. She felt like a child whose hand had been slapped. With an indignant sniff, she rolled away and presented him with her back. Kane made no effort to recapture the distance she put between them. Abby couldn't decide if she was more angry or hurt. It took forever before she fell into an exhausted sleep.

Kane didn't allow himself the luxury of sleep that night. He knew the instant Sam awoke. Through the watery light that seeped in through the shack's only window, he watched the other man stumble to the door and open it. He hitched his arms high above his head, then strode outside.

Kane was waiting just outside the door when Sam returned from the bushes. Overhead the sky was blue and clear. Last night's storm was just a memory.

"You know, I was just thinkin', Kane, this is quite a change for you, isn't it?" He tipped his chin toward the shack. His laugh set Kane's teeth on edge. "Don't recall you ever traveling with a woman before."

Kane shrugged. "Took a fancy to the lady down in Rawlins," he said lazily. He saw that Abby had appeared in the doorway. A hand at her brow, she shielded her eyes from the morning glare. There was an odd tightening in his stomach. Even from here he sensed her uncertainty.

"Rawlins. That where you've been keeping yourself lately?"

A half-formed idea began to buzz in Kane's mind. "Not staying in any one place too long. Can't afford to, if you know what I mean."

Sam clapped him on the shoulder. "On the run again?"

"Let's just say I have a pressing need to lay low for a while."

Sam's gaze settled on Abby. "Having the girl along might slow you down."

The barely disguised lust in his eyes made Kane see red. With an effort he tamped down the violent urge to wrap his fingers around Sam's scrawny throat. "I don't think so. No, I don't think so at all. In fact—" He let a hard smile drift across his lips. "—she might come in handy if some fool chances to recognize me."

Abby was sitting on the bed when he strode inside a few minutes later. "Where is he?" she asked without preamble.

"Outside getting his horse ready."

"He's leaving?"

"Yes."

She released a fervent sigh of relief. "Thank God," she murmured. Her eyes widened as Kane dropped down before their gear, heaped in the corner. In shock she saw him rummaging through her things.

He hefted her revolver in his palm before shoving it into his saddlebag.

"Kane, that's mine!"

"Not for the present, sweetheart. Hostages don't have weapons of their own."

Every vestige of color drained from her face. "Dear God," she said faintly. "You told him who I am . . ."

Kane cursed himself when he saw. Quickly he crossed the room and caught her by the elbows. "I might be a low-down skunk," he said roughly, "but I'm not that low. I told him I picked you up in Rawlins—I let him believe you're my hostage. He thinks I'm running from the law." He took a deep breath. "We're going with him, Abby."

She couldn't hide her horror. "Go with him? My God, are you out of your mind? We can't!"

"It's the best way to find out if he's after your brother. Hell, it's the best way to *keep* him from your brother!"

Footsteps sounded outside. There was no time to argue, no time for anything, Abby realized sickly . . .

Within minutes she was mounted before Kane on Midnight's back.

An awful thought crowded her brain. Kane claimed he hadn't told Sam she was Dillon's sister. But what if he changed his mind? He certainly owed no loyalty to her. What if Sam discovered the truth—that she was Dillon's sister?

Her life would be forfeit, she realized numbly. Sam would have no qualms about killing Dillon's sister . . .

Sam's appearance had changed everything, she

thought with a sudden wash of reckoning. What little control she had had over her fate had been snatched from her . . .

Her very life rested solely in Kane's hands.

Her stomach knotted. She stared with single-minded fascination at the length of rope coiled around the horn of Sam's saddle. She'd told Kane last night she trusted him . . .

Now it seemed she had no choice.

Chapter 13

⎯⎯◜◯◯◝⎯⎯

They didn't stop until the sun was a fiery ball almost directly overhead. They had descended into a sun-baked plain. The land was dry and cracked. Here and there a scraggly tree jutted toward the sky. The cool, rain-washed morning air had turned hot and burning. Kane watched as Sam strode off toward a huge boulder.

He reached up to pull Abby from the saddle, unconsciously measuring the slightness of her waist. He resisted the compulsion to linger when her hands drew away from his chest as soon as her feet were on the ground. Wordlessly he watched as she walked away, her easy, long-legged stride rather stiff. That was unusual for Abby. The hours in the saddle never seemed to bother her. He frowned, wondering what was the reason for her discomfort . . .

It dawned with crystal clarity.

He was at her side before he knew it, pulling her around to face him.

"Are you all right?" His voice was gritty. He spoke through lips that barely moved.

Startled, she stared up at him. "Of course," she said faintly. "Why wouldn't I be?"

"You know why." The sweep of his eyes slid

downward. Abby felt her cheeks sting with heat. She couldn't say a word.

Kane silently cursed. Last night came back in scorching remembrance. Her stricken, shattered expression the instant he'd torn through her maidenhead flashed before his eyes. An odd tightening crept around his chest. He knew he'd hurt her, both then and now. Her glazed expression hadn't been from sublime ecstasy—far from it.

His fingers tightened on the curve of her hips. "I didn't want to hurt you," he said, very low. "I didn't mean to . . ."

Abby averted her face. She couldn't look at him—she just couldn't!

"It's just that I thought . . . How was I supposed to know you'd never . . ." Jesus, he sounded like the fool he was. And this conversation was having a dangerous effect on him. His loins had begun to tighten and swell. If only she would say something . . . anything!

Her gaze drew level with the bristly tangle of hairs at the base of his throat. She could look no higher. Vivid in her mind was how she had lain beneath the dark fur of his naked chest, pleasantly rough against the tips of her breasts. To her shame, her nipples grew all tight and tingly.

"Abby." He ground out her name.

She swallowed convulsively. "I'm . . . fine," she said faintly.

His fingers dug into her hips. "Are you sure?"

She nodded, reluctantly meeting the steely probe of his eyes. Her tongue came out to moisten her lips, pink and wet. His blood began to heat. His heart began to pound.

"You're not . . . sore?" His voice was very low. The question made him sweat. He remembered how it felt, imbedded deep inside her, clasped within the velvet prison of her womanhood. She'd been so small, so tight. Tension constricted his entire body as he waited.

She was embarrassed. He could see it in the way her gaze shied away. The breeze played with a tendril of her hair, feathering it across her cheek. She brushed at it distractedly, then lowered her hand to her side. A surge of longing shot through him.

He captured her fingers in his. "Abby—"

"Kane, please . . ." She couldn't think with him so close. She could scarcely even breathe. "I don't think this is something . . . we should be discussing . . ."

His grip on her hands tightened. "Dammit, Abby—" His voice roughened. "I need to know that you're all right."

An odd little tremor coursed through her. His concern did that to her—*he* did that to her. With a heated rush she recalled the size and breadth of his manhood, the full, straining pressure of him buried deep in her flesh. Her throat grew parched, in a way that had nothing to do with thirst.

He *had* hurt her. Oh, not terribly, but enough that the memory was still there. Only now . . . it didn't seem so awful . . . She'd been . . . oh, almost disappointed . . . Because until that moment, there had been so much pleasure, more than she'd ever dreamed . . .

Her cheeks were flaming. "I'm a little—sore," she whispered haltingly. "But it's better now . . . than this morning."

She tugged to free herself. Kane wasn't yet ready to let her go. He moved, his nearness overpowering. Abby's breath wavered. He was so close she could see the outline of dark silver that ringed the pure pewter of his eyes. His scent was not unpleasant—horse, musk, and all man. She swayed, her senses swimming dizzily.

Kane pinned her against him with a growl of frustration, molding her against the lean contours of his body. Her eyes caught his, endlessly blue, awash like a summer sky. Miraculously, he glimpsed no bitter accusation. No hateful condemnation. He lowered his head, aware of his blood running rampant in his veins. Her breath was as shallow as his. Her lips were parted and waiting . . .

A burst of mocking laughter filled the air. "Well, well. You two are mighty cozy, aren't you? And it's not even dark yet!"

The pair broke apart as if a knife had cleaved them in two. What would have happened had Sam not shown up, Kane wasn't sure. God, right now he didn't even want to think about it!

Moments later they were off once again.

Riding double with Kane was torture. Her bottom was nestled between his muscled thighs, riding against his blatant masculinity. No matter how she shifted and squirmed, trying desperately to stay erect, there was no escaping it—there was no escaping *him*.

Nor was she sure she wanted to. Every time she recalled what she had done last night—what *they* had done—her emotions scattered in every direction. She had been vulnerable then. Distraught and despairing. She'd needed someone . . . she'd needed *him*. She'd wanted him to make love to her—wanted it with an intensity that even now left her breathless. The knowledge was both heady and a little frightening. She'd sacrificed her virtue—to an outlaw. Why wasn't she ashamed? Why wasn't she horrified?

Soon they began to climb into the high country. The trail they took was apparently used very little. Rough and uneven, it jolted her very bones. The sun was so bright and glaring her eyes ached.

By the time they halted that evening, she was exhausted, both mentally and physically. She scarcely noticed the pristine blue waters of a mountain lake a hundred feet away. Kane dropped down from Midnight. He tugged her down, then immediately swung away without looking at her even once. Feeling snubbed, and battling a ridiculous hurt, she stepped forward. Her cramped muscles screamed in protest. Pain like red-hot needles shot up her legs. She staggered. A hand like a vise closed around her arm. Thinking it was Kane, she glanced up, an instinctive thank-you on her lips.

The words died unuttered. Gleaming ebony eyes bored into hers. With a gasp she wrenched away. Sam laughed, a guttural sound that chilled her to the bone, then walked away. Moments later a shot rang out. Abby's heart lurched until she realized Kane was standing just a few paces behind her. Sam strode back, a furry jackrabbit dangling from one hand, his rifle in the other.

Sam lowered himself to the ground and started skinning the rabbit. It was hardly the first time Abby had seen a rabbit skinned. Yet Sam approached the task with such relish that she found herself staring in horrified fascination. In seconds his fingers were smeared with blood. Her stomach churned sickeningly. She whirled and came face-to-face with Kane.

"We need some wood for a fire," he said brusquely. "See to it."

His high-handed arrogance brought her upright. She stiffened her spine and fixed him with a glare. A furious retort leaped to her lips; the only thing that stopped it was the silent warning glimmering in his eyes, reminding her of Sam's presence.

A lazy, taunting smile curled his lips. "Oh, and don't even *think* about running off, sweetheart. I guarantee you wouldn't like how I'd have to punish you." His insolent gaze traveled over her, leaving no part of her untouched.

Sam hooted with laughter. Abby's temper began to boil. Sam's laughter wasn't half so bad as Kane's leer. She had the feeling he was actually enjoying this! Her fingers itched to slap the smirk off his face. She marched off before she did exactly that.

Luckily, firewood was plentiful. They hadn't yet reached timberline so she didn't have to wander far before her arms were filled with dry branches and twigs. The delicate line of her jaw firmed. She stared out where the soft glow of evening touched the clouds with amber fire.

She'd like to do more than just *think* about running off. She'd like to do exactly that and to hell with Kane and his edict! But he was so damn smug, she thought bitterly. He knew she wouldn't leave with Dillon still out there somewhere.

There was a fire already burning when she returned. The rabbit roasted on a primitively fashioned spit above it. Abby dropped her pile of firewood just outside the circle of stones, determined to ignore Kane.

When the rabbit was done, she found a relatively private place behind a small boulder. She sat alone, ignoring the two men behind her. Though the meat was stringy and rather tough, she forced herself to eat, knowing she would need her strength. When she finished, she tossed away the bone and wiped her hands on her riding skirt.

A shadow fell over her.

"This seems as good a time as any for a bath," Kane drawled. "Get that fancy soap of yours, will you, sweetheart?"

Abby was tempted to snap at him to get it himself. She was dirty and dusty, hot and disheveled. It didn't sit well that he wanted to use her precious sliver of lavender soap.

Snapping blue eyes clashed with smoldering gray. Abby delayed as long as she dared, then spun around. Muttering under her breath, she fumbled through her belongings, closing her fingers around the soap. She turned and tossed it to him, only barely resisting the impulse to fling it at his head with all her strength.

He caught it neatly. "I thank you, sweetheart." There was a flash of white teeth in that dark face. "Now all I need is someone to wash my back."

Abby gaped. It took an instant before she grasped his meaning. She shook her head, her mouth dry as dust. "You can't mean me—"

His smile held little humor. "Honey, I sure as hell don't mean Sam."

Abby sucked in a harsh breath. From the corner of her eye she could see Sam looking on with interest.

He wiped his mouth with the back of his hand and leaned back on his elbows to watch. Did Kane really expect her to bathe him? No! She couldn't . . . she *wouldn't.*

"Time's a-wasting, sweetheart." There was an edge of steel in his tone that hadn't been there before.

Abby didn't move. Her expression was distinctly wary. His was distinctly unnerving.

He tapped his fingertips on the gun tied to his thigh. "I'd hate to have to make you, sugar."

His tone was all the more deadly for its quiet. Time stretched to a standstill. He confronted her with frightening intensity, all the while, his fingers tapping . . . tapping. Abby was stunned by the unyielding intent revealed in his eyes. In that instant, he appeared every bit as terrifying as Sam.

Her heart froze in her chest. Kane wouldn't hurt her, would he . . . *Would he?* All at once Abby didn't know. Because before her was the man she'd been so certain she would find and hadn't . . . until now. She sensed a ruthlessness that pierced her to the quick. Nor had she let herself speculate what crimes he'd committed—she hadn't dared. But now her mind ran rampant with the possibilities. Robbery. Rape. Maybe he was even a killer, like Stringer Sam . . .

She grappled for composure, grappled for courage. Through some miracle she found it. Her chin angled high, her shoulders squared, she stepped forward.

Inside she was quaking.

A steep trail dropped down to the lake. Half-way down, Abby's feet nearly skidded out from under her. Kane hauled her up beside him. He didn't let loose of her elbow until they reached the water's edge.

The lake was small, only a few acres at most, pure and clear. A pine-studded hillside rose from the opposite shore. Under other circumstances Abby might have caught her breath in sheer delight, but not now. Her nerves were screaming.

Kane began to strip. He dropped his shirt carelessly on the grassy bank. His fingers fell to his pants. Hastily she averted her head.

Water splashed. In all honesty, Abby didn't mean to look. She just couldn't help herself. Naked, he was an awesome sight. His legs were lean and roped with muscle, netted with hair. She couldn't tear her eyes away from the smooth, naked expanse of his back. She had discovered for herself last night that his buttocks were as firm and round as they looked . . .

"It's your turn now, sugar."

Abby's eyes jerked upward. He had stopped, turning to face her. Water lapped the bony ridge of his hips. Above the water the hair on his chest grew curly and thick. His jaw was dark and bristly with several days growth of beard. He looked dark. Dangerous. Raw and overwhelmingly male. Despite everything, a quiver shot along warm, forbidden places.

"You heard me, Abby. Strip."

Abby wet her lips. "What if I don't?"

"You'd damn well better."

Abby stood like a trapped doe. The pounding of her heart seemed to jolt her entire body.

"Don't push me, Abby. Don't test me. Because

there are times a man is capable of just about anything."

His tone was so pleasant, at first she didn't perceive it for the threat it was. But when she did, something seemed to give way inside her.

"I can't," she cried wildly. "Kane, you know I can't. He—he's watching!"

There was no need to ask who *he* was. Kane's gaze flickered to the hilltop. She was right—he *was* watching, still gnawing on a hunk of rabbit.

"Wear your underclothes."

Abby was perilously near tears. "I can't! I told you last night, Kane, I—I don't have any others!"

His eyes narrowed. "They'll dry, sweetheart. Now strip, or else I'll come and do it for you."

Abby searched his face for some sign of compassion—there was none. He appeared utterly merciless, hard to the bone. He hadn't brought his gun, but if he really wanted her dead, he didn't need one . . . All he had to do was wrap those powerful fingers around her neck . . .

Biting back a sob, she fumbled with the buttons of her blouse, wanting desperately to hide herself as she undressed. But where could she turn? she wondered half-hysterically. Stringer Sam was behind her, Kane before her . . . She remained where she was, conscious of how Kane absorbed her every move.

Stripped down to thin cotton drawers and her chemise, she waded ahead. As soon as she drew close, hard fingers curled around her arms. He moved so they stood face-to-face. She didn't back down from his gaze. Instead she faced him with a bravado that made a painful pride swell within him.

But she couldn't entirely hide the indignant hurt in her eyes. And her soft mouth was tremulous, though he could see her trying to press her lips together in an effort not to show it.

Hardening himself against her, he lifted her hand and dropped the soap in her palm. He turned so that his back was to her, carefully shielding her from prying eyes.

Abby hesitated for a moment, uncertain what to do next. There was no cloth to soap him, so she did the next best thing. She dipped the soap in the water, then lifted it to his shoulder. Her first tentative touch made her snatch her hand back. His shoulders were thick with muscle, gleaming dark gold in the waning sunlight. And he was so hot!

She drew in an unsteady breath and started again. Beneath her fingers, his shoulders tightened and flexed; her other hand came up as well, smoothing the lather across his back. At first her movements were quick, almost jerky. But by the time she reached the small of his back, the motion of her fingers was slow, almost methodical. Cupping handful after handful of water, she rinsed away the suds, feeling shaky both inside and out. His skin was smooth and sleek, but the muscles beneath were solid and hard.

Kane gritted his teeth. The feel of her hands sliding over his skin, kneading and stroking, soothing and massaging was incredibly arousing. God, but he despised himself for putting her through this! He despised everything he was, everything he'd done. And Abby did, too, because he could feel her trembling before him. In fear? Disgust? He couldn't stand the thought of either.

He wanted to drag her arms around his neck and kiss her until nothing else existed—not Sam, not Dillon. He ached with the need to lose himself in her fiery warmth, to erase the pain he'd given her last night and replace it with pleasure. But Sam was watching . . .

Sam.

Slowly he turned. "You're not quite finished yet, sweetheart." His tone was flat, as emotionless as his eyes.

His coldness was like a blow. God, she thought brokenly. Why was he doing this? Why was he being so—so hateful? She didn't mind what he'd asked of her; she couldn't hide what she'd felt. She'd liked washing him. She liked touching him . . . But he was so distant. So remote.

She stared up at him, tears and dismay keenly evident. "I can't," she whispered.

"You can, sugar. And you will."

"I won't!" In defiance she drew back. He snared her by the wrist, pulling her against him.

Though his face was shadowed, she could feel the hunger that leaped in him. *He wanted her again.* Her gaze slid down, unwittingly confirming what she felt. Her eyes widened. Through the water she could see him—swollen, thick with arousal. She inhaled sharply.

"Kane," she whispered. "Kane, please—"

Please.

That single word sent his mind flooding back . . . He wondered bitterly if Lorelei had looked like this, her eyes huge and wounded, if she had pleaded for her life . . . as Abby was pleading. He could almost see the thoughts vaulting through her mind.

His lips twisted. She thought he was heartless. Cruel. But he'd done nothing to hurt her, nothing but impose his will over hers ... and that was nothing to what Lorelei had endured. *Lorelei*. A wrenching pain ripped through him.

She had been brutally beaten. Savagely raped. And Lorelei hadn't possessed even a fraction of Abby's fire and spirit. She wouldn't have fought back ...

Some dark, nameless emotion crept over him, like a shadow across the sun. He was suddenly furious; furious with Lorelei for dying, for turning his life into a living hell ... furious with Abby for tempting him, for reminding him of all that was better left behind.

"Kane, please—"

That stricken cry came again. Kane closed his mind to it. He closed his mind to everything but the feel of her. He pinned her against him, weaved his fingers through her hair and turned her face up to his, holding her immobile. Abby had one terrifying glimpse of glittering silver eyes before his mouth came down on hers, hotly demanding.

Her precious soap fell from her fingers. She clutched at him weakly, trying to push him away, but his arm was so tight about her back she couldn't move. She could scarcely even breathe. Her heart cried out as she sensed the fierceness in him. He rubbed his chest against hers, abrading her nipples even through the damp cloth of her chemise. With his palm he ground her against his hardness. She was gasping when he finally raised his head.

She stumbled back, fingertips pressed against quivering lips. She stared at him with eyes that stung painfully. "I hate you," she choked out. "God, I hate you!"

She surged through the water, nearly falling twice in her haste to get away from him. She struggled into her clothes and fled without a backward glance.

A confusing, unfamiliar emotion knotted his insides as he watched her flee. It lingered all the while he dressed, all the while Abby sat huddled before the fire, staring into the flames. Sam was snoring heavily when he spread out his blanket beneath the tree. He dropped hers at the far end, then crooked a finger at her.

She got to her feet, her expression mutinous. "You can't expect me to sleep next to you!"

He bowed mockingly. "Indeed I do."

Her glare turned hotter. "I'd sooner bed down with a snake!"

His laugh was a terrible sound. "Honey, you already have." His features turned grim when it appeared there might be another standoff. A tussle was something he preferred to avoid. He was sorely afraid it might escalate into something much, much more . . .

Just when he was convinced that was his only recourse, she marched forward and obliged him. Throwing her blanket over her shoulders, she pointedly turned her back on him.

But she shivered and shivered, so long and so hard Kane was sorely put not to wrap his arms around her and pull her close. It was a long time later before she finally stopped shivering. Her deep, even breathing told him she'd fallen asleep.

With a sigh of resignation, Kane succumbed at last. Slipping his arm beneath her head, he rolled her gently against him, molding her snugly against his side, tucking her head into the hollow of his shoulder. God, she smelled so good, all warm and sleepy. And he wanted so badly to whisper his regrets.

His breath stirred the baby-fine hair at her temple. She released a watery little sigh and burrowed even closer. Overcome by the compelling need to touch her, he let his knuckles graze the curve of her cheek.

They came away wet with tears.

His arms tightened. "Abby," he whispered raggedly. And then again: "*Abby* . . ."

His eyes squeezed shut. Holding her like this was sweet heaven. Sweet hell. It was better this way, he told himself, better that she was convinced he was a cold, unfeeling bastard.

Only the price was far steeper than he'd imagined.

It was up to him to protect her from Sam, and keep on protecting her until this wretched affair was over . . .

But who the hell would protect her from him?

Chapter 14

The next day passed in a blur. Abby was so tired of riding she didn't care if she ever saw a horse again in her life. Her bottom felt bruised. Her head throbbed. Her entire body hurt. Worst of all was the empty ache in her heart.

She prayed that they were nearing Sam's hideout. She prayed that Dillon was nearby—and safe. They had to be close . . . Please, God. Because the thought of spending another night with Stringer Sam terrified her as nothing else ever had . . .

And then there was Kane. Since Sam had joined them, he had become a stranger, a frightening one at that. There was a razor-edged sharpness in him that he hadn't revealed until now—or maybe she just hadn't wanted to see it. He had scared the living daylights out of her last night, and she was furious at him for doing that to her. Nor did she understand how he could be so deliberately nasty and callous . . . and then hold her the night through.

She had a dim, fuzzy memory of strong arms enfolding her tightly against the sleek hardness of his shoulder, of soothing, stroking hands, of warm, comforting lips. She awoke once a long time later, dazed and disoriented. He nuzzled her forehead, the warm, musky scent she'd come to associate only with him swirling all around her, and whispered her name . . . or had it only been wistful imaginings?

Traveling with Sam and Kane was taking its toll on her nerves. She didn't like the way the two men eyed each other with wary caution. There was a seething undercurrent between them, a tension that existed far beneath the surface. It made her distinctly uneasy.

Mid-afternoon they stopped atop a rocky bluff. Far below a sunken valley zigzagged across the land. On one side craggy, saw-toothed peaks reared into the skyline. The other was marked by a sheer fire-red wall of stone. The wind whistled and wailed, as lonely and desolate as the surrounding landscape.

Abby slid from the saddle, her mouth dry and aching with thirst. She walked away on wobbly legs, needing to attend to her private needs. Kane's eyes dug like tiny needles into her back, but he made no move to follow her.

Sam was gone when she made her way back. Kane sat atop a flat-topped boulder, long legs thrust out before him, his profile as stark and barren as the mountains. Her steps slowed as she approached, yet she made enough noise so as to alert him to her presence. He didn't glance around, as she thought—hoped?—he might. Feeling rather tentative and unsure, she lowered herself to the knobby surface—close, but not touching him.

"Where is he?" she asked.

"Checking to make sure there's no one around."

"We're nearly there, aren't we?"

He nodded. There was no need to say more.

Several seconds passed before she spoke again, her voice very low. "Is he—" She hesitated. "—as bad as they say he is?"

For a moment Kane said nothing. He turned, at last giving her his attention. Abby had the sensation she'd startled him with her question. Finally he gave a harsh laugh. "Believe me, you don't want to know."

She bit her lip. "I've heard some of the things he's done—robbing. Cheating. Stealing."

Kane jerked his gaze away once again. Sam and his killing had always turned his stomach. But Sam was a master at eluding the law—and at the time, staying alive was the only thing that mattered . . .

"I've also heard that he . . . that he kills for no reason . . . other than to kill." She shuddered, thinking of the length of rope coiled on his saddle horn. "That he *likes* to make people suffer. That he likes to hear people scream . . ."

Yes! he wanted to shout. *It's true, all of it.* He was suddenly furious with her for dragging up the past, for dragging out the memories he'd purposely shut away.

He lunged to his feet, wheeling on her almost violently, hauling her upward by the arms. "Why do you want to know, Abby? Do you want to know if *I* did all those things?"

Abby was half-afraid to breathe. She stared at the white lines etched beside his mouth, a telltale sign of his anger. Her breathing slowed to a trickle. "Did you?" she whispered, half-afraid to even speak.

"I rode with his gang for a year, Abby." He took a perverse satisfaction in telling her. "What the hell do you think?" He couldn't tell her he'd only done what he had to do to stay alive. So-called *decent* folk like her didn't understand. Or maybe they just *wouldn't*.

She turned her head aside. "I don't know what to think anymore." She squeezed her eyes shut, her voice stifled. "I'm just . . . trying to figure out why someone would choose that kind of life—running from the law—why *you* chose that kind of life."

Kane said nothing. He just stood there, his features a mask of ice. Her mind traveled fleetingly back to that night at the shack. It seemed impossible that this hard-featured man was the same one who had held her comfortingly, kissed away her tears . . . made love to her with such melting passion.

Her eyes opened, wide and mutely beseeching. "Why did you stay with him, Kane? And why did you ever join up with him in the first place?"

He pushed her away, his gaze scraping over her. "I might ask you why all the questions all of a sudden? Why the concern? Did it finally dawn on you what kind of man I am?"

Abby just stood there, shaking. Trembling. Never in her life had she been so miserable. Tears stung her eyes. She blinked them back. "I—I'm just trying to understand you. But you just won't let me close, will you? You won't let me see what's really inside you!"

"You wouldn't like what's inside, Abby. Take my word for it."

"Why don't you let me be the judge of that?"

His jaw locked. "What the hell do you want from me, Abby? An admission of guilt? You want me to list my sins one by one? I couldn't, because there's too goddamned many. Besides, I don't know why the hell you'd want to know—why you'd even care."

"I *do* care!" she cried. "Can't you see that?"

"I told you before, Abby. You don't know what I am. You don't know *who* I am."

"Oh, I know, Kane. I know more than you think. You want me to think the worst of you." She battled to keep the quaver from her voice. "Is it just me you won't let close? Or are you like this with everyone? Dammit, tell me!"

His hands clenched and unclenched at his sides. He was tempted—God, he really was! It took every ounce of willpower he possessed not to drag her close, to pour out all the anger and hurt dammed up inside. But to tell her about Lorelei—about everything—would open up his soul to her, and that was something he just couldn't do. She would scorn him, shun him, treat him like the scum he was.

And he couldn't stand to see the condemnation in her face.

"Why the hell should I? You're no different than anyone else, Abby. You'll believe what you want to believe."

Never had he been so cold, so utterly inflexible. It was as if she could see him throwing up walls and barriers, anything he could to shut her out.

Something snapped inside Abby. She was furious that he would treat her so—and after she had given him what she had shared with no other man. Her body. Her heart . . .

Pure rage fringed her vision. "I can't believe I ever let you touch me—I must have been out of

my mind!" She was screaming, her voice thick with
the threat of tears that lay just beneath the surface. "I hate the way you are! I hate your orders,
your demands. I hate the way you keep trying to
scare me! Do you hear me, Kane? I hate you!"
She launched herself at him, hands raised wildly,
fingers curved like talons.

She never touched him. From out of nowhere an
arm shot out, clamping about her waist and lifting
her clear off her feet, hauling her back against a
sweaty male chest. There was a burst of ribald
laughter.

"What's the matter, old man? Lost your touch
with the ladies?"

Sam! Abby went wild then, kicking, struggling,
trying in vain to pry his forearms from beneath
her breasts. Blindly she slammed her head back; it
hurt but she felt his head snap. That vise-like arm
around her waist tightened so that the breath was
driven from her lungs in a soundless *whoosh*. She
gasped, the world going black around the edges.
Her body went limp. Her struggles ceased. The
pressure eased and she hauled in a stinging lungful
of air.

"Let her go, Sam."

Her feet dangling helplessly, Abby swallowed,
her gaze riveted on Kane. All his attention was
focused on Sam. His voice was as flat and emotionless as his eyes. His features might have been
hewn of granite.

Sam was undaunted. "Looks to me like the lady's
a little too much for you."

"I like a challenge as much as the next man,"
Kane stated flatly. "Now let her go, Sam."

Abby's feet touched the ground, but Sam didn't release her. When she would have wrenched away, his other arm came around her as well. Hot breath rushed past her cheek. "But the question is . . . you still got what it takes to break a skittish mare? It sure seems like the lady don't like you too well." He laughed, a sound that curdled Abby's blood. "Me, I like a woman all feisty and pepper-hot."

Kane's eyes flickered. "She's mine," he said with deadly quiet. "I made that clear from the start."

Sam made a sound of disgust. He gave her a none-too-gentle shove. Abby landed on her hands and knees in the dirt. Tiny stones ground into her hands but she paid no heed.

Sam eyed her lustfully. "Tell you what—" He sounded almost reasonable. "—I'll take the lady off your hands right now. You can have her back at midnight. It wouldn't be the first time we've shared a woman for the night." Abby pushed herself back on her haunches in time to see his leering gaze rake over her. "Why, the way she had her hands all over you last night had me hotter than a poker—and just about as hard, too. I'll keep her hands full, yes indeed."

His hand cupped his groin. He added something so blatantly obscene Abby could never have repeated it—even in her own mind.

Later she would wonder how a man could move so fast. There was a whirl of movement, a flash of light. The next thing she knew Kane stood behind Sam, his elbow locked around his neck; the flat of a gleaming knife lay drawn across Sam's whiskered throat. Sam stood frozen, his eyes bulging. He was as stunned as Abby.

"You know I don't much care for your mouth," Kane said quietly, almost silkily. "Did I ever tell you that, Sam?"

"You were never much for talking, Kane." Sam's voice came out a raspy whisper. "Hey, I was just having a little fun . . . The girl's all yours, I swear. I won't lay a hand on her—hell, I won't even look at her!"

Abby couldn't move. She recalled Kane's cold-blooded efficiency the night he'd killed Jake. His expression was much the same. His eyes were thunderhead-gray, cold and merciless.

"You don't have much of a reputation for keeping your word, Sam. Maybe I ought to just kill you now and be done with it."

Sam swallowed—a mistake. A thin trickle of blood appeared on the razor-sharp edge of the knife.

Abby made a faint, strangled sound.

Kane's gaze flickered to Abby. She was back on her haunches, her face bloodless, the fright and horror she felt at his violence stark and vivid. Every muscle in his body was rigid with the effort it took not to kill Sam then and there—the urge was so overpowering he could almost taste it. Yet how could he with Abby not three feet away? She already thought he was an animal. She would hate him forever.

Christ, who was he trying to fool? She hated him already . . .

He ground his teeth in frustrated rage. Sam didn't deserve to live. Yet he couldn't kill him, not before Abby, not the way he deserved to die. But it wouldn't hurt the bastard to do a little sweating for once.

"What do you say, Sam? A quick, neat slice would make it easy on both of us." Deliberately he paused. "On the other hand, you've made more than a few souls suffer on their way to the hereafter. Maybe it's time you got just a little taste of how they felt."

Sam was pale. "Don't get hasty now, Kane. Remember that little job we agreed you'd take care of? If you kill me now, you'll never get paid that hefty little fee we agreed on."

There was a long, drawn-out silence before Kane spoke, his tone lazy. "Double it and I might consider it."

"I'll triple it. Cash on the spot, as soon as it's done!"

A heartbeat went by. Then another and another. Kane slowly drew the knife away from Sam's throat. "You got yourself a deal, Sam." He retreated, alert for any threat the other man might pose. Sam stepped forward, his movements jerky.

"Think I'll take a last look around before we head down into the valley." He spun around and walked away, but not before Kane glimpsed the venomous rage in his eyes. Kane's mouth thinned. *Great!* he thought, crossing to Abby. *I should have killed him. Now I'm going to have to watch my back twice as hard.*

He frowned as he reached her. She still appeared dazed. "Are you all right?" He extended a hand to help her up.

She ignored it. She tipped back her head and regarded him with unblinking eyes. " 'That little job we agreed you'd take care of,' " she quoted. "What did he mean by that?"

The concern was gone. His face wore that closed,

forbidding expression she had come to recognize.

"He didn't mean anything," he said curtly.

"Don't lie to me," she whispered. A sick coil of dread was slowly strangling her insides. "He was talking about something—some*one*. And don't try to tell me he wasn't."

"Dammit, Abby—"

"It's Dillon, isn't it? He was talking about Dillon . . ." A numbing cold began to seep into her chest. She began to tremble. "What did he do? Ask you to kill Dillon?"

"Abby, keep your voice down—"

"He did, didn't he? He wants you to kill my brother!"

Kane went utterly still. He hated himself for putting that awful look on her face. He had no trouble reading her mind. She was calling herself every kind of fool for trusting him. He shoved his fingers through his hair. "Abby, you have to understand—"

"Oh, I understand, only too well! He offered you *money* to kill my brother . . . God, Kane, whose side are you on—"

He pulled her to her feet, gripping her shoulders. "Abby—"

With a jagged cry she tried to wrench away. "Don't touch me!"

"Dammit, will you just listen . . ."

He got no further. An ear-shattering explosion rent the air, followed by another, and then another like the echoing rumble of thunder.

Gunfire.

For a mind-splitting instant they stood paralyzed, staring into each other's faces. "Son of a bitch!"

The expletive accompanied the none-too-gentle motion of Kane's hand on her shoulder. She toppled heavily forward behind the weight of Kane's body. Stunned, she lay face-down behind the granite-faced boulder.

"Stay here!" he yelled in her ear. "And don't move until I get back!" He hunched down in a half-crouch and charged toward the sound of the bullets.

Fear encircled her heart. Abby had only one thought—Sam had found Dillon ... or Dillon had found Sam ...

There were shouts and footsteps—and the deadly staccato of gunfire came again. Sheer terror propelled her upright. She rushed forward, trailing Kane by a dozen steps. He disappeared around a jutting spur of rock. She followed blindly, only to be brought up short scant seconds later by the sight of two men scuffling, rolling wildly across the barren, dusty earth, one with hair as black as sin, the other with hair only a shade darker than her own ...

Dillon.

She had no recollection of screaming his name aloud. It was the culmination of her worst nightmare. She realized sickly that the gunfire had ceased. There was a rifle poking from the saddle of a horse—Dillon's strawberry roan. Sam staggered upright; Dillon surged forward just as Sam whirled. His knee came up and connected with Dillon's chest. Abby gave a garbled scream as he hurtled to his back.

Abby's skin was pure ice. She stood as if paralyzed. Horror stripped her mind of all thought. She could only watch and wait as Dillon struggled to his feet just as Sam ripped the rifle from its berth. His teeth pulled back in a feral grin, the rifle barrel swiveled slowly toward Dillon . . .

It all seemed to happen in slow motion. Another figure had appeared—Kane, his Colt raised high, sighting down the barrel . . . Her mind screamed out a warning . . . Dear Lord! . . . They stood only a foot apart . . . Did he aim at Dillon or Sam . . . ?

She sagged to her knees. The gun exploded. There was an answering shot—or was it only an echo? The very ground beneath her knees seemed to echo and vibrate; the acrid smell of smoke burned her throat and blurred her vision. When the haze cleared she saw Stringer Sam sprawled face-down in the dirt.

But so was Kane.

Chapter 15

H e lay on his side. Somehow she was on her knees next to him. Blood welled through the fabric of his shirt, thick and oozing. Alarm erupted inside her. She pressed her hands against his chest. Her fingertips came away crimson. "He's bleeding," she cried, feeling as if she were flying apart inside. She began to sob. "Oh, God, help him! He's bleeding!"

Suddenly Dillon was there, shouldering her aside. He ripped Kane's shirt apart, revealing a blackened hole in the flesh of his left shoulder, perilously near his heart. Bile rose to Abby's throat. She pressed ice-cold fingers to her mouth to keep from vomiting.

Dillon's expression was hard and intent. "Jesus," he breathed. "We've got to stop this bleeding . . ." He cursed. "Damn! There's no exit wound. The bullet's still in there."

Abby began to shake. Kane's eyes were closed, his lashes a dark crescent against skin that was white as a sheet. All she could think was that he looked just like Pa, in the very instant the Lord had taken him away.

"He's going to die," she moaned. "Oh, God, he's going to die and it's all my fault."

"Abby, there's a clean shirt in my saddlebag. Get

it—and hurry!" When Abby didn't move, he turned on her. Grabbing her shoulder, he shook her hard. "The nearest town is a four-hour ride from here," he told her sharply. "He'll be dead by the time we get him there. If he's going to live, you're going to have to help me!"

Somehow that penetrated Abby's daze. She listened intently to Dillon's low instructions, then scurried to obey. When she knelt down once more beside Dillon, Kane stirred at last. His lashes fluttered but didn't open. Abby laid her hand against his unshaven cheek. "Kane," she whispered. "It's okay. You'll be all right."

He gave a low moan. A spasm of pain twisted his lips.

Dillon uncapped the whiskey bottle she'd brought from his belongings. In his other hand was a small, vicious-looking knife with a curved tip; the blade gleamed silver in the sunlight.

"The bullet has to come out," Dillon said tersely.

Abby's jaw went slack. "Don't tell me you're going to take it out!"

"It's you or me," he said grimly, ripping the shirt into strips. "And I don't think you're in any shape to do it."

"But you're not a doctor!" she cried. "Dillon, how—"

"Abby, didn't you hear me?" He wound a swath of cloth into a small pad as he spoke. "We don't have any choice—there's no time to get him to a doctor. If there's any chance at all for him to make it, we have to do it *now*. I've seen it done a dozen times before—I'll just have to do the best I can."

Her stomach pitched violently as he began to wipe away the blood, then held the pad firm in an attempt to staunch the bleeding. She had helped out at the ranch a hundred times for different injuries. Normally she wasn't so squeamish. She fought the wild panic that surged within her, struggling for calm. Dillon was right. They had no choice if Kane had any chance at all of survival.

She smoothed her hands on her knees. "Just tell me what to do," she said levelly. *Lord*, she prayed, *don't let Kane die. Please, just help me through this— help him.*

When the bleeding had eased off, Dillon liberally doused the knife with the whiskey—and Kane's shoulder as well. Abby's eyes widened as he straddled Kane, sitting squarely atop his legs. Gripping the knife, he nodded at Kane's head.

"Try to hold him as still as you can," was all he said.

The knife descended. Abby tried hard not to look. As Dillon began to probe the wound with his knife, Kane's head jerked up off the ground. He let out his breath in a low, whistling sound that was almost a sob. Her lungs burning, Abby wanted to cry along with him. Instead she cleared her mind of all thought and concentrated on holding him still. The only way she could do that was to brace her knee on his good shoulder.

Dillon probed deeper. Kane's entire body convulsed. Abby thought fuzzily that he must have sensed what they were doing; although his arms and limbs went rigid as a stone pillar, he didn't try to fight them. His eyes squeezed shut. The tendons in his neck stood out. A sound that was inhuman ripped from his throat. Abby bit down so hard on her lip she tasted blood. She darted an anguished glance at his face. His flesh was colorless beneath his tan, stretched taut across sharply jutting cheekbones. His lips were contorted in pain. Then, mercifully, she felt his body go limp. He lost consciousness.

That made it easier—at least for Dillon. He gave a triumphant whoop as he extracted the bullet and gave it a toss. By then silent tears streaked Abby's cheeks. She wiped them away as Dillon began to carefully bandage Kane's shoulder with the strips from his shirt.

Finally he rocked back on his heels, wiping away the beads of sweat that dotted his upper lip. He glanced over at her and flashed a crooked grin. "We did it." He rubbed his jaw, frowning suddenly. "Christ, who is he anyway?"

Abby took a deep breath. Her fingers curled unconsciously around Kane's hand where it rested on his chest. "His name is Kane," she whispered. Softer still, she added, "He used to ride with Stringer Sam's gang."

"Stringer Sam!" Dillon leaped to his feet. "What the hell—! Did the bastard kidnap you?"

Her gaze slid to Kane. She shook her head. The merest hint of a smile crossed her lips. "It wasn't like that at all, Dillon. In fact, you might say it was the other way around . . ."

Her smile withered. She swallowed convulsively. "Dillon," she whispered. "Pa's dead . . ."

Later Abby reflected it was the longest night of her life. She wept in Dillon's arms as she told him how Stringer Sam had killed Pa and was hot on his trail. But his lips were thin with disapproval by the time she'd finished.

"An outlaw, Abby! Didn't you realize what he might have done? He could have killed you! What the hell made you think you could trust a man like that?"

"At first I wasn't sure I could," she admitted. "But Kane isn't—well, he's not evil, not in the sense that Sam was evil." She shivered. "You had only to look at Sam and know he was a horrible man."

She paused, staring out where dusk gathered along the horizon, pink and amber and glorious. "Kane said he wasn't a wanted man in this territory," she said quietly. "I don't know why he's wanted by the law elsewhere—maybe he's a horse thief, or a bank robber—I don't know. But whatever it is, I—I have this feeling it weighs on his conscience—that he regrets it. He saved me from those awful men, Chester and Jake. And he killed Sam—my God, Dillon, you'd be dead if it weren't for him! As far as I'm concerned, he deserves another chance." She met her brother's gaze, her own anxious. "I promised him you wouldn't put him in jail. You won't, will you?"

Dillon's eyes narrowed. There was something in her tone he couldn't quite place . . . He glanced from the man lying prone near the fire back to his sister. "You don't have any doubts about him, do you?" he said slowly.

"I trusted him with my life," she said quietly. "And I trusted him with *yours*."

Dillon hesitated. Abby wasn't flighty and frivolous, like some women. She had a good head on her shoulders. She wasn't one to place her faith lightly in someone else . . .

He sighed. "I can't very well jail a man who saved my life. That sure as hell would weigh on *my* conscience."

A rush of relief so intense it was almost painful swept through her. Abby kissed his cheek, then checked on Kane, who had yet to regain consciousness. Though she wanted desperately to curl up beside him, she didn't dare—their physical relationship was the one thing she hadn't shared with Dillon. She shook out her bedroll near the fire and soon fell into an exhausted sleep.

Dillon left at dawn to ride into town to notify the authorities of Stringer Sam's death. Kane still hadn't roused, and Abby was beginning to get worried. Mid-morning she set a pot of coffee on to boil. When she straightened, she discovered Kane's eyes trained on her.

His gaze was bleary and pain-filled. She rushed to his side, dropping to her knees beside him.

"Jesus," he muttered, "it feels like somebody stuck a branding iron into my shoulder. What the hell happened?"

"Stringer Sam and Dillon were struggling. Dillon got knocked to the ground. Stringer Sam grabbed Dillon's rifle and turned it on Dillon. You shot Sam, but then he turned the rifle on you."

"I remember now." Kane's eyes half-closed. He winced as he tried to move his shoulder. "Did the bullet go clean through?"

"No. Dillon . . . He took it out." Just thinking about it made Abby shiver all over again.

It was a moment before Kane spoke again. "I take it Sam's dead."

"Dillon buried him yesterday evening," she said quietly. "He rode into town to send a telegraph to the territorial sheriff and bring a doctor back to look at you."

He grimaced. "Don't need a doctor if the bullet's out." He tried to prop himself on his elbow to raise himself up. Beads of sweat popped out on his brow.

Her hand against his good shoulder, Abby pressed him back. "Oh, no you don't," she admonished firmly. "You're in no condition to get up just yet."

He didn't argue; that alone was testimony to his weakened state. Abby wet a handkerchief with water from her canteen, then returned to bathe his brow. She frowned—he was so warm!

She ran the cloth down the tendons of his neck. "You were lucky." She hesitated, her voice very low. "It scared the life out of me when I saw you lying there. I—I thought you were dead."

His eyes opened to stare directly into hers. "I may be yet when your brother finds out who I am."

Abby returned his gaze steadily. "He already knows—" A hint of a smile curved her lips. "—though he didn't until *after* we dug the bullet out."

"Jesus," Kane muttered. "I'm surprised he didn't push me in alongside Sam then."

Abby's lips firmed. "I told you he won't put you in jail—and he won't. Even if he wanted to, I wouldn't let him."

Another time, and Kane might have voiced his skepticism. As it was, he was simply too damn tired to care right now . . .

Abby watched as he drifted off to sleep once more. He woke again near noonday. She managed to get him to eat some of the beans she'd fixed, but he hadn't finished more than half before he'd dropped off again. She hovered near his side until Dillon returned early that evening. A stab of dismay shot through her as she saw he was alone.

"Where's the doctor? Why isn't he with you?"

Dillon dropped to the ground. He rubbed his hand across his forehead with a grimace. "He wasn't due back until tomorrow morning. His wife gave me some bandages, and some salve that's supposed to help it heal. She said to watch for redness and a green discharge—said that's what you don't want to see."

Abby looked ready to cry. Dillon patted her shoulder awkwardly. "Look, she said if he made it through the first day, likelier than not he'll make it through okay."

Abby didn't argue—she couldn't bear to think that Kane might die. He roused when she changed his bandage and spread the pungent salve on the wound; he ate and then slept once more. Her fears eased somewhat when he awoke the next morning looking a little less haggard. He sat up to eat, refusing any help from her or Dillon.

When he'd finished, Abby took his plate, then excused herself to go wash up in the stream. Dillon poured a cup of coffee; wordlessly he handed it to Kane.

Unsure what to expect from the other man, Kane watched Dillon resume his place on the other side of the fire. Every sore, aching muscle in his body was on guard.

"Abby tells me you used to ride with Stringer Sam."

Kane braced himself and met the other man's gaze. Surprisingly, he discerned neither accusation nor condemnation. But the unwavering directness he read in Dillon's eyes made him only slightly less uneasy.

A faint red flush crept into his cheekbones. "I won't lie to you," he said shortly. "I was framed for something I didn't do. I ran and eventually hooked up with Sam. I rode with him for almost a year. We parted company six months ago."

Dillon rested his forearm across his knees. "Mind telling me why you left?"

"I did what I had to do to stay alive," Kane said evenly. "Sam would just as soon kill a man as look him in the eye. But his way wasn't mine. I got out before I got dragged down any further."

Dillon's ice-blue eyes never strayed from Kane's features. There was no doubt that Kane could be a dangerous man—hard, maybe even cold. But that very same instinct told him it was just as Abby believed—Kane wasn't evil, not in the way that Sam had been.

"Abby said you're not a wanted man in this territory. Is that true?"

"Don't ask me why. Maybe because we spent a lot of time in the Dakotas. Or maybe because every lawman this side of the Mississippi was itching to get his hands on Sam." Kane gave a harsh laugh. "God knows I'm sure as hell not lucky."

"Oh, but I think you are." Dillon's tone was matter-of-fact. "There's a sizable reward out for Stringer Sam. You're entitled to it. But I'm afraid you'll have to make the trip to Laramie to get it."

Kane's lips pulled back over his teeth. "What! Collect a reward so you can throw my hide in jail? Thanks, Marshal, but I'd like to stick around a few more years."

Dillon didn't bat an eyelash. "I promised Abby I wouldn't do that, and by God, I won't. You took care of my sister and you saved my life. I'm willing to turn a blind eye to whatever happened in the past. But you cross the line in the future, now that's another story."

Kane pushed aside a niggling pang of shame. Did he dare tell him there was a warrant out for his arrest in New Mexico—that he'd escaped from jail? He'd been stunned when Abby told him it was Dillon who had removed the bullet from his shoulder. It might be that Abby's brother was a decent sort, even though he was a lawman—it might be that he wasn't. Kane decided it might be wise to reserve judgment for a while. As for going back to Laramie with them, well, that was where this whole thing had started. He might as well return there as anywhere.

That he would soon be saying good-bye to Abby was something he refused to think about.

The next morning he pronounced himself well enough to travel. Abby vented her disapproval as he voiced his intention. He paid no heed, but struggled to his feet with a grimace, shunning both her help and Dillon's.

They headed out an hour later; Abby rode behind Dillon. It was almost noon before they reached the nearest town. Abby suppressed a wry smile as they rode down Main Street. They were a rather disreputable-looking trio, she reflected. The two men were rough and unshaven, distinctly on the unsavory side. Her own appearance was no better. She was covered with dust from head to toe. Her clothes were wrinkled and filthy; they looked like she'd slept in them, which she had, for more nights than she cared to remember.

Dillon insisted they take the stage back to Laramie. Abby was heartily relieved. She hadn't been looking forward to the long ride home, nor was she certain Kane was in any shape to handle it. She held her breath when Dillon made the announcement. She half-expected Kane to argue. She was secretly relieved when he didn't.

Unfortunately, the nearest stage line was another four hours away. It was early evening when they stood on the platform, waiting for the stage to arrive. Dillon had moved away to check on the horses.

At noon, she and Dillon had rigged up a sling to restrict the movement of Kane's shoulder. Abby had argued that he should see the doctor before they departed, but Kane curtly declined.

Now she approached him once more. "The stage won't be here for nearly an hour. There's plenty of time to get that wound dressed properly."

He didn't bother to look at her. "It's fine, Abby."

Her chin came up a notch. "It's hardly a pretty sight, Kane, and I'd say it's far from healed," she said sharply. "In fact, it probably still hurts like the very devil. A doctor could probably give you something to ease the pain, too."

One corner of his mouth curled up. "Consider it penance for my many sins."

Abby's jaw clamped tight. The man was impossible!

Abby settled herself next to Dillon in the stagecoach, while Kane took the seat across from them. They were the only passengers. The hours slid by, one into another. A deep purple haze of twilight draped the earth. Beside her, Dillon was quiet and subdued.

Disturbed by his mood, Abby touched his sleeve. "What's wrong?" she asked quietly.

Dillon remained silent. Abby twisted slightly on the seat, straining to see him. His profile was stark and barren, his eyes bleak.

"I—I thought you'd be glad that Stringer Sam is dead." She spoke tentatively. "Dillon, he'll never hurt anyone again."

At last he spoke. "You're right. He'll never lay a hand on anyone again. But it's too goddamned late for Rose, isn't it?"

Rose. Abby caught her breath. Oh, but she should have known ... Since Rose had died, Dillon had been so—so different. There were times—times like now—when she glimpsed a brooding hardness that hadn't been there before. Abby hated feeling so helpless, but Dillon wouldn't even try to let her help.

"I know it hurts to think about it," Abby said softly. "But Rose is gone. Stringer Sam is dead. Dillon, it's over."

But it wasn't, Dillon thought blackly. Because while the world had rid itself of one less piece of scum, there was still one left ... And the memory of Rose wouldn't rest easy until that man lay cold in his grave, as cold as Stringer Sam.

"Dillon—" Abby probed as gently as she could. "—maybe it would help if you would just talk about it."

The line of his lips hardened. There was so much Abby didn't know. But he couldn't. Not now. Maybe not ever.

He thrust his hands through unruly dark-gold hair. "What do you want me to say, Abby? My God, Pa's dead! And I keep thinking that if I hadn't gone after Sam, Pa would still be alive."

"And *you* might be the one dead," she reminded him. "It was you Stringer Sam came to the ranch to kill."

He stared down at his hands. "I don't know if I'll ever forgive myself," he said, his voice so low and so raw she hurt inside. Her chest ached; she knew Dillon felt responsible for Pa's death—maybe even Rose's death—in much the same way that she felt responsible for Kane being shot.

Her gaze slid fleetingly to Kane. His head was tilted back against the seat, and his eyes were closed. He looked a little uncomfortable, his long limbs folded between the narrow seats, but she sensed he was asleep.

Her hand slid out to cover Dillon's. She was very much afraid nothing she could say would ease his guilt. Only the passage of time could dull the hurt he felt right now, but she had to try. Swallowing the lump in her throat, she offered the only reassurance she could and prayed it was enough.

"Pa loved you, Dillon. You had a job to do. Pa understood that—and he was proud of you! I'm sure that wherever he is now, he doesn't blame you. You're safe, and that's all that matters." She squeezed his fingers. "I think Pa would agree, don't you?"

He sighed. "How did you get so smart, little sister?"

"I guess I take after my big brother," she said with a watery smile.

Abby was glad to note that although his mood remained somber, some of the bleakness had left his features. She pillowed her head against his shoulder and let the rocking rhythm of the stage lull her to sleep.

She didn't know that Kane wasn't asleep at all. His shoulder throbbed like hell. He felt extremely awkward eavesdropping at such a moment. Oh, he'd tried not to listen, but his hearing was just a little too keen at times. He'd heard every word the pair spoke; he'd seen her misty, tender smile, a smile she had yet to bestow on him. And try though he might, he couldn't vanquish the burning in his veins. He envied their closeness. He envied Dillon for being the recipient of such obvious love and adoration.

He jammed his hat down over his forehead, thoroughly disgusted with himself. Jesus, if that didn't beat all—he was jealous of her brother!

It was two mornings later when the stage pulled into Laramie. Dillon nudged Abby awake. She straightened, whisking stray wisps of hair from her cheeks and behind her ears as her eyes went straight to Kane. He was stirring as well. Abby tried to cover her anxiety as they disembarked from the stagecoach.

Kane looked awful, his eyes bloodshot and

rimmed by fatigue. But he seemed steady enough as he stepped from the coach. Dillon had rounded the wheel to retrieve their horses. Abby gnawed her lip uncertainly. Was Kane merely tired? It had been a long, exhausting trip for all of them. She hoped that's all it was, but it wouldn't hurt for him to see a doctor.

She slipped her fingers into the crook of his elbow so that he was forced to halt. "We have an excellent doctor in town—Dr. Foley. In fact, his office is right around the corner—"

He squared off to face her. "How many times do I have to tell you?" His jaw was set stubbornly. "I'm fine, just fine!"

Dillon stepped back into sight. He tossed a coin to the boy who led Midnight and his roan away from the coach, then turned to Kane. "Let's head on over to my office and we'll get you squared away." This time Kane didn't argue. His head was pounding and it required all his concentration just to put one foot in front of the other.

A cheerful whistle greeted them at the marshal's office. There was a young man in his early twenties behind the desk, Doug Avery, his feet propped jauntily on the desktop. The chair came down with a thud as he recognized Dillon. He popped up like a jackrabbit.

"Marshal!" A grin appeared from ear to ear. "We didn't expect you back until late this afternoon. The whole town's been abuzzin' like a nest of bees since we got your telegram the other day—to think you was the one who finally rid the countryside of that vermin Stringer Sam! Heard he was damn good with a gun—but you proved he wasn't near as good as you." He beamed and grinned again.

"I'm afraid I don't deserve much of the credit," Dillon said calmly. "If it weren't for our friend here, I might be lying six feet under instead of Stringer Sam." He inclined his head toward Kane, who had eased into the nearest chair.

Doug took in Kane's unsmiling countenance, gulping when he recognized him. "You mean he . . ." His mouth opened and closed. "Well, I'll be damned," he finished weakly.

"Do me a favor, Doug." Dillon scribbled something on a piece of paper. "Go over and see Mr. Percy at the bank. Kane here's anxious to claim his reward."

Doug was out the door in a flash. Abby nearly groaned. The tale about Kane would be all over town before Doug ever reached the bank.

The three of them were alone once more. Abby moved to whisper something in Dillon's ear. When Abby stepped back he cleared his throat. "It seems I also owe you for helping Abby track me down. It took a good piece of your time—is four hundred dollars agreeable?"

Kane's head came up slowly. The reward for Stringer Sam was one thing; taking money from Abby and her brother was another.

"I didn't come to Laramie for a handout," he said stingingly.

"It's hardly a handout," Dillon said evenly. "My sister hired you to find me. It's payment for services rendered, no more, no less."

Kane had trouble meeting the other man's direct gaze. He had the feeling Dillon wouldn't be so generous if he knew what he'd done with his sister.

Dillon glanced at Abby, who gave an encouraging nod. "In fact," he went on rather stiffly, "Abby and I have talked it over. We'd like you to stay at the Diamondback until you're fully recovered."

Kane lumbered heavily to his feet. He looked from one to the other. He couldn't believe he was about to turn down cold hard cash. He'd never been noble before—why now? But he didn't need anyone's pity, especially not theirs.

His lip curled. "You think I don't know the only reason you're even making that offer is because I saved your life? Hell, everybody in the household would probably run screaming out the door if they thought an outlaw like me intended to sleep under your roof. You dug that bullet out of my shoulder and as far as I'm concerned, that makes us even."

Dillon's eyes glinted. "Anybody ever tell you you've got a chip on your shoulder, fella?" He laughed grittily when Kane bristled. "Well, I don't suppose there's any use telling you you've got a job waiting at the ranch whenever you want it."

"You sure as hell got that right. I told you, I don't need any charity from the likes of you two."

Dillon's spine went ramrod-straight. His eyes narrowed dangerously.

Before he could say anything, Abby stepped between them. "Dillon, please." The seething tension that flared between the two men had her holding her breath, afraid of what might happen next. She struggled for a calm she wasn't at all sure she could muster. "Do you mind if I have a word with Kane?"

"Not at all." He hitched his thumbs into his belt. He didn't move.

Abby sighed. "Alone," she said pointedly.

Dillon scowled. She could see he wasn't certain he liked the idea, but she refused to back down. "All right," he relented finally. "I'll get things squared away with the bank on that reward."

The door slammed shut. Abby wasted no time but immediately whirled on Kane. "Dillon was right," she said hotly. "You do have a chip on your shoulder."

"You think I should take that four hundred dollars, don't you." It was a statement, not a question.

"Of course I do. You earned it."

"Well, well. You just can't wait to be rid of me, can you?"

She wanted to scream in vexation. "That's not it at all!"

He ran a hand over his unshaven chin and pretended to ponder. "What then? Wait—let me guess! If I take that four hundred dollars, then I guess that makes me greedy and selfish. But if I refuse it, then that makes me a damn fool, doesn't it?"

"You're a fool, all right—a fool not to take what you're owed!"

"What I'm owed!" His insolent gaze swept to her breasts and belly, burning through the layers of clothing, stripping her naked. "Sugar, you're forgetting one thing," he sneered. "I've already been paid in full!"

His implication was clear. Abby flinched as if she'd been struck. He looked like death warmed over, but he was as arrogant as ever—and his tongue cut as deeply as ever. He might as well have called her á—a whore!

She welcomed the biting anger that rose, fast and furious.

"You know, you're right, Kane. Don't take that money. Go out and rob a bank instead—you'll certainly get a whole lot more!"

"Fine!" he shouted, already marching toward the door. "Maybe that's exactly what I'll do!"

"Good!" she taunted, trailing behind him. "See if I care! See if anyone cares—"

She broke off. He'd stepped outside onto the sun-bleached planks of the sidewalk. But something was wrong. His posture was no longer arrogant. His gait was stiff and wooden-legged . . .

Kane passed a hand before his eyes. What the hell was going on? It was no longer sunny and bright outside. There was fog swirling all around. He could hear Abby, her voice rising, then fading; it was eclipsed by a dull roaring in his ears. Abby's face flashed before him, then receded.

"Kane?" His eyes were dull and unfocused. *"Kane!"*

His knees began to buckle.

Abby did the only thing she could. She propped her shoulder beneath his and slid her arms around his waist. He leaned heavily. Her back bowed. She staggered beneath his weight.

Dillon had just emerged from the bank. "Dillon!" she screamed. He spotted her and broke into a dead run.

He reached her just as Kane collapsed.

Chapter 16

"Y ou say you traveled from near Buffalo?" Dr. Foley shook his head. "It really is a miracle he made it so far. He must have the strength of an ox."

They were in Dillon's old room at the Diamondback, where they'd brought Kane after he lost consciousness. The wound in Kane's shoulder had reopened. When Dr. Foley peeled away the blood-soaked bandage, Abby took one look and nearly fainted. Clumps of crusted blood mingled with fresh blood and oozed freely from the place where Dillon had gouged the bullet from his shoulder. The entire front of his shoulder was purpled and bruised, but the flesh all around the bullet hole was fiery red.

Dr. Foley muttered under his breath as he blotted away the blood. "From the looks of it, he's been bleeding a while off and on. It really should have been sutured . . ."

"We did the best we could," Abby defended both herself and Dillon weakly. "But we were four hours from the nearest town . . . Dillon rode in to try to get the doctor to come back with us but he was gone . . . When we caught the stage, I tried to get him to see the doctor but he just wouldn't go . . ."

"Oh, I'm not blaming either you or Dillon, dear.

Without the two of you, why, the man might already be dead! But I think the trip here was more than his body could handle. He really should have sought medical attention as soon as possible."

Her arms hugging her middle, Abby looked on from the rear of the room as he cleaned and stitched the wound to keep it from tearing open again. Dorothy stood just behind him, assisting when needed. By the time the basin on the bedside table was filled with bloodied rags, Abby was holding her stomach to keep from retching.

All the sick fear she'd felt when Kane had first been shot had come hurtling back. "He won't die, will he?" She forced the question through blood-less lips.

Dr. Foley straightened and wiped his hands on the towel Dorothy handed him. "I don't think he's in any imminent danger, unless infection sets in. I'll leave medicine that should help prevent that. What concerns me right now is his loss of blood—his weakened state won't help his recovery. I suspect it's going to take quite some time before he regains his strength."

Abby's tone was anxious. "Shouldn't he be awake by now? He's been unconscious an awfully long time." All through Dr. Foley's ministrations, Kane hadn't roused even once. Abby couldn't help wor-rying—it disturbed her.

"He's in much less pain this way. Sleep is nature's way of healing the body. Let him rest while he can. He'll likely wake up thornier than a cactus."

Both women listened carefully to his instruc-tions. He left laudanum and medicine on the bed-side table. Abby escorted him to the front door.

"Don't be afraid to send for me if his condition worsens. You know where to find me."

"I will, I promise." Abby nodded her thanks.

He pinched her cheeks. "You look like I could knock you over with a feather, young lady. You need a good night's rest as much as your young man in there. See that you get it, all right?"

Abby nodded. It wasn't until much later that she realized Dr. Foley had called Kane "her young man." If she hadn't been so tired, she might have smiled.

She hurried back to Kane's room. Dorothy was pulling a crisp white sheet up over his chest. The very sight of him sent a shaft of fear through her. Was it her imagination, or was his skin only a shade darker than the bleached muslin sheet?

She pushed a small wing chair toward the bedside. Dorothy hurried to help her. When they were finished, Abby straightened, brows raised quizzically. "There's no need for you to stay, Dorothy," she said with a faint shake of her head. "I'll sit with him."

For a moment Dorothy said nothing. Abby's frenzied distress when they'd carried Kane inside had given her a bit of a shock—it didn't take long before the reason became very clear. Abby had never been one to hide her feelings; her eyes gave her away every time. Dorothy laid her hand on Abby's shoulder. "Just give a holler if you need me."

Abby nodded. Her gaze didn't waver from Kane.

Outside the sky shone brilliant and blue. A noisy bluejay scolded his mate. A restless wind whipped through the gnarled oak tree outside, rustling branches and whipping leaves. Her mind wiped clean of all but the man before her, Abby's hand crept atop his where it lay on the sheet.

It seemed odd to see him so silent and listless, his powerful muscles dormant and still. She'd have gladly endured his rancorous taunts, if only this hadn't happened—if only he were safe and unharmed!

She brushed a sweat-dampened lock of hair from his forehead. "I told you you should have seen a doctor," she whispered. "But you wouldn't listen, would you?" Men, she thought, half-angry, half-despairing. Why were they always so convinced they knew best? Why did they think they had to be forever tough and strong? Why did they think it shameful to show any sign of weakness, no matter how small?

So much had happened, she thought helplessly. And now this! A piercing stab of guilt rent her breast. If he'd only suffered a flesh wound, she wouldn't have been so worried. But what if he *died*? The thought was like a knife twisting over and over inside her. Oh, this was all her fault! She should never have involved Kane. She'd had no business dragging him into her troubles, let alone the kind of danger he'd had to face.

Her hand crept into his. She weaved her fingers between his and squeezed, as if to impart her life's vigor into his. Minutes sneaked into hours. Dorothy tiptoed in with a tray for dinner, but Abby could scarcely eat a bite. By the time evening dimmed the horizon she could hardly keep her eyes open. Still, she couldn't bring herself to leave him. She dozed; a firm hand at her shoulder woke her.

Hands on her hips, Dorothy glowered down at her. "When was the last time you had a good night's sleep?"

Abby gave her a lopsided smile. "Do you know, I can't even remember?"

"Then it's been a durn sight too long," Dorothy said sternly. "Scoot now. I've got your nightie all laid out and the covers turned back."

"I can't. What if he wakes up? What if he doesn't remember where he is, or—or what happened?" She pushed a hand through her tangled hair. How could she explain? "I don't want him to be alone," she said finally.

"And he won't be." Dorothy pointed to the rocking chair in the corner. "I'll be sitting right there, catching up on my knitting. If he wakes up, I'll give a yell that'll surely wake the boys in the bunkhouse."

A current of understanding passed between them. Abby rose and gave Dorothy a hug. "Thank you," she whispered.

In her room she dropped her stained, filthy clothes in a pile and tugged her plain cotton nightgown over her head. She crawled between sheets that smelled of sunshine and fresh air and bit back a groan. Her bed felt heavenly, comfortably soft and cozy. But she knew she'd never sleep a wink, not in a million years . . . That was her last thought.

She didn't wake until almost noon the next day. She washed hurriedly and changed into a clean blouse and skirt. She didn't take the time to braid her hair but left it loose over her shoulders. She hurried from her room, anxious to see how Kane had weathered the night.

Dorothy was in the midst of changing his bandage. Abby's stomach lurched at the sight of his swollen, raised flesh, crisscrossed with ugly black stitches. While the wound didn't look any better, neither did it appear worse.

She moved to the bedside. "How is he?"

Dorothy's expression was somber. "Dr. Foley came early this morning. Said he's doing about the same. But he's been a little restless this morning." Abby laid a cool hand on his forehead. She frowned. He seemed rather warm.

That wasn't the case by late afternoon. His temperature shot up. His skin was dry and burning. He started to thrash from side to side, moaning and tossing his limbs.

"Kane—" She half-sat on the edge of the mattress and pressed her hand against his good shoulder, trying to quiet him. His features were flushed and contorted, his body rigid and unyielding. With a snarl and a mighty sweep of his arm he sent her tumbling to the floor. Stunned but unhurt, Abby scrambled to her feet. If he kept this up, he would tear open his wound once again. She had to get him quiet! Racing to the door, she screamed for Dorothy.

It took Dorothy, Lucas and Grady, one of the ranch hands, to hold him while Abby tipped a glass of water laced with laudanum to his lips. It seemed to take forever before he swallowed what she hoped was enough. With a nod she dismissed the others.

It wasn't long before the laudanum took effect. Abby poured fresh, cool water into a basin and carried it to the bedside table. There she wet the cloth and bathed his face and throat. Wetting it again, she dragged it slowly across his chest and arms. Over and over again she repeated the movement, seeking to cool his feverish skin. Her quiet murmuring soothed him. The tension constricting his muscles loosened.

She bathed him until she was certain her arms would fall out of their sockets. Dorothy relieved her for a short while, and then she was at it again. It was nightfall before his flesh seemed cooler, his color more natural.

Her shoulders sagged with relief. She laid her fingers against the raspy hardness of his cheek and smiled. "Thank heaven," she said aloud.

It gave her a start when she realized his eyes were open, his stare wide and unblinking. Before she knew what he was about he'd clamped his hands around her wrists and dragged her close. Their eyes locked. It was as if he were seeing her for the very first time.

"Lorelei?" he whispered.

"No, Kane." She was half-afraid to speak. "I'm Abby, remember? Abby!"

He paid no heed. In the blink of an eye his expression changed to one of sheer disbelief. The hair on the back of Abby's neck prickled eerily. He stared at her, but clearly he saw someone else.

The grip on her wrists tightened painfully. "It can't be," he said hoarsely. "It can't be . . ." The muscles in his throat worked rhythmically. "Did you know they're going to hang me?" His tone grew frantic. "They're going to hang me . . ."

He released her. "No!" he cried. "You can't do this! Lorelei . . . I loved her . . . Don't you know I loved her? You can't do this . . . I don't want to die . . ."

Scalding tears slid down her cheeks. She cradled his face between her palms. "Hush," she said raggedly.

"Don't let them hang me." His eyes were wild

and glazed and pleading. "Please don't let them hang me." He threw an arm across his face. Dry, racking sobs tore from his throat.

Abby closed her eyes, as if to drown out the sound of his torment, the tightness in her chest nearly unbearable. She wrapped her arms around him and clung, willing away the tremors that racked his body. But even as her heart went out to him, a bone-deep despair crept over her.

Lorelei, whoever she was, was someone Kane had once loved deeply . . . For the life of her, Abby didn't know why the knowledge hurt so much.

But it did. God help her, it did.

It was a faint tugging on her scalp that wakened her. Rousing slowly, Abby realized she must have dozed. She raised her head and spied darkly tanned fingers inching through the wild tangle of her hair where it lay on the mattress.

She sat up. Kane was awake and watching her, his eyes shadowed but clear. With his fingertips he skimmed the dampness from her cheek. Although he was foggy and dazed, his heart contracted. Tears? For him?

Abby pressed a hand to her cheeks. Her eyes were scratchy and swollen. No doubt her face was blotchy and red. She felt suddenly shy and awkward. "I must look a fright."

His gaze was moving hungrily over her features—or did she only imagine the hunger? But she knew she didn't imagine his mumbled "You look beautiful."

There was a huskiness to his voice that had never been there before. Abby thrilled to it.

"Are you hungry? Dorothy fixed hot broth, in case you woke up—" She broke off at the mute question in his gaze. "Dorothy's the housekeeper. We brought you here to the Diamondback after you passed out. Do you remember?"

He grimaced, shifting a little. Pain like a white-hot brand shot through his shoulder. "I remember the ground coming up at me and that's about it." His voice was low and hoarse.

"The wound in your shoulder reopened. Dr. Foley said it was a wonder you made it this far. He cleaned it and sewed it closed so it wouldn't tear again." She wet her lips. "You must be hungry," she said again.

He shook his head. "Thirsty more than hungry."

Abby poured a glass full of cool water from the pitcher across the room. She sat on the bed and slipped an arm around his shoulders, levering his head up and touching the glass to his fever-parched lips. He drank thirstily, swallowing almost the entire contents of the glass. His head fell back upon the pillow. Abby half-rose, intending to set aside the glass.

Kane turned his head. He blinked at her, his eyes bleary. "Don't go," he mumbled.

Abby sank back down. His hand groped across the blanket, blindly searching. She clasped his palm between both of hers. With a sound that was half-laugh, half-sob, she rubbed her cheek across his knuckles.

She stayed by his side the night through. Dorothy crept in at dawn's first light. Kane was sleeping peacefully, as he had most of the night. Dorothy shooed Abby to her room to lay down. Abby didn't argue; her shoulders drooped with fatigue.

It was late morning when she awoke. She washed quickly and changed into a gaily patterned blue skirt and a white blouse. She was still braiding her hair when she stepped into Kane's room. Dr. Foley was there, bending over Kane, wrapping a new bandage around his shoulder. Dorothy stood nearby.

She entered with a rustle of skirts. "How is he?"

"Better than I expected," Dr. Foley said, smiling cheerfully, "especially since Dorothy tells me he had quite a fever yesterday. I'd say his temperature is just about back to normal, and his color is good." He winked at her. "Anytime you'd like a job as a nurse, you just let me know."

He turned back to Kane. "You can have broth today, solid food tomorrow. I'll stop by and take those stitches out in a week. By then you'll be good as new. Just don't take it in your head to get too frisky on these two ladies. You can get up and take a turn around the room this evening, but no further." He started toward the door, then waved Abby off when he saw she meant to follow. "I can see myself out. No need to bother."

Dorothy left as well. She smiled briefly at Abby and closed the door quietly behind her.

Their eyes caught and held. Dr. Foley was right, Abby thought fleetingly. He *was* much better. He lay propped against a mound of pillows, watching her approach. His features were gaunt but there was an alertness about him that hadn't been there yesterday. Abby laid a tentative hand on his forehead. His skin was cool to the touch.

"How are you feeling?" she asked softly.

"Like hell," he muttered in his usual blunt manner.

Abby smiled. She couldn't help it. The relief that flooded her was immense. He was going to pull through. She could have shouted with relief and happiness.

He glared at her. "You think it's funny? I suppose you like seeing me in pain."

She banished the urge to grin from ear to ear. "You must be starving," she murmured smoothly. "I'll bring you some broth—"

"I had broth this morning," he informed her crossly. "Frankly, I'd like something a little more substantial—no, make that a *lot* more substantial—"

"Not a chance," Abby said firmly. "The doctor said not until tomorrow and that's that."

She smiled; he glared. "Now then," she said lightly, "I'm sure Dorothy has some broth warm in—"

"Dorothy. The housekeeper?"

"Yes. The lady who sums up the extent of our household staff—" She couldn't quite keep the censure from her tone. "—the lady who didn't run screaming out the door when she discovered that you, dangerous outlaw that you are, would be spending the next few nights under our roof."

He had the grace to drop his eyes; nevertheless, he managed to have the last word. "She's as bossy as you are," he muttered. Abby didn't mind, though. She picked up her skirts and swept from the room—Kane was going to be fine and nothing could dim her joy right now.

She soon discovered Kane was smarting because he couldn't feed himself. Rather than have him waste his energy arguing, she decided to let him try it. But it was obvious the slightest movement pained his shoulder. By the fourth spoonful, his hand began to shake so dreadfully it spilled all down the front of the napkin she'd placed on his chest. He let out a vivid string of curses. Without a word Abby took up the handle and spooned the fragrant broth into his mouth.

He voiced no protest when she brought a basin of warm water to the bedside table and announced her intention to give him a bath—at least not until she lathered a cloth with soap.

He swore. "Dammit, I don't want to smell like a two-dollar whore—"

She whirled on him, fire in her eyes. "For heaven's sake, watch your tongue," she snapped. "Besides, as I recall you demanded I use this very same soap the last time you . . . the last time we . . ." She stopped, realizing that particular memory was better left undisturbed.

It was too late. Their eyes caught and held endlessly, reflecting the same sizzling awareness that kindled inside both of them. Kane was the first to glance away. Abby lowered herself to the edge of the bed, her posture unnaturally stiff.

Kane didn't look at her as he spoke. "Maybe you should call Dorothy."

As hesitant as her expression was, her response came swiftly. "I'll do it." *I want to*, she almost said, only barely curtailing the words. Relegating such an intimate task to someone else—even Dorothy— just didn't bear thinking about.

She soaped his arms first, careful to avoid jarring his shoulder, trying hard to distance her mind from the task at hand. Her heart fluttered—and so did her breath. His skin was very dark against the white sheet folded flat against the plane of his belly, just below the hair-enclosed hollow of his navel. He was lean and tough, all strong, hard male.

Not once did she allow her hands to touch his bare skin—she kept the barrier of the washcloth between them—but her fingers displayed an embarrassing tendency to linger along the roped hardness of his muscles. Trying to subdue her feelings was even harder; twice she glanced up to find Kane's eyes on her face, his features strangely somber. His scrutiny flustered and disturbed her. If only she knew what lurked behind those silver eyes; if only she could see into his mind and discover his very thoughts.

If only she could see deep within his *heart* . . .

Next she soaped the beard-roughened stubble on his face and throat. Picking up a long, glinting razor and strop, she drew the edge down the strop several times. When she turned back to Kane she found him still watching her, one brow raised high.

"I don't suppose this is a good time to ask if you know how to use it." He spoke from the corner of his mouth.

Her smile was slow but breathtaking. Tiny lights appeared in her eyes, lighting them to blue silver. Kane felt as if he'd been kicked in the gut. This was the first time he'd seen her smile—really smile. A purely selfish pleasure rushed through him. He felt greedy and intoxicated.

"Let's just say this is not a good time to pick a

fight with me." She couldn't quite keep the thread of amusement from her tone. "Just hold still and don't move, all right?"

The razor scraped slowly from his sideburn down to his jaw. Kane couldn't have moved if he wanted to. Her brow was furrowed in concentration. The tip of her tongue darted out, pink and wet, as she applied herself to her task. The neckline of her blouse gaped slightly, offering him a glimpse of white satin and the delectably rounded top of her breast, tantalizingly close to his chest. He branded himself a cad for looking, yet what else could he do? He didn't dare turn his head.

A delicious fantasy burst in his brain. He saw Abby astride him, her hips clamped tight around his own. Her hair was glorious and unbound, rippling over her naked shoulders, her nipples peeping impudently from between honey-gold strands that brushed the taut skin of his belly. Her breasts swayed gently in tempo with the eager glide of her body over his thrusting hardness . . .

Beads of sweat popped out on his forehead by the time she finished. Sick or no, his body displayed an all-too-familiar reaction to her nearness.

He swallowed. He'd cut his own throat before he'd let her shave him again. He'd never considered shaving an erotic experience . . . until now.

She finished blotting the last of the soap from his cheeks, then paused.

"What is it?" he asked gruffly. "Don't like what you see?"

"It's not that," she said quickly. She smiled slightly. "I'm just not used to seeing you clean-shaven."

The admission slipped out before she could stop it. She flushed, all at once uncomfortably warm, when she realized her hand still rested on the sun-bronzed hardness of his chest. It looked dainty and fair, curled against the dark forest of hair on his chest and belly. Despite his illness, he made her feel small and weak—not that she minded, oddly enough. He had only to look at her and she felt all shivery inside.

"I don't imagine your brother is thrilled I booted him out of his room." Kane glanced around the bedroom. The furnishings were tall and spare, of dark polished wood. A pair of antique rifles hung on the opposite wall. Clearly it was a man's room.

Abby withdrew her hand to the safety of her lap. "Not at all," she said quickly. "Dillon doesn't sleep here at the ranch. In fact, he hasn't lived here for years. He has a small house in town. It makes it easier—with him being marshal and all."

Kane digested this news silently, watching as she moved to straighten the lace doily on the bureau. She'd have liked to stay and keep him company, but she sensed he was tired. She quietly withdrew and left him to nap.

She returned that evening with more broth. He talked her into bringing him a portion of the stew that she, Lucas and Dorothy ate for dinner. It certainly seemed to do him no harm; in fact, he seemed much stronger than he had all day. She decided this was a good time to get him on his feet.

She tapped a fingertip against one pearly-white tooth. "Maybe I should get Lucas—"

"Lucas?"

"Dorothy's husband. He's the ranch foreman."

"What for?" he demanded. "There's not a damn thing wrong with my legs. Just help me get on my feet and I'll be fine." Abby wasn't so certain, but she decided to keep quiet. He pushed back the covers with his good arm and lowered his legs to the floor. Bright spots of color appeared on her cheeks. His naked chest seemed to jump out at her. Despite his illness, his raw masculinity leaped out at her, making her feel all jittery inside. She was sincerely grateful he still wore his drawers.

He got to his feet. He swayed unsteadily and Abby instinctively slid her arm around the steely expanse of his waist. When his head cleared, he took several short steps.

"Damn! My legs feel like mush."

"It's because you've been off your feet so long. You're doing fine. The next time you're up you won't feel so weak."

He turned his head. His chin grazed feathery-soft wisps of hair at her temples. The scent of wildflowers and her soft, yielding body against his did nothing to ease his dizziness. By the time they'd walked around the room three times his shoulder was throbbing and his head whirled so he could scarcely think. He collapsed onto the bed with a muttered curse.

"Hell! I can't walk. I can't even feed myself. What the hell kind of man am I?" He squeezed his eyes shut, fighting the blackness that threatened to snare him once again.

A gentle hand brushed a lock of hair from his brow. Small fingers interlocked with his. *My kind of man,* whispered a voice as soft as fleece.

His mind spun and drifted. Surely he was dreaming. Abby never would have uttered such foolishness—never in a million years . . .

Chapter 17

The next day Kane showed a remarkable improvement, the third still more. Abby decided he was well enough to eat in the dining room with the rest of them. Lucas had joined them for dinner. Abby explained that he and Dorothy had always eaten with the family.

A week ago Kane would have accused her of lying if she'd told him she ate with the hired help. Suffering pangs of guilt, he now shamefully ducked his head as she said the blessing.

He was downright nervous, though he hated to admit it, even to himself. It had been a long time since he'd sat down to a meal with decent people. But at least Dorothy wasn't the fire-breathing dragon he'd first thought. And Lucas was friendly and amiable; it wasn't long before the tight knot in his stomach was gone. He listened quietly when the conversation turned to ranch business. Abby and Lucas discussed the expected yield for next year's herd—and the market price as well. It was clear Abby was no novice when it came to building a herd. When he commented on it, Lucas gave a shout of laughter.

"Son, this little gal was up in the saddle when she was three and riding herd when she was no bigger than a beanpole. Her pa used to brag she was a match for any cowhand a hundred miles around."

Heat scorched Abby's cheeks. Kane absorbed this latest bit of news with mounting insight. Somehow, it fit. She wouldn't be content to sit on the porch and give orders. And he knew for a fact she wasn't afraid to get her hands dirty.

But he'd done her a disservice, he realized grimly, for nothing about this woman was as he'd thought. She wasn't spoiled and pampered; she was smart and strong and sassy, a woman quite unlike any other.

All along he'd reviled her for what he'd considered her preconceived notions about him. But he was just as guilty—no, far *more* guilty—of judging her unfairly than she had been of judging him.

The knowledge left a bad taste in his mouth.

Dorothy and Lucas insisted on cleaning up. A hand curled inside his elbow, Abby showed him into the parlor, a warm, cozy room filled with sunshine, braided rugs and several big overstuffed chairs. She returned to the kitchen after he eased into the settee opposite the huge stone fireplace. Kane glanced around, calling himself every kind of jackass, because even in this he'd been wrong. He'd expected her home to be far more grand and pretentious. Instead it was homey and comfortable . . .

The kind of place *he* would have liked to call home.

Where the thought came from, he didn't know. But he was thoroughly annoyed. Damn! What was wrong with him? He might have been a homebody once, but that was years ago—and with Lorelei. A lot had changed since then—*everything* had changed since then.

Abby returned carrying two cups of coffee. She placed his on the small table before him, then perched on the other end of the settee. "That was quite an enlightening meal, wasn't it?" Her tone was falsely bright. "I suppose I should have warned you—Lucas can be rather frank, sometimes a little too frank. But at least you know the truth about Abigail MacKenzie . . . I'm afraid she's not much of a woman."

Kane stopped in the midst of reaching for his coffee. He glanced at her sharply. "Why on earth would you say that?" he demanded.

"Why else? Because I'm twenty years old, I grew up on this ranch, and just about the only man I've ever spent time with was Pa." Abby looked away and whispered, "I've never really had a man come courting me." Her lips trembled slightly. "Dillon says it's because most of the men in town are scared to death of a woman who's better with a gun and a lasso than needle and thread."

Some strange emotion unfurled in his chest. This was a side of Abby he had yet to glimpse. He had seen her vulnerable, yes; but never quite so exposed and powerless to fight back. Usually she was so brave and capable . . . His heart twisted. Didn't she know she was sweet and softly feminine, all a man could ever want? Any man worth his salt wouldn't be threatened by her starch and sass—he certainly wasn't. It merely made her all the more exciting . . .

She ran the tip of her finger around the china cup. "Remember the night you said my daddy probably packed me off to some fancy Eastern school for ladies?" She didn't give him the chance to answer. "Well, you were right. But the truth is, I was only there for a month before the headmistress, Mrs. Rutherford, sent *me* packing home. She told Pa there was no way in hell I'd ever be a proper lady. She said I couldn't sing. I couldn't dance. She said I walked like a—" Abby couldn't quite hide the quiver of her lip. "—a cow . . ."

The thought of someone so humbling his proud, fiery Abby made Kane see red. The woman must have been mad—most likely jealous! At the same time, the mere mention of her loose, leggy walk pitched him into a realm of purely sensual awareness. Her presence these past days had taken its toll. He had only to glance at her and remember how it had been between them—the sweet, wet heat of her lips beneath his, the way it felt to be buried deep inside her creamy sheath. And he'd dreamed how it would feel to have those deliciously long legs wrapped around his . . .

But a sudden thought occurred to him. "You keep talking about your father," he said slowly. "Where was your mother?"

She set aside the coffee. "She died of pneumonia when I was seven. But I'm afraid I don't remember much of her. Dorothy and Lucas didn't work for us then. There was just me and Pa and Dillon. But Dillon is ten years older than me. He scouted for the army after the war, so while I was growing up, he was gone most of the time. Pa's the one who raised me."

Her head was bowed low, eyes downcast. Her hands lay clasped in her lap, the pose oddly defenseless. A wistful sadness shone in her expression. It didn't take much to know she was thinking of her father.

He watched her rise and move to the window. Pushing aside the lace curtain, she peered through the glass.

His voice cut through the quiet. "You miss him, don't you?"

She swiped at one cheek. The merest hint of a smile grazed her lips. "I guess it shows, doesn't it?"

Kane was on his feet before he was even aware of it. He wanted to reach out and hold her, to say . . . what? Abruptly he checked the impulse, clenching his fists, his features tightening almost bitterly. His conscience stabbed at him. Who was he to offer her comfort or tenderness? Who was he to offer her anything?

"Pa and I had something . . . I don't know what to call it except special," she went on. "Maybe it's because it was just the two of us for so long. I don't mean to say that Pa didn't love Dillon as much as he loved me," she clarified quickly, "because he did. But Pa always said Dillon would rather be off hunting down outlaws and searching for adventure than chasing down a stray calf."

Kane stood off to one side. "Your father disapproved?"

She hesitated, resting her forehead against the glass. "I don't think it was so much disapproval," she said slowly, "as it was disappointment."

There was a small pause. "Dillon doesn't have the same feeling for the land that Pa and I had," she said slowly, almost to herself. "But this ranch meant everything to Pa. He worked hard to make it what it is today," she added feelingly. "I can't fail him. I—I won't."

She stared off into the distance, where the amber glow of the sunset dappled acre after acre of grassland. Sheer determination etched the proud lines of her profile.

The blackness in his soul yawned deeper.

Once . . . once he'd felt the very same emotions that drove Abby at this very moment. He experienced the same bond with the land, the urge to succeed, the desire for success. He'd wanted nothing more than to preserve and protect what was his . . . It hadn't mattered that he'd gained what he had through marriage. He'd wanted to prove his worth to himself . . . and to Lorelei.

He came up behind Abby, losing the battle not to touch her. His hand settled on one shoulder. "What will happen to the ranch now that your father is gone?"

"It belongs to both Dillon and me now. For the most part it will be business as usual. Day-to-day operations will be under my direction instead of Pa's. Any major decisions will be handled by both of us."

She turned. His nearness, as well as the familiarity of his touch, lent her courage. She searched his face. "Have you thought any more about Dillon's job offer?"

Abby knew the instant the question emerged that it was a mistake. His hand fell away from her shoulder. He spoke in a monotone.

"Your memory's mighty short. I turned it down, remember?"

She stared at him, hurt and dismayed, but willing herself not to show it. "Of course I remember," she said at last. "I just thought you might have reconsidered—"

"What's to reconsider?" His features shut down from all expression. He had stepped back, and it was as if she could see him pulling into himself . . . and pushing her out.

"Oh, I don't know." She raised her chin, her tone as cold as his. "But I seem to recall that night at the Silver Spur you said you planned to see if any of the ranchers around here needed a hand."

"I changed my mind." He turned and walked back to the settee.

Abby's eyes drilled into his back. Did he really think he could dismiss her so easily? "No," she said very deliberately. "I think *I* changed your mind, Kane. So why don't you just admit it?"

That snagged his attention, all right. His head came up. His lips twisted. "Oh, come on, Abby. Do you really expect me to stay on as one of your hired hands? Or have you forgotten what happened between us? And what would your brother say if he knew I took his little sister to bed? Hell, he'd be hauling out his shotgun!"

She caught her breath. She hadn't expected him to mention that particular incident; neither of them had dared to speak of it since that terrible morning after . . . But more than once she'd caught him staring at her when he thought she didn't see. And she knew the memory was there, simmering just beneath the surface as it did with her, always . . . *always*.

Her mouth was suddenly dry as dust. "I don't

see why that should make any difference." She wet her lips, wondering what he would say if she begged him to stay, the way she yearned to . . . "Kane, surely you realize . . . this could be a fresh start for you . . . a chance to start over . . ."

Ruthlessly he closed his mind against her. Christ! Didn't she realize he didn't dare stay? He was like a lovesick calf around Abby. Oh, he recognized the symptoms—he'd experienced them once before. He'd start thinking about settling down, building a home, a future . . .

No, he couldn't fall in love. He *wouldn't*. But it seemed he couldn't help himself either.

Guilt shafted through him. It struck him that he could scarcely recall what Lorelei had looked like—what it had felt like to hold her, to make love to her. When he closed his eyes, all he could see was Abby, her face turned up to his, eyes tear-bright and wanting. All he could feel was Abby, her form soft and sweet-smelling . . . the kind of woman he'd always wanted.

The kind of woman he didn't deserve.

It was laughable, really, to think a man with his past could want a woman like her. Savagely he asked himself what the hell he could offer her. Not a goddamn thing—nothing!

Not even the respect of his name.

But Abby wasn't about to let him off so easily. "You know what?" she said suddenly. "I think you're scared, Kane. Deep inside I think you're afraid. I think that's why you're running—why you keep running. From me. From everything."

Anger brought him surging to his feet. "Just because I have no intentions of staying here doesn't mean I'm running, sweetheart."

"The hell it doesn't! Remember the night Sonny was killed? You were the one who said we can't go back—we can't change what happened, so we have to learn to live with it. Isn't it time you learned to live with yourself—with your past?"

His silence was brutal.

"God, when I think of all we've been through . . . and I know next to nothing about you, Kane—God, I don't even know where you're from!" She blinked back hot, scalding tears.

He saw them and cursed. "What is this? You spill your guts—I spill mine? Well, turn off the tears, sweetheart. They might have worked before but they won't work now. It's no use prying and digging, Abby, so don't even try!"

He turned his back on her and strode toward the stairs.

Abby was behind him all the way. "Dammit, Kane, you—you can't just push me aside like this! I gave you what I gave to no other man . . . I'm not one of your—your whores to be used one night and cast aside. I won't let you use me like this! I deserve an explanation if nothing else."

They were on the landing now. She punched him squarely in the back. "Dammit, look at me!"

He whirled on her. She reared back and would have lost her balance if he hadn't caught her arm. Eyes afire, he stared down into her face. "You want to know why I'm running? Why I'm wanted by the law? Why I'm afraid my past will someday catch up to me?"

"Yes! I—I know you, Kane. I can't believe anything could be as terrible as you think. I can't believe you would *do* something so—so terrible that you feel you have to hide it from me!"

His laugh was false and brittle. "No? What about murder, Abby? What would you say if I told you I was wanted for cold-blooded *murder?*"

Chapter 18

*M*urder . . .
  The word hung between them.

Abby's heart skipped a beat, but her mind raced on. A choking fear constricted her throat. All at once she recalled what he'd said that night with Sam, the night he'd frightened her so . . .

There are times a man is capable of just about anything. Her breathing came slow, then fast. She suspected it was true—Kane was indeed a man capable of many things . . . but cold-blooded *murder*?

No, not that. Not *Kane.*

For Kane, this moment was everything he had feared. Her reaction was everything he had *known* it would be. Her face was bloodless, her eyes wide and dark. He made a sound low in his throat and spun around.

He didn't get more than two steps before she snagged his arm. "Kane, wait!"

He tried to shake her off. "Let go, Abby. I'm no damn good—maybe now you'll believe me!"

"Don't say that!" Her nails dug into his forearm. She was as fierce as he.

They were standing at the door to her room. She pushed him inside and slammed the door shut. She stood for a moment, her spine and hands pressed against the door. She pushed him none-too-gently toward the bed. To her shock, he didn't argue, but obligingly dropped down on the mattress. Abby took a place opposite him in the room's only chair.

"Now," she said evenly. "Who was it you supposedly murdered?"

His gaze came up to tangle with hers. "What! You don't believe I'd kill anyone? Honey, I'm an outlaw—a renegade!"

Lord, how she hated his mockery! She was only now beginning to understand that it was directed at himself as much as her. Abby was suddenly deeply ashamed of her doubt, no matter that it had been fleeting.

"You may have killed someone out of self-defense," she said coolly. "But cold-blooded murder?" She shook her head, her eyes locked with his. "I don't think so, Kane. No, I don't think so at all."

His eyes were the first to slide away. He let out a long rush of air. He no longer seemed angry, just immensely tired.

"Her name was Lorelei." He paused, then said heavily, "She was my wife."

Abby inhaled sharply. So Lorelei was his wife . . . No wonder he'd loved her. And then to be accused of her murder . . . !

"Tell me what happened," she said softly.

He was silent for so long she feared he would refuse to answer. He thrust his fingers through his hair and scowled. "Christ," he muttered. "I don't even know where to begin."

"Where did it happen?"

"New Mexico."

Her eyes were steady on his face. "Is that where you're from?"

He shook his head, then stretched out on the bed. "I grew up in Georgia." He hesitated, then said slowly, "I didn't have the kind of life you had, Abby. Maybe you didn't have a mother, but you had a father and a brother who cared for you. My family was nothing but poor white trash. I never knew my father. My mother was drunk more than she was sober. She took off when I was just a kid. I spent most of my childhood begging because I was hungry—and then being shoved aside by people who thought they were better than me."

Abby didn't know what to say, and so she said nothing. Somehow she'd suspected as much.

"When I was twelve I ran off and joined the Confederate Army as a courier. By the time it was over I'd seen enough bloodshed to last me a lifetime. I decided to head west. For years I just drifted, taking jobs when and where I could find them, leaving when I felt the urge to move on. I finally ended up in New Mexico, working on a ranch breaking horses for a lady who'd just lost her husband . . ." A shadow passed over his face.

Abby bit her lip. "Lorelei?"

Kane nodded. "I started working there a few months after her husband died. Lorelei was young. Inexperienced when it came to running the ranch. She started coming to me for advice. Pretty soon we were spending a lot of time together." His voice trailed off. A faraway look appeared in his eyes.

Abby swallowed. There was an awful constriction in her throat. "You fell in love?"

Again he nodded. "We were married within six

months. There was some nasty talk in town about her marrying a hired hand—" He shrugged. "—but neither of us cared."

Abby watched as he hitched his good arm under his head. He stared at the ceiling, but a strange hardness crept into his eyes. She probed very gently. "What happened then?"

"I came home one day and found her lying in a pool of blood, a bullet through her heart. The next thing I knew the sheriff was there, hauling my ass off to jail on a murder charge." His words were clipped and abrupt. "The whole town was real quick to come up with a motive, too. They were convinced I married Lorelei and then killed her just to get control of the ranch."

Abby was appalled. "That's terrible! My God, you'd just lost your wife! How could they be so cruel? So unfair? Especially when there was no evidence—"

"Oh, but they thought there was plenty. A few days before, Lorelei had paid a visit to her attorney, a man named Allan Mason. She had had him draw up the paperwork adding my name to hers in the ownership of the ranch. She had also planned to change her will so that if she died, the ranch would be mine."

She watched as he swung up from the bed and went to stand at the window. There was an uneasy knot in the pit of Abby's stomach. "Planned to?" she echoed. "Weren't the changes completed?"

"No. Her attorney testified she hadn't signed the documents and so the legalities were never completed. Hell, it was the last thing on my mind! She was the one good thing to come into my life . . ." He stopped. She couldn't see his features, but his posture was so stiff she could almost feel his tension. She stared helplessly, aware of his pain as keenly as if it were her own.

She was half-afraid to speak, yet she had to know. "Didn't you have a trial? Maybe if you'd told them—"

"Oh, I tried, Abby. But no one wanted to listen. I discovered the hard way that justice is a word for people with power and money. There was no justice for the common man—not for me. I was an outsider, the way I've been all my life—a drifter who happened to be lucky enough to marry the boss. I was tried, convicted and sentenced to hang before Lorelei was even cold in her grave. It didn't matter that I wasn't responsible. I wasn't even there when she was killed! But in the eyes of the law, I was guilty. I didn't want to hang for something I didn't do. So I broke out of jail and ran."

"And you've been running ever since." She didn't realize she spoke aloud until he half-turned. His eyes snared hers, cool and opaque.

A chill ran through her. "Kane, who do you think killed Lorelei—and why?"

A taut silence descended. "I don't know," he said at last. "It was months later before I figured out someone killed Lorelei and set me up to get both of us out of the way—probably to get their hands on her ranch. I woke up day after day knowing her killer was out there somewhere. But I was tired of fighting what I couldn't see, tired of fighting what I didn't know. Hell, I was so damn concerned with just staying alive that at first I didn't even let myself think about who murdered her." He gave a short, self-deprecating laugh. "I guess that tells you what kind of man I am. My wife is murdered, and my only concern is where the hell I'm going to find my next hiding place!"

Abby's heart twisted. There was a world of guilt festering inside him. Didn't he know it was time to let go?

"Is that how you ended up with Stringer Sam?" she whispered.

He nodded. "I was at rock-bottom when I hooked up with Sam and his gang. But Sam was damn good at eluding the law. At the time, staying alive was all that mattered."

He sounded so cold, so distant. His profile was stark and barren. Her heart bled for him, for all he had suffered.

She rose, standing alongside him, compelled by the overpowering need to touch him, but not quite daring to. "When are you going to stop punishing yourself for something that wasn't your fault?" she asked quietly.

He stared at the twisted snarl of tree limbs outside the window, his lips drawn in a relentless line. "I didn't even have the courage to try to fight back. You were right, Abby. I was running . . . I'm *still* running."

"You were desperate—desperate to survive." Grasping for courage, she stepped before him. Her pulse skittering wildly, she placed her fingers lightly on his chest.

His tone was haunted. "I've changed. God knows I was never a saint, but . . . all those years of running from the law . . . God, Abby, I've done things I could never tell you about, things I could never tell anyone. If I died today, I'd go straight to hell with no hope of redemption. Doesn't that scare you?"

She shook her head. Her eyes clung to his. "What scares me is the thought of never seeing you again."

Kane stared down at her, at her small hand curled so trustingly against his heart. Where was the stinging condemnation, the disgust and revulsion he'd been so certain he would find? Her eyes were wide and unwavering; the shimmering hope reflected there made his insides coil in dread. Panic such as he had never known shot through him. So much trust. So much faith. He didn't deserve it. He didn't deserve *her*.

The memory he'd deliberately thrust aside came alive once more. His hand rose slowly, skimming the cotton-covered valley of her spine, resisting the urge to stray lower, clear to the curve of her buttocks. He remembered exactly how she felt there. He'd taken his palms and settled them over those gentle curves, in that mind-shattering instant he'd taken full, hot possession of her . . . and dear God, he wanted to do it all over again. He wanted to taste her just one more time. Just once . . .

"You shouldn't say things like that," he said roughly. "Hell, I shouldn't even be here with you. What would Dorothy and Lucas say if they knew where we were?"

She didn't care. The realization washed through her, nearly bringing her to her knees. She remembered all too clearly that horrifying instant when he'd been shot—she feared he was dead and the agony that tore through her was devastating. And these past few days, knowing he was in pain made her hurt inside just as much.

Oh, she'd tried to hide from the truth. She'd told herself it was simply because they had come through so much together.

But the night she'd let Kane make love to her, she had given him a part of herself that would always be his . . . and his alone. But now there were no more misgivings—all doubt fled her mind. She could hide from the truth no longer.

She loved him. It didn't matter who he was, or what he had done. *She loved him.*

Her tongue slid over the generous curve of her lower lip. "I heard the door slam ages ago. Dorothy and Lucas went back to their house." Her voice was a breathless whisper in the stillness of the room. "They won't be back till morning."

Her other hand crept up to join the first. Beneath her fingertips, the rhythm of his heart picked up its pace.

His chest expanded with the ragged breath he drew. "You don't know what you're doing, Abby."

Her eyes clung to his. "Oh, but I think I do."

Her unsteady smile wrung a groan from him. God, if only it were so simple! He wished like hell her hair didn't look like sunburst gold, her eyes like sun-washed sky. He wished like hell he wasn't like a man hypnotized, starved for the touch and taste and feel of her. He hated the sudden churning of desire that ripped through his gut, the aching hunger. He hated knowing only this woman could slake the hunger that burned inside him. He wished any woman—any woman but this one—could slake it. But only this one would do. Only her.

He fought to keep his hands at his sides. "Are

you saying what I think you are?"

In answer she clumsily fumbled with the buttons of his shirt. One popped free, then another and another. "You stayed with me when I was hurting, Kane. You held me and made me forget . . ." His lips were only a breath above her tremulous mouth. "Now it's my turn to do the same for you."

The last button slid free. She nuzzled her cheek against the hair-roughened plane of his chest. Kane gritted his teeth against a rush of pleasure so acute it nearly brought him to his knees.

"Kane," she whispered. Her mouth, warm and sweet, opened against his skin. Her breathy sigh stirred the hair across the flat brown disk of his nipple. Then she was kissing him—the hardness of his collarbone, the musky hollow of his throat, the side of his jaw where it clenched so tight . . .

Damn, he thought helplessly. Damn.

He squeezed his eyes shut. "God, Abby, what are you doing to me?" His voice was tight and dry. Blindly he caught her against him, curling his fingers possessively around her nape and urging her face to his. The kiss they shared was ravenous and fierce, fiery and tender all at once. Her mouth parted, shyly at first, timidly joining his bold foray.

He dragged his mouth away reluctantly. He rested his forehead against hers, his breathing ragged and labored. "I want to make love to you, Abby." His voice vibrated all through her, low and intense. "I want to make it good for you, the way it should have been the first time—"

Her fingers on his lips shushed him. "It *was* good. You made me feel things I never thought I could feel."

With a groan he kissed her again, but this time his hands were busily engaged, and far more deft than hers had been. Warm air spilled over her as her blouse was drawn from her shoulders. She felt a tug on the ribbon that held her chemise closed. Her breasts spilled into his hands, her nipples already hard and straining. He circled each with his finger-tips; they swelled taut and eager against his palms. A cry of sheer pleasure inched up her throat.

Her skirt and drawers went the way of her blouse, pooling in a heap at her feet; her shoes and stockings came next. Abby's heart set up a wild stampede as his fingers set to work on his own clothing. She had one heart-stopping glimpse of his body, bronzed and gloriously naked, before she was swept up in his arms.

Very slowly he lowered her to the bed. Eyes like molten flames roamed the length of her. Abby blushed fiercely but made no effort to hide her-self from his devouring gaze. The thought that she pleased him made her feel all hot and giddy inside. There was an odd melting sensation deep in her belly. He pulled her to him, sealing her lips with a deep, drugging kiss. Abby wound her arms around him and clung, keenly aware of the heavy pressure of his arousal snug against her belly.

They were both gasping when he raised his head. "Touch me, Abby." There was a hint of ragged harshness to his voice. "Touch me . . ." He caught her wrists and dragged her hands down to his chest.

His urgent demand unleashed a quiver of sen-sation all along her nerve endings. The idea of exploring his lean, hard body was tantalizing, but also rather intimidating. She suspected Kane's experience was far more vast than what little she had to offer. She bit her lip.

"I—I want to," she confided breathlessly. "But . . . oh, Kane, I know you've been with—with other women. And I don't know anything . . . I can't possibly compare—"

He rolled to his back, taking her with him. His gaze seared hotly into hers. "There's never been anyone like you, Abby. *Never*."

"Not even Lorelei?" The question slipped out before she could stop it.

His eyes darkened. "Not even Lorelei." He tangled his fingers in her hair and brought her mouth down to his. He kissed her, a fervent, soul-shattering kiss that said all that words could not—and rewarded her with a tenuous courage.

She trailed her fingertips across the binding hardness of his biceps, steel sheathed in satin flesh, then slid her fingers through the dense mat of hair on his chest, thrilling to the rough-silk texture, careful of his bandage. The quickening of his pulse, the rapid rise and fall of his chest, emboldened her. The muscles of his belly clenched when she pursued a daring pathway even lower, clear to the heat and heart of him . . .

Her first measuring caress sent a jolt through both of them. Abby trembled; his length and breadth made her shiver with awe—but excitement, too. Holding her breath, she indulged her curiosity, gasping at the contrast—ridged, straining steel and velvet-tipped smoothness.

Kane bore her dainty exploration with his eyes squeezed shut, his head cast back, his features

taut with restraint, his fingers digging into the soft
flesh of her hips. He was burning wherever their
skin touched . . . and empty and aching wherever it
didn't. Blood pumped thickly through his veins. The
desire to push her back, to drive his shaft to the hilt
and take her hard and fast was almost overwhelming. But he'd taken her that way before and he was
determined that this time he would banish the hurt
and give her the pleasure he'd cheated her of the
first time. Except the feel of her small hand curled
around that part of him—gliding, stroking her tacit
approval—inflamed him almost past bearing. He
was only a heartbeat away from spilling himself.

With a swiftly indrawn breath, he moved her
hand to safer territory. Lightly he nipped the smooth
curve of one bare shoulder.

"It's my turn now." His low, throaty whisper
rushed past her ear. Passion glazed his eyes, making
them silvery-bright and brilliant. His expression
ignited a fiery blaze within her.

He turned her on her stomach and brushed aside
her hair. She gasped as he pressed a feathery kiss
upon her nape. Heat rippled through her as he
slid down the length of her spine, his mouth and
tongue lingering here and there, and then again at
the warm valley where her buttocks swelled soft
and firm.

And then she was being turned again. His hands
were on her breasts, cupping, squeezing, teasing.
Her fingers sank into his hair when at last he took the
dusky, swollen peak of one breast into his mouth,
tugging, nipping, suckling, first one nipple and then
the other. She bit back a moan, seized by a wanton
fire that burned from the inside out.

The backs of his fingers skimmed the flat of her belly, grazed her silken fleece. He ran the callused tips of his fingers down the insides of her thighs, clear to her knees and back again. One daring finger plundered further, tracing the furrowed cleft of her womanhood, the treasure between—torrid, tormenting strokes that made her go weak inside, her limbs boneless. A damp, liquid heat spiraled through her, settling there between her legs, even as a sharp, piercing ache shot through her middle. Her hips began to circle and writhe, unconsciously seeking his searching hand.

A jagged moan caught in her throat. He raised his head. A sense of wonder filled her. She saw the same uncontrollable passion that swept through her mirrored in his hot gaze. He kissed her, the contact wild and heady; she could taste the hunger in his mouth, as ravenous as her own. It made her tremble to think that this man, dangerous as he was—desperate as he was—wanted her so.

He braced himself above her, his knees spreading her wide. A low, guttural sound of need and desire tore from his lungs. The sleek, round crown of his shaft breached the waiting folds of her woman's flesh. His penetration was excruciatingly slow, driving them both half-mad.

Her nails dug into his shoulders. Her breath skittered out in a rush. There was no pain this time, only a primitive need to join with this man, to be filled with his essence and strength. She stared at his face, unable to look away. She could see the tension constricting his features, feel the tautness of his shoulders; she sensed the iron control he exerted in order to keep his desire in check.

Something inside her came undone. A tremendous outpouring of emotion rushed through her, spreading through mind and body and heart. She buried her head against the solid curve of his shoulder, in that instant uncaring that she bared her soul to him.

"I love you!" she cried against his throat. "Oh, Kane, I . . . I love you."

He half-closed his eyes, his features almost anguished. "Abby." He groaned her name as if he were in agony. "Oh, God, Abby . . ."

He thrust home, his control all but gone. He could feel the sleek, wet heat of her passage stretching, expanding to accept the plunge of his body. She was so small, so tight. It had never been this good before . . . never. Engulfed in dark, sweet ecstasy, he lunged mindlessly, driving himself deep—so deep she would never forget this night . . . never forget him. He yearned for nothing more than to brand himself into her body and heart as surely as she was branded into his.

Abby moaned. So this was love, she thought dazedly. Reckless and wild. Wondrous and glorious. Caught in the same raging inferno as Kane, she cried out, feeling the clasp of her body around his tighten and contract, again and again and again. And then she was exploding, hurtling through space, as if the world were falling away all around her. Her pleasure doubled as she felt him shudder, a heartbeat before his scalding release drenched her womb in heat and fire.

He buried his head against the damp hollow of her shoulder, loath to move. She combed her fingers through the dark hair that grew low on his nape. Nothing had ever felt so right, she thought, still floating in the languorous aftermath. Surely he had felt it, too—that delicious sense of oneness. They belonged together, she realized fiercely. Tomorrow, she vowed, tomorrow she would tell him . . .

But in the morning he was gone.

Chapter 19

❦

Kane stood high atop a lonely bluff, his gaze trained on the white ranch house nestled in a stand of scrub oak. A wide covered porch held up by stout columns ran the width of the house. A lazy plume of smoke trailed skyward from a massive stone fireplace. Several horses lazily grazed in the largest of two corrals. Beyond the cluster of buildings, rich grassland ran back into the hills.

His mind was filled with just one thought— he'd taken a hell of a chance coming back to New Mexico.

At length he turned away. Midnight glanced up from where he'd left him tied to a bush. Kane retreated several steps, then knelt down in the grass. He stared down at two overgrown grave markers, tugging on the dried, parched grass until he could see the letters etched into the stone.

Self-disgust churned in his belly. Kane hated himself at that moment. He had seen to it that Lorelei was buried next to her first husband, Emmett, but this was the first time he had returned to the site of her grave.

He cursed himself for being a rotten, no-good bounder. What kind of man was he to leave as he had, not knowing who had murdered her?

You selfish bastard, jabbed a scathing voice. *She was your wife. You owed it to her to try to figure out who murdered her—and why. And you didn't even try . . .*

Guilt gnawed at him. Maybe he should have come back years ago. He thought of the hollow emptiness of that first year without her. He woke up every day knowing her killer was out there somewhere. But he'd been so tired of fighting what he couldn't see. Tired of fighting what he didn't know. And so in the end, he had emptied his mind and heart of all feeling, of all memories.

He bowed his head low. "I'm sorry, Lorelei," he whispered, his voice raw. "I'll make it up to you. I swear I will."

He'd failed her, he realized starkly. But he couldn't do the same with Abby . . .

He rose, then untied and mounted Midnight, his heart sealed with a brittle determination. It was nearly dark when he approached the outskirts of town. Kane was secretly glad for the enveloping cloak of darkness as he rode toward Willie's, the local saloon. He dropped down from his saddle into the dusty street and tethered Midnight to the weathered gray railing. His spurs jingled as he mounted the steps, his hat ducked low over his eyes. His posture was ramrod-straight, that of a man sure of himself and where he was going. But inside he was sweating. What if he was recognized? What if they threw his hide in jail?

Yet Kane knew he had no choice. He couldn't live with the man he'd become. He had to clear his name or die trying. Not just for himself, but for Lorelei.

But most of all for Abby.

Spirals of hazy smoke and raucous male laughter drifted through the swinging doors. He rubbed the bristly beard that had sprouted in the last two weeks, grateful it obscured his features. A few idle glances swung his way as he stepped inside; none lingered. He attracted little attention as he made his way to the bar—with luck, the patrons would think he was just passing through on his way to Albuquerque.

He stepped up to the bar. The barkeep appeared, wiping his hands on a towel. "What can I get for ya?"

"Whiskey," was all Kane said.

"Comin' right up."

Seconds later, his whiskey in hand, Kane made his way to a table in the corner, where he was less likely to be noticed. He sat, taking a sip of the burning brew. He surveyed the room, taking care that his gaze didn't dwell on any one face too long. He recognized a few, but most were unfamiliar. A lot had changed, he acknowledged distantly. The town was spread out more than he remembered. He'd passed a number of houses near the school house that hadn't been there four years earlier, and a new hotel.

His whiskey finished, Kane rose. He made his way toward the door, his mind surging ahead. He didn't think it was wise to stay here in town. Tyler Flats was only five miles west. He'd ride there and put up for the night. There was time enough to start asking questions tomorrow—

His shoulder slammed into a man who'd just stepped up onto the boardwalk. Kane's head came up. Beneath the dusty brim of a Stetson, a young man with narrow features and a reddish-brown mustache peered at him. Kane silently cursed. *Son of a bitch*! The man was Rusty Owens. He'd worked with him on Lorelei's ranch; they'd once been friends.

The other man stepped back. He nudged the brim of his hat upward, his expression faintly puzzled.

"Say, mister, don't I know you?" The question was no sooner voiced than his eyes widened. Recognition dawned.

His feet braced slightly apart, Kane's hand was already on the butt of his Colt. "I don't want any trouble, Rusty," he warned, very low. "Let's just go on around to the back of the saloon, real slow now. Keep your hands where I can see them."

Rusty obliged, his hands spread away from his body. Kane was right on his heels, watching for any sudden move. Once they were behind the building, he stopped.

"Okay. That's far enough." He relieved Rusty of the gun strapped to his thigh, slipping it into the waistband of his gun belt.

Rusty raised his hands and turned slowly. "There's no call for alarm. I won't let on who you are, I swear. We were friends once, remember?"

A filmy stream of light from the upstairs window lit the other man's face. Kane could tell he was nervous by the sheen of perspiration above his mustache.

"I remember." Kane's eyes never strayed from the other man's face.

Rusty swallowed. "Look, Kane, for what it's worth, I never believed you killed Lorelei. Any

fool could see how it was between you two. Hell,
a man doesn't shoot his own wife when he's crazy
in love."

Crazy in love. The words made Kane's heart
squeeze. He'd loved Lorelei, yes. But not the way
he loved Abby . . .

Rusty's gaze never faltered. Kane felt the tight
coil of tension within him begin to unwind. Trust
didn't come easy after so long, yet instinct told
him Rusty hadn't changed—Rusty had been one
of the few who had clamored for his release from
jail.

Kane slowly extended his hand. "You're right,"
he said quietly. "We were friends once. I'd like it
if we could be again."

Rusty released a pent-up breath and seized his
hand in a hearty grip. His wide grin lasted only an
instant, though.

He shook his head, his expression somber. "I
gotta tell you, Kane, you took a hell of a chance
comin' back here. That beard hides a lot, but there's
still a few folks might remember you."

Kane's tone was as hard as his features. "I came
back to clear my name. I won't leave until it's
done."

Rusty rubbed his jaw. "It won't be easy," he
ventured. "I asked a lot of questions when you
were sittin' in jail and got nowheres. Seems to me
the only way to clear your name is to find out who
really killed Lorelei."

"My idea exactly," Kane said grimly.

Rusty gave him a long, slow look. "Say, why
don't you come back to my place? Mary Beth and
I don't have an extra bed, but if you don't mind a

few chickens scratchin' around, you can bunk out in the barn."

Kane raised his brows. "Mary Beth?"

Rusty beamed. "My wife," he said proudly. "Been married a year now. Bought ourselves some land just west of town." He grinned. "You're lookin' at a farmer now, but we hope to buy a few head of cattle next year."

So Rusty had a wife now. Kane wasn't surprised; Rusty was an amicable, likeable fellow. But the threat of being caught again was very real. He might well be putting Rusty and his wife in harm's way as well.

"I don't know," Kane said slowly. "It's mighty generous of you to offer, but I don't want to put the two of you in danger."

Rusty flashed a grin again. "I'll take my chances. Besides, this way you'll have a chance to think things through, without worrying about some damn fool finding out who you are before you're ready for it."

Kane took off his hat and thrust his fingers through his hair. "All right," he agreed reluctantly. "But just for tonight."

An hour later he found himself in Rusty's kitchen, scraping the last of a mouth-wateringly delicious beef stew from his plate. He swallowed appreciatively. His gaze lifted to the diminutive dark-haired woman who was Rusty's wife.

He laid down his fork and smiled across at her. "Best meal I've had in years, ma'am."

Mary Beth flushed with pleasure. She was plump and rosy-cheeked, and it was readily apparent there would soon be an addition to the family.

Rusty scraped his chair back. He piled the empty

plates together and carried them to the washtub.
"I'll see to those later," he said firmly. "You're
supposed to rest whenever you can, but if I know
you, you've been on your feet since sunup."

Mary Beth sighed. "Sometimes," she scolded gently, "you know me a little too well."

Kane refilled his coffee cup. "When's the baby
due?" he asked.

Rusty resumed his seat next to Mary Beth. He
reached out to pat her round belly with a familiar
hand. "This little rooster's about to hatch any day
now," he said with a chuckle.

Mary Beth swatted his hand away. "A rooster?
Who's to say it's not a hen?"

Rusty's expression softened. He slid his arm
around her shoulders and pulled her close. "You
know I don't much care either way, as long as you're
both all right."

Kane deliberately averted his eyes. An odd sensation knotted around his chest. Rusty and Mary
Beth were obviously very much in love, and didn't
care who knew it. A knife-like pain spliced through
him. That, he realized, was what he wanted for
himself and Abby. A home, filled with love and
warmth. And like Rusty and Mary Beth, the chance
to have a baby of their own . . .

His mind came to a skidding halt. *A baby.* Kane's
palms grew clammy. That was something he hadn't
considered—and he knew damn well Abby hadn't.
Lord God, she might even now be carrying his
baby . . .

Christ! Maybe he'd been wrong to leave. But he
wanted his life back. He wanted his name back. He
wanted the chance to live his life without constant-
ly looking over his shoulder.

He was only half-aware of excusing himself. Outside on the porch, he dragged in a lungful of stinging night air, trying to clear his spinning thoughts. Was this a fool's errand after all? The only way to clear his name was to find Lorelei's murderer. And how the hell was he supposed to do that? He had no idea where to begin. Lorelei had had no enemies that he'd known of. He'd discounted robbery long ago; there had been nothing missing from the house.

Rusty joined him out on the porch a few minutes later. Kane stared up at the inky night sky. "What happened after I escaped?" he asked quietly.

Rusty let out a long breath. "It's been so long now, it's hard to remember," he admitted. "Seems like there was a big uproar for a couple of days."

"Led by anybody in particular?"

"Not as I recall," Rusty began. All at once he stopped short. "No," he said slowly. "No, that's not right. There was somebody who was pretty vocal about Sheriff Keenan sending out a posse."

Kane grimaced. "The sheriff never liked me to begin with. He was damned eager to see me strung up."

"Oh, he was a mean-spirited coot if there ever was," Rusty agreed. He was silent for a moment, then suddenly snapped his fingers.

"Allan Mason, that's who it was. He's the one who insisted the sheriff send out a posse—even went along, as I recall."

Allan Mason. There was an elusive tug deep in Kane's brain. Allan Mason had been Lorelei's attorney.

Kane was silent for a moment. "I rode past the

ranch on my way in. Looks like it's been kept up pretty well." He paused. "What happened to it once I was gone?"

"It was put up for auction and sold to the highest bidder." Rusty's features were grim. "And I'll give you one guess as to who that was." He stared at Kane expectantly.

The pieces began to fit together . . . Suddenly it all made perfect sense . . . "Christ! Don't tell me it was Allan Mason."

Rusty nodded. "Never thought about it before, but it's a hell of a coincidence."

Kane cursed himself for a fool. Lord, he should have known. But at the time, all that mattered was finding a way to stay alive . . .

His laugh was harsh. "More than a coincidence, I'd say. I remember Lorelei rode into town to see Mason just a few days before she was killed. Said she planned to have my name added to the title for the ranch. Hell, that was even used as evidence against me!"

Rusty rubbed his chin. "You know what I think? I think maybe Mason decided to get rid of her, and lay the blame on you so's he could buy himself her ranch—and dirt cheap, too, from what I heard!"

"You're probably right. But how the hell am I supposed to prove it? Nobody believed me four years ago—they thought I was just a drifter lucky enough to marry the boss, and then got rid of her so I could get my hands on her ranch." He moved down the stairs, then paced in a tight circle.

"Allan Mason is a goddamned saint in this town. Who the hell would believe me over him?" He kicked savagely at the dust. "I don't have a damned thing to go on! It would be Mason's word against mine."

"But if the sheriff were to hear it for himself—"

Kane's lip curled. "The sheriff! Hell, if I show up on his doorstep he'll string me up in the nearest tree!"

Rusty shook his head. "I don't think so," he said softly. "No, I don't think so at all."

Kane shot him a venomous glare. "Man, you're loco! You know damn well he would!"

The merest hint of a smile lurked on Rusty's mouth. "No," he stated calmly. "You see, Keenan's dead. And the sheriff who took his place just happens to be my brother-in-law . . ."

Saturday nights at the ranch were always quiet as a tomb. Most of the ranch hands rode into town to spend their hard-earned money drinking, playing poker and whoring. It would be morning before they staggered back to the bunkhouse, smelly and still half-drunk, many of them broke—but happy as a bee in a field of clover.

Allan Mason had every intention of joining his boys in town, but he was in no hurry. He had learned to take life easy, to snatch at opportunity as it came his way. He strode into his study, a brandy in his hand. A smug smile of satisfaction creased his lips as he eased into the chair behind the wide mahogany desk. He glanced around, admiring the pine-paneled walls, the rich dark furniture.

He leaned back and laced his fingers over a belly given to excess. Behind him, a cool evening breeze fluttered through the curtains at the window. A mirthful laugh erupted. He had more than he'd ever dreamed of . . . and it had cost him so little! Oh, yes, he gloated, this ranch had been a real steal . . .

"Maybe," came a lazy drawl from behind him, "you'd care to share the joke with me."

Cold steel butted the back of his neck. Mason froze. "What the hell?" he gasped.

Slowly the intruder stepped around him and into the circle of lamplight. Mason gaped as he beheld a face he'd never thought to see again.

"Big of you to keep up the place while I was gone, Mason. Looks like you've kept things real nice."

Mason swallowed. "You're a fool to come back here, Kane. There's a noose in town just waiting to stretch your neck."

Kane just smiled, a smile that made Mason's blood run cold. "You're already wanted for one murder, Kane. Do you really want to make it two?"

"Ah, but we both know I didn't kill Lorelei. Don't we, Mason?"

The man said nothing. Kane raised the barrel of his Colt until it was level with his heart. His eyes were glittering shards of onyx. "I won't ask again, Mason. We both know I didn't kill her, don't we?"

Time spun out endlessly. The air was laden with expectancy. For one horrifying moment, Kane feared he had come all this way for nothing—that Mason would refuse to cooperate. But just when he'd nearly given up hope, Mason burst out, "All right, I—I'll tell you. I know you didn't kill Lorelei."

Kane's gaze narrowed. "It was you, wasn't it? You killed her—or did you have someone else do it for you?"

"It was me," he admitted, his voice very low.

More than anything Kane wanted to reach across the desk and curl his fingers around Mason's pudgy neck. With an effort he restrained his fury. "Speak up, Mason. I can't hear you."

"It was me."

"Louder."

"I just told you, it was me! I killed her—I shot Lorelei! Now just—just put away the gun!"

Kane's fingers unclenched around the handle of his Colt. He had to force himself to slide the weapon back into its holster.

"Just to set the record straight, I'd like to know why."

The immediate threat to his life now removed, Mason's eyes blazed. "Why? Because she was a fool, that's why! She could have had me, but she turned to you—a dirty, no-good cowboy—as if I wasn't good enough for her!"

The stirrings of an old memory resurfaced. Dimly Kane recalled Lorelie telling him that she'd been seeing Mason after Emmett had died. She'd said it was hardly serious, and so it had slipped his mind.

Kane's expression hardened. "She came to see you about having my name added to hers, so that we were co-owners of the ranch. And her will . . . She told me she'd changed her will, too, and named me as her heir. That's when you decided to murder her, didn't you?"

Mason's lips drew back over his teeth. "This ranch is worth a fortune! Why should *you* have it—hell, why should she? She proved she was a slut when she let you into her bed. She would never even let me touch her! She didn't deserve it, any more than she deserved me! Oh, but I showed her," he taunted. "If I couldn't have her, I'd damn sure get my hands on her ranch. And then there was you—so much a man you ran like a lily-livered coward." His gaze slid to the gun Kane had replaced in his holster. "Hell, you're too much a coward to shoot me now!"

Kane smiled tightly. "Oh, there's no question I'd like to. But I think the sheriff might have some say-so in what happens to you now."

"The sheriff," Mason sneered. "He'll never believe you. He'll believe me, just like before."

"That's where you're wrong," proclaimed another voice. "In fact, looks to me like Kane here was tried for a crime he didn't commit. And I'd say I've heard enough to lock you up and see that you're tried for murder."

Mason's eyes bulged. He hadn't seen the shadowy form that had slipped in through the open window. He leaped to his feet and stared at the sheriff as if he'd been struck dumb.

The sheriff, a lean, raw-boned man with keen blue eyes, pulled out a pair of handcuffs. "Yes, indeed, looks like I'd better wire the judge and see about setting a trial date."

A rush of giddy relief swept through Kane. It was over, he realized. He could finally get on with his life. He was free. Free to go back to Wyoming . . .

And back to Abby.

Chapter 20

〜〜✄〜〜

At first the hurt was more than Abby could stand. She couldn't believe Kane had cleared out, packed his belongings and left, with no explanation . . .

With no good-bye.

She remembered vividly the exact moment when she stood in the barn, staring in disbelief at Midnight's empty stall. It seemed like yesterday that she had desperately wanted to scream aloud her pain and heartache. But all she could do was weep—silent, scalding tears that made no sound.

Six weeks later there were no more tears left. Her anguish had given way to a bitter resentment.

She experienced a wrench of shame every time she thought of how completely she had given herself to him—how she had held nothing back . . . In the cold light of day, Abby was under no illusions. Despite the unforgettable night they had shared, she knew he wouldn't be back. After all, he'd made no promises; nor had he given her any reason to hope he felt the same. Certainly *he* hadn't been foolish enough to profess undying love.

July passed into August, and August into September. Kane had been gone less than a week when Buck Russell began calling on her. The first time was to express his sympathies for the loss of her father. The second was to escort her to Sunday services in town. Out of courtesy more than anything else, Abby had asked him to stay for dinner. Dillon hadn't been pleased when he found out Buck's visits had become almost a daily occurrence.

"How come he's sniffing around your skirts now, little sister? Why after all this time?"

"You haven't liked him since the time he bloodied your nose over that Hawkins girl when the two of you were fifteen," Abby said crossly.

His jaw thrust out. "He's no bargain, Abby. He was a womanizer even then. Hell, he still is! He's a regular at the Silver Spur. Believe me, I know. Why, Pa wouldn't have let him anywhere near you!"

"Whatever faults Buck Russell may have, he's a shrewd businessman," Abby said challengingly. "He knows this land and cattle like the back of his hand—in fact, he's a damn good rancher. Even Pa thought so."

"He's not the right man for you, Abby. You know it as well as I do. Hell, we both know it's the Diamondback he wants!"

Abby's lips tightened. She wasn't going to blind herself the way she had with Kane. She suspected it wouldn't be long before Buck Russell proposed marriage. Buck might not be a prize, but he knew how to run an operation the size of the Diamondback. These past two months had taught her she couldn't handle it all herself. She needed someone she could rely on day after day—not someone like Dillon who lent a hand only when he could spare the time—and more importantly, because he felt he *had* to, not because he wanted to.

"You know as well as I do the Diamondback meant everything to Pa," she said sharply. "I'm simply looking out for the future—"

"The future," he snorted. "Sounds to me like you've got a lot more on your mind than an escort for the Saturday-night shindig!"

"And what if I do? I'm twenty-one years old. It's high time I got married!"

"Not to the likes of Buck Russell!"

For the life of her, Abby didn't know when she'd ever seen Dillon more furious. But there was no use pining for what could never be—if she'd learned nothing else these past weeks, she'd learned that.

Dillon paced around the parlor. Finally he ground to a halt on the braided rug before her. "What about you, Abby? What about what *you* want? A pen full of steers and acres and acres of grassland won't keep you warm at night. It won't keep you company when you're old and gray!"

Her laugh was short. "My, my, this is certainly a change. When did you decide to start cozying up to home and hearth?"

He glared at her. "This isn't me we're talking about here, little sister—it's you. Which reminds me . . . What about Kane?"

Abby drew a sharp breath. Kane was the one thing she didn't want to discuss, not with Dillon or anyone else. She struggled for a calm she was far from feeling. "Kane has nothing at all to do with this," she said shortly.

Dillon's eyes narrowed. "Don't play innocent with me, Abby. I had a feeling something was going on the way you fell apart when he got shot. Then when he was here at the ranch you hardly left him alone for two minutes! It was pretty damn obvious you were sweet on him."

Abby flushed painfully. She hadn't realized she'd been so obvious... But Dillon's reaction was puzzling. She had been so convinced the very idea of his sister associating with a man like Kane would have blown the lid off his temper.

"It's probably better that he did go," she said, her voice very low. She had told Dillon about Kane's wife and how he'd been framed for her murder. "Even if he didn't kill his wife, he rode with Stringer Sam—"

"Even the best of men make mistakes, Abby. Sometimes a gut reaction is the only thing a man can rely on." He gave a harsh laugh. "Believe me, I know. And if I had thought Kane was a cold-blooded murderer, he wouldn't have set foot on this ranch. He sure as *hell* wouldn't have stayed in this house with you. And there's a part of me that wonders if Kane wouldn't be a damn sight better for you than Buck Russell."

His defense of Kane made her want to hang her head in shame.

"I'm afraid I can't agree," she told him quietly. "Besides, Kane's gone. And it's just as I said—I have to look out for the ranch."

Dillon rolled his eyes. "So we're back to that again, are we?"

His condescending tone sparked the fuse on Abby's temper. She jumped to her feet. "Let's be honest with each other, Dillon. Why don't you just admit this ranch doesn't mean a damn thing to you—it never did!"

Dillon stared at her. But his mind had drifted

back in time . . . Once, he thought vaguely, once
he might have been able to settle down here, the
way Pa had wanted . . . A knifelike twinge cut into
his heart. How different things might have been, if
only Rose had lived! With her at his side, he might
have been happy here. Pa's dream of making the
Diamondback a family operation might have been
his dream, too. But Rose was gone. And so was Pa.
And his life had been forever changed . . .

With an effort he dragged himself back to the
present. "What do you want me to say, Abby?"
His voice was gritty with suppressed emotion. "Do
you think I didn't think long and hard before I
signed up to scout for the army? You were just a
kid so you don't remember. I knew how much Pa
wanted me to stay here and work the ranch with
him. But I just wasn't cut out for ranching, for this
kind of life." He paused. "You're like Pa," he said
finally. "This land, this ranch, meant everything to
him—"

"Pa didn't die for this land, Dillon. He died for
you."

That was the one thing he didn't need to hear,
and in that instant, he bitterly resented his sister
for that brutal reminder.

"Look," he said, his voice very low. "I'm doing
the best I can—"

"And so am I, Dillon. So am I. I need someone
to help me run this ranch. Someone I can depend
on. Someone I can rely on."

His gaze sharpened. "Are you trying to make
me feel guilty?" he demanded. "I just couldn't do
things Pa's way. I've got my own life to live, and
I'll thank you to stay out of it."

"And I'll thank you to stay out of mine," she retorted coolly.

He swore. "Christ, Abby, you're a fool if you sell your soul for a goddamned piece of land!"

"I'm old enough to make my own choices, remember?"

His eyes were cutting. "Looks to me like you've already made it." He snatched up his hat and stalked toward the door.

That had been this afternoon. Abby was still rather upset when Buck came by that evening. Lately it seemed that whenever she saw Dillon, all they did was bicker and fight. She wasn't about to mention the conversation to Buck, though. They sat outside on the swing that hung from the porch rafters. Darkness gathered all around. Abby was quieter than usual but Buck paid no notice. He was busy talking about the stock he planned to purchase in Denver in several weeks.

Now she felt the slide of his fingertips against the thin calico of her blouse, around and around the curve of her shoulder. "Ever been to Denver, Abby?"

"A long time ago with Pa. I was just a kid, though." Abby resisted the urge to squirm out from beneath his touch. It flashed through her mind that she'd never felt that way with Kane. Irritated with the thought, she reminded herself that Buck was a handsome man. Most women would have been proud to have him come calling the way he had lately.

"Oh, it's a wild town sometimes. Always somethin' going on. You'd like it, I think." He paused. "Maybe you'll get a chance to see it—sooner than you think."

His tone was low and intimate. Abby found the avid boldness of his look unnerving. "Perhaps," she murmured. She summoned a faint smile. "Buck, I hate to be rude. But I have an early day planned for tomorrow, and I'm sure you do, too."

"I guess I do, at that." A hand at her elbow, he helped her up. His hand remained cupped there as they crossed to stand in the center of the porch. His fingers tightened ever so slightly.

"How about a little good-bye kiss to see me off?" he suggested.

Tall and dark-haired, Buck towered over her by nearly a foot. He really was a handsome man, Abby noted with a curious detachment. Razor-sharp blue eyes gleamed beneath rich brown hair. His features were elegant but masculine. One had only to glance at him to know he was a thorough, capable man. But it was his air of brash confidence that sometimes annoyed her to no end.

"Well, Abby. How about it?" His words were soft and cajoling. His arms were hard about her back and wholly determined as he pulled her close.

She hesitated. Again her mind sped straight to Kane. The next instant she berated herself fiercely for her lack of control—and lack of enthusiasm. Certainly it wasn't as if she'd never been kissed before ...

"Very well," she murmured. Closing her eyes, she turned her lips up to his.

His kiss wasn't the chaste peck she expected. His mouth came down on hers, moist and full. Abby inhaled sharply and attempted to draw back. He caught her chin between thumb and forefinger. "Not so fast," he murmured smoothly. "I've waited a long time for this. Why not make it worthwhile?"

His mouth again trapped hers. Though his hold was not hurtful, he allowed no retreat. His kiss was stark and sensual, both persuasive and seductive—it spun through Abby's mind that he certainly knew his way around women. Yet while she felt no distaste, neither did she feel any pleasure. Indeed, she felt strangely numb, as if she watched from a distance. The pressure of his mouth deepened. His hands skimmed down her spine, feathering over her buttocks. He urged her against his lower body a scant second before he released her.

He ran a finger down her cheek, eyes dark and smoldering. "Why don't we have a picnic down by the river tomorrow afternoon after church, just the two of us?" He didn't give her the chance to agree or disagree. "I'll stop by at two o'clock."

He disappeared into the night. The sound of hoofbeats filled the air. Abby blinked, just a little stunned. She'd been feeling rather guilty that his kiss left her so unaffected—and he hadn't even noticed!

"What the *hell* did you think you were doing letting him paw you like that?"

She froze. Her eyes strained, sifting through the gloomy shadows surrounding the house. Just when she was convinced she'd conjured up that silk-steel drawl out of some perverse longing, he stepped forward. The light spilling out through the parlor window caught him in its glow.

Kane.

Her heart had forgotten how to beat. Her legs felt like Dorothy's fresh-made jam. His features were drawn, his clothing dusty and travel-stained. He looked leaner than ever. Even as her eyes drank in the sight of him, all she could think was that it was just like him to forego the courtesy of a greeting.

Her spine straightened. Her chin came up. "A gentleman would have made his presence known instead of spying on us like that!"

He shook his head. He was smiling, a smile that didn't quite reach his eyes. "How many times do I have to tell you, sweetheart? I'm no gentleman."

Lord, he was as maddening as ever. "I am not your sweetheart and I'll thank you to stop calling me that once and for all!"

He hitched his chin to the west, where the other man had ridden off. "I'm curious, sweetheart. Was that Buck Russell?"

He was coming up the steps now. She sensed something hard and dangerous in his manner, something that made her want to turn tail and run for all she was worth. Instead she stood her ground with uneasy caution.

"What do you know about Buck Russell? How do you even know who he is?"

"Midnight threw a shoe just outside of town. The smith was just bursting at the seams when he found out I was headed out here. He was only too willing to bend my ear with some mighty interesting gossip."

Abby surveyed him warily. Kane's easy tone belied the tempest alive in his eyes.

"He said you and Buck Russell are real tight these days. Rumor also has it there might be a wedding real soon."

Abby felt like grinding her teeth. Was Buck

responsible for that rumor? She had the sneaking suspicion he was, the arrogant fool!

"Well?" Kane demanded. "Has he asked you to marry him?"

Abby's temper began to simmer. Who did Kane think he was to reappear in her life again like this—making demands, insisting on answers—as if he had every right to do so!

She glared her dissatisfaction. "I don't see what business it is of yours."

"I'm making it my business," he said between his teeth.

"Well, don't!" She spun around and marched into the house.

Kane was right behind her. When she realized he had followed, she whirled and gave him a look designed to make him feel lower than a snake.

He grimaced. As if he didn't already . . . They stood just inside the parlor. It took every ounce of willpower Kane possessed not to reach for her. A muscle in his cheek contracted.

"Dammit, Abby, tell me. Did he ask you to marry him?"

Too late Abby realized her silence had given her away. God, how she hated the satisfied gleam in his eyes.

"Just because he hasn't *yet* doesn't mean he won't. In fact, I expect he'll propose any day now. And when he does," she informed him heatedly, "you may rest assured you *won't* be the first to know. Because I'll say it again, Kane—what I do or don't do is none of your affair!"

She was angry—Kane could see it in the defiant tilt of her chin. "And what if I make it my affair?"

Even as he spoke, his gaze roved her face hungrily. She was thinner, the hollows in her cheeks more pronounced. Even in the dim light, he could see how pale she was—her eyes were bigger and bluer than ever. Was it worry over him that caused the changes he saw? The thought sent his heart soaring.

The next minute she was ripping it to shreds.

"I can't think why you would want to. You made your choice the night you left here, Kane. You were so eager to leave . . . . You could have stayed on but you didn't . . . Well, this time I don't care. Go. Stay. Do whatever the hell you like. Just *stay out of my life!*"

For the longest time he didn't say anything. He just stared at her, his eyes as anguished as hers.

"I can't do that, Abby."

She gave a brittle laugh. "Oh, yes, you can. You already proved you had no trouble at all walking away from me and not looking back. After all, I had it from your own lips—you're a drifter! Why I expected anything more is beyond me. I guess I'm just the world's biggest fool!"

"No. You're no fool, Abby. But you will be if you marry Buck Russell."

She went white about the mouth. "What do you know about it?"

His lips twisted. "All I need to know. You said it yourself. Your half-ownership of the Diamondback makes you a wealthy woman—and rather attractive in the marriage market, I'd say. Looks like you won't have to worry about not being courted after all, sweetheart. Even if you turn down Buck I imagine there'll be a dozen others just waiting in line after him."

Abby gasped. He inferred too much—that no man would want her for herself. Before she had stopped to think, she'd dealt him a stinging, open-handed blow to the side of the cheek.

Stunned at the extent of her own violence, she pressed a shaking hand to her mouth. "Damn you!" she cried, her voice breaking at last. "Damn you anyway, Kane! Why did you ever come back? Why didn't you just stay away?"

Kane steeled himself inside and out. "I had to come back," he said, very low. "We were ... together more than once, Abby. Don't you know there could have been ... consequences?"

She lowered her hand slowly to her side. "Consequences?" she whispered.

He made a disgusted sound. "A baby, Abby. A baby!"

"Oh." She glanced away, certain she was as red as the sunset had been earlier. "You don't need to worry," she announced in a high, tight voice that sounded nothing at all like her own. "Besides, what were you going to do? Make an honest woman out of me?"

Hot color crept beneath the bronze of his skin. "What if I was?" Guilt seared him, like acid eating away at his insides. There was a time when he *had* wanted to walk away. Until that last incredible night, he'd had every intention of leaving Abby— and never coming back. And he might have been able to, if only she hadn't said she loved him.

But he couldn't lie to himself forever. His time with Abby had awakened a long-dormant need inside him. His whole life he'd longed for nothing more than to be accepted, the same as everyone else. He wanted a home, roots, and a family—things he'd never dared dream about before ... Now it was *all* he thought about.

Only now this wasn't coming out at all like he'd planned. She was furious. He'd expected that, but he hadn't expected the situation with Buck Russell ... Damn, but she hadn't wasted any time either! And now his own temper was riled ...

Abby was too shocked to notice his defensiveness. Her mind was spinning. Was he asking *her* to marry him? She sank into a chair, suddenly too weak to stand any longer.

"You came back here to see if I was expecting a baby ... to marry me?"

"Yes, goddammit! Why is that so hard to believe?"

Marriage—to Kane. Lord, it would have been everything she wanted . ... But there was a rending pain in her heart. He hadn't come back because he loved her—not even because he cared, just a little ... He'd felt *obliged* to marry her.

"Oh, my." An hysterical laugh bubbled up inside. "Well, you don't need to worry, Kane. There's no need for you to even try to be noble. There's no baby—no need to make such a *sacrifice* as marrying me. Besides, you're hardly a good catch—here one day, gone the next. And you're an outlaw, no less! Buck is a much better prospect, don't you agree?"

He hauled her up and out of the chair so fast her head spun dizzily. "Aren't you going to ask me why I disappeared, Abby? Where I've been all this time?"

"No!" Defiance blazed in her eyes. She tried to jerk free. He wouldn't let her.

"I'm not an outlaw," he said harshly. "Do you

hear me? I'm not a wanted man anymore! I went back to New Mexico to see if I could clear my name. I didn't murder Lorelei and I figured it was time I stopped paying for a crime I didn't commit. Thanks to a friend, I found out her ranch was put up for auction after I escaped—and guess who bought it? Her attorney, Allan Mason, and dirt-cheap, too! He set me up, Abby. He framed me for her murder just to get his hands on her ranch!"

His fingers bit into her shoulders. "Maybe I was wrong to leave the way I did," he went on roughly. "Maybe I should have told you. But I didn't know if I'd be able to clear my name—hell, for all I knew, I could have been shot down the minute I walked into town! And I thought you'd try to keep me from leaving and I didn't want that! I remember you said that night that if I stayed, it would be a chance to start over for me—and you were right!

"But first I had to free myself of my past—I had to stop looking over my shoulder!" He floundered, searching for the right words. "I—I wanted to feel worthy of you, Abby. So I had to leave—I had to go back to New Mexico and finish what happened there once and for all. I never meant to be gone so long, but I had to stay and testify at Mason's trial. And once he was convicted, the judge declared me the rightful owner of Lorelei's ranch. It took a while, but I sold it because I didn't want to come to you with nothing but the clothes on my back—I didn't want you to think I was after *your* money or your half of the ranch. Maybe you can't understand it. You've never had anyone treat you like dirt! But I wanted to come to you with my name as clear as my conscience. Don't you see, I did it for you!"

In an anguished kind of way, Abby *did* understand. His pride had forced him to it. Only if he hadn't been so stubborn, if he had listened to her just once, he'd have known that his past didn't make one whit of difference in her feelings for him! And right now all she could see was that salvaging his pride had been more important to him than she was.

"You did it for me," she choked out. "Kane, how can you say that? Do you have any idea what you put me through? I was out of my head with worry. You left before Dr. Foley even took the stitches out. I had visions of you lying dead alongside the road! That night . . . I thought we had something special . . . I thought you felt it, too . . . God, I—I told you I loved you . . . And what did you do . . . You just left me without a word! . . . Do you know what it was like, knowing I'd never see you again . . . thinking you didn't care . . ."

The words were a torment for them both. He felt the deep, shuddering breath she drew. He knew she was convinced he'd been unforgivably cruel. Maybe he had. His guts twisted. But he'd make it up to her, if only she'd give him the chance. He started to tighten his embrace, to soothe with lips and hands all that he had laid bare, but she thrust herself away.

With the back of her hand she wiped the tears from her cheeks. The angry hurt she felt was like fire in her lungs. "You thought I was spoiled and pampered, Kane. All the time we were after Stringer Sam, you were convinced I thought only of myself. But who were you thinking of when you left? Did you ever think how I might feel? No! You were the selfish one, Kane—you!"

His eyes never left her face. "What do you want from me, Abby? You want me to beg? Fine. I'm begging you. Marry me." His voice was gritty, as gritty as his vision. Fear had a stranglehold around him, the awful fear that he was about to lose the only thing he'd ever really wanted. "I—I can't live without you. I don't even want to try. Being with you ... it changed me. Maybe because you believed what I couldn't believe anymore—that I wasn't the devil's own hand. Maybe because you saw what I thought was gone forever."

Oh! So now he was proposing out of gratitude? For saving his soul from damnation? Abby wasn't sure if she should laugh or cry. Yet his manner was anything but humble. He looked as if he were fighting mad.

Inside her heart was breaking. Lord, but she'd been a fool. She had trusted him with her life and with Dillon's. But trusting him with her heart was something else entirely—and something she wouldn't do again!

Her breath came raggedly. "You're mad to think I would even consider becoming your wife! Why, my pa would never have considered you a fit husband! So just—just get out and don't come back!"

Kane went rigid. His eyes pierced hers, as if to see clear into her heart. "You mean that, don't you?"

"Yes!"

There would be no reasoning with her, he realized. She was dead-set against him, and he knew from experience she wouldn't relent.

An icy tightness settled around his heart. His

lips barely moved as he spoke. "Have it your way, sweetheart—you usually do anyway." He whirled and stalked out of the parlor, slamming the door behind him.

Only then did Abby realize what she'd done . . . She collapsed in a flood of angry tears.

Chapter 21

Dillon wasn't surprised to see Buck Russell's sorrel stallion hitched in front of the Silver Spur. His mouth curled in disgust. The hard line of his jaw thrust forward, he shoved aside the slatted wooden doors and stepped inside.

As always, the crowd was noisy and rambunctious. A half-drunk barmaid warbled an off-key tune to the trill of the piano. An occasional shout from the poker table punctuated the uproar. Dillon's gaze drilled through the smoky haze, finally settling on the table in the far corner. Sure enough, Buck Russell was there along with several of his cowboys, his long legs lazily sprawled beneath the table. Polly, a buxom brunette, sat on his lap, her hand inside his shirt.

Dillon cussed under his breath, a long, fluent curse that did little to vent his frustration. This was the man Abby wanted for a husband? The rutting bastard couldn't keep his fly closed if the damn thing were nailed shut!

Four long strides carried him across the floor.

The two cowboys scrambled to their feet. Polly hurriedly uncurled herself from Buck's lap. Buck appeared nonplussed at Dillon's appearance.

Then an easy smile spread across his handsome

face. He waved the others away. "Evening, Marshal." Pulling his cigar from his lips, he gestured Dillon to the seat across from him. "Can I pour you a drink?"

"Not tonight, or any other night, Russell." Dillon's tone was terse. He remained standing. "I think it's time you and me had a little conversation."

Buck raised a brow. "Something seems to have your dander up, Marshal. If one of my men has—"

"This doesn't have anything to do with your men. Let's just say I'm mighty curious as to why you're sniffing at my sister's skirts all of a sudden."

Buck merely laughed. "Marshal, apparently you haven't taken a good look at your sister lately. She's a beautiful woman. Intelligent. Well-educated and well-bred—"

"And also half-owner of the biggest spread in the Territory. We can't forget that now, can we?" Dillon didn't bother to hide his mockery.

Buck was still smiling, but his eyes had gone diamond-hard. "We all have ambitions, don't we, Marshal?"

Buck had just confirmed Dillon's suspicions. It was the ranch Buck Russell was after; Abby was merely the means to attain it. The hell of it was that she knew it—she knew and still she didn't care!

It was all he could do not to haul the other man from his chair and plant a fist squarely in the middle of his jaw.

Buck blew a ring of smoke into the air. "In case you're wondering, I'm not entirely the rascal you think. I've kept my hands to myself. I'm not about to forget she's a lady. After all, a man like me has certain standards that must be met when it comes to taking a wife. I've made no secret of that."

A wife. So it was true. He *did* plan to marry Abby. Buck's pronouncement gave Dillon little satisfaction.

Deliberately he placed his hands flat on the table. He leaned forward so that they were nearly face-to-face. His voice was deadly quiet. "I can't stop Abby from marrying you, if that's what she wants. But I think if she does, she'll be making the biggest mistake of her life. So I'll say this once, Russell. You hurt her—*ever*—and it won't matter one damn bit that I'm wearing a badge. I'll see that you pay." He turned and walked out without a backward glance.

Dust flew behind his heels as he strode back toward his office. For the life of him, he didn't understand Abby. Why was she so determined to put the ranch ahead of her own happiness? Didn't she know that marriage was more than a business proposition—more than a herd of cattle and money in the bank? She deserved far better than that land-grubbing swine, Buck Russell. She deserved to be happy.

She deserved to be loved.

He stalked into his office, his expression dark as a thunderhead. Duke Severins, his new deputy, looked up from behind the desk as he entered. He gestured toward the chair in the opposite corner.

"Got a visitor, Marshal."

It was Kane. Dillon's eyes narrowed as the other man got to his feet, looking dusty, travel-stained and weary. His gaze slid back to Duke.

"Why don't you take a break for a while?" he suggested. "I'll hold things down here."

Kane had yet to speak. Dillon dropped his hat on the wall peg and took a seat behind the desk. "This is quite a surprise, Kane." He propped his booted feet on the corner and leaned back. "Abby gave me the impression you'd cleared out for good."

"Abby likes to come to her own conclusions sometimes. In this case it was hardly the right one."

Despite his foul mood, Dillon's lips quirked. "Saw her already, eh?"

"Oh, I saw her, all right. She didn't exactly roll out the welcome wagon."

"I told Abby this afternoon I thought she was sweet on you. Got the feeling it wasn't exactly a one-sided affair."

Kane's gaze sharpened. "It sure as hell isn't," he said slowly. He seemed to hesitate. "That doesn't bother you?"

Dillon's smile withered. "Let me put it this way. If you hadn't left, I think I'd have a few less problems." He motioned for Kane to pull up a chair. "Where the hell have you been all this time?"

Kane grimaced. "Can you believe I was trying to be noble? I went back to New Mexico to try to clear my name."

"Did you?"

Kane nodded.

"Well, well. Now that sounds like something to celebrate." Dillon opened a drawer in his desk and pulled out a bottle of strong Irish whiskey and two glasses. He filled both with a generous portion and handed one to Kane.

Kane accepted it with a grimace. "I'm not so sure," he said with a short laugh. "Abby's got herself in a dither because I left without telling her.

I didn't say anything because I didn't know if I'd even make it back." He went on to tell Dillon of all that had happened in New Mexico.

By the time he'd finished, the lines in Dillon's forehead had eased, while Kane's had deepened.

"I didn't want to raise any false hopes in case I ended up in prison—or dangling at the end of a noose. But Abby doesn't see it that way."

Kane fell silent. Damn! She still cared. He knew it. If she hadn't cried, he might have believed otherwise. But even with tears streaming down her face, she had denied him. What the hell was he supposed to do?

He stared into what little of the amber-colored liquid remained in his glass. "Shit," he muttered aloud. "I can't go. Yet how the hell can I stay when it looks like she's about to tie the knot with somebody named Buck Russell!"

Dillon shook his head. "I'm afraid I may be to blame for that," he admitted. "Pa left half the ranch to each of us, but I wish to hell he'd left me out of it. I'd turn my half over to her, but how can I? She knows a lot about ranching, especially for a woman. But the Diamondback's too much for her to handle. She needs a partner. I help out when I can, but I just don't have the time or the inclination." His lips thinned. "It's common knowledge I got no call for ranching. Buck Russell probably figures if he marries Abby, he'll have it all for himself."

Kane was just a little puzzled. "Sounds like you don't have much use for Buck Russell."

"Damn right I don't. He's a cold, heartless bastard. All he cares about is land and power and money. The only reason he wants to marry Abby is so he can get his hands on the ranch. I tried to tell Abby he's not the man for her." He snorted. "The stubborn little fool won't listen! Says she's got the future to worry about." He slammed his hand down against the desk. "You can't let her marry him, Kane. You have to stop her somehow!"

Kane was startled. "I think she's a lot more likely to listen to you than me—"

"Oh, but I think you could be a hell of a lot more persuasive than I could. Do whatever you have to. You understand what I'm saying? I won't stand in your way."

Kane stared at him, almost unable to believe what he was hearing. "Why are you doing this?" he asked quietly. "Why would you possibly take my side against Buck Russell?"

"For the best reason in the world." Dillon looked him straight in the eye. "Better a man who loves her than a man who doesn't."

Kane looked down at his hands. He laughed, an odd note in his voice. "Guess it shows, huh?"

Dillon's eyes softened. "I wouldn't have it any other way. This is my sister we're talking about, remember?" A glimmer of understanding passed between them. Strangely enough, Kane didn't feel at all foolish over his confession.

Dillon's smile faded. "Now," he muttered, not bothering to disguise his impatience, "we just have to figure out a way to get Buck Russell out of the picture."

Kane swirled the whiskey in his glass. His mind drifted to Lorelei's ranch, the ranch he'd just sold in New Mexico. He'd insisted that Rusty take a healthy chunk of the profit—after all, he owed Rusty his freedom—but he was still a wealthy man. His jaw hardened. Yet what good was money, if he didn't have Abby?

The idea came out of nowhere; it caught and took hold . . .

He was on his feet before he realized it, staring at Dillon. "What a minute," he said slowly. "You said something before, about turning your half of the ranch over to Abby."

Dillon's lips thinned. "I would, if Buck Russell was out of the way."

"I've got a better idea," Kane stated calmly. "Why not sell it to me?"

Buck proposed the next afternoon.

They sat beneath the shelter of a copse of trees, near the bank of the river. Fluffy white clouds floated overhead. Birds flitted to and fro, high above their heads. There was just enough breeze to cool the warm air and keep the heat from being stifling. It really would have been so very idyllic, even romantic, she mused vaguely. But although the setting was everything a woman could ask for . . .

The man was not.

"Well, Abby? How about it? You willing to marry me or not?"

To Abby's dismay, the muscles of her throat locked tight. A flurry of panic gripped her mind. Was this right or wrong? Dillon wanted out. Buck wanted in.

It struck her then . . . If she married Buck, she would be spending a lifetime tied to this brash, imperious man. Instinct warned her that his own needs would always come first—never hers. Dear Lord! How could she say yes?

Her mind screamed a resounding no. But her traitorous lips were another story. "Yes," she heard herself say, as if from a very great distance. "I'll marry you, Buck."

A big hand squeezed her knee. "Just think. The Triple R and the Diamondback." His laugh was bursting with satisfaction. "Honey, nobody in this whole territory is gonna be bigger 'n better than us!"

The rest of the day passed in a daze. Abby felt curiously numb and lifeless. They had a light supper at Buck's place; for the life of her Abby couldn't have recalled what they ate. It was dark by the time they returned to the Diamondback.

Buck walked her to the front door. The inside of the house was dark. Abby guessed that Lucas and Dorothy had gone back to their own place for the night.

Buck's hands settled heavily on her shoulders. He turned her to him. "It occurred to me this evening that Denver would be a hell of a good place for a honeymoon. Might as well mix a little business with pleasure."

Buck had pressed her several times during the evening to set a wedding date. She had been deliberately evasive. Now her breath caught.

"That's less than two weeks away, Buck."

Broad, leather-vested shoulders lifted in a shrug. "Don't see any point in waiting. Besides, it'll be hard to fit in a wedding once we start fall round-up."

Abby curbed her annoyance. In his arrogance, it never occurred to him that she might change her mind.

In the moonlight, his eyes glimmered. "Now," he murmured, "how about another kiss?"

Abby stiffened, but he paid no heed. His mouth came down on hers, hard and demanding, his tongue intrusive. She made a faint sound low in her throat but Buck was intent on his own pleasure. She would have pushed him away but his arm had clamped tight around her back. Her hands were trapped so tightly between their bodies she couldn't move.

Her lips felt throbbing and bruised by the time he'd lifted his head. He ran a finger down her jaw. " 'Night, sweetheart," he drawled.

A moment later the buckboard rolled away. Abby remained where she was, one hand pressed against her breast, trying vainly to still the turmoil in her heart.

"You know, I'm getting real tired of that man helping himself to what's mine. If you don't put a stop to it, sugar, I will."

Abby's heart jumped. *Kane.* His voice came from the shadows just off to her right. Even as she strained to see, he strode into view. Lord, but he was infuriating. Who did he think he was, spying on her—again!

He took a seat on the top step, his back braced against the post, his wrist hitched across his bent knee. An arrogant smile curved his lips as he held her gaze. His offhand manner rattled her temper. She bit back the retort that sprang to her lips. Instead she smiled sweetly.

"I guess I was wrong, Kane. It seems you *are* the first one to know, after all . . . You see, Buck asked me to marry him today. Naturally, I accepted."

His smile was wiped clean. He was up and on his feet with a swift economy of movement. He captured her wrists and pulled her close. His features bore a mask of anger, yet his words weren't what she expected.

"Don't do this, Abby. Don't marry him to spite me."

Abby's eyes flashed. "That has nothing to do with it!"

"Then why? Because you need a man to help run this ranch? I can do that, Abby. I *will* do it, if you just give me a chance."

"You?" Her laugh was scraping. "Why, Kane, you're hardly a good prospect. I never know when you're going to appear and disappear!"

He ignored her jab. His grip on her wrists tightened. "You don't love him. You know you don't."

"I'm going to marry him, Kane. And you can't stop me!"

"You're right. I can't. But I think there's something that just might stop *him* from wanting to marry you."

Her struggles stopped. A prickly unease raised the hair on her neck. "What do you mean?" she whispered.

Something that might have been regret flashed in his eyes. "I saw Dillon last night after I left here. We had quite a talk, your brother and I. Dillon's convinced Buck's only reason for marrying you is to get his hands on the Diamondback. No doubt he thinks Dillon will just bow out and he can do as he pleases."

Abby winced. That was something that might prove true—she simply hadn't wanted to consider it.

"But Dillon won't hand over his half of the ranch to Buck," Kane continued. "Do you know why?"

Abby had gone utterly still. She shook her head, her widened eyes on his face.

"Because Dillon sold his share of the ranch to me last night. I'm your new partner."

Chapter 22

Disbelief washed over her. "No," she said faintly. "You're lying."

"We're meeting at the bank at ten sharp tomorrow morning to finalize the papers."

She shook her head. "You're lying," she said again. "You don't have that kind of money—"

"I do now, Abby. I told you last night, I sold Lorelei's ranch in New Mexico. That's what held me up for so long getting back here."

A blind, irrational anger swept over her. She wrenched away from him. This time Kane made no move to stop her.

"God, I hate you both, you and Dillon! Who do you think you are, to do this to me? Do you think I've got nothing to offer a man but this ranch? Am I a homely old spinster that no one could possibly want for any other reason?"

Kane regarded her soberly. Her pride, he realized, had been sorely bruised. "Of course not," he began, stretching out a hand.

She slapped it away. "Don't touch me!" she spat. "Do you really think Buck won't marry me because of that? Well, I think you're wrong—you're forgetting I still own half this ranch!"

He sighed. "Abby, come tomorrow morning it'll be nice and legal."

"And maybe come tomorrow *evening* my marriage to Buck will be nice and legal! He wanted to be married by the time he left for Denver in two weeks, so I doubt he'll mind pushing up the date. Why, Reverend Gaines would marry us right now if we asked him!"

Kane swore softly. "Dammit, Abby, why do you have to make this so hard? I'm asking you to be my wife—to hell with Buck Russell!"

"I'd never consent to marrying you, Kane, never!"

Pure fury tightened the white line of his mouth, but his insides had gone cold. By God, he wouldn't beg. He tried that last night, and he'd be damned if he'd do it again. "You won't marry Buck Russell either. You don't love him."

Abby trembled. It was galling that he knew her so well. She said the only thing she could think of, the thing she sensed would hurt him the most.

"I don't love you either," she cried. "And I *will* marry him because whether or not I love him doesn't matter. He's a better man than you, Kane! I cringe to think I ever let you touch me!"

A muscle in his cheek ticked. A fierce light blazed in his eyes. Fear seized hold of her. She began to back away. "Kane—"

"You're a liar, Abby." He advanced toward her, smiling that mocking smile she so loathed.

She flung out a hand. "Stay away from me, Kane!"

"And I'm going to prove it," he continued as if she hadn't even spoken.

She bolted inside the house. She snatched up the rifle near the front entrance and brought up the barrel just as he cleared the hallway.

"Hold it right there!" she cried. "I want you to leave, Kane—now!"

He'd stopped cold. "I'll leave," he said quite pleasantly. "As long as you go with me."

"I'm not going anywhere with you ever again! I'm through with you, Kane!" She pointed the rifle at his chest.

"We've been through this before, Abby. You won't shoot me." He began to move forward.

She swallowed. He was so calm, so sure of himself—and of her. Nerveless fingers gripped the rifle stock more tightly. "Don't, Kane. I—I warn you, you'll be sorry!" She was on the verge of hysteria.

He made no answer. But the distance between them was closing. The barrel of the rifle wavered . . . but not that arrogant smile.

Whether she dropped the rifle or he grabbed it, Abby couldn't say. The next thing she knew the rifle had clattered to the polished wooden floor. She was caught up against a hard male form and swept from her feet. Swift, purposeful steps bore her up the stairs to her bedroom. Before she had a chance to catch her breath she'd been dumped in the middle of her bed.

By the time she pushed herself upright, he had lit the lamp in the corner. Eyes locked with hers, he slowly unbuckled his belt.

Before her stunned, incredulous scrutiny, he stripped, swelling and quickening before her very eyes. The sight of his bold, jutting arousal galvanized her into action. She leaped from the bed.

It was no use. He toppled her back onto the bed with the heavy weight of his body. Abby tried to push him away, shatteringly aware of their closeness, of his warm, hard nakedness.

She gave a choked half-sob. "No! I don't want you, Kane. I don't want this!"

Soft, husky breath reverberated against her lips. "We'll see, sweetheart. We'll see."

Her bodice was already halfway undone, her clothing no barrier at all. Within seconds she lay as naked and bare as Kane.

His gaze swept the length of her, lingering on the tremulous thrust of her breasts. Waves of hot and cold flashed through her. Her thoughts grew wild and panicked. No! She couldn't let him do this. If she did, it would happen all over again. She'd never be able to forget him ... She would never stop loving him. Somehow she had to put an end to this before it was too late ...

He lowered his head. His lips hovered dangerously near hers. "I used to lay awake at night and think about how it was, Abby. About how soft you were here ..." With his thumbs he skimmed the sensitive tips of her breasts. Her body betrayed her; they quivered and strained for his touch. She closed her eyes against the sight of her traitorous flesh swelling ripe and eager into his palm.

"And how sweet you tasted here—" His tongue curled around her nipple, a wanton caress that stole her breath.

It spun through her mind that the gentleness of his touch was at complete odds with the cold, relentless purpose in his eyes, the harshness of his whisper. Yet she couldn't fight the insidious heat that engulfed her. She couldn't fight *him*. Her body remembered all too well the pleasure he had given her.

He raised his head. Triumph flashed through him as he observed her parted lips, the ragged trickle of her breath. He swept his hand down her belly, threading his fingers through the soft fleece that guarded her womanhood. Flames of blistering heat shot through her as one daring finger taunted with brazen, silken strokes that called forth a wealth of passion's dew. Kane could hardly breathe as he felt the proof of her desire.

He slid down her body. "Do you know what it's like to want someone so bad you hurt and burn inside? Do you?" His voice was a low growl against the hollow of her belly. "Tell me, Abby. Tell me!"

But he gave her no chance to respond. He shifted suddenly. He spread her thighs with the bulk of his shoulders. Air escaped her lungs in a scalding rush.

"No." Her protest came weakly. "Oh, no . . ."

Her mind reeled. She couldn't believe that he would actually . . . Lord, it was too intimate, too daring and irreverent, too . . . She pushed at the knotted muscles of his shoulders but there was no denying him.

His breath scorched the silken flesh of her inner thigh. Boldly he found what he sought, the rough velvet of his tongue a sizzling flame of wet fire. Her body was a stranger's; dimly Abby heard herself crying out, again and again. A burning ache ignited inside her; there in that place he possessed so fully. She began to writhe and moan, her senses screaming for release.

But he wasn't yet ready to end her torture.

He levered himself over her. "Do you want me to stop?" He rubbed the thickened ridge of his manhood against her sleek dampness, tormenting them both.

"No," she gasped out. "No!" Her eyes were glazed and wide open. Her nails dug into the hardness of his arms, as if to capture and keep him there forever.

He caught her lips with his. "Do you want me?" he said into her mouth. "Do you?"

Abby could no longer deny herself. She could no longer deny him. "Yes," she panted. "Dear God, yes!"

"Tell me. Tell me *I'm* the one you want—not Buck."

"I want you," she moaned. "Kane, please . . . I want you."

"Look at me," he ground out. His eyes were black and burning.

Helplessly she raised her eyes. Her hands lifted. Her fingertips skimming—gliding—she explored the hollows of his cheeks, the blade of his nose.

In that mind-splitting instant, Kane knew . . . Her words were just that—words. No matter how much she denied it, she still loved him. It was there in the shimmer in her eyes, the gentle movement of her hands on his face, the tremulous offering of lips she could no longer withhold.

He braced himself above her, hard and achingly full, knowing if he didn't take her soon he would explode. "Hold me," was all he could say.

Her arms crept around his neck.

An odd look washed across his features. Regret? Surrender?

His eyes squeezed shut. His fingers dug into the softness of her bottom. He slid inside her, all velvet-encased steel. She cried out and wrapped her legs around his, wordlessly urging him deep . . . still deeper. Then he was driving. Thrusting. Dark and desperate, the tempo of their union wild and fierce.

Again and again he plunged into her, filling her even as he was filled with a flood of emotion too great to contain. His low groan welled up from deep in his chest. "Oh, God," he moaned. "You're mine, Abby . . . mine . . . You know that, don't you . . . Mine . . ."

Her hips met his, time and again, as frenzied and urgent as his. Her fingers rode his buttocks, the churning and bunching of sleek muscle. Tremors raced along his spine, tremors that echoed clear to where he lay buried so deep inside her. She shattered around him; her pulsing spasms rushed him toward the edge. He shuddered and spilled himself inside her again and again, hot and honeyed, scalding and splendid.

Drained and exhausted, he rolled from her, but not before he'd pressed a kiss to her half-open mouth. He smiled slightly. She was still gasping and struggling for breath. He reached for her, wanting to cradle her close for the rest of the night.

At his touch, her body went rigid.

She lurched upright. Kane was left staring at the naked lines of her back. Her shoulders were heaving.

His heart skipped a beat. "Abby?"

She jumped up and grabbed the quilt from the bed, shielding her nakedness before whirling to face him. Tears stood in her eyes. A dry, ragged sob tore from her chest.

"How could you do this to me?" she cried. "Did you really think you could seduce me into changing my mind?"

His feet hit the floor. He reached for his pants, his jaw clenched hard. "Seduce you! What the hell kind of nonsense is that? All I wanted to do was show you how right we are together. You need me, Abby, as much as I need you—"

"No!" It was no longer a matter of need or want. It was a matter of pride and he'd bruised hers sorely. "I'm through with you. Do you hear me? You may very well own half this ranch, but you don't own me! I want you out, Kane, out of my bed and out of my house. So just go . . . Go and don't ever come back!" She was crying now, but Kane was too furious to care. He shoved his arms into his shirt, grabbed his boots and shoved his way past her.

Not until he was outside again did he let loose of the bitter storm in his heart. A blistering curse filled the air. He glanced back at the house, his eyes glittering like frost.

She had made her feelings very clear—she thought it was over between them. He had the sneaking suspicion hell would freeze over before she would admit she was wrong. And he was very much afraid she was stubborn enough to go ahead and marry Buck Russell. The very thought of her with another man was like a crushing blow to his heart.

He couldn't lose her. Not now. Not ever. And he damn sure couldn't let her marry Buck Russell . . .

He could think of only one sure way to stop her.

Two hours later Abby was still tossing and turning. A restless stirring churned in her breast. The bed was too big, her heart too empty, her mind too full of all that had happened tonight. Worst of all, she ached with the memory of Kane's lovemaking, the way his touch stole her breath, the ripe yielding of her body giving way to his stretching, filling heat . . .

Her heart squeezed. Why had she sent Kane away? Why had she denied herself what she wanted most? Who was she deceiving but herself? Why had she let her wounded pride stand between them?

She still loved him. Dear God, she'd never stopped.

But in her urge to strike back at him, she'd said some terrible things to him. A piercing ache shot through her. Would he ever forgive her? Would she ever forgive herself? If only she hadn't sent him away! He had come back not once, but twice. Would he come back again? She battled the urge to cry. She was very much afraid he wouldn't . . .

She couldn't marry Buck. Kane had opened her eyes in that respect, at least. In some dark place deep inside, she wondered if she could have gone through with it, even if Kane hadn't reappeared.

Punching her pillow, she rolled to her back and stared at the ceiling. Shadows leaped from every corner. The night lay steeped in silence, a silence so absolute she heard the nicker of the horses in the paddock. It was strange, because the sound seemed so much closer than usual.

Her eyes flew open. She froze. There were soft footfalls coming down the hall—or was it merely the thrumming of her pulse?

Eyes straining, she leaned up on an elbow. "Who's there?" she called sharply.

The footsteps, more distinct now, came closer. She felt her heart laboring, her lungs struggling to breathe. All she could think was that she was about to be robbed—or worse!—and Kane was nowhere around . . .

The creak of the door made her jump. She gasped as the broad-shouldered outline of a man slowly filled the doorway. Against the gloom of the night, his features were indistinct.

The glitter of cold, silver eyes was very, very familiar.

Her shocked gaze turned to a glare, as searing as her tone was icy. "I thought I told you to leave!" She slipped from the bed and faced him bravely, very glad she'd taken the time to slip into a nightgown.

He ignored her and stepped into the room. "I won't let you marry Buck Russell," he said calmly.

Her lips tightened mutinously. She snatched up a shawl from the bedpost and tugged it around her shoulder, her resentment surfacing in full force. "If that's what I want, you can't stop me!"

"I think I can, sweetheart."

A scathing retort trembled on her lips. But it struck her that he was so very calm, so very controlled. There was an utterly inflexible air about him that gave her pause. In the meantime, his gaze flickered over her. "I'd get dressed if I were you," he said curtly. "Unless you intend to tell your children and grandchildren you became a bride dressed in your nightgown and bare feet."

Abby blinked. She made no move to obey. Surely she hadn't heard right. Maybe this was all just a dream . . .

"Fine," he muttered. "It doesn't matter to me one way or the other."

He ducked and swept her over his shoulder. Abby's eyes flew wide as the world turned topsy-turvy. She pounded his back with her fists. "Kane! For heaven's sake, are you crazy? Put me down! I'm not going anywhere with you . . ." They were on the stairs now; the jouncing of his shoulder into her belly drove the air from her lungs. She was breathless and dizzy by the time they reached the parlor.

He set her on her feet in the center of the floor.

"You see, Abby, I *can* stop you from becoming Buck Russell's wife."

Her eyes blazed her defiance. "I'd like to know how!"

"It's very simple, sweetheart. You can't marry him if you're already married to me." He stepped aside, revealing a mousy-looking man perched on the edge of the settee. He was trussed up hand and foot, a gag between his teeth.

The man was Reverend Gaines.

Chapter 23

❧

The world around her buzzed and grew dim. For a heart-stopping instant, she feared she might faint. This was no dream—it was all too real. The reverend's presence squelched any doubts she might have had that Kane wasn't serious . . . deadly serious as evidenced in the fearful brown eyes that even now issued a soulful plea in her direction. Kane expected her to marry him.

Here. Tonight. *Now.*

She cast him a look filled with reproach. "Dear Lord," she cried. "Did you have to kidnap the poor man!" Three steps took her to the reverend's side. He was, she noted, as inappropriately attired as she. She removed the cloth wedged between the man's lips.

He gasped in a grateful breath of air. "Miss MacKenzie! Thank heaven you're here. This—this madman stormed into my house, dragged me out of bed and demanded I leave with him! When I refused, he threatened me with bodily harm!"

Abby's chin jutted out. "Is this what you'll do to me if I refuse to marry you?" Her gaze bounced back to Kane, her tone withering. "Tie me up and gag me?"

"If he hadn't been so damned stubborn I wouldn't have had to lay a hand on him. I brought him here to marry us. And by God, I'll do whatever I have to."

His expression was stony. Clearly he meant every word.

She gave a strangled cry of rage and turned her attention to the reverend's hands—at least she thought it was rage. All at once she didn't know. Her emotions were a hopeless muddle. She wasn't certain if she should be angry or elated, incredulous or indignant, anxious or confused—it seemed she was a little of all those things.

Her fingers were so clumsy she couldn't undo the loose knot that held the reverend's wrists together. Kane made a sound of impatience and pushed her hands aside. She straightened, her knees so weak she could hardly stand.

The last knot loosened. The rope slipped from the reverend's ankles. Kane wasted no time pulling the unfortunate man to his feet. "Get on with it, man!"

Reverend Gaines's eyes nearly bulged from his head. "I—I neglected to bring my Bible!"

The fierceness of Kane's features pinned him to the floor. "I can't believe you don't know what needs to be said!"

Reverend Gaines was growing paler by the second. "But there are no witnesses," he blurted. "How can I perform a marriage ceremony without witnesses?"

Kane swore under his breath. "Wait here!" he said gratingly. The sweep of his gaze encompassed both the reverend and Abby. He strode from the room. Seconds later the door slammed behind him.

It seemed like he was barely gone before he returned. This time Dorothy and Lucas trailed behind him. Lucas was yawning, still buttoning his shirt. Dorothy was clad in a voluminous nightdress. Her eyes lit up when she spied Abby. Her arms encircled the younger woman in a fierce hug. "Abby, I'm so happy for you. I knew he hadn't deserted you—I just knew it!" She stepped back, still beaming.

Kane took his place beside Abby. He didn't bother looking at her as he tugged her hand into the crook of his elbow. Hazily she heard Reverend Gaines's wavering beginning.

"Dearly beloved . . ."

Her mind was spinning. Was this really happening? She clutched her shawl more tightly around her shoulders. She stole a glance at him, disconcerted to discover him watching her. She searched his face for some sign of tenderness, or even affection, but his expression was hidden behind the screen of his eyes. He was grim and unsmiling, hardly the picture of a man in love! Oh, she knew he desired her. Was that why he'd gone to all this trouble to see that they were married—simply because he wanted her in his bed? The very thought tore at her heart, yet what else *could* she believe?

She began to tremble. She bent her head to hide the sudden tears that sprang to her eyes, unaware of the faint choked sound she made.

"Stop."

The word sliced the air like the sound of a bullet; Reverend Gaines stumbled to a gaping halt. Lucas stared at Kane with an unsettled frown, while Dorothy held her breath.

Kane turned slowly. Something inside him twisted as he spied the moisture welling and overflowing in her beautiful blue eyes. Every muscle in his body grew rigid and tense as he faced her.

"I can't force you to marry me, Abby. I thought I could but I can't." His voice was low and rough with the effort it took to check his emotions. "I'll walk away now, if that's what you want. But you have to tell me you don't want me—that it's over— that what we had meant nothing."

Abby wept the harder.

"You love me, Abby." With his eyes he dared her to contest the truth. "I know you do, so why the tears? Why is the thought of marrying me so awful? Why is marrying Buck Russell preferable to marrying someone you love?"

She stifled a sob. "I never really wanted to marry Buck. I—I don't think I *could* have married him, not after seeing you again. It's just that I was so hurt and . . . and don't you see, it's not me, it's you . . . I—I don't know why you're doing this . . ."

His hands came out to cradle her shoulders.

"Look at me, Abby."

She didn't—she couldn't. She was afraid that if she did she'd start bawling all over again.

He pulled her against his chest, burying his lips in the chestnut-colored cloud of her hair. "I love you," he said unsteadily. "Why do you think I went off half-cocked when you said you intended to marry someone else? Why else would I drag a preacher out of bed in the middle of the night?"

But Abby heard only one thing. *He loved her*. Joy poured through her heart, filling her every pore with light and warmth.

"Kane . . . oh, Kane, why didn't you tell me? If you had just told me I couldn't have refused you *anything* . . ." She began to sob. "Oh, Kane, I love you, too. I—I never stopped! I just hope you can forgive me for the awful things I said . . . I didn't mean it when I said Pa wouldn't have considered you a fit husband. It doesn't matter what you were— what you did—what matters is the man you are today—"

He pressed his fingers to her lips. "You don't have to explain," he said gently. He smiled crookedly. "You're not still angry I bought out Dillon's share of the ranch?"

Her eyes darkened. She touched his cheek. "You don't have to do that, Kane. You don't have to prove anything to me. All I want is you."

His arms tightened. "I know," he said, very low. "But I want to. I'd like to think of us as partners— a new start for both of us, just like you said."

Abby's heart turned over. "I like the idea," she said softly.

He kissed the tips of her fingers. "Dillon's not here to give you away. I just hope he'll forgive me for not being able to wait any longer to make you my wife."

The hungry tenderness in his eyes stole her breath. She laughed shakily. "I don't think *I* can wait any longer."

His lips captured hers, slow and sweetly rousing. He kissed her as if nothing else in the world mattered. As always, Abby felt the world melting away around her. She clung to him, her heart taking flight, soaring like an eagle on the wind.

There was a loud cough next to them. "Excuse me, but I think the two of you are in need of my services after all."

They broke apart. Abby blushed fiercely. Kane was totally unrepentant, refusing to let her step from the binding circle of his arms. He cast the reverend a rather pointed look.

"Yes, and I *do* think this ceremony has gone on quite long enough."

Reverend Gaines hastily made the sign of the cross. "I now pronounce you man and wife," he gulped. "You may kiss the bride."

Kane wasted no time doing exactly that. He swept her from her feet and took her mouth in a deliciously long, unbroken kiss that didn't end until he laid her on the bed in her room.

It was a very long time later that Abby reflected . . . She really *had* been married in her nightie and bare feet. But she didn't mind . . .

Somehow she didn't think their children and grandchildren would mind either.